DOGFACE

A NOVEL

Jeff Garigliano

DOGFACE

A NOVEL

Jeff Garigliano

MACADAM CAGE

MacAdam/Cage
155 Sansome Street, Suite 550
San Francisco, CA 94104
www.MacAdamCage.com

Library of Congress Cataloging-in-Publication Data

Garigliano, Jeff.
 Dogface : a novel / by Jeff Garigliano.
  p. cm.
 ISBN 978-1-59692-258-7
 1. Juvenile delinquents—Fiction. 2. Shock incarceration—Fiction.
I. Title.
PS3607.A746M36 2008
813'.6—dc22

                        2007015666

Paperback edition: January, 2008
ISBN 978-1-59692-259-4

Manufactured in the United States of America.
10 9 8 7 6 5 4 3 2 1

Book and jacket design by Dorothy Carico Smith.

PART I

CHAPTER 1

The first rule: no crying. Special Forces don't cry. Navy SEALs don't cry. Loren once read about how this Green Beret in Vietnam had to cut his own foot off with a k-bar (that meant knife—Loren looked it up) after he stepped into a punji trap. The guy laced his boot back up over the bleeding stump and kept humping through the jungle, and did he cry? Not even once.

Still, when Loren hits the sprinkler head at a full run and goes sprawling he feels his eyes well up. It's part pain, part humiliation, and he tells himself, *No crying, no crying, do not cry.*

"You OK?" Tim trots up from behind, lugging the gas can.

Loren rolls over and grunts. Half the toes on his right foot are throbbing, and he thinks running might be a problem the rest of the night, but other than that he'll live. Stupid sprinkler. They were crossing the fairway, and even with the moon it was impossible to see, dark metal, no hose attached, no water coming through. It was a punji sprinkler, almost—set by the enemy greenskeeper and waiting patiently to trip Loren up.

He gets to his feet and they keep moving, to the line of trees along what Loren's pretty sure is the seventh fairway. Reconnoiter undercover—that's a rule too. Never stay visible for long, especially when the moon's out. It's slightly humid, and the night air smells like fertilizer. Loren can hear sprinklers ratcheting around nearby. The wet grass appears silvery in the moonlight, and he looks over to the fence where they stashed their bikes and sees two sets of black footprints leading straight to him, plus a big smear like an asterisk where he wiped out. The front of Loren's shirt is soaked.

He's checking the map when Tim says, "Hey, do you want to take the can for a while?" Tim opens and closes his fingers. He's been carrying the gas since they bought it an hour ago. Loren wanted a plastic container—another rule on these missions was to stay fast and light—but the tattooed girl at the register said all they had was metal. Loren made a big deal of their car-ran-out-of-gas story, more than anyone would if he were really old enough to drive. After he repeated it a second time the tattooed girl blinked at them and said all they had was all they had. So Loren bought the steel can and two gallons of regular unleaded, filling it to the brim.

In the bushes, rubbing his hand, Tim says maybe they could go with a little less, like maybe one gallon's enough. But Loren tells him that on covert ops you either fill your canteen all the way or empty it. Otherwise it makes sloshing noises.

"If you want it full then why don't you carry it?" Tim says.

"You're carrying it in, I'm carrying it out," Loren says. "We decided."

"We didn't decide. You decided."

"In an operation like this 'I' and 'we' is the same thing. I'm in command, so I decided, but it's really like *we* decided."

Tim says that's not fair, but Loren goes back to the map, signaling that the subject is closed. He doesn't have a flashlight—not allowed unless you have a red lens, better for your night vision—so he's trying to read by the faint glow of his watch. It's not easy, and the map's not exactly U.S. Geological Survey. The road they came from isn't on there, and there's no north, and in fact it's not even a real map—just a scorecard with a line drawing of the course layout on the back. Loren took it from the golf pro's car one morning last weekend, when the pro and Loren's mom decided to sleep in.

"Because the can's heavier now than it will be when we're done," Tim says. "So I only get the heavy part."

"It's good for you. Just switch hands."

"I already did."

"Then switch back."

"I think you should carry it for a while."

"No way. You don't change duties in the middle of a mission just because it's hard. Do Delta Force guys complain because their boots pinch a little? Do they stop in the middle of the desert and ask for ice cream? Carry the can, and the next time you're doing something hard you'll know you can do it, because you did this."

Tim's coming along, Loren thinks, but he still needs help with the basics. Like this recent insubordination, for example. This questioning of orders. Or showing up for tonight's mission in a white T-shirt that on a dark golf course would have been like a homing beacon. He might as well have worn a string of Christmas lights. Loren gave him one of his black T-shirts and explained again that they own the night—they come and go like the darkness, and they are never seen, ever. "That's what strikes fear," he said. Tim said the T-shirt was a little too small but he'd wear it anyway.

Just then an engine starts somewhere close. Loren drops the map, and Tim crouches next to him. They watch a single headlight wheel around toward them like a lighthouse. The night greenskeeper? Loren's done some low-level reconnaissance and found that the man doesn't usually go out to change the sprinklers until 2:00 a.m. or so, staying close to the shed until then and smoking pot and listening to sports radio talk shows. If that's him, he's early tonight, and maybe not as wasted as they were counting on.

Loren freezes as the single headlight gets closer, heading down the fairway they just crossed. Those footprints in the wet grass might be a problem, but it's too late now. The greenskeeper drives past in a maintenance cart, dragging a bunch of canvas hoses behind it like a giant squid. He slows down at the footprints, glances in both directions, and then accelerates again.

Once he's gone, Loren hears something spattering on the ground behind him. Tim has uncapped the gas can and is dumping it out into the grass. The sweet chemical smell blooms around them and makes Loren's eyes water again.

"Tim, what the fuck?"

"I'm just lightening my load."

"Don't. We need all that."

Tim looks evenly at Loren and keeps pouring. "You can carry it if you want." It's an open challenge, disobeyal of a direct order, but there isn't time to address it right now. The gas is spilling out, and they started with only two gallons, and Loren wasn't even sure that would be enough.

"OK," Loren says. "OK, I'll carry it. But you're taking the can home when we're done. The whole way—no bitching."

Tim says deal.

Loren starts off with the can, and Tim says it's the other way, this is the fifth tee and they want to go right, not left.

"How do you know?" Loren reaches into his pocket for the map again.

"There's a bench right there." Which is true enough. Hole 5. A par 3, 186 yards from the men's tee, 137 from the women's. It's all printed on the slats in yellow paint, along with an ad for a hardware store.

Loren tells himself to get it together. It's important to listen to your men, but more important that they trust you to lead them when things get hairy. "OK," he says, like he's confirming it to himself. "OK then, let's get going."

*

It's not that Loren hates the golf pro. It's not that he wants to trash every square inch of the shitty course the pro boasts about to Loren and his mom like it's Pebble Beach. But from the start Loren has known the guy's a hand job. Like the way he's always tan, even in winter. Or the license plate on his car that says, "BRDY4ME." Or that he wears nothing but polo shirts—he must own about a million of them, Loren's never seen him in anything else. They're all bright colors, pinks and sky blues, stuff that would never work in the jungle. One of the first times they met, the pro tried to make conversation by asking what teams Loren played on in school, and Loren said junior varsity misdemeanors. It only got worse from there.

For Loren's fourteenth birthday a few weeks ago, the pro got him—and Loren was pissed that he didn't guess this in advance—a yellow polo shirt with the golf course logo on it. They were at a Chinese restaurant, and the pro lectured Loren and his mom on how to use the chopsticks. Loren's mom gave him her present, a book—*Death Before Dawn: Memoir of a Green Beret.* (He had written down the title for her; last year, she got confused and bought him a coffee-table book about the coast guard.) Then the pro whipped out a wrapped package that turned out to be the polo shirt, canary yellow, brighter than the sun. A little cartoon golfer was knitted onto the front, swinging an oversize club. The shirt had about the same odds of wearability by Loren as a miniskirt. Only after his mom glared at him did he say thanks, as flatly as he could.

And then the pro said to put it on.

"That's OK," Loren said. "I want to save it for a big day."

"Nonsense. I'll get you another one for then. Put it on. You can wear it home."

Loren's mom gave him the look, the expression he'd seen before, which said, *You-know-I-really-like-this-guy-so-please-don't-pull-anything.* So Loren put it on. The pro gestured at him with the chopsticks and said he'd have to get Loren out on the course for a lesson or two. Then he divided the check up three ways and told his mom she was on the hook for two-thirds. That night, after the two of them went to bed, Loren took the polo shirt to the bathroom and wiped his ass with it.

*

The U.S. Navy SEAL trident is complicated, especially when you're trying to trace it in wet grass using gasoline.

"It's like a big fork," Loren explains to Tim. "Plus there's this fierce eagle and a globe." Compared to other uniform insignia it's huge—almost like a belt buckle. Among Loren's more prized possessions is an actual trident worn on the uniform of an actual SEAL. He bought it at an army-navy store, and when the guy didn't seem too knowledgeable about the program, Loren stopped asking questions. He's looked at the pin long enough to memorize the pattern, which he's drawn into notebooks and etched into desks at school. The army's Delta Force is probably more of a badass organization, but they're so secretive they don't even have a logo. The army refuses to acknowledge that they exist (even though books have been written about them, books that Loren owns). At one point he considered just writing "Delta Force" in the grass with gasoline, but he wasn't sure two gallons would be enough, and the trident would probably strike more fear anyway.

Except Loren's afraid the trident won't look right. He's pacing out the pattern on the first tee—right in front of the clubhouse and in direct view of the window the pro looks out all day. He pours some gas every few steps and spreads it around on the wet grass with his boot. But the fluid is clear, and in the darkness it's impossible to see what he's already drawn. Plus the spout is too free-flowing, probably OK if all you want to do is fill up a lawn mower, but no good for any kind of detail work. He knows what he wants—the end result should look like a giant, red-hot brand was pressed down into the grass from above—but he's not sure this is the best way to create that.

Tim's standing guard duty, which right now means he found a crooked stick and is taking pretend golf swings from the ladies' tee. The course sits next to a marsh—the first hole is lined with reeds that must be filled, Loren thinks, with about a million stray balls. Even on top of the gasoline scent the air smells swampy. Halfway down the first fairway, two sand traps appear gray in the darkness like a pair of lunar lakes. Loren's socks are wet all the way through, either with dew or with gas, and he wonders if his boots might go up in flames when he lights the trident. Didn't he see that in a Roadrunner cartoon one time?

A few curious geese emerge from the reeds and waddle over, honking softly and poking their dark beaks out like they're taking measurements.

"Tim, get these things out of here," Loren says. He's almost ready and doesn't want any collateral damage.

Tim tries to shoo the geese away, but there are suddenly more, fifteen or so, walking over the gas-soaked grass and moving around Loren like a river around a rock. Tim makes a lunge to scare one, and another doubles around and pecks him in the calf. The honking is getting louder, and when the birds flap their wings they look suddenly huge and intimidating. Both Tim and Loren scramble around now, trying to divert the flock, and Loren thinks this is the kind of stuff you never see in Special Forces movies. Fucking geese—you can't control every variable. When most of them have finally waddled past, Loren rushes around in the newly shit-spattered grass and tries to finish the pattern.

He'd originally wanted something high-end and sophisticated for ignition, but all they could find were matches, a cheap pack from the QuikMart with an ad on it that says, "Make $$$ Working From Home!" Tim's standing nearby, but he gets distracted when he finds a ball in the long grass next to the ladies' tee. Loren tells him to pay attention and gives him the briefing again about their means of egress—basically, run back to the fence where their bikes are and hop over. Finally Loren lights a match, says, "Fire in the hole," and tosses it.

The match goes out before it lands.

Loren lights another and repeats, "Fire in the hole," and again it goes out before it hits the ground. They definitely need something better for this. By the fifth match, Loren's not saying anything anymore. Tim starts playing hacky sack with the stray golf ball, and Loren tosses the matches and watches them go out, one after the other. He moves closer to the gas each time, thinking it might be better just to touch one to the ground, but that idea makes him nervous. He has gasoline up and down his sleeves and probably soaked into his jeans too. He's seen burn victims on the internet—crinkly skin that's black as tar, faces wrapped up like a mummy. There's no medic or corpsman out here, and Loren has no idea where the nearest phone is, which means it might be a long bike ride to the emergency room. Plus he can't really trust Tim in a crisis. Tim cries sometimes—which there's a rule against.

"Tim, do you want to do this?" Loren says. "Just light the match and touch it to the grass."

Tim shakes his head. "No way. I'm the guard, remember?"

On Loren's fourteenth match the greenskeeper comes back. He must have seen the matches sparking. Tim yells—actually part squeak, his voice is changing—and Loren realizes the mission is coming apart. The headlight comes on, the mini-engine revs up, the cart starts closing fast. The greenskeeper yells something that Loren can't make out. There's still time to abort, just take the can and disappear into the marsh. No real damage—they could come back another time and do it better. More recon, a better pattern, more gas in a lightweight plastic can.

Instead Loren lights one last match and sets the rest of the pack on fire. It goes off like a pyrotechnic, blue and yellow, and he drops it to the grass.

The gasoline ignites with a *whoomp* that's almost concussive—

Loren feels a kind of shock wave pass through his chest—and a flash of light that reflects off nearby trees. The greenskeeper is thirty yards away when it goes up, close enough that Loren can make out his shout of "Holy Mother!" He steps off his little cart as it's coasting to a stop and falls down, losing his glasses. The flame doesn't burn for long. For some reason Loren imagined a bonfire kind of thing, but it's more like a quick blue thump and then a lot of hissing, and then another big thump when the gas can explodes. A big chunk of it goes flying past Loren's head.

The geese start honking wildly. The burned shape on the grass doesn't look much like a trident—more like a big, sloppy oval with some extensions. It almost looks like Florida. The golf pro will think he's been attacked by radical grapefruit growers. Still, Loren thinks, the point is made. They got here and did something, a small piece of harassment, and now he's got to get his men out safely. Actually just one man, or more accurately, one kid.

Tim, following orders at last, is trying to pick up a piece of the gas can to carry out, but it's too hot to touch. The greenskeeper's reaching around for his glasses and yelling, "Hey!" Loren and Tim turn to go, and Loren realizes another factor he didn't consider—the explosion was so bright that when they look away from it and face the darkness they're blind as bats. But he points Tim in the direction of some open space and says, "Run."

CHAPTER 2

After dinner the Colonel sits at his dining room table, forging medical records. His goal is to get through a dozen each night, though it's rare when he finishes more than two or three. The records were requested three weeks ago by the state—he was given seven business days to hand them over, along with Camp Ascend! fire inspections and emergency-exit maintenance logs, etc., etc.—and lately the calls have gotten so persistent the Colonel has stopped answering his office phone. A job like this, he feels, can't be rushed.

For each record he puts down the name of a Camp Ascend! attendee, then makes up some realistic-sounding medical information about him. Didn't Drew Garrity have an identifying scar on his neck? Wasn't Susan Gert, fifteen, about five-foot-seven and 119 pounds? Didn't they both have blood pressure of about, let's see, maybe 117 (which the Colonel picks because the digital clock in the kitchen says 8:17 in red block letters) over 86 (because that was the year he and Kitty got married)?

Both kids free of allergies, check, neither one currently taking any medications, check. The Colonel puts down one visit to the infirmary each, Drew for a sunburn—prescription: aloe lotion—

and because he can't think of anything else, because he has a lot of bee stings and already ran through the roster of foliage poisons (oak, sumac, ivy), he says screw it and gives Susan Gert a sunburn too. That's reasonable, right? Two sunburns on people who just happen to be next to each other in the alphabet?

Finally, he adds a few of his special realistic touches—the kind of details he thinks will convince a certain nagging state agency that these records are legit. He crimps the corners on David's record and puts his coffee mug on Susan's, sloshing it around to leave a ring. He also puts a few drops of cough syrup onto the outside of both folders, in different places, then puts them in the "done" pile and caps his pen. Eighty-five more to go.

*

Camp Ascend! has been open for only sixteen months, but the Colonel first got the idea three years ago, when he was doing community service for the credit card operation. It was before he'd adopted the "Colonel" title, when he was just E. Raymond Kellogg ("aka Eddie Ray Kellogg, aka Earle R. Keller, aka Eduardo K. Fernandez," as it read in the indictment). He plea-bargained the whole thing down to thirteen counts of fraud and agreed to five hundred hours at a youth home, where his primary responsibility was driving the sluggish, ancient, no-AC van.

The home took in every manner of weirdo teenager, with all kinds of complicated piercings and dreadlocks and baggy tent clothes. About half the kids were sullen brooders who never made eye contact and never said anything, whose favorite activity seemed to be staring at the floor with their arms crossed and shoulders slumped, and the other half just would not shut up. The Colonel was the sole community-service person on staff, so the kids called him Al Capone. He met regularly with his court-assigned counselor and told her that, yes, he was getting a lot out of his time there, that he found it "spiritually renewing" to see these youngsters work through their issues, when the only real benefit was the gasoline he charged to the van account and somehow, whoops, wound up putting in his own car instead.

But one day something did happen—the kind of event the Colonel realized even then could send him in a new direction. He was driving a couple of kids back from school. The van was half-empty and rattling like a coffee can with rocks inside. The Colonel was late and expecting to get yelled at again by the director, so he ran a couple of lights on the way. When they finally got back to the home, one of the fathers was in the parking lot, waiting.

It was a surprise visit—the father was leaning against a bike rack, hands in his pockets, and the kid, on the bench seat behind the Colonel, was mortified. Apparently he was a lot wealthier than he'd let on, because idling nearby was a gleaming silver Bentley. The kids filed into the building, the one ignoring his father entirely, and after the Colonel parked the van, the father called him aside.

"Look out for my boy," the man said. "Can you do that?" He had a graying mustache and shallow lines around his eyes. The Bentley idled so quietly you could barely tell it was running.

The Colonel was about to explain that he didn't really work there, that he only had seventy-one hours to go, but instead he shrugged and said sure.

"He doesn't listen to me," the father continued. "I can't even get him to tie his shoes. But it's not like I don't want to be involved here. So I'm asking you to make sure he's all right. Just watch out for him, that's all."

Then he held a bill out—a fifty, straight from the ATM, with edges so crisp you could have used them to slice cheddar. The Colonel saw the brassy flash of a money clip before it disappeared into the man's pocket. The other staffers apparently all got similar offers and rejected them, outraged that someone would think they'd adjust their care based on a bribe. The director held a special house meeting after the father left, to make sure the boy was OK and ask how he felt about the experience, during which the Colonel stood in the corner. The fifty was folded perfectly flat in his pocket.

It was nothing less than a revelation. Because if his life and his business ventures had a central theme, a philosophical North Star, it was that it's always easier to convince people to *give* you their money than to steal it. The more the Colonel thought about it, the more he realized that this was opportunity leaning on the doorbell, that there was a certain kind of parent (distracted, successful, ideally with some extra cash) who didn't know what else to do with a bad kid— or maybe just a *mixed-up* kid; you wouldn't want to say they were bad, the Colonel recognized right away that marketing would be crucial. And pricing, you could probably set the bar pretty high, given the emotional state of parents once they understood that the flesh of their flesh, the fruit of their loins, had what the director of the youth home liked to call "special needs."

When his five hundred hours were up, the Colonel did a little research and learned that he couldn't possibly open the kind of youth home he'd worked at. There were all kinds of regulatory issues—those places got funding from the county and the state, plus they were in populated areas, so they were easy to monitor. But a lawyer he knew, who'd played a minor role in the credit card operation (ultimately getting disbarred and doing two hundred seventy-five hours at a soup kitchen), said he'd poke around a little, maybe there was another way. Two weeks later the lawyer called back with good news, and the Colonel started shopping for property.

The place he finally found couldn't have been more perfect: an old music camp on 165 isolated acres, which had been abandoned in a hurry after a chemical refinery nearby was declared a Superfund site. Something about soil and leaching—the Colonel didn't ask too many questions. The camp had sat idle for more than two years, collecting mold and not a lot of buyer interest, so when the Colonel stumbled onto it he put in an offer at Louisiana Purchase per-acre rates and signed the deed seventeen days later. Along the northwest property line there's a bunch of bright orange EPA markers with skulls painted on them, but he brings in bottled water for the main house and doesn't lose too much sleep over it.

When the music students left they fled like it was Pompeii, leaving behind clothes and instruments and marching uniforms. In the performance rooms in the barn are tangled black music stands and upright pianos docked in the corner like barges. If the wind kicks up, stray pieces of sheet music blow around the property—the trombone line for "Livin' la Vida Loca," "Eleanor Rigby" for strings—snaring themselves in long-untrimmed hedges or wrapping around the Colonel's shin. He was startled on one of his early trips to see something that looked like a bone, cylindrical and sun-bleached, at the edge of the parking lot. It turned out to be the corroded middle segment of a flute.

Even if the place had been in perfect shape when the Colonel took over, it wouldn't be any longer. The amount of upkeep required was staggering. It was like nature got accelerated out there, like they were under constant siege. Cricket colonies, plagues of hornets. For a while, during the first few classes, they had a maintenance man from town who used to drive out for minor repairs. (Kitty, in particular, who's used to a higher standard of luxury and hates being stuck out in the woods, would call him at all hours and complain that the new water heater he put in was better but not really *hot*, not really powerful enough.) But when Donovan caught the maintenance man spying on Kitty at the pool one day, he repositioned the man's nose on his face, and since then they've been completely on their own.

At its height, the Gerald R. Schaeffer Camp for Musical Instruction could house about ninety kids, but now that it's Camp Ascend! the Colonel can only scrape up fifteen or so at a time. Sometimes the number drops on the first day, when parents take one look around and say they'll take their chances with Catholic school. It's understandable—the Colonel can admit that his brochures and website might give a slightly inflated sense of the place. He puts a lot of emphasis on some geographical elements, like horse trails and a waterfall, that don't exist and never did.

Which is why he doesn't get too upset when parents balk at the last minute, and why his feelings didn't get hurt when one father recently called the facilities a shit hole, or when another family arriving last session didn't even get out of their car. As long as they understand the Colonel's policy on refunds, which is No Refunds, Ever. He charges seventeen thousand dollars for a six-week session, all checks payable to one E. Raymond Kellogg (leave the "Colonel" part off, please). For those parents who change their minds, well, the Colonel believes in customer service, so he'll smile and gladly give them directions back out to the highway.

*

When the phone rings, he doesn't answer.

He's on the front porch, smoking a cigar. A sliver of moon floats over the serrated edge of a line of pine trees to the west. The moonlight is barely enough to make out the boxy outlines of the student cabins—in silhouette they look like Monopoly houses, identically square and small and grouped in little clusters. Starting tomorrow two of those cabins (the two that aren't falling down) will be filled, or at least occupied, with the next class of Camp Ascend! attendees—nine total, including one last-minute addition, a Loren Something, who the Colonel can't remember if that's a boy or a girl. He'd hoped for more, but nine times seventeen thousand, that's not bad.

Inside the house the microwave is beeping, meaning Kitty's heating up her lotion. From the backyard, he can hear the nine-hundred-dollar bug zapper she bought from a catalog. It's struggling to keep up with the volume of insects, popping continuously, like a transformer on the blink, and the Colonel doesn't even want to think about the growing heap of tangled insect bodies piled up underneath it. (He can have someone from the new class take care of that.) Any minute, he thinks, the mosquitoes will stop being bothered by the cigar smoke and he'll have to go inside.

After the seventh ring the phone stops and Kitty appears on the other side of the screen.

"It's for you," she says.

"Who is it?"

She shrugs. "Some woman."

"Which woman?"

"One of the moms, I think. That one who's been calling."

Kitty opens the screen door slightly and reaches her slender arm out with the cordless phone. Even after twenty years of marriage he thinks his wife is beautiful. She's in a kimono that shows a little V of tan skin inside the lapels. Her hair is up, and her extremely well-pedicured feet are bare, with shiny carmine toenails in descending sizes like a fanned-out display of gems.

Kitty doesn't work, doesn't exert herself too much other than complaining about the remoteness of Camp Ascend!, so she has a lot of time to spend on personal grooming. A few times a week, she'll get another shipment of at-home spa treatments—the latest is an exfoliating mask from Germany which is battery-powered and makes her look like the Phantom of the Opera, though its strongest effect is probably on the Colonel, who actually gets light-headed when he thinks about the $319 it cost him. Kitty says the at-home experience is nothing like an actual spa—the products aren't as good, and when there's no attendant you have to figure out how to get yourself into the heated chamomile-tea wrap with ginkgo, ginger, and cucumber extracts, and it's always too cold or too hot or it leaks. Other than grooming, she fills her days by watching satellite TV and flipping through catalogs and sunning herself at the swimming pool left over from the Gerald R. Schaeffer music camp, underneath a big sign that says, "*Adagio!* No running."

"Will you take the phone?" she says. "I don't want to get bit."

"Why'd you even pick it up?" the Colonel says.

"Donnie's asleep," Kitty says. "I didn't want the ringing to wake him up."

"So turn the ringer off."

"Are you going to talk to her?"

The Colonel takes a big puff of his cigar and exhales in the direction of a mosquito. He says she should just tell the woman he's busy.

She stares at him for a minute, then says into the phone, "He'll be right with you," and tosses it into his lap.

Insolence! She doesn't respect him! After all he's done, the life he lets her live up here, the forty-seven thousand dollars he spent so far to fix up the pool. What he should do right now is hang up and go straighten this out with Kitty, but instead he picks up the phone and says hello like it's a question.

"Finally," the woman says. "Colonel, it's Miriam Diehl. I've been calling and calling—to be honest I can't believe I'm finally talking to an actual person about this."

The Colonel can't believe it either. He has a procedure for dealing with disgruntled parents, and that procedure is to ignore them. Mrs. Diehl has been calling a couple of times a day for two weeks, getting the answering machine and alternately talking and sobbing until the tape runs out.

"Well, we're pretty busy up here," the Colonel says, rubbing the bridge of his nose. "Lots of—"

"Do you remember my son?"

"Of course I do," he says. Was it Evan Diehl? Adam? He thinks about going in to check the half-completed stack of medical records—the Colonel's already up to the Gs so the kid would be in there—when she tells him it was Matthew.

"He was there in March and April," she adds.

"Right, of course. Great kid—I thought he got a lot out of the program."

"Don't start your stories. Just listen for a minute, if that's possible for you. As soon as Matthew came home last spring I knew there was something wrong. He was so much quieter than normal. I told myself it was nothing, but when he came out of the shower one morning I saw that one of his toenails had fallen off. He didn't want to talk about it, but finally he told me that one of the guards up there stomped on his foot. The guard was wearing boots."

"Are you sure?" That must have been Donovan. The Colonel doesn't like to wear boots. He thinks they chafe.

"Yes, I'm sure," Mrs. Diehl says. "The podiatrist was too. So that was one thing. I was ready to go to the police right then, but Matthew begged me not to. He told me it was over and we should just move on. And as crazy as it sounds, I listened to him. He seemed so upset. But then there were some other things too."

"Like what?" The Colonel watches a mosquito float around his face and stabs at it with the cigar.

"Like he has nightmares."

"A lot of kids have nightmares, Mrs. Diehl. I did. I still do sometimes—"

"No, you're not *listening*. I don't want to hear your stories. He has nightmares almost every night, and he wakes up yelling the most awful things. And there's more—he started missing things lately. Things I say to him. I know my son, and something wasn't right. So I took him to a doctor, our family doctor, who's known us forever and simply would not make something like this up, and he says Matthew has something wrong with his hearing."

"I'm not sure I see how that—"

"He says Matthew must have had some kind of trauma up there. 'Physical and emotional trauma,' is what he said, and he thinks I should send him to a neurologist next and maybe even a psychologist. Now, I want to know the truth. I want you to tell me what happened to my son."

"Well, Matthew was a difficult case. I'm looking at his file right now—" He glances around the porch for something to ruffle, pages of a catalog or whatever, but comes up blank. Two more mosquitoes take up formation in front of the Colonel's face. "And, hmm, it seems like he was responding to the program...Right here: 'Diehl responding well to the program. Considered a leader in his peer group. Expressed during therapy that he'd like a stronger relationship with his...'"

"With his what?" the woman says.

"Well, it says he'd like a stronger relationship with his mother. That's you, right?"

Pause. "I don't believe you."

"His record's right here in front of me. Look, long story short, all our cases are tough, but some are tougher. What I can do is this. I have another class starting tomorrow, and you know what? A spot just opened up, just this afternoon. Someone up there must be looking out for you, Mrs. Diehl, and looking out for young Matt. Sometimes a second session can be beneficial, and because you're a repeat customer, here's what I'm prepared to do: I'll knock off...call it 5 percent from the full tuition price if you'll just tell me, right now over the phone, that you want that spot. Just a show of good faith— I made one, now you make one."

"Is this an infomercial or something?"

"What?"

"Here I am telling you my son was hurt, was psychologically *scarred*, in that POW camp you're running, and you say I should put him through it again? Are you insane?"

"What's your idea of a fair solution?"

"My idea is to get a lawyer."

"Great. Good. I encourage legal representation, but just make sure you show that lawyer the release you signed before your son started. Remember? It's about seventeen pages long? You initialed every page and signed the back one? Is that ringing any bells? Because I think any attorney you find is going to take one look at that and say '*Buona fortuna.*' They'll say good luck and Godspeed, because you're on your own. Mrs. Diehl, please. We're professionals. You trusted us, and we appreciate that trust."

Now she's sobbing again—a series of muffled exhalations working their way down in pitch. Above the threadbare pines the moon is the color of tarnished silver, and something's rustling, some kind of animal, near one of the cabins. The Colonel rubs off the smeared remains of a mosquito near his elbow.

"Mrs. Diehl, I have a lot I need to take care of here, so if you'll excuse me—"

"*Why won't you tell me what happened to my son?*" She screams so loudly that the phone vibrates in the Colonel's hand. She yells at him that this is her only child she's talking about, and he's hurt and she just wants to know what happened, that's all, no lawyers, she didn't mean that, but she wants to know right now what happened up there and she's not getting off the phone until he tells her.

So he hangs up.

What happened to her son—the truth is, the Colonel doesn't know. He knows the rough outline but not the specifics. He knows, for example, that Matthew Diehl spent some time in the rehearsal rooms in the barn, which are soundproof and windowless (it's surprising how much like cells they are), and now escape-proof, since Donovan installed new dead bolts on all the doors. Three on each side of a long hallway, built by the Schaeffer Foundation expressly for musical instruction and solitary drills, so that Pavarotti and Jimi Hendrix could be in adjacent rooms and neither would be bothered by the other.

Donovan's taken only two or three kids into the rehearsal rooms the whole time the camp has been running, but Matthew Diehl was one of them. The Colonel remembers seeing Matthew on the ground one afternoon during the fourth week of his session. Donovan was kneeling on his back, saying he could get up when he finished eating all of the dirt in his mouth plus one more big mouthful. Then he got taken to one of the rehearsal rooms, and that's where the Colonel's knowledge of the situation gets a little vague.

Did the kid get water? Food? Was he allowed to go to the bathroom? The Colonel could acknowledge that, yes, OK, he could have been more diligent about staying on top of that situation (even though Donovan held the only set of keys). But he didn't, because whatever happened in the rehearsal rooms seemed to work. Matthew Diehl came out three days later, a little shaken up but with no marks on him, nothing the Colonel could see, and for the remaining three weeks of the session, he fell over himself to obey orders. He marched his laps around the compound, he cleaned the bug zapper with his bare hands, and he weatherproofed the first-floor window frames of the Colonel's house using a Q-Tip.

The Colonel almost had to admire how effective it was. You didn't need to punish all of them, just one—severely. You needed to find out which kid had influence over the others and then focus on him. Once he was broken down, the rest of the group would line up for you, like little iron filings on a magnet.

*

The mosquitoes are in full-scale attack now, a tiny Luftwaffe, and the Colonel retreats back inside. As he's coming through the screen door he hears yelling. It's Kitty, somewhere upstairs. The Colonel bolts up the steps two at a time and finds her in her kimono, kneeling in the hallway behind a hamper. "A bat," she says. "In the bedroom. He's still in there."

The Colonel's first reaction is to start talking. Start lying.

"That's a good omen," he says. "It's a blessing on the house in some places."

"Right," Kitty says. "Like in Transylvania. Go kill it." She's clutching the lapels of her kimono to her throat.

The Colonel swallows. "Maybe it'll find its own way out. Is the window open?"

"No."

"Well, maybe it'll open the window and then fly out."

"*Go kill it.*"

Instead he keeps talking, trying to calm her (and himself) down by pretending it's natural. "Listen," he says. "We're out here in their territory, and it's only reasonable that they'd want to come into a nice house like this and take a look around. He's probably more afraid of us than we are of him." Which even he himself doubts, given how scared he is of things like this—bats and mice and raccoons. He's scared of everything in nature, really.

Downstairs the phone starts ringing, probably Mrs. Diehl again. The Colonel says he should go pick that up, but Kitty yells at him to get into the goddamn bedroom right now.

"Just once," she says. "Just take care of one thing."

He opens the bedroom door and slinks in, and immediately the theory of relative fright falls apart, because the bat doesn't seem scared at all. It's flying steady circles around the ceiling light—veiny, translucent wings flapping. It looks almost like a Halloween prop, a piece of floppy black rubber attached to a string. The Colonel looks down at the carpet, half expecting to see bat droppings, a little crusted mound of guano, but instead there's just the German exfoliating mask, buzzing away. Kitty has the air-conditioning cranked up, as always, and the room is cold enough to store meat. The bed's made, with a little impression on the rust-colored comforter where she was lying down and exfoliating, and next to that is a catalog for restaurant-quality coffee machines. Lately Kitty's been complaining that she misses good coffee, that there's no Starbucks around for 700 million miles so she has to make her own.

Slowly, the Colonel moves toward the bed, sliding along the wall and expecting the bat to swoop down and sink its rabid fangs into his scalp. He remembers something about bats having radar. Or maybe it's smell—they have a strong sense of smell but no hearing at all. One of those. There are so many things like this to keep track of in life, he thinks. Too many details. He's not a detail-oriented person, he's an idea man, and the details are what sometimes trip him up.

When he finally gets to the catalog, he doesn't know what he's going to do with it—order the bat a coffee grinder? Kitty has an item circled, the Pasquini Livia Auto-90 espresso machine, Italian-made, $1,400. Jesus—she's killing him with this stuff. He crouches down by the bed and rolls up the catalog, patting it in one palm. It's clear to him that he's never getting that bat out by himself. He just needs to prove that he made some effort. Maybe if they leave the thing alone for a while it'll die. How long could that take? He crouches down, pulls part of the comforter over himself, and bangs the catalog against the radiator a few times, hoping the noises will sound convincing in the hall. The bat doesn't seem to notice—it keeps flying jagged circles around the ceiling light. The Colonel rips out the page Kitty circled in the catalog, wads it up in his pocket, and runs for the door.

In the hallway, Kitty looks at him warily. She has an expression she uses at times like this.

"I couldn't get him," the Colonel says. "He's a wily one."

"Are you kidding me? What do we do now?"

"I think if we leave him in there he'll either go out the same way he came in, or else maybe die. If we're lucky."

"So where are we supposed to sleep?"

"Pullout couch, I guess."

"That's your plan? We're out here living like pioneers, and your approach is to just surrender parts of the house to whatever comes in?"

From the back bedroom, Donovan appears. He's wearing a T-shirt that says, "Huntington H.S. Marching Cougars," and his hair's pressed up on one side of his head and pressed down on the other. As he comes down the hallway toward them, the Colonel says another of his countless prayers of thanks that Kitty and her brother don't look alike. Donovan's forehead is pitched back, and his jaw juts out in a way that makes him look not fully evolved. His shoulders slope down to long arms, and his legs are disproportionately short. Their shouting must have woken him up. He sleeps odd hours and in strange places, sometimes in a cabin, sometimes in the barn. When the camp is in session, he'll stay up for three or four days straight, doing God knows what, then sleep for thirty-six hours at a stretch. The Colonel has no idea how he does it.

Kitty starts explaining about the bat, but Donovan cuts her off. "I know," he says. "I heard."

He walks past them into the bedroom and closes the door. The Colonel shouts in to ask if he wants a weapon or something.

"There's a catalog in there," he says. No response.

The house is suddenly calm—the only sounds are the muffled hum of the air conditioners and the bug zapper popping and, remotely, Mrs. Diehl leaving another weeping message on the machine downstairs. The Colonel has mosquito bites up and down his arms. He and Kitty look at each other and say nothing.

After a minute Donovan emerges, carrying the crumpled bat in one bare hand as casually as if it were a set of car keys. At the bottom of the stairs he goes outside, the screen door slamming behind him and echoing through the house, and the Colonel knows they won't see him until the kids start arriving tomorrow morning.

CHAPTER 3

For a week Loren waits for the punishment to come down. He waits to hear a knock on his bedroom door, the pro on the other side in assistant-principal mode saying, *Loren, your mom and I need to talk to you.* He waits to come home one afternoon and find the two of them at the kitchen table with no food or place mats out, just bare wood and nervous hands and the strong sensation they've been sitting there for hours. After a few days of nothing, he even tries to force a confrontation by filing thin lines halfway through the titanium shafts of the pro's new eleven-hundred-dollar Ping irons. It was perfect—he used a hacksaw blade that was as thin as a wire, so the cuts were almost invisible, but as soon as you took one swing they'd snap like old bones. Unfortunately, the pro started keeping his clubs at work instead of in his trunk, and if they did break he acted like it never happened.

Weirdest of all is that his mom and the pro know about the golf course. Loren *knows* they know. The insurance company left a message on the answering machine about the "little barbecue out there on the first tee," and Tim's mom called Loren's mom three times that night, even though they don't like each other and never have. (Whenever Loren goes over to Tim's house he's not allowed inside.

If there are meals involved Loren gets a paper plate of food handed out through the screen door, and he sits in the driveway with Tim and Tim says, "What do you expect? They think you're going to blow up their kitchen.")

Five days after the golf course mission Tim's parents go public with his punishment—he's being shipped off to a Quaker prep school in Delaware called Friends of Friends. He'll be gone before the weekend, and in the meantime he can't spend any time with Loren, not even on the phone.

"But it's summer," Loren says into one of the old PRC-90 radios they bought at an army-navy store. "Quakers go to school in the summer?"

"The school has some extra program," Tim says. "Everyone else comes back in September."

"Do you have to wear wooden shoes?"

"I don't know," Tim says. "Maybe." He says the Quaker thing is a bummer but he's not all that surprised. His parents have been threatening for more than a year.

When a week passes and Loren hasn't heard anything from his mom, he thinks maybe she's going to Try Something New. That's happened in the past, whenever Loren's gotten into trouble and she doesn't know what else to do. "Nothing seems to work with you, Loren," she'll say, "so we're going to Try Something New." Occasionally that means something she's read—she has shelves and shelves of books around the apartment, memoirs about being a single mom, guides on how to raise adolescent boys. Unfortunately she doesn't make it all the way through a lot of them, and sometimes she does-n't get past the introduction.

Mostly, however, when she says Try Something New, that means Defer to the Boyfriend. And because she's dated men with wildly different approaches about how to raise kids, Loren has gone through huge swings of permissiveness and clampdown.

A year ago, on a warm Thursday in May, he and Tim took Tim's parents' Explorer and decided they'd explore a little on their own. They skipped a day of eighth grade and drove to the beach with a big thermos of vodka and Sunny Delights (Loren called them Russian Summers). Loren's mom was dating an out-of-work actor who said he was "preparing for roles" a lot but who mostly sat on the couch watching game shows and calling out the answers. The beach was Loren's idea—he was the one who drove, and he was the one who accidentally backed the truck into a yield sign—but even though Tim's parents went ballistic and grounded Tim for two months and issued the first of the Quaker-school threats, Loren received zero punishment. Instead he got a heart-to-heart on the couch with the actor, who told him it was good Loren realized he should have a little fun in his life. The actor said he used to do stuff like that growing up, even crazier stunts, if Loren wanted to know the truth, and then told a couple of stories that Loren didn't believe, things that sounded like they'd gotten exaggerated—why would anyone spray-paint a horse?—though Loren tried to play along and laugh when he was supposed to.

But six months later, the actor was gone and Loren's mom started dating a bank manager, who respected her decision to have Loren while she was a senior in high school but didn't respect much else about her life, or anything about her son's attitude. So when Loren got up from the dinner table without asking to be excused, the banker said he should be grounded for nine days—a week and two weekends—and Loren's mom said OK.

Once, under the strategy of Try Something New, she even signed up for a Big Brother. She saw a commercial and called the 800 number, and a few weeks later a local college student named Ethan showed up. Loren was skeptical but Ethan seemed OK. He was always on time and a better athlete than Loren would have guessed by looking at him. The first few times they met, Loren called him Mr. Rogers, because of the cardigan sweaters, but then they went up to Ethan's campus one day and ran the obstacle course the football team used (Loren's idea), and Ethan basically lapped him without even breathing hard.

Ethan said he'd been recruited to play football but didn't like the coach, didn't like the "politics" of the game anymore. He had an antimilitary bent that somehow didn't bother Loren as much as it would have in other people. He said, for example, that the U.S. Special Forces were probably responsible for more innocent people being killed in Latin America than Pinochet and Noriega combined (Loren had to look both names up). But the two of them usually *talked* about stuff like this, instead of arguing about it, and Ethan actually listened to Loren. He also had a knack for getting Loren to do things without yelling or nagging. Like the manners thing—ten push-ups every time Loren forgot to say please for something, or thanks. After three or four months Ethan even convinced him—again, without seeming to try—that Loren might want to maybe study sometimes, just a little, instead of doing no work and skating by with low Bs.

At first his mom watched the whole thing unfold and didn't get involved. But as Loren started behaving better, she got more intrigued. It was almost—Loren realized this months later, after thinking about it a lot—like she just couldn't resist. Like she didn't want Loren to have anything good that she couldn't have too. So she started wearing smaller and smaller shirts whenever Ethan came around, and then one day Loren got home and found the two of them in the kitchen, half-dressed on the kitchen floor. It was practically incest, his mother and his Big Brother. Loren wasn't even spying—the junior high had a gas leak that day, so all the kids got sent home at 1:30 instead of 3:15. His mom yelled that Loren was a sneak and Ethan ran out of the apartment, carrying his wadded-up cardigan. He got kicked out of the program, stripped of his Big Brotherhood, and later wrote Loren and his mom separate five-page letters to apologize. Loren didn't bother reading his. Instead he wrapped it around an M-80 in the woods and blew it into confetti.

*

Twelve days after the golf course incident, Loren comes down to breakfast to find his mom and the pro waiting for him. The pro's plate is empty, just some yellow smears of egg yolk on it. He's reading the sports page and picking orange-juice pulp from between his teeth. Loren's mom's food is mostly untouched.

"What would you say about going camping this weekend?" she says to him. She says this like they've already been making plans and she's throwing out a new option—instead of the beach, how about camping? "Maybe we could find someplace up north," she continues. "Walk around, see some trees."

As far as Loren knows, his mom has never been camping in her life. She's not looking at him when she says this. Instead she butters her corn muffin intently, with a little more concentration than usual. The tendons in her wrist stick out. Loren sees crumbs falling and thinks—time for Something New?

"That sounds like fun," the pro follows up, like he's reading lines off a cue card. "Just the three of us." The sports section is folded into fourths, with some OJ pulp smeared onto the margins.

"What do you say, Loren?" his mom says. "Want to go camping?" She keeps buttering the corn muffin until it disintegrates, then puts the knife down and blinks at him.

Does he want to go camping? He definitely wants to go camping. He already has all the gear, or most of it, and he knows for a fact that the pro doesn't really like the outdoors unless it's heavily landscaped. Maybe they'll get out there and actually listen to him for once. But Loren also realizes that the golf course fire isn't completely behind him, and he's not sure how this factors in. The last few nights, he's heard them up late in his mom's room, talking in low voices. He bought a stethoscope from a medical-supply place and tried listening through the wall (though all he could make out was the pro saying his name a couple of times and the word *Columbine*).

"You don't have to work this weekend?" he asks the pro.

"What're vacation days for?" the pro says. "I've got some time saved up. I can cancel all my lessons and catch up when we're back."

Loren's hesitant, but maybe the New Thing here is his mom trying to connect with him on his level. Maybe at some point during the weekend he'll have to pull up a log and sit through some stupid lecture. Whatever it is, he figures, he'd be better off handling it in the woods. He's more comfortable out there.

"OK," Loren tells them. "Sure, let's go. Should I pick the place? Because I heard about this one up near Hansenville where you can park and it's only a short hike in. Like less than a mile. But it's a state park, so you have to reserve in advance I think."

Silence. His mom considers the crumbled pieces of her muffin and tells him they'll figure all that out. "Just start packing," she says.

*

The rental car is a two-door red Pontiac with plastic everything. The pro said he didn't want to run up the miles on his lease, and Loren's mom's car probably wouldn't make it there and back. They're heading north on the highway, expansion joints thumping under the tires, and every twenty miles or so an exit rolls past. From his perch in the backseat Loren can see his mom's ponytail against the headrest. Her window is open a few inches, and the wind has pulled a few strands of brown hair free. The radio plays an oldies station that's slowly overtaken by static as they drive north, but the music is clear enough for the pro to tap his hairy knuckles on the steering wheel.

Loren tries to keep himself occupied but there's not much to do. He already searched through both of the marsupial seat-back pockets and found nothing but a gas receipt and a hardened, lint-covered ball of old gum. The backseat is tiny, and Loren stretches out by propping his feet up against the opposite window. He can tell the pro wants him to take them down so he purposely leaves them there, even though after a few minutes the position isn't comfortable anymore.

They get passed by a pickup with a dog hanging out the passenger side, ears flapping. The pro goes around a gleaming silver tanker truck that looks like a giant Tylenol capsule, and Loren watches the Pontiac's reflection slide along the underside as they pass, like a red marble moving through a syringe. The pro has a tendency to drift slowly out of his lane and then veer back. Each time he does it both Loren and his mom reach out for something to hold on to. It's a little like tacking in a schooner, and Loren can feel himself getting woozy.

For long sections of the drive nobody says anything. "Where's this place again?" Loren asks. They haven't told him the name of the campsite.

"Carlyle County," the pro says. "Another two hours or so."

"And they have tents and coolers and stuff? A place to buy food?"

"All that's taken care of," the pro says. "Everything's arranged."

In the trunk is nothing but his backpack and two small overnight bags. Something's up, but Loren hasn't figured out what. If they really are going into the woods, he pictures the two of them having real problems—his mom is wearing flip-flops. Whatever it is, though, he figures he can handle it.

They stop at a diner that's about two-thirds chrome, inside and out. The menu says it's famous. When Loren can't decide between chicken parmigiana and waffles, his mom stuns him by saying he should just order both. "It's OK," she says. "Get whatever you want." Which by itself is as strange as anything that's happened in the past week. Usually she gets mad when he asks to get an appetizer. The pro is about to protest but Loren's mom silences him with a look. He says he needs to make a phone call anyway so she should just order him a club sandwich. Loren watches him wander around the parking lot trying to get reception, peering at his cell phone and pointing it over his head like it's a flare.

When the food comes Loren starts eating and his mom sips her coffee and watches him with a weird expression. She knows something, Loren can tell. Two nights ago, she insisted on lining up all his gear on his bed and helping him load his pack, even though she probably knows as much about camping as she does about space travel. She had some official-looking page that seemed like it had been ripped out of a pamphlet, listing everything he was supposed to bring. Boots, T-shirts, extra socks. On the back was an even longer list of stuff he couldn't bring. No flasks. No metal cutlery. No flammables or lanterns or box cutters or blades of any kind.

"Where'd you get that?" Loren asked her.

"This? Tom was doing some research. I guess the campsite sent it to him."

"It seems kind of specific."

She said some of these places have strict rules, and then she asked to see his boots. The boots. Ever since the golf course, they'd been in Loren's closet, sealed in six plastic grocery bags. He told his mom he could just pack them later but she said no, she wanted to see them now, she had to decide if he might need new ones. When Loren finally gave in and took them out of the bags they had dried mud and grass on them, and they reeked of gasoline. It spread quickly through the room, the fumes were practically visible, and something seemed to shift inside her. She didn't react—she didn't get mad or yell. Instead she looked around the room at his Special Forces posters, his camouflage ponchos hanging in the closet, the ammo boxes he uses to store CDs, and with a sigh she said those boots would probably work.

A half hour after they leave the diner, Loren already regrets the chicken-waffle combination. They're off the highway and on a smaller, two-lane road, and the pro's drift-and-swerve steering has gotten worse. At one point the Pontiac gets so far out onto the shoulder that he has to skid to get it back onto pavement. Loren and his mom both grab for a handhold, and she asks him again to please slow down.

"We're almost there," the pro says. "I just want to keep moving, OK?"

Loren feels woozier than before, especially now that he's got a full stomach. He's never been carsick before, but his head feels like it's hollow and he finds himself swallowing a lot. He tries to roll down the window but the pro has the child locks on. When he asks for some air the pro opens one window three inches and then closes it back an inch.

The breeze helps a little but not much. Loren tells himself to look out the window, but that doesn't work either. The roads keep getting smaller and windier. The pro makes turns, looks for landmarks. He's reading directions off a sheet of paper and asking Loren's mom to keep an eye out for road signs. They go through narrow canyons lined by rock walls with perfectly straight grooves in them, where road crews packed the dynamite. Loren has a gauzy thought that that must be a fun job. You get to be outside all day, blowing stuff up. No radio station has come in for a while now—the pro hit scan about ten miles back and since then the green numbers just keep cycling. Sunlight flickers down through some trees onto the ground below, blinking light and dark, which somehow makes Loren feel even worse. Twenty minutes, the pro says. Twenty minutes and they'll be there.

"I think we might have to pull over," Loren announces, though his words get lost in the rushing air of the barely opened window. No one in the front seat hears him. He's holding his mouth up to the window and taking deep gulps and thinking about the dog he saw hanging out of the pickup truck a while ago. A face full of fresh air like that—no wonder the dog looked so happy. The pro misses a left and has to make a veering U-turn and Loren's face gets pressed against the glass, then yanked away sharply as the car reverses. He feels like he's being flung around at the end of a lasso.

He doesn't want to admit it, but his claustrophobia is kicking in. The backseat of the rental is tiny, and the child locks on the windows are freaking him out, and he realizes that he couldn't get out of the car if he had to. If the pro missed a turn really badly and the car plunged off a bridge and into a river (neither of which he's seen the entire drive, but still), Loren thinks that he would be seriously, seriously fucked. He'd have to kick out a rear window. Or he'd have to climb into the front seat and save his mom first and then save himself and go back for the pro if he felt like it.

"Can we pull over?" he says again, louder this time.

"We're close," the pro says. "We're almost there."

"I think I'm going to spew," Loren says. "Can we please pull over for two minutes? What difference does it make when we get there?"

The backseat is definitely getting smaller.

His mom says, "Tom, if he's going to be sick...."

The pro keeps driving and says, "Cecile, we talked about this, remember? United front—we agreed."

"This isn't the same thing. We're not even there yet."

Loren wants to ask what they're talking about, what united front? But his head is swimming and if he opens his mouth, lunch is coming out. He feels himself pressed back into the seat as the car accelerates.

"It's fine," the pro says. "If he throws up he throws up—it's a rental. But he's not getting out of the car. We'll be there in a few minutes."

Outside, the trees start to look different. At first Loren thinks it's just him, his ballooning head, but no, the trees really are all mangy and sick-looking, like you could push them over if you wanted to. The pro slows down near a sign for something called the Schaeffer Camp for Musical Instruction, and to Loren's surprise he turns in.

There's a run-down gate with three men sitting on folding chairs, each of them in a dirty white sash. One of them wears a T-shirt that says, "Official Jack Daniels Tasting Team." The pro gives a name—Loren's name instead of his own, another strange thing—and a man with a clipboard scans down his list and waves them through. No other words get exchanged. Loren can feel the other two eyeing him from their chairs, and he turns to watch them get smaller in the back window, their bodies sliced up horizontally by defrost wires inside the glass.

The property looks neglected, almost abandoned. The road is unpaved and bumpy, and the rental car bottoms out a few times. On either side are more dying or already-dead trees, though most of them somehow remain upright, like they don't even have it in them to fall over. The radio hooks on to some station now, a staticky commercial for mustard, and when Loren's mom reaches to turn it off he can see that her hands are shaking. Stuff is gurgling around in the back of his throat and he's thinking about his mom's flip-flops and the overnight bags and the lack of a tent.

Just start packing.

After what seems like forever they reach the parking lot. It's paved, though just barely, with weeds poking up through the asphalt and newish-looking white slanted lines that look like they were put down with a paintbrush. Loren wants to hold out until they get out of the car but the pro swerves into a spot and he knows he can't, no way.

Before the car even stops he throws up against the mostly closed window. His mom lets out a shriek, the pro throws the car into park, and they both scramble out. The inside bulb comes on. Loren's lunch is sprayed in a grayish-pink spatter down one side of the backseat, and he pushes the passenger seat forward and sags out of the car so at least the second wave ends up outside.

A minute or so later, when he stops heaving and looks up from the ground, bleary-eyed and weak, he sees something and understands. He realizes in an instant what's happening and how stupid he was to believe they were ever going camping.

What he sees is another kid about his own age, being led by his parents out of the parking lot toward some buildings, wrists held behind his back by a set of silver handcuffs.

CHAPTER 4

"Where are they?" William's mom says. "Tell us and we'll leave right now. We don't even have to get out of the car."

William slumps in the backseat and ignores her, listening to the clicking of the engine as it cools down. The parking lot is nearly empty—maybe ten cars scattered across spaces for a hundred. The trees surrounding it are tall pines, which would look almost stately except for the bare patches on them, and the grayish-yellow needles heaped underneath. Above the treetops, a line of ragged clouds floats past in formation.

William's mom stares at him for few long seconds in the growing silence, then spins around in the passenger seat to face front again. She crosses her arms with a huff, and her silver pineapple earrings bob around her head like tiny speed bags. They're her favorites—William's surprised she's wearing them to a place like this.

"You know, part of growing up is taking responsibility for your actions," his father says into the rearview mirror. "Owning up to your mistakes. Otherwise you never learn from them."

"We're worried that you're going down the wrong path," his mom says.

The paths again. They love to talk about the paths.

William responds by asking if they know what kind of trees these are. "They look like maybe pines," he says. "Right? But sick ones."

His father shakes his head. He's wearing glasses that turn dark in bright light, and right now they're at a halftint, making him seem bug-like in the mirror. William wishes it bothered him a little more to go out in public with stuff like that—stuff that makes William cringe.

"What would you do right now if you were us?" his father says.

"I'd start the car and drive me home," William says.

"Great. We're on the same page there, but you know what has to happen first. Your version of the story. That's not too much to ask."

William sneezes twice, then a third time. It's a bad sign. They haven't been on the property fifteen minutes and already his allergies are kicking in.

"We don't want to do this," his mom says.

"Then don't."

"Our family has never had a thief in it," his dad says. "That's not who we are."

They're never going to get anything out of him, and William knows it. He doesn't think they're going to leave him here—he's an only child and not exactly hearty—and he's willing to call their bluff. Everything he's seen so far has been weird to the point where it almost seems set up, arranged by his parents just to scare him. Those homeless guys at the gate, the parents leading their son away in handcuffs. A hundred feet away a red car just pulled up, and a kid is now draped out of the backseat, throwing up.

"William," his mom says. "You have one last chance. This is it."

She's facing forward, staring out the windshield at nothing.

William shrugs and reaches for the door handle. His mother lets out a long sigh and follows. When his father gets out of the car, William watches his glasses turn completely dark in the bright sunlight.

*

"He's faking," the pro says over the hood of the Pontiac. "He's trying to get out of this, but it won't work. I don't care if he throws up his organs—we're checking him in and he's staying."

Loren's sprawled on the pavement, clothes soaked warm, spitting out strings of saliva and trying to clear his head.

"He's not faking, Tom," Loren's mom says. "He's just carsick." She walks around to the driver's seat and gets Loren the soda she bought at a rest stop hours before. The cup has turned waxy soft and the soda's flat and beige, with melting ice diluting it to semisweetness. Loren takes small sips to rinse his mouth out. It tastes better than he would have guessed. He hands the cup back, humbly grateful.

"Are you going to make it?" his mom says. She has little worry lines pressing in around her mouth. The Pontiac ignition chimes softly, dumb and insistent.

Loren nods. "I'm OK. What is this place?"

"It's…a break. You get a break from us, and we get a break from you. It's a place where you'll be for a few weeks. I've got the brochure in the car somewhere. And it might not even be that bad. There's horse trails and a waterfall."

"Great. I can go swimming with handcuffs on."

A family of red-haired people, two parents and a son about Loren's age, stare at him as they pass, walking toward a set of railroad-tie steps at the far corner of the parking lot. Above the steps, some buildings are visible through the thinning trees.

"This was his idea," Loren says to his mom. "Right?"

"Tom's? Sort of."

"What does 'sort of' mean?"

The pro speaks up. "I heard that Cecile. Loren, this was her idea."

She glances over and tells the pro they'll talk about it on the way home. To Loren she says, "Look, it was this or call the police. The golf course was bad, really bad. He almost lost his job because of it.

He wanted you in a juvenile center right now. So I bargained him down and he found this place instead."

"Where'd you get the money?"

"I cashed in grandma's account."

"But she left that for me. It was supposed to be for college."

The chiming stops. Loren looks over and sees the pro dropping car keys onto the passenger seat. He reaches into the glove compartment and takes out a can of something, shiny and black. Loren's gack-covered clothes are giving off a smell.

Special Forces would do something here. Commandeer the Pontiac and barrel out of there, or just disappear into the woods. Loren's read stories about John McCain and Admiral Stockdale, how they were hauled into POW camps with broken bones all over, basically half-dead, and even then they managed to put up a fight. Name, rank, and service number only, right? Except Loren doesn't have a rank or service number, so that limits him to just his name. The important thing is to resist without doing anything stupid. Don't give in, but don't make your situation worse either.

The pro leans on the hood and looks through some papers in a folder, and Loren's mom moves a few feet away to dump out the remaining soda. The woods are so close, maybe fifty feet to the edge of the lot. So close that he can see sap on the trunks, dark sticky lines tracing cracks in the bark. If Loren were feeling better he could easily outrun the pro—he could probably outrun him backward, Loren's always been fast—but right now he's not sure. Those bare patches in the trees would be a factor, not a lot of cover, but he could figure out his next step when he got in there. Resist when you can, but don't do anything stupid.

As quietly as he can, Loren rolls to his feet and starts running. His mom yells, "Tom!" and there's a sound of scuffling feet behind him. As an escape attempt, it definitely falls in the category of Stupid, because Loren's so light-headed he can only make it about eight diagonal steps before sagging back down onto the pavement.

The pro comes running over and holds the black shiny can over Loren's face and squeezes. It's pepper spray, but something's wrong with the nozzle—nothing's coming out. Loren is flat on his back already anyway. The pine trees whirl above his head. He can hear his own fuzzy heartbeat thumping.

"Just calm down," the pro says. "Just take it easy. You're here and there's no getting around it." He keeps shaking the can and peering into the nozzle. The pavement is hot under Loren but it feels good right now. He thinks he could just lie here for hours, absorbing heat, gathering strength. Then he'd be able to do something. He tries to stop the pine trees from spinning and thinks, OK, not now but later. Resist later.

The red-haired family is at the top of the steps now, staring back at Loren with their mouths hanging open.

"Jesus," his mom says. "What this must look like."

"Stay strong, Cecile. We knew this would be hard." The pro turns to Loren. "You stay weak."

Loren thinks his mom might be softening on this idea. She looks at him on the ground for a long moment and the wrinkles around her mouth, the tiny fault lines, get one degree deeper. For the first time in his life she almost looks old. As long as he can remember his mom has gotten special treatment because of her looks. At restaurants waiters bring her free desserts, and men in suits try to pick her up at the ATM. Loren always got a kind of reflected flattery from it—he's proud that she's beautiful—but sometimes it goes too far. Loren once thought a man behind them in line at the supermarket was being pushy, too aggressive in trying to talk to her. His mom acted like it was no big deal, but when the man made a comment about her butt Loren turned around and threatened to bust some Delta Force moves on his head. Which actually worked—the man did leave Loren's mom alone, and even left the store, but only after he shoved Loren into a potato chip display.

In the parking lot, if she hesitates at all about following through with the plan, she doesn't hesitate for long. Instead she crouches down and tells Loren it's going to be easier for everyone if he just goes up to the camp willingly. "Now," she says. "I mean it."

"I don't have any choice, do I?"

She doesn't even shake her head. She doesn't need to.

"OK," Loren says. "I'll go. Just let me get my stuff."

They help him to his feet and walk him slowly back to the car. The pro's guiding him, a hand on his back, which somehow bothers Loren more than anything else he's been through so far. He thinks about wheeling around with a downward chop. It only takes seven pounds of pressure to break someone's collarbone—he read that somewhere.

In the passenger seat he sits, blinking and empty-headed. The plastic, new-car smell is fighting with the vomit smell. "I'll get your backpack," Loren's mom tells him. Cicadas are ratcheting in the woods, and something on the car seat sticks up into his leg, something sharp. When Loren reaches under him he realizes it's the Pontiac keys, and he gets an idea.

The trunk slams and the pro says, "Ready?" When Loren stands up he's got the keys in his pocket. Quick as a thief—no noise, no strange movements. He's not even sure what he's going to do with them yet. Maybe if he's left alone for a few minutes he can try to get away. Assess your materiel. Commandeer assets. Resist when you can.

At the base of the railroad-tie steps, Loren takes the backpack from his mom. It feels like it weighs three hundred pounds, but he tells himself he can handle it. A small stream drains back down the hill, slaloming around rocks and disappearing at the bottom into a rusted metal pipe. On the steps Loren sees something weird—little musical instruments carved into each piece of wood. Tiny tubas and French horns, bass drums and snare drums, a line of clarinets. Most of the shapes are filled in with leaves and dirt. The pro reaches down for a pine needle and starts poking it into the nozzle of the pepper spray can. When they get to the top step Loren hears a hissing noise and the pro says, "Hey, I got it. Hey it works!"

They walk past some cabins, gently sagging in on themselves and looking to Loren as if they were slowly deflating. A few have plywood boards nailed over the windows and others have missing panes of glass, like knocked-out teeth. His mom keeps glancing back and forth between what she sees around her and the brochure in her hand. The grass underneath their feet is so brown and dead that it crunches.

Higher up the path sits a larger house, white with black shutters, which seems to overlook the property and is in slightly better shape. Better, at least, than the cabins. The house gives off a steady hum of air-conditioning, and through the upstairs windows Loren can see into two of the rooms, where identical ceiling fans are spinning at the same speed. It's like looking at the inner gears of a watch.

There's a swimming pool on the property, which contrasts with the rest of the camp in that it's perfectly maintained. Brilliant, clear water, no leaves floating in it, not even an insect that Loren can see. It's a topaz gem in a junkyard. On the paved patio surrounding it are two chaises—varnished teak with bright red canvas stretched taut across the frames. They're both set up to face the deep end of the pool like an ad for a tropical vacation. A sign above them says, "*Adagio!* No running." Loren doesn't know what the word means— it sounds like a kind of pasta.

Beyond the pool is a barn, also in surprisingly decent condition, with not-too-faded red paint and a complete set of intact windows, and next to it on the ground is a huge circle of hexagonal paving stones with dead grass sprouting through the cracks. The whole thing is maybe a hundred feet across—some kind of outdoor performance space, or at least that's what it used to be. Near the center some initials have been grooved into the stones, "GRSCMI," and above them stands a rickety card table with a box of supermarket doughnuts on it and three half-filled Mylar balloons sagging at the bottom of a length of twine like fish on a string. A sign, hand-lettered and taped to the table, reads: "Welcome to Camp Ascend!"

A bored-looking woman stands behind the card table. "You're late," she says to them. "Kitty" is written on her name tag in spiky script.

"We got lost," the pro says. "And then we got hung up in the parking lot. Anyway we're here now. That's all that matters."

"Where's Loren?" the woman says. She's wearing expensive-looking shoes and a one-piece white zip-up thing like an Elvis suit. Her face is extremely tan, the color of wood, and tiny droplets of sweat bubble up through her makeup.

"Here," he says. Name, rank, and service number—nothing else.

"What?" the woman says. "Are you kidding? OK, hold on. We have you down as a girl."

Loren's mom says, "Well, he's not."

"OK, OK," the woman says, crossing a line out on her list and writing something in its place. She holds the pen with all five fingers, and her nails are so long they click against each other.

A definite surprise, Loren thinks: the place is coed. He feels a little better, but his feet are still heavy and his head seems weightless. He has the rental-car keys in his pocket though. That's something— a charm, a ticket out of here. He looks around the property to get his bearings and sees a small animal dart out from under one of the cabins and into the woods, dragging something behind it. Kitty keeps scratching at her list. The pro takes a big bite of powdered doughnut and white sugar dusts onto his shirt. Loren's mouth is so dry that his tongue is sticking to various parts of it. A powdered doughnut right now would be like eating a handful of sand. His throat would seize up.

The woman clicks her pen and hands the pro and Loren's mom blank "Hello" name tags. "You two are in there," she says. "The barn. You'll meet with the Colonel. It's inside on the right." Then she turns to Loren. "You come with me, to the cabin. You can drop your stuff. The other kids are already there."

Loren picks up his backpack and follows her off the ring of stones and back toward a cluster of cabins. The straps of the pack cut into his shoulders. He thinks about bolting here, but it's a long way back to the car and he hasn't had a chance to check out the security yet. The woman, Kitty, doesn't seem too concerned about an escape, though. She stays in front of him, wobbling slightly in her high heels. Loren glances back, thinking he might see his mom, but instead all he sees is the side door of the barn closing.

"It's that one," Kitty says finally, pointing to one of the less decrepit cabins. "Go inside and wait." The wooden steps sag a little as Loren climbs them—two, plus a gap in the middle where the third one's supposed to be. A shiny dead bolt is fastened to the outside of the door frame, conspicuously new, slate gray and thick as a thumb. They'll be locked in, he realizes.

The cabin is dim inside and smells like dust. Loren sees five kids about his own age, sitting on their hands on the floor like they're condemned. They look up at him but no one says anything. The red-haired kid from the parking lot is there, plus two others who look a lot alike—probably twins. A fourth rocks back and forth in a weird, unsettling way. Loren's seen animals do the same thing in run-down zoos. He steps past them all, floorboards creaking under his boots. The cabin has twelve low beds, six on each side, some of them claimed by a duffel bag or a suitcase.

At the far end of the cabin is a window with bars across it, which lets a gridded trapezoid of sunlight shine onto the floor. Loren sets his pack on the bunk closest to it—already he's thinking about reconnaissance and escape routes. The bunk has a blue-and-white striped mattress on it, dingy and not much thicker than a newspaper, with rust stains leaking out from metal buttons. A set of black sweats, tops and bottoms, lies folded near the foot of the bunk. It's warm and airless inside the cabin, and the only sound comes from the cicadas outside, overtaking each other in waves.

On the floor by the adjacent bunk, Loren notices some writing.

In faint pencil are the words, *ALL DOWNHILL FROM HERE.* That's probably true enough. The last letter has a squiggly line leading away from it and disappearing under the next bunk, like a piece of string. He wants to kneel down and investigate, but he's distracted by one of the twins, who sniffs the air and announces that Loren stinks. It's the first thing anyone's said since he walked in.

He ignores the comment and asks the other twin, "What's in the rest of the cabins?"

"How should I know?" the twin says.

"Shut up!" another kid says. He has nervous eyes. "They told us no talking."

More rocking from the rocker.

"Who told you no talking?" Loren asks.

"The guard. The big one."

"But he's not here, right?"

The red-haired kid gestures up behind Loren to a camera mounted high in a corner of the cabin. A single green light next to the lens blinks steadily. As a test Loren walks in front of it, staring up. Then he waves. When nothing happens he sits down on his bunk.

"We're supposed to sit on the floor," the nervous kid says. "On our hands. He told us no getting on the beds."

"He didn't tell me. If he comes in I'll say I didn't know."

"But we're supposed to tell you. He told us to tell everyone who comes in."

"I thought he also told you no talking."

Pause. "He did."

The rocker is rocking a little faster now.

"If he catches you it's not my fault," the nervous kid says. "I told you no beds. Everyone heard."

Loren tells the kid to just take it easy, and then, as a test, he lies back down on the mattress, half expecting the camera to start beeping. The bed is lumpy and thin—it feels like lying on uneven ground. After a few seconds he puts his boots up on it too, crossing them as nonchalantly as he can. The nervous kid's eyes go wide.

The twins notice this and give each other a look. They both have really nice bags—matching high-tech backpacks with about fifty straps and mesh webbing and carabiners in different colors clipped all around them. The kind of gear you could take up Mount Everest.

There's movement underneath the cabin, some animal making scratching noises. Loren stamps one boot on the floor and it stops. He puts his hands behind his head. His stomach is basically back to feeling OK. The vomity clothes aren't bothering him either. He's acting normal, acting relaxed.

The twins pull their hands out from under their butts and drape them back onto the mattresses behind them. They look like they're about to get up too, when Loren hears approaching footsteps near the cabin, dead grass crunching. He slinks down onto the floor and says, "Someone's coming."

*

The Colonel leans back in his office chair and starts talking about honor and accountability.

"These are things that a lot of kids just don't see nowadays," he says. "Stuff they don't understand. So what we do here—what we *try* to do—is push them a little and hold them responsible for their actions. How do we do that? Good question. First off, no television. That means no MTV, no Comedy Central, no video games. For some of these kids, that alone is a big burden."

The couple in front of his desk nods solemnly. The Colonel's already forgotten their names—he's not good with details like that. They're holding their name tags in their hands, so no help there. The woman has a brochure for Camp Ascend! rolled up in her hand, and the man wears a bright blue polo shirt with a surprising amount of powdered sugar on it. This is the ninth and last set of parents the

Colonel has to meet with today, and they all get the same honor-and-accountability speech, stolen almost word for word from the director of the youth home where he did his community service. He heard it so many times that when he decided to launch Camp Ascend! he could write down whole sections from memory, and the gaps he filled in with stuff he found online.

Classical music plays on the stereo in his office. The Colonel knows precisely jack squat about music and can't even keep the names straight (the current disc is Shosto-somebody), but he found a crap load of classical CDs left over from the music camp and likes to play them on days when the parents come in. It helps create the right atmosphere and convinces them that he's cultured, a man of many interests.

The office itself is a luxury. Most of his previous businesses were run from kitchen tables or storage units, or out of the backs of vans. Initially the Colonel had big plans to buy some new furniture, but so far he's only gotten around to a few minor changes. He brought in a fax machine (an old one, with wheels that squeak), which he considers a necessity out here in the woods. Parents fax in applications and legal waivers, and he communicates with his banks via the machine as well.

A lot of the old photographs around the office remain in place—big eight-by-tens of kids sitting around a bonfire, or having splash fights at the pool. Before the first class the Colonel took down about half the pictures, every one that showed a musical instrument, along with the framed conductor's baton in black velvet and the brass placard that said, "The Maestro Will See You Now." In their place are squares of unfaded paneling, which he'll have to do something about at some point.

"You were a Marine, huh?" the man across the desk says. "Ever see any action?"

"A little, but I don't like to bore everyone with war stories."

"Vietnam?"

If the Colonel had been drafted he would have crawled on his hands and knees to Canada. He would have sold his grandmother to the Pentagon as a sex slave. But it never came to that—he was a little too young.

"Yeah, I went," he says now. "Mekong. Khe Sanh." He lets the words trail off and then shakes his head slowly, which is supposed to show that something big happened to him over there, something significant, and also that the experience might be painful to dredge up so please don't ask. Over the speakers, one of the Shosto-whatever songs ends and a crowd starts clapping softly. It sounds like rain.

"Well, anyway," the man says. "We did want to say thanks for taking us in at the last minute like this. I know you probably have to turn people away sometimes."

"All the time," the Colonel says. "All the time. We can only help so many families, unfortunately enough."

"This place has been open, what, about fifteen years?"

The Colonel hesitates. Camp Ascend! opened sixteen months ago, but he doesn't know whether this is a trap or merely a dumb person. He tries to keep these meetings as short as possible—they don't really serve any purpose, other than to convince people that there's nothing wrong here, nothing amiss. After the parents leave today he has to drive out and give the three homeless men at the gate a ride back to town. Every time a new group of kids checks in the Colonel swings by the shelter and hires a few bums for the day, to provide security and make it seem like the camp is fully staffed. Twenty bucks each, plus a six-pack to the one who can keep his mouth shut the most. It's money well spent.

"About that long," the Colonel says. When there's no noticeable reaction he rules out "trap" and puts a mental check mark next to "dumb person." The man across the desk nods and cracks his knuckles. He's got powdered sugar under his fingernails.

"What about a doctor?" the mom says. "Is there someone here if the kids get hurt?"

Women usually ask the better questions, the Colonel's found. He thinks it's because they're nurturers. Kitty's not but most women are.

"Not right at this minute, no. Ordinarily, yes. He got called into town on some business. But I can show you the infirmary if you want."

Another good-natured lie—there's no doctor at the camp, and the infirmary has been locked up for months. Every horizontal surface in the room has a layer of dust on it, and hornets have gotten in there somehow. It's reverted back to nature. If the couple says yes, they want to see it, then he'll come up with something else. *You know what? I just realized the doctor has the only set of keys. He keeps prescription drugs in there, so we're pretty strict about access.*

They don't seem interested though. "You're sure?" the Colonel says. "Well, I'll tell you this—even when the doc is here, he's pretty bored, because the kids never get hurt."

"Never?"

"Not in our"—he gives Doughnut Dave a significant look—"*15 years* of operation. We like to keep someone around, but the place is so safe it's not really necessary."

The woman seems mildly reassured and says, "Where's the waterfall, Corporal?"

Corporal? He blinks at her and decides to let it go. "About two miles north," he says. "It's flowing pretty good right now, because we've had some rain."

"Mail? Phone calls?"

"No, and no. The program here is challenging, and we don't want the kids sending scary letters home. That's a distraction, and we've found it's better for everyone—you, the kids, and especially us—if there's no contact. I'll tell you what, though. Give me a call from time to time. Not too often, but every other week. I can keep you updated on, ah"—he looks down at a sheet on his desk—"Loren's progress. How she's doing, how she's feeling, any special requests she might have."

"Loren's a boy," the mom says. There's an edge in her voice.

The Colonel gives an automatic smile. Did he know that? They probably would have mentioned it when they made the arrangements, right?

"Yes," the Colonel says. "Of course he is." Move on! Press ahead! Don't dwell on mistakes. "So I should probably ask if there's anything special we need to know about this Loren," he says.

"Let's see," the mom says. "He's…sensitive, and he's got a different way of looking at things."

The man snorts and crosses his arms. When the Colonel looks at him, he shrugs and says, "He's not my kid. She gets the blame."

"Don't start," the woman says.

The Colonel's seen these conversations turn into family therapy before. It happens a lot, and while it eats up some time, his curiosity is usually enough to let the people go at each other for a while. The things he's heard people say, the dirt that gets aired—right in front of him! This mother smokes pot, this father shoplifts. This mom's having an affair with the contractor, or the maid, or both. Two months ago a woman tried to punch her husband, knocking over a chair and two pictures of music campers on a day hike.

Unfortunately, the current discussion doesn't get anywhere near that rough. The man simply reaches into his shirt pocket and pulls out a Polaroid, slightly crumpled and shiny. He flicks it across the Colonel's desk like a card dealer.

"What's this?"

"Insurance photo," the man says. "Just so you know what you're up against."

"It's all black." The image looks like someone's hand was over the lens.

"That's right. A day before this it was Augusta National. A county course, OK, but lush, well maintained. A fucking emerald. And then this little sensitive, creative thinker of hers comes along and torches it."

"Tom."

"Four hundred thousand dollars in damage. Hedges, all new sod—"

"*Tom.*"

"I just want the Colonel to know he should watch the kid around anything flammable, OK? I just want him to keep fire extinguishers handy and put away the oily rags, and that's all I'm going to say."

"If only," the woman says. "Just stop talking, will you please?"

The Colonel hands back the Polaroid and says, "Listen. We're experienced in handling cases like this. We have a program, a process, and after a few days he'll be a lot less likely to go looking for fires to start, I promise."

"What exactly are you going to do?" the man asks.

The Colonel hedges a bit. "The basics. No TV, though I guess I already mentioned that. Also discipline, accountability. We try to tire them out a lot."

The woman stares at him as his words trail off. After a long moment she shifts in her chair.

"That's it?" she says. "That's your program?"

"Like I said," the Colonel tells her. "We stick to the fundamentals."

"You know what?" the woman says. "I'm starting to have some doubts about the whole idea."

The Colonel sits back in his creaky office chair and steeples his fingers in front of his face.

"Cecile, we've been through this."

"I know. And we both agreed. But I've never been away from Loren for six weeks, and I'm having a harder time with it than I thought. And looking around this place doesn't make me feel any better. Everything is so, I don't know, *run-down*."

"It's not supposed to be the Taj Mahal," the Colonel says.

"Sure, but would a coat of paint kill anyone? Some soap and water? I mean, those cabins, are they going to be standing much longer? Because it doesn't look like it."

"Listen," the Colonel says. "I understand completely. But just so you know, we have a pretty strict policy about refunds."

"We didn't give you any money yet," the woman says.

The Colonel freezes. She's right—he remembers now. They were a last-minute addition. He made an exception this time and said they could worry about the financials when they got here.

The man reaches into his shirt pocket where the Polaroid was and pulls out a folded cashier's check.

"I think this was a mistake," she says, reaching for the check. "I'm sorry if we wasted your time. Tom, let's go."

When she stands to leave, the Colonel says loudly that he can't let her do that.

"What do you mean?" the woman says. "Of course you can."

The Colonel feels a darker impulse bubbling up. He knows he can be hapless sometimes, but when there's money involved, money he can *see*, his caveman instincts start to come out. The caveman philosophy says that you do what's necessary to bring meat back to the fire. Some people are capable of those things, and the rest, probably 98 percent of the population, don't have the nerve, so they wuss out and say they're "following the rules" and "being a decent member of society," all that crap. The check is a seventeen-thousand-dollar chunk of meat, and the Colonel's not just going to let it walk out of here. One time during the credit card operation, he found out that a junior associate was skimming and had him beaten with a two-by-four. The man's vision was blurry for months, and that was for less money than this.

"Right," the Colonel says. "It's a free country, you can leave anytime you want. But before you walk out of here, indulge me in one quick story."

The man and woman look at each other.

"Please," the Colonel says. "It won't take long."

They remain standing but turn to face him.

"We had a family come through here a few years ago," the Colonel says. "The, ah, Sousas. Ever hear of them?"

Blank looks.

"They signed their son up for the basic program, same as you. On that first day, his parents sat across this very desk from me and said the same things I hear you saying now. 'The windows are dirty, the grass isn't green enough.' They asked to pull their son out, and I let them. Any idea what happened next?"

Silence. Skeptical faces. He wishes they'd say something, anything, because it would give him time to think. Instead he has to dream up stuff on the fly.

"That same kid quickly graduated from firecrackers to BB guns to assault rifles," the Colonel says. "Three of which he brought to the high school one day seven months later, where he took his earth science teacher hostage."

Details! Seven months, earth science. Every story lives or dies on the specifics.

In the doorway, the mom's face turns grave, but the Colonel keeps pressing.

"Two-hour standoff. The SWAT team got called in. The boy refused to surrender, until they took him out with a knee shot. He'll never walk right again, and most of his walking these days is around the grounds of a psychiatric hospital, where he'll stay until he's very, very old."

The mom's back on the fence now—he can tell. You do what you have to do.

"His mother, Mrs. Sousa, is now on our board of advisors. She's made it her life's work to help parents avoid the mistake she made that day. We can call her right now if you want. I've got her on speed dial."

He picks up the phone and holds the handset out to them. The woman chews her lip but stays rooted in place. Her eyebrows are pressed together.

"No?" the Colonel says. "OK, I won't push. But let me tell you something. I lie awake nights and think about how much of that was my fault. That's why I can't let you just walk out of here—I couldn't live with myself if it happened again. If you really want to go, I can't stop you. But before you leave, ask yourself whether your son, Loren, might be at risk for that same type of dangerous behavior. And whether you're willing to gamble with his future because of a little faded paint."

He sets the handset gently down onto the phone and sits back in his chair again. Sometimes a caveman doesn't need the club. Sometimes a trap works better.

The mom takes a deep breath and turns the check over in her hands.

"Just take care of him, OK?" she says. "He's my only kid, and he's really not a monster, just a little…."

"Mixed-up?" the Colonel offers. Marketing. You could never say the kids were bad.

"Exactly," she says. "He's mixed-up."

"We see that all the time," the Colonel says. "Lots of mixed-up kids in the world. He'll be fine. I'm actually curious to meet this Loren."

And for the first time in the conversation, he's not lying.

*

If you're supposed to feel violated by the process of being frisked, Loren doesn't. He and the other five kids are lined up outside their cabin, and it's just the way he's seen it in cop shows—feet wide, hands up against the wall. The shingles of the cabin are surprisingly cool in the shade, pressing little grooves into his palms. Behind him Donovan, the guard, is holding out a shoe box. He looks more like an ape than anyone Loren's ever seen before. That sloped forehead, and the extra-long arms—it's like he should be swinging from trees. Donovan's wearing desert camouflage, five different shades of tan, which Loren thinks doesn't make much sense, given that they're in the woods. Maybe he's waiting for all the pine trees to die.

"Whatever's in your pockets, now's the time to hand it over," Donovan says. "You get one chance. After that you'll be patted down, and anything I find besides lint means an automatic strip search. So don't fuck around."

He starts working his way down the line, holding the shoe box in front of each kid. When he gets to the twins they give each other a glance and then take a long time emptying their pockets, producing a one-hitter made of mahogany and brass, a Zippo lighter, and two folded hunting knives each, plus billfolds with a respectable amount of money in them. Over his shoulder, Loren sees a green Amex card as it drops into the box.

"When do we get this stuff back?" one of them says.

"Not until you leave," Donovan tells him.

"We know how much money's in there," the other one says. "The exact amount."

"Congratulations. No more talking."

Next to them the nervous kid dumps in a handful of change and breath mints and a comb. "How do you know which coins are everyone else's and which are mine?" he says.

Donovan says the next person who opens his blowhole is going to regret it. After the last kid empties his pockets Donovan puts the box down in the grass and goes back the other way in line, patting each kid down in turn.

The bottom foot or so of the cabin is green with moss, and the shingles are rotting. When Loren shifts his hands, little shards of spongy wood stick to his palms. He's strangely not nervous. He already hid the Pontiac keys in the cabin, tied to the bottom of an empty bed frame two bunks down from his own. If someone really searched for them the keys would turn up, but he doesn't think that's likely.

There's a noise behind him and Loren turns to see three girls lining up outside another cabin fifty feet away. They're putting stuff into another shoe box held by the high-heeled woman in the Elvis suit, Kitty. She puts the box down and yawns and says something to the girls, and after some confused glances they start frisking each other. Not surprisingly all three come up with nothing. Then they file back into their cabin.

So six boys and three girls. One mean male guard and one bored female guard/administrator. Seriously decaying infrastructure. Loren's assessing his situation, gathering intelligence. When Donovan finally makes his way down the line and stands behind him, Loren puts his feet deliberately close together. Then *bam*—they get kicked back out wider. He doesn't even see the kick coming. Donovan starts patting him down, and Loren says, loud enough for everyone to hear, "I don't usually do stuff like this on the first date."

It gets a few laughs, but Donovan puts his ape face up next to Loren's ear and says, "You just earned a spot at the front of the conga line."

"The what?"

"You'll see. After the parents leave."

Once he's finished, Donovan marches everybody back into the cabin and tells them to change into the black sweats set out on each mattress. Loren's probably more grateful than anyone else to be out of his clothes, which are damp and vomity-smelling, but that feeling vanishes when he puts the sweats on. They're...not clean. They're dirty from the last group, or the last few groups, and they smell like old sweat. Plus they don't really fit. A few kids try to roll up the sleeves, but Donovan, watching from the doorway with his arms crossed, says the sleeves need to stay down at all times.

"I don't want to see any more of you than I have to," he says. "This is your uniform—the only thing you're allowed to wear here. You get one set, and we'll tell you when you can wash them. If you rip yours, or destroy them, or damage them in any way, your next option is a wool sweater—which trust me is dirtier and smells worse. So don't screw around."

He takes a few steps inside and continues, pacing between the bunks.

"Now," he says. "I want you to take the bag you brought here and pull out all the socks and underwear. Everything else stays in. That means any other clothes, any books, DVD players, pictures of your cat—I don't want to see that crap. Then zip up the bags and line them up on the center plank of the cabin. We'll lock them up, and you'll only get access if you put in a formal request and if one of us feels like taking you over there. OK? Do I make sense? Good."

The kids all start rifling through their bags, and Loren immediately goes for some extra things he figures he'll need. He sets out a small pile of wool socks, and underneath it he stashes his Swiss army knife and a hundred-foot length of tactical rope (which Special Forces guys use, strong enough to pick up a boat), plus a tiny compass and a pack of matches. The water filter would be good to keep—it makes him more or less self-sufficient in the woods, at least for a few days—but it's bright white and the size of a soda can, so probably too big to stash. He also gets the Pontiac keys when Donovan goes back outside for a second and ties them inside his sweatpants, bound together with the waist string so they won't jingle. All the other contraband goes under his mattress. As he's stuffing it all down there, something pokes him in the hand. It's a clarinet reed, yellowed with age, like an artifact. He's staring at it when Donovan appears behind him and grabs the reed.

"Did I say anything about digging under your bunk?"

"No."

"Are you looking for lost change?"

Loren shakes his head, and Donovan walks on.

The twins already have their high-tech bags down on the center plank. The red-haired kid is done next, breathing heavily and thumping his rolling suitcase onto the floor like it's a safe. He doesn't have a whole lot of outdoor experience—Loren can tell. The one with the nervous eyes, same thing. He's wearing brand-new hiking boots, basically blisters waiting to happen. They still have the plastic price tag loop, like a circle of heavy-duty fishing line, laced through one of the grommets.

Loren lines up next to them and drops his pack, wondering where the other guards are, or if there even are any other guards. The place is so deserted, what's to keep the kids from just scattering like roaches? If Loren took off on his own, sprinting for the rental car, he'd likely get caught. But if they all took off at once Donovan could only catch one or maybe two of them, right? Even if there were surveillance cameras all over the property, those weren't the same as actual people who could chase down an actual kid. The twins could probably be persuaded—they seem like they're up for anything—but the red-haired kid might not be. The one with the nervous eyes, no way. And the last of the six boys, the kid who was rocking on the floor, is a bigger mystery. He doesn't even have a suit-case or a backpack—just a brown grocery bag with some clothes stuffed into it. It gets dropped onto the plank and he lines up with the rest of them.

Kitty is suddenly outside the cabin.

"Everyone gone?" Donovan says.

"All but one couple," she says. "Lost their car keys. The tow truck's coming soon, I think. It's clear as long as you go straight up into the woods."

"OK," Donovan says. "Bring the girls over."

He marches the six kids outside and lines them up, with Loren in front. The three girls file out of their cabin. They're now wearing the same not-clean black sweats as the boys, with the sleeves rolled down. One of the girls looks at Loren as they pass. She has bright eyes and the blackest hair he's ever seen, with a purple streak dyed into one side. When all nine kids are in place, Donovan gives them a length of white rope that they have to hold in their right hands. If anyone drops the rope, Donovan says, it gets tied to that kid's wrist.

If a second kid drops the rope it gets tied to all nine wrists. This is the conga line, Loren realizes. This is how the place can operate with only a few guards. Donovan points Loren in the direction of a trailhead barely visible in a line of trees, and Loren sets off.

For the next two hours they march laps along a thin dirt trail that traces a rough oval around the main part of the property. It's about two miles, give or take, and overgrown, so he has to clear sections of it as they go, stomping onto high weeds and bushes with his boots. This is why it's worse to be in front. Before long the rope is tied around all nine wrists, and because it's not long enough, the kids start tripping on each other. The twins keep saying, "What the fuck?" over and over again, and Donovan keeps telling them no talking. Loren falls twice because of the footing and once because the nervous kid, who's right behind him in line, steps on his heel.

At a certain point on the oval, the trail rises onto a low ridge, and the dying pines give way to a clear view of the parking lot on one side and the rest of the compound on the other. It looks like a village almost—cabins, the big house, the barn, the adjacent ring of stones. The pool, luminous and sky blue, seems even more out of place. The kids hit this same point every half hour or so, and on the first pass Loren looks down into the parking lot and sees his mom and the pro, arguing over the hood of the Pontiac. The next lap, a flatbed truck is pulling in—yellow flashing lights, gold leaf script on the door. And the third time, when the trail has finally been stomped clear and the kids have all gotten the knack of walking in step to minimize the stumbling (Loren's idea), and the sun is softening in the sky and Loren's growing exhausted but resolving that he will not complain—not like the nervous-eyed kid, who's whimpering that his heel is one big blister, and not like one of the girls, who's short and heavy and red-faced from the exertion—he looks down and sees that the parking lot is empty.

INTERMISSION

*I*n the Colonel's office, late at night, the fax machine comes to life. A green "RCV" light starts blinking, and rubber-nubbed document-feed wheels squeak into motion. Today the machine has already produced a deposit-transfer confirmation ($47,000 from First Bank of the Caymans over to Belize Federal), and another pleading letter from Miriam Diehl about her son, but the fax that comes in now is longer. It's from the disbarred lawyer, the Colonel's old partner in crime on the credit card operation, with a note at the top that says: "Saw this on the box a few weeks ago & thought you'd be interested. Could be good for your business or bad, but either way, maybe more attention coming? (By the way, you owe me $8,700 for helping you set that place up.)"

Then eighteen more pages spool out. The chemical smell of toner fills the room, and the squeaking, rubber-nubbed wheels serve up sheet after sheet of paper until they get tangled up in the collection tray. The Colonel will straighten the pages out tomorrow, rearrange them in order and read the document start to finish, but right now the ink on them is literally not dry.

SHOW: Straight from the Heart (10:00 p.m. ET) — KLS
April 14, 2005 Thursday

HEADLINE: Teens on the Edge: When parents put their kid into a
wilderness camp, are they getting effective treatment or just a very
rough—and very expensive—kind of babysitter?

ANCHORS: PAULINE VERO; MONTY ONG

ANNOUNCER: Now, from KLS Studios, Pauline Vero and Monty
Ong.

MONTY ONG: Good evening, I'm Monty Ong. Welcome to
another edition of *Straight from the Heart.*

PAULINE VERO: Tonight, we look at every parent's nightmare—
what happens when a teenager in the house gets out of control?
This is more than just taking the car when they're not supposed to.
We're talking about drugs, crime, kids who just don't listen no
matter what you tell them. If you're a parent, is there any place you
can turn?

MONTY ONG: Well, Pauline, an increasing number of parents are
putting their kids in so-called wilderness camps. It's tough love
with a twist—the teens are living out in the woods, being pushed to
some extraordinary lengths, both emotionally and physically. But
does it work? Tonight, *Straight from the Heart* finds out. We follow
three troubled teens through one such program, start to finish.

   With the cooperation of all three families and a camp facility
in Montana called Ridgeline that's among the more respected in

this largely unregulated business, reporter Bill Jervin goes into the wild. He's there to watch three very special, very troubled teens as they find out about themselves—and find out about life.

BILL JERVIN: (VOICE-OVER) The sun beats down like an enemy on this barren, red-rock campground miles from civilization. The teens sent here come from all across the country, but getting here, it seems, was the easy part.

COUNSELOR #1: You have to make it across the stream one way or another. No one's carrying you. That rope bridge is the fastest way, but if you want to walk across and get soaked, that's your choice.

MARC MCLURE: Are you high? No way. Seriously, no (deleted by network) way am I climbing on that thing.

JERVIN: (VO) Marc, a sixteen-year-old from Evanston, Illinois, wasn't always this way.

MRS. MCLURE: The most wonderful child you could imagine. Everyone loved him. He just laughed and laughed. He smiled all the time.

JERVIN: (VO) And how about lately?

MRS. MCLURE: (sighs) Lately he's Mr. Tough Guy. Always with the defiance and the acting out. I can't tell him anything. No one can tell him anything.

COUNSELOR #1: Those wet boots now weigh about three times what they did when they were dry. That's what's known as a conse-quence. You made your choice, now you have to live with the consequences until they dry out again.

MARC MCLURE: Yeah, well, bite me, OK? I didn't (deleted by network) ask to get sent here.

JERVIN: (VO) David Wheeler, our second teen, is fifteen and grew up outside Boston. As a child, his mother says, he was almost too well behaved.

MRS. LEANNE WHEELER: Oh yeah, very shy, very quiet. We couldn't get him out of his shell sometimes. But lots of friends. I'm not saying he didn't have friends or anything.

JERVIN: (VO) And how would you describe him these days?

MRS. WHEELER: Sullen, gloomy, sad. Did I already say sullen?

JERVIN: (VO) Finally, meet Alanna Fritsche, from York, Pennsylvania. Just sixteen, she's been battling severe mood swings for years.

ALANNA FRITSCHE: Sometimes I'm like, fine, you know, for days and days. And other times I just want to line up all the (deleted by network) mean, stupid people I see—they're everywhere, you don't even have to look hard—and just like line them all up and put one long stake through all their hearts. (Pause) I think I might like that.

JERVIN: (VO) It's day one here at Ridgeline. Our three teens are among a dozen shepherded into a small room, where they hand over their belongings and get outfitted with the gear they'll need for the coming weeks. Ridgeline is fairly typical in what it charges—about $4,700 for the three-week program. What is different is that the kids here get top-notch equipment.

COUNSELOR #1: That sleeping bag has two sides, see? One's thicker than the other. So when it's cold out, you use the thick side as your blanket. On warmer nights, you just flip it. Make sense?

DAVID WHEELER: (grunts)

JERVIN: (VO) Two hours later, after a van ride and short hike to the campsite, the kids set up their tents and reflect for a few minutes about their situation.

MARC MCLURE: This place blows.

ALANNA FRITSCHE: I feel OK. I feel good. They can't get to me. They're gonna try but they can't.

MCLURE: Really, it blows bad.

DAVID WHEELER: (silence)

JERVIN: David, anything you want to say for our cameras?

WHEELER: (shrugs) (walks away)

JERVIN: (VO) And so they settle in for their first long night. The counselors take away their boots and flashlights, so they can't run off. Tomorrow, their real challenge begins.

(Commercial break)

JERVIN: (VO) Despite yesterday's heat, Alanna, Marc, and David awake to a chill, and a sense of exactly what they're in for over the next three weeks.

COUNSELOR #1: If you don't put the tent stakes back into the bag the right way, they'll never fit.

MCLURE: The stupid things don't fit anyway.

COUNSELOR #1: They do. I promise you they fit.

MCLURE: Then why don't you just (deleted by network) do it?

JERVIN: (VO) Forced to be self-sufficient for the first time in their lives, the three get guidance and instruction from the counselors but not much in the way of help. No one's here to bail them out of anything. A few hours later, on the trail, it only gets worse.

WHEELER: I'm stopping.

COUNSELOR #2: David, that's the first thing I've heard you say since you got here. It's good that you're starting to open up, but sorry—you can't stop.

JERVIN: (VO) Their packs weigh almost forty pounds each, and the sun is scorching—by 10 a.m. it's already ninety degrees out. Today's hike is eight miles over hilly terrain, including a difficult climb they must complete before lunch. The kids who show up at Ridgeline aren't jocks—many of them have never exercised in their lives. Yet they're constantly pushed by the counselors to keep going.

MCLURE: (yelling to the sky) This sucks!

COUNSELOR #1: Did you hear that echo? That's nice.

WHEELER: I'm not kidding. If I don't stop I'm going to die. (sits down)

COUNSELOR #1: You're not going to die. Listen, you need to put your pack back on and keep going. Marc, hold on a sec. No one's going anywhere and no one gets lunch until David gets off the ground. You're all in this together. So David, what do you want to do?

WHEELER: I just said. I'll hang here.

COUNSELOR #2: There's food just ahead.

MCLURE: You said that an hour ago.

FRITSCHE: It's true. You did.

COUNSELOR #2: But this time it's real. Anyway, you won't know either way until David gets up and keeps hiking. No one eats until then. Alanna, stop picking at your face.

JERVIN: (VO) While this may seem like rough treatment, camps like Ridgeline specialize in using physical exertion to break down the defenses these kids have built up. Dr. Thomas Bruehl is the director of the Center for Adolescent Development at Middleton University.

BRUEHL: I suppose it could work, in the right circumstance. You can't say that it definitely won't work. The question is, where's the line? How far do you go with it? And how do you know that some of these operators aren't just punishing the kids out of cruelty, or to make a buck?

JERVIN: (VO) After half an hour and some tears, David finally says he'll keep going.

WHEELER: I'm fine. Let's just (deleted by network) go.

COUNSELOR #1: We're proud of you, David. All of us.

WHEELER: Big whoop. Whatever.

JERVIN: (VO) To celebrate finishing the first full day, the group gets a treat at the campfire that night.

COUNSELOR #2: It's a muffin. Homemade.

MCLURE: What's in it?

COUNSELOR #2: Soy, applesauce. Good stuff like that. It's all natural.

MCLURE: It also sucks ass.

FRITSCHE: They aren't good. I mean, thanks and all, but, you know....

OFF-CAMERA VOICE: I'll have yours if you don't want it.

FRITSCHE: (laughing) (tosses it)

JERVIN: (VO) And so, the rarest of gifts from these troubled kids, a smile.

(Commercial break)

JERVIN: (VO) Day seven, and the guides say Marc has made real progress in dealing with his anger.

COUNSELOR #2: Oh yeah, a lot less attitude, a lot less lip. He's definitely responding to the program.

JERVIN: (VO) (Pause) Then he throws his backpack off a ravine.

COUNSELOR #2: Now you did it. Now I'm mad. So here's what happens next: everyone's going to wait here while you go collect all that gear and hump it back up. I'm serious. While you're in the program that pack belongs to you—it's your responsibility. So go down and get it. We'll wait.

MCLURE: I'm not (deleted by network) going anywhere, you (deleted by network). I didn't (deleted by network) ask to come here. This whole (deleted by network) place can (deleted by network) my (deleted by network).

JERVIN: (VO) When he takes a swing at one of the counselors, we're asked to turn the cameras off while they restrain him. On occasion, the counselors say, the extreme physical exertion triggers feelings the kids aren't fully prepared to deal with. Meanwhile, at the McLure house in Illinois, Marc's parents worry about how their son is holding up.

MRS. MCLURE: We've been trying to keep busy. Not think about it too much.

MR. MCLURE: We cleaned out his room a little bit.

MRS. MCLURE: I told my husband not to go in there, but he said—

MR. MCLURE: It's my house, I'll go wherever I want. Some of the stuff we found you can't believe. A pipe for marijuana. It was as big as one of those things for the highway, with the orange....

MRS. MCLURE: A traffic cone.

MR. MCLURE: Right. As big as that.

JERVIN: (VO) Back at Ridgeline, forty minutes later, the cameras are rolling again, and a few of the other teens in the group have agreed to help Marc climb down the ravine and collect his pack.

MCLURE: It's over. It's no big deal. I'll just do whatever the (deleted by network) they say until it's time to go home.

COUNSELOR #1: He's a tough case, I mean it. Big shell around him. We see this kind of thing all the time. He'll break eventually.

JERVIN: (VO) But while the guides at Ridgeline are all experienced outdoorsmen, they don't have any formal training in dealing with adolescents and teenagers.

COUNSELOR #2: We got a few books to read before we started. Mostly I skimmed.

JERVIN: (VO) And unlike social workers, they're not licensed by the state. Ridgeline has a better reputation than most of these camps, but few are regulated by any government agency, state or federal.

COUNSELOR #2: Look at it this way. If it's this or wait until your eighth-grader picks up his next felony, you start making some hard decisions real fast. The parents just need to trust us. We know what we're doing. (turns) Hey, unless you want your guts to seize up you better not be drinking out of that stream! Sorry. Where were we?

JERVIN: (VO) After two weeks, fourteen days and nights in the wilderness, the kids seem just as stubborn as before. Marc still struggles with the tent stakes every morning, and David Wheeler talks more to himself than to any other person. Is there hope of finding transformation in the woods? Coming up next on *Straight from the Heart.*

(Commercial break)

JERVIN: (VO) It's now the third and final week of the program, and the guides have some big news to announce.

COUNSELOR #1: We didn't tell you this before, but the last day is coming, and there's a chance some of you might not be going home.

WHEELER: Huh?

FRITSCHE: (drops her canteen)

COUNSELOR #1: That's right. Some of you could get sent to a juvenile detention facility. Three-month stint. The decision is up to us—your parents gave us that option.

MCLURE: What the (deleted by network)? How come you didn't tell us before?

COUNSELOR #1: We wanted to get an accurate read on how you responded to the program. Now, we've seen some progress, but not a lot. Nothing we'd call significant. So if you want to go home any-time soon, all of you, I suggest you start doing what we tell you, when we tell you. Does that make sense?

WHEELER: (shrugs)

MCLURE: Yo, I think it's (deleted by network) up, but I'll walk on my hands if that's what it takes to get out of here.

JERVIN: (VO) As expected, the threat brings results. At the campfire that night David Wheeler finally begins to open up about his feelings.

WHEELER: Sometimes it's like not easy, you know? To deal with life and school and all this family stuff. But I know I need to try, so I just say, you know, (deleted by network) it. Let's get to it. Let's get on with the living part of life. (pause) (sighs) Is that enough?

COUNSELOR #1: That's very good, David. Thank you for that. Who's next?

JERVIN: (VO) By day seventeen, the changes are significant in just about everyone in the group.

MCLURE: Seriously, I'll carry an extra pack if that's what you want. I mean it. Gimme that thing.

FRITSCHE: I can honestly say, honestly, that my moods are getting better. See? (half smiles to the camera). Will you guys tell the counselors that my moods are getting better? Will you tell them that when you see them and we're not around?

JERVIN: (VO) With just seventy-two hours left to go, the counselors want to see if the changes are real. So they send each kid toward their final challenge: two days alone in the woods. No food, no help. Just a lot of solo time to reflect.

COUNSELOR #1: It's designed to let them think about where they were before showing up here, and where they want to be when they leave.

COUNSELOR #2: It's also a nice break for us.

COUNSELOR #1: But mostly it's for the kids.

COUNSELOR #2: Right. Definitely.

JERVIN: (VO) The counselors have a surprise: each kid is handed a bag of M&Ms.

COUNSELOR #1: This represents your drug of choice. Think of it as a little bottle of pills. So when you're out there and you're hungry, the point is to not give in. Prove to yourself that you can face down temptation. Any questions?

MCLURE: What if I never took pills? What if I just smoked a lot of pot?

FRITSCHE: Can I switch my drug of choice to peanut M&Ms instead?

JERVIN: (VO) One by one, the kids are led out into the woods, where they'll be monitored by guides watching with binoculars. Again, their boots get taken to keep them from escaping. After just a few hours, the kids forget the presence of the guides and become themselves.

COUNSELOR #1: They're supposed to write in their journals and meditate. We teach them breathing exercises.

JERVIN: Is that what they're doing out there right now?

COUNSELOR #2: Mostly the girl is sleeping. And swatting mosquitoes.

COUNSELOR #1: Marc tried to catch a squirrel with his hands and got scraped up a little. Score one for the squirrel.

JERVIN: And David Wheeler?

COUNSELOR #2: Lots of mumbling. He climbed a tree and then climbed back down.

JERVIN: (VO) When the second day is completed, a horn sounds and the group collects back at camp. There's a sense of accomplishment, relief, and a few tears.

COUNSELOR #2: You guys made us proud out there. We knew you could do it.

COUNSELOR #1: What about the M&Ms? What about your drug of choice?

WHEELER: (eyes down) I ate mine.

FRITSCHE: Me too, like an hour after I got out there. Then I ate the wrapper.

MCLURE: A bird took mine.

COUNSELOR #1: Marc.

MCLURE: What? It did, OK? Don't be a (deleted by network) about it.

JERVIN: (VO) The next day, when the parents arrive to pick their kids up, there are hugs all around. But the final decision hasn't been made yet about who's going home and who will be sent to another juvenile program.

MRS. MCLURE: I think it's fifty-fifty right now. Maybe sixty-thirty that he goes home.

MR. MCLURE: That doesn't add up to a hundred.

COUNSELOR #1: The big question for us is whether Marc's going to go back to his old friends and his old habits.

MRS. MCLURE: Oh absolutely. I'll make sure of that.

COUNSELOR #2: No, that's bad. That's not what we're shooting for here.

MRS. MCLURE: In that case—no, he won't.

MRS. WHEELER:…really love you David.

WHEELER: Yup. OK.

FRITSCHE: Know what I want more than anything right now? A milk shake.

MRS. FRITSCHE: It's hard for me to tell. She certainly seems more stable. I'd know, right? I'm her mother.

FRITSCHE: Look, I'll take responsibility for whatever I've ever done wrong in my life, ever. Even stuff I didn't do. I blew up the space shuttle, OK? I shot Tupac. Let's just get out of here.

MRS. FRITSCHE: Lanny, we have to wait and see what they say.

JERVIN: (VO) The entire group convenes for the final announcement. David Wheeler is allowed to leave. Alanna Fritsche too.

MRS. FRITSCHE: Oh thank God.

JERVIN: (VO) But Marc McLure is not.

COUNSELOR #1:…question of whether he really, truly has changed. We're not convinced.

MCLURE: No way. No (deleted by network) way!

COUNSELOR #2: See? This is exactly what we're talking about. This whole anger thing.

MCLURE: You're the (deleted by network) one making me angry. Why didn't you tell me sooner?

MRS. MCLURE: Marc, listen.

JERVIN: (VO) As the rest of the group heads to their cars, Marc is asked to wait inside, where two men will escort him to the juvenile facility in Denver. He gets one last hug from his parents, and then the door closes.

MR. MCLURE: Would I do it again? I don't know. This hurts. This hurts so much I don't know what to think.

FRITSCHE:…and french fries. And a cheeseburger. With bacon.

MRS. WHEELER: I feel like I just won the Powerball. I got my son back.

JERVIN: David, anything you want to say to the camera? Anything at all?

DAVID WHEELER: Just…I don't know. I'm happy I guess.

JERVIN: (VO) So as the families head to their cars for the long trip home, some of them are finally able to put this struggle behind them. But others, unfortunately, are not.

SCROLLING TEXT:
• Six months later, David Wheeler is back in high school.
• He's passing most of his classes and playing on the junior varsity soccer team.
• Alanna Fritsche is in a group home outside Richmond for girls with acute emotional problems.
• She's been drug-free since leaving Ridgeline.
• Marc McLure ran away from the juvenile facility after just four nights.
• His parents do not know where he is.

PAULINE VERO: Wow, great story, Bill.

JERVIN: Thanks, Pauline. You know, I really found myself rooting for these kids. After spending a few weeks with them, you start to see that some of them, deep down, might not be as hopeless as they seem.

VERO: I can imagine.

JERVIN: Still, I wouldn't trust any of them with my wallet.

VERO: (laughs)

MONTY ONG: Next week on *Straight from the Heart*—"Mormons and Marriage: How Many Wives are Enough?" Until then, I'm Monty Ong.

VERO: And I'm Pauline Vero. Good night.

PART II

CHAPTER 5

Loren is dreaming about his mom again. It's the same dream he always has. He's eight or nine, and it's their first day in a new place. His mom got a promotion—no more waiting tables, she made it to manager—so they could finally switch to a better apartment. "A real home," she calls it, with a parking spot in front and a washer and dryer in a tiny closet. Loren even gets his own room. In the old place he had a corner of the den closed off with curtains and string, but now he has a bed, a door, everything. His mom tells him that this time it'll be different. They'll be happy here, she says. They'll stay a long time.

In the dream, Loren runs around the stacked-up boxes and his mom tells him not to knock anything over. She's in the kitchen, unpacking spoons. Movers file in and out, and the building super comes to change the locks. The super has shiny black hair that's parted ruler-straight, and he smells like food. Loren doesn't get how that word works—super what? When he asks, the man says just plain super. He looks at Loren's mom, whose back is to them, and says, "Super at lots of stuff."

His mom doesn't know it yet, but the super's bad—Loren can tell already. It takes the man a long time to change the locks, and

Loren realizes it's because he mostly just stands in the hallway, watching Loren's mom through the gap by the door hinge. Loren notices things like that. He always has. And when she tells him that this time it'll be different, this time they'll really be happy, he acts like he believes her but really he doesn't—and he'll be right. In a few weeks, the super will start calling a lot, and then knocking at weird times, and when he finally lets himself in one night, Loren's mom will have to call the cops. After that, another move, and she'll look back at this place and say they were never happy here. It wasn't a real home. They won't even stay six months....

He's woken abruptly by a crashing noise, which turns out to be Donovan, whacking a cymbal with a wooden coat hanger. Loren squints his eyes open and remembers where he is—Camp Ascend!, day three.

"Let's go, let's go!" Donovan yells. "Get in your sweats and onto the center plank."

The lights come on and he starts clomping around the cabin, pounding the cymbal like a crazed, mechanical monkey. His poncho is dripping, and his boots leave wet marks on the floor. Outside the windows the sky is still dark.

Loren groans and rolls out of bed. In the bunk next to him, William, the red-haired kid, doesn't get up. Instead he pulls his blanket over his head, until Donovan comes over and blows an air horn down through it like a weapon. The sound is so loud it makes Loren dizzy.

Donovan announces that the horn's going to stay on until everyone is dressed, which definitely speeds them up. In less than a minute all six kids are lined up on the plank, and Donovan opens the door. The three girls are waiting, huddled in the darkness in their ninja sweats. The rain makes a whispering noise on the grass. Donovan leads the kids to the bathrooms, where they're given exactly thirty seconds to wash up (he holds a stopwatch and counts down), and when everyone's back outside he makes them form two columns.

"March in place," Donovan says. "Right now. Go."

Loren's already noticed that Donovan tries to mimic the stuff that happens in Marine Corps boot camp, but his version always comes out wrong. Like the commands he uses—everything's close but just a little off.

The kids shuffle in place for a moment, going nowhere, smelling the bathroom plumbing, while Donovan walks down the line, getting in each kid's face to scowl. Then he cracks his neck in both directions and says, "OK, go straight," and all nine kids step forward.

The ring of hexagonal stones is not even a hundred feet away, but Loren wishes it took longer to get there. He's still sore from yesterday. For all his talk about Special Forces, he doesn't get much exercise. He tends to do it in spurts, trying out something he's read about and then moving on when it turns out to be harder than he guessed. Once he read that Navy SEALs do five-mile timed runs in the sand, wearing boots, so when he was twelve he went down to the fake lake near his mom's apartment and tried to do some laps around the perimeter in his work boots. Before he'd gotten halfway around he started to feel strange twinges in his heel, which kept throbbing even after he slowed to a walk and then to a limp, and by the time he got back to his bike it made him wince just to put the kickstand up. When the doctor told him it was a stress fracture, Loren had never heard the term before.

"Spread out," Donovan says, once they're on the ring. "Two lines, facing me."

Loren puts himself in the back row and winds up behind Ty. On the stones are a lot of crooked, bumpy lines that turn out to be slugs—Loren can feel them squishing under his boots. The kids peer down at them, and one or two girls make *eww* noises, but Donovan tells them all to be quiet.

"Can't we clean these off first?" Loren says.

"No talking."

There's a metal chair in front of the ring, which Donovan tips forward to spill the pooled rainwater from the seat. When he flips the hood of his poncho over his head, some more rain trickles down the ape features of his face. Finally he settles into the chair and crosses his boots out in front of him, straight-legged.

"OK, march in place again. Ready? Go."

They start marching, feet thumping against the stones. Loren's sweats are nearly soaked through already.

"Now run," Donovan says.

A few confused glances among the kids. This is a new one.

"Run where?" Loren says.

"Here," Donovan tells them. "Where you are. Run in place."

The drumbeat of footsteps accelerates and gets louder. Donovan leans back in the chair and tells them to keep their knees up. "Every minute you all don't have your knees up is a minute that doesn't count," he says. "Arms out in front. Like zombies."

They put their arms out, which makes the exercise even stupider. Loren's feet hurt, and he's surprised at how fast his arms get heavy. It feels like he has weights dangling off them. Water splashes up all around the kids, and Loren tries to maneuver to a spot with a shallower puddle. After a few minutes the pace slows, until everyone's basically trotting in place. In front of Loren, Ty isn't even lifting his feet off the stones anymore—instead he does a stationary moonwalk—but Loren tries to keep going and prove to the hand job in front of him that he can take it.

The sky is brightening from black to light gray, and the tops of the pine trees are partially hidden in mist in a way that reminds Loren of a fairy tale. The rain seems like it's coming down harder, but Loren can't be sure.

Donovan slouches in the chair and finally says stop. "That's pitiful," he says.

The kids huff into the rainy air, hands on their hips. Ty's sweatpants sag, exposing a winking sliver of butt crack.

"Let's try squat thrusts," Donovan says. "Twenty-five of them." He points to Ty. "You, Freak Show. Keep count for the group. Ready? Go."

The kids start, putting their hands down into the squished slugs, and at seventeen Ty loses count.

"Wait, that's fifteen," he says. "Right?"

"You just said fifteen. Two things ago." It's Becca, the chubby girl, protesting. She hates the workouts more than anyone. Her face is tomato red.

"Just call it eighteen and let's keep going," one of the twins says.

"No, start over," Donovan tells them. "You still have to do twenty-five."

"No fucking way," the other twin says.

"Now it's fifty. No more talking."

There's a moment of mute protest, the kids all staring at Donovan in disbelief, and Loren half expects some signal for them all to charge him. That's how it works, right? That's how mutinies happen? But the moment passes. Ty hitches his sweatpants up and they start all over again. The rain is definitely coming down harder now.

*

Already Loren has figured out that the place is not what it seems, that there's something not quite right about Camp Ascend!. Like the fact that there's zero maintenance done—the buildings are basically falling down around them—or like all the music stuff he keeps finding. He's known something was wrong from the first night, when they were introduced to the Colonel.

A few hours after the parents left, after Loren's mom and the pro finally got the Pontiac towed away, Donovan led the kids into a big rehearsal room in the barn. The room had tiers that wrapped amphitheatrically around a podium in front, covered by a stained carpet with wadded-up sheet music and food wrappers all over it, and little black flecks of mouse shit in the corners. The kids sat in silence, even after Donovan left them alone and locked the door.

They hadn't had a chance to wash after their first conga line, so they were still dirty and sore. The idea of exactly what their next six weeks would be like had settled on them like a hangover, and no one felt like talking.

Loren glanced around the room and tried to go through the names he'd picked up. In Vietnam, the POWs were always challenging themselves to memorize the names of everyone in captivity. It kept their minds sharp, and if they got released early they could report back to the families at home. But so far Loren had only rough intelligence, and only on a few kids.

He knew that the one who rocked was named Ty, and that he'd already been to a few camps like this. Sitting next to him were the twins—EK and RK, for Eric and Robert Kaladjian. RK was older by seven minutes, and bigger (they weren't identical), and EK was more of a wiseass. They were from Los Angeles and their father was some big shot at a paper company.

And behind them sat the girl with the bright eyes and the purple streak in her hair. She had her sleeves rolled up neatly, a padded band around each biceps, and her forearms looked perfectly circular. The only thing Loren knew about her so far was her name—Liz.

Suddenly they heard a hiss coming from speakers mounted in the ceiling, followed by marching-band music. Loren didn't recognize the song—it wasn't "Hail to the Chief" but something like that. The door opened and Donovan took one step in and turned sideways. He stood almost at attention and yelled, "Everybody get up!"

The Colonel followed behind him and walked to the podium. After all the buildup Loren almost couldn't believe what he was seeing. This was a retired marine colonel? He looked like he was wearing a Halloween costume. No marine would leave his hat on indoors, or let stray bits of hair curl around the edges. He was missing one collar insignia, and he had his belt turned around, so the sword was not only on the wrong hip but pointing in the wrong direction. It nearly tripped him on the way in.

Donovan disappeared into the hall, and the music stopped. The Colonel told them to take a seat. He must have seen a lot of war movies, or prison movies, because for a long moment he just stood, looking out at them and relishing the moment. Loren blinked in disbelief. The left shoulder of the Colonel's dress blue jacket was faded lighter than the right, from being stored somewhere in the sun. Finally, he spoke.

"Welcome to Camp Ascend!," the Colonel said. "Your home for the next six weeks. I know who you all are, and you know who I am, so let's skip the introductions. I also know why you're here, every one of you, and you know that too, so that's another thing we can skip. What's most important right now are the rules."

He crossed his hands behind him and turned to pace, and the sword knocked against the podium. The twins, sitting next to Loren, gave each other a glance. The Colonel moved the sword out of the way and continued.

"First," he said, "no talking. Don't take it personally—we just don't want to hear you. Don't talk to us, don't talk to each other, don't talk to yourselves. In the cabins at night, where you'll be locked in, you can talk quietly but always remember that we're watching and listening. We have cameras and microphones all over the grounds here, so be careful what you say."

The Colonel had not stopped pacing, and as he approached the podium the next time he grabbed the sword by the hilt and held it as he turned.

"Also, expect to march. Laps around the perimeter, 1.7 miles each. Whenever you do something wrong, that's the punishment. Or that's *one* of the punishments. If you haven't pieced it together yet, our plan is to keep you tired. Fatigue is our friend. You'll work out every morning, supervised by the drill sergeant here, who I believe you've already had the pleasure of meeting."

He nodded at Donovan, who was leaning against a chalkboard with permanent musical staffs on it. Loren could see old, half-erased musical notes on the board. The horizontal bars behind Donovan's head made him look like he was part of a police lineup.

The Colonel noticed Liz and stopped pacing.

"Are your sleeves rolled up?"

Liz looked down at them.

"It looks like yeah, they are."

"Don't be smart. It'll work against you here. Roll them down please, right now. We'll wait."

Liz let out a sigh and rolled down her sleeves. Loren watched her skinny forearms disappear.

"Thank you. Do you see that, everyone? If you follow the rules and do what we say, you'll be all right. This place is not as bad as it probably seems right now. Remember the rules and we'll all have a fun six weeks. Which brings me to my biggest rule—no escaping. Please don't even try, because then we'll have to punish you all, severely, and nobody wants that. Besides, you'll never make it out. It's twenty-one miles to the first paved road, and farther to anyone who might help you. If you think you can go through the woods, you're wrong. There aren't any trails out there, but there are animals. Even if you had a chain saw and Sacagawea to lead you by the hand, you'd never pull it off. We'll be monitoring you, as I said, and if we think you might escape, we'll take away everyone's boots, all eight of—"

"Nine," Donovan said, looking satisfied with himself. "It's nine this time."

The Colonel took a deep breath. "Right. Thank you, Mr. Math." Then, to the group, "Think about it this way—you could have a two-day head start and we'd find you. So really, don't try to escape. Not on your own, not as a team. No one's ever gotten out, and the few people who've tried were dragged back here and wound up regretting it. Is that clear?"

Silence.

"Everyone nod your heads."

"Nod!" Donovan ordered, stepping forward and uncrossing his arms.

The kids started nodding. Loren merely rolled his eyes, and he noticed that Liz didn't bother to nod either. From the front of the room, Donovan glared at him.

"That's not all," the Colonel said. "We've got some other options too. One of my personal favorites—we can extend your stay. We'll call your parents, tell them it's going well but that you might need a few more weeks of treatment. That's happened before. We've had people with us as long as four months. Think about that, everyone. Four *months*. Everyone else goes home to tell stories about this place while you stick around for another class or two. When things get rough around here I want you to keep that in mind. You can follow the rules, do what we say, and you'll go home on time."

"How is that legal?" It was Liz, speaking up. "I mean, we have rights."

Donovan started to say something, but the Colonel held up his hand.

"No, no. It's a good question. But the answer, basically, is no, you don't. Not the kind of rights you think, anyway. I can't rent you out to the townies for slave labor, and I can't sell you to the circus, much as I might want to sometimes. But I can clearly extend your stay. There's paperwork, signed by your parents…where are the twins? Right, signed in your case by your father's administrative assistant, but for the rest of you signed by your parents, and that paperwork makes it official. So when we tell you to do something you have to do it. You *have* to. If you don't we'll force you, and that might not be fun. Now, none of this is meant to scare you. Actually that's not true. It is meant to scare you, but I don't want you to walk around here scared all the time…"

He closed his eyes and straightened out his thoughts. "What I'm trying to say is, if you behave, this place is easy. It's summer camp. If you don't, it's more like prison. The choice is yours, but if something bad happens, it'll be your fault either way. Everybody got that?"

The group sat silently. Ty began to rock in small motions. William bit off a fingernail and discreetly spit it to the side. Donovan whispered something to the Colonel, who said, oh yeah, there was one more rule.

"Forgot to mention," the Colonel said. "No looking Donovan in the eye. He can look at you, but you can't look back at him. It's a respect thing."

Donovan nodded, then whispered something else to the Colonel, who sighed and said OK.

"And you have to call him sir."

Donovan started to whisper something else, but the Colonel brushed him away and said enough. "Let's wrap this up. Go start the music."

Donovan walked out. A few seconds later the speakers started hissing, the marching-band music began, and the kids stood as the Colonel made his exit. No problems with the sword this time, though one of his boot laces was untied. The flopping end clicked against his heel. It was the last part of him to leave the room.

*

For the first few days Loren tries to pay attention and make some sense of the camp, but it's not easy. There's no real schedule—most mornings they're woken before sunrise by Donovan, smashing the cymbal and blowing the air horn, but then sometimes they're allowed to sleep in, with no explanation. They get twenty minutes in the morning to clean up after the ring workout, rinsing off under a thin trickle of lukewarm water that pools under their feet on rust-stained, moldy floors. It's well water, the Colonel explained, and they're having a dry summer, which is why the showers are limited to ninety seconds each. The kids are supposed to throw their dirty sweats into a big cardboard box and pull clean ones from another box next to it, though some days the clean sweats don't make it out. Kitty's responsible for laundry, and if the weather's nice she doesn't get around to it and they have to go back for the dirty sweats, sifting through the smelly pile and trying to figure out whose were whose. The twins call it Dumpster diving.

They're all assigned chores around the property. Already Loren's had to clean the wheels of the Colonel's Jeep Grand Cherokee with rags tied to the end of a wooden drumstick, and the girls have been scrubbing bathroom grout in the main house. Loren thought this might open up options for guerilla resistance, though it's hard to tell exactly how just yet—the Colonel seems to assign the jobs without any plan or system. Loren's read that in real POW camps the routine is kept unpredictable as a form of low-level psychological pressure. It's a mind-fuck element—it creates unease and prevents the prisoners from plotting. But he can't tell how much of that is intentional here. Donovan and the Colonel can barely keep the cabins from falling down, let alone design elements of the operation that are calculated to seem random.

Because Loren hasn't figured out much about the place yet, his early acts of sabotage have all been solo. His second night there, when the other kids were brushing their teeth before bed, he deliberately "forgot" his toothbrush, and Donovan said he could go back to the boys' cabin for it.

"Sprint," Donovan said. "You have one minute."

In the empty cabin, Loren put some boot polish on the end of a broomstick and reached up to smear it over the lens of the security camera. A giant wad of polish, and then he waited for the inevitable reaction, for some alarm to go off, or for a guard no one had seen before to come huffing out in a gray uniform, radio squawking. Instead there was nothing. After a few long seconds Loren reached up and tapped the camera with the broomstick. It made a hollow, tin sound. It wasn't a camera at all, just an empty metal box with a battery-powered light to make it seem real. Same as everything else

about Camp Ascend!—half-fake and half-stupid, equal parts bully-
ing and inept.

He was about to head back to the latrine when he saw the penciled lettering on the floor next to his bunk: *ALL DOWNHILL
FROM HERE*, with a long, squiggly line disappearing under the bed
like a piece of string. Loren was late already, but his curiosity was
enough for him to kneel down this time.

Under the bunk, the line straightened into an arrow pointing to
a knothole in one of the floorboards. Reaching a finger into the
knothole, Loren pulled, and to his astonishment the board lifted
free. No nails, no screws—it was a way out. An escape hatch. He did-
n't know if the plank had been pried loose during the band-camp
days or by a Camp Ascend! inmate, but either way it didn't matter.

Loren dropped the board back into place and rubbed at the letters with his boot, trying to smudge them out. The fake camera
blinked down at him, and Loren raised his middle finger back in
return. Two days in and he had already cracked the code. He
thought about telling the other kids about what he'd found but
decided not to—not just yet.

*

Liz thinks they're on their way to dinner, and she's hungry. It's late
afternoon on day three, about twelve hours after the slug workout,
and Donovan's marching the kids across the compound toward the
cafeteria. He's in a good mood, even whistling a little.

So far Liz's position on the camp is that she keeps waiting for it
to get hard. It clearly sucks, it's clearly a hassle, with about eight
hundred pointless rules that would be laughable if they weren't
enforced by a big, dumb guard. But on the whole she hasn't seen
anything here that she can't do. Like the morning sessions on the
ring—all around her the kids flail and huff and gasp for air, and Liz's
main thought is, *Stop bitching. This is not that bad.* At night in the

girls' cabin, whenever Becca shifts into whine mode (which seems to make up about 80 percent of her conversation), Liz just tunes out. It's not that she's happy about ending up here, but there's no point talking about it.

Her biggest issue so far is the food—though that's true just about anywhere she goes. Riap, the Indonesian cook, makes some weird things that he probably thinks kids would like, but it all has a weird twist, like yam fries, or pork rolls, or, one night last week, pizza with fish on it (including heads). And Liz's main problem is that there's never a lot of vegan options. Still, if she has to survive for six weeks on vegetables and bread, fine. It's better than eating dead animals.

Her stomach's grumbling right now. Everyone's always famished by this point in the afternoon, but Donovan surprises her by marching the kids past the cafeteria and over toward the pool. The rain has come and gone all day, and under the cloud-covered skies the pool looks silent and abandoned. Kitty hasn't been out, though her chaises are in their usual positions by the deep end. Next to the chairs is a stack of wet, wrinkled catalogs, and a glass with a lemon wedge submerged in two inches of grayish rainwater.

A fence surrounds the pool—chain-link, chest-high—and Donovan lines the kids up about ten feet away from it. Two rows, five in the front and four in the back, facing the water. Once they're in place, standing at attention, he leans back against the fence and says don't move.

The kids glance around. Donovan just looks at them.

Liz thinks there's an outside chance they'll go swimming—she loves to swim but hasn't been in a pool all summer. Or maybe the point is to rub the kids' faces in the fact that they *can't* go swimming. They can look at this pristine pool, stare at it, and know they'll never be allowed in. But she gets a clue of what Donovan's really up to when the mosquitoes start to land. The kids slap at them, and Donovan tells them again not to move.

"You're in formation," he says. "That means no swatting. It's undisciplined."

The humidity must do something to bring out the mosquitoes, because they swarm pretty quickly. Liz can feel them on her face, hear them flitting by her ears. Bugs are everywhere on the property—moths, mantises, spiders the size of mice. The whole place is like empire of the insects. The beams in the cabin above her bunk are pitted with termite damage that looks like old acne, and there are two spots on the perimeter lap where the midges always gather in furious, flitting clouds that blur the air. Liz has to remember to hold her breath each time they pass, or else she inhales big, bitter mouthfuls of them.

The mosquitoes now are the worst of all, though. Within minutes, she has bites up and down her neck. Her wet skin feels soft, easier to bite into.

"We're going to get malaria," Jeremy, the kid with the nervous eyes, says under his breath. Becca slaps at her neck, looks at her hand, and rubs it onto her hip.

Donovan says, "Stand still for five minutes and you're done. That's it. But every time someone slaps, you get another five minutes." He's in a curiously good mood.

One of the metal fence posts near the kids is bent in near the top, Liz notices now. She can't figure out why.

Someone slaps again, and Donovan says, "That's another five minutes." Slap. "Another five. You're up to half an hour already."

Next to Liz is William, who seems to attract mosquitoes like a bug lamp. William is allergic to a lot of things Liz thought were supposed to be good for you, like sunlight and grass and milk. His neck is dotted with bugs, but William is one of the few kids who does not flinch.

"The next slap I hear means everyone has to roll up their sleeves," Donovan says.

On cue, there's a smack from the direction of the twins.

"That's it," Donovan says. "Get them up."

The kids start folding their cuffs, but Loren, two spots down from Liz, doesn't move.

"You, Dogface," Donovan says, pointing at him. "Let's go. I gave you an order."

Loren says, "I thought we were supposed to keep our sleeves down at all times."

"Not now," Donovan says. "I just told you, get them up."

"But the Colonel told us to keep them down. He said that, we all heard him. And he outranks you."

Donovan starts to say something and then stops. He smiles. It's warm, almost genuine, and Loren half smiles back, like he just won something. A small point but he outsmarted Donovan and they both know it. Donovan chuckles, and the twins start laughing and the laughter spreads. It's been a long day, and the kids are all tired and punchy. Liz has an uneasy feeling.

In three strides, Donovan walks over and picks Loren up by two giant fistfuls of his sweatshirt, then turns and throws him like a rag doll. Loren is suddenly airborne, legs kicking, body tracing a low arc, until he hits the fence and crumples to the concrete on the other side. For a few seconds he doesn't move, until finally his breath starts to come back in wheezing gulps.

Through the diamond pattern of the chain link, Liz can see him blink in slow motion. His eyes are tearing up—he's trying not to cry, she can tell. Donovan isn't laughing anymore, no more warm smiles. The metal fence post that Loren hit is now bent inward a few degrees, just like the one next to it, and Liz figures it out now. She realizes that Donovan—who marched them over here, who gave them an order he knew no one would be able to follow—just wanted to make an example of Loren. This has happened before, with previous classes. Donovan set the whole thing up.

CHAPTER 6

"This won't work," Donovan says.

"It'll definitely work," the Colonel tells him.

"Watch." Donovan crosses his arms and watches his brother-in-law wrestle with an old box fan they found in the basement. The fan was covered in dust, and the screen around the blades was shredded. They're in Donovan's bedroom, the hottest room in the house. His windows face south and his ceiling is sloped, so on sunny days the heat soaks in and turns the room into an oven, and even at night, like now, the air is so hot it practically shimmers. His air conditioner broke two days ago.

Sitting on his bed in a glaze of sweat, Donovan can look around the room and see everything he owns in the world. One twin mattress, with some sheets he hasn't gotten around to washing lately—a gray silhouette of dried perspiration runs down the middle—and some dumbbells he hasn't touched in months, and a suitcase full of clothes, mostly cammies. Plus one old radio that he uses to listen to baseball games, though the compound is so far out in the sticks that they only get reception if the weather's perfect, and even then the radio makes strange Sputnik noises, clicks and whistles, and the announcers sound like they're calling the game through kazoos. All on a slanted floor with a ratty-ass rug and old magazines to cover the spots where the nails stick up.

"Outlet?" the Colonel says.

"Over there. Behind the boxes."

The Colonel's got the fan in place, though it doesn't fit right, so Donovan knows he'll have to stuff T-shirts into the gaps. It makes more sense to push the fan to one side of the window frame—that way you have only one gap, not two—but Donovan's content to watch the Colonel screw this up on his own. He'll fix it later, same as always.

When he showed up at the compound eighteen months ago, Donovan thought he was finally in on the ground floor of a solid operation. He'd tried to go into business for himself a few times—good ideas come to him, he considers himself an idea person—but usually he's this close to hitting it big when something swims up and bites him in the balls. The watches, for example. How hard could it be to get ten thousand fake Rolexes into the country from Korea? Donovan sees them sold on street corners all the time. Someone must know how to do it. But the Colonel didn't want in on that deal—he never wants in on the stuff Donovan dreams up—and the wrong customs officer opened the right box and Donovan lost every dollar, plus got the piss beat out of him by four huge Koreans. The fighting dogs he wanted to breed? Another raw deal. The fake passports? Jesus, don't even get him started.

At the beginning of Camp Ascend!, before the first kids showed up, the Colonel told Donovan that he wouldn't be getting a salary, that instead he'd get "equity," which the Colonel had to explain meant ownership. "So from this date forward you are a manager-owner, and thus entitled to a cut of all future revenues," the Colonel said. Somewhere in the Colonel's safe is a piece of yellow legal paper that says: THIS DOCUMENT MEANS THAT DONOVAN A. FRENCH NOW OWNS FORTY PERCENT (40%) OF CAMP ASCEND!. That's it. Two signatures at the bottom, in blue ink that skipped in spots. The Colonel said it was good they put it on legal paper, because that made it official.

The catch was that Donovan had to put up some money to buy his way in. "Kitty and I bought the property already," the Colonel said. "We're doing marketing, all that crap. So if you want in you have to pay for it." Kitty stepped in for her brother and talked the Colonel down a bit, and after Donovan sold his Camaro he still had to come up with fifteen thousand dollars, which was exactly fifteen thousand more than he had. "OK," the Colonel said, "I'll front you the money but you have to pay me back. You can give me fifteen thousand this month, or sixteen thousand next month, seventeen thousand the month after, and onward from there. See how it works? On a percentage basis the interest actually goes down every month, so it's a good deal. Only cause you're family."

Since then, the Colonel kept telling Donovan that once the start-up costs were covered, they'd be rolling in money. "It's pure profit," he said. "A stream of cash. You just have to reach out and take some, like a bear catching salmon." Though they're sixteen months in now, on their ninth class, and the Colonel doesn't yet seem to know when those costs might be paid. Meanwhile, the amount Donovan owes keeps going up. When he needs spending money he has to take it out of Kitty's purse, like a little kid grabbing change. She steals it herself, from the Colonel's safe (she knows the combination), so Donovan doesn't feel guilty about his secret raids for twenty or forty or sixty dollars. But every once in a while, like this situation with the air conditioner, he realizes exactly how badly he's being screwed.

"I think we're good to go," the Colonel says, stepping back from the fan. "You're going to need a ski jacket in here pretty soon."

"Just turn it on," Donovan says.

The Colonel pushes a button and his finger comes away black. The fan slowly starts spinning, and a faint cloud of dust blows into the room. The motor groans like a plane doing acrobatics, and the blades move a little faster. Before they're even going full speed Donovan can see bugs getting sucked in—a lot of them—through the shredded screen. A few make it through intact, but others get chopped up, with little broken bodies landing in a wedge pattern on the carpet.

"Nope," Donovan says, standing up. "No fucking way."

"It's fine," the Colonel says. "Put some newspapers down. You can get a kid in here to clean up the dead ones each morning."

"What about the live ones?" Donovan says. Bugs circle between them, and more are coming through. The room is filling up with insects. "And anyway, it's still a thousand degrees in here. You're sweating through your shirt."

"Then sleep on the couch downstairs if you want," the Colonel says.

"Kitty watches TV late at night. You come down in your tighty whities sometimes. I don't need to see that shit."

Donovan doesn't feel like explaining again that he has to be up at four every morning to run the kids. He can go a few nights without sleep, but eventually it catches up with him.

"I'm trying to come up with some solutions here," the Colonel says. "I don't hear anything from your end."

"My solution is, you give me one of the other air conditioners in the house."

"I told you, we don't have any extras."

"You have seven. Two in your own bedroom."

"But we have two people in there," the Colonel says. "And you know Kitty likes it cold."

"So what if I ask her and she says yes? You'll give me one of those?"

The Colonel hesitates. "Not fair. She's your sister. You know she'd give it to you."

"So why don't you then?"

"Because this is a business, and you can't let family stuff get in the way of that. It clouds your judgment."

The fan clanks once but keeps running. The air in the room is starting to move, but it doesn't feel any better. It's like being under the hood of a car with the engine running. A black-winged beetle crunches through the blades and lands on the carpet in two twitching pieces.

"Or how about this?" the Colonel says. "I'll sell you an air conditioner, but you have to pay that back. You can add it to the loan."

"I'm not paying you a damn dime," Donovan says. "If a hole opened up in the roof right here, you'd make me buy the wood to fix it?"

"Look, you wanted to be a partner, so I made you a partner. This is what it's like. You don't get a salary, and when stuff breaks you have to cover that expense."

"Then maybe we should change the deal," Donovan says.

"You can't change halfway through. That's why they call it a contract."

"That contract's bullshit. I got shafted and you know it."

The Colonel just shrugs. "You signed it," he says.

Donovan knows the Colonel would break the limp-dick contract in a second. The thing about the Colonel is that he has no integrity, no honor. That's why Donovan feels like he *can't* break it—he wants to show the Colonel he's better than that. So as much as he bitches about the shitty terms, he doesn't do anything about them. As a strategy, he's not sure it's working, but at least it gives him some lines to go by.

He opens his suitcase and starts tearing through his clothes. It's so hot in the room that he thinks paint's going to start peeling off the walls. When he finds a pair of cutoff cammies, he grabs them and heads for the door.

The Colonel asks where he's going.

"The pool. Maybe I'll get a snorkel and sleep underwater."

"Up to you," the Colonel says. "But listen—one more thing, before you go."

Donovan thinks he's going to ask about the kid he threw into the fence post yesterday afternoon. The one with the girl's name,

Loren. He hit a little harder than Donovan intended—he has a way of plucking on Donovan's nerves, there's one in every class—and maybe it got back to the Colonel already. Usually Donovan likes to keep that stuff private, especially the first big shock at the fence each new session.

Instead the Colonel says, "Do you remember a kid named Matthew Diehl? He was here a few months ago. I think he was bad at first, kind of a troublemaker, but then better at the end."

"Lots of kids come through," Donovan says. "They're hard to keep track of."

"This one's easy for me, though, because his mom keeps calling. She says something happened to him up here, that he was maybe, I don't know, *hurt* a little. Does that sound right to you?"

Sometimes when the Colonel's talking Donovan doesn't know how on guard he needs to be. Little traps in every sentence. He doesn't remember the kid, but if someone got hurt he's pretty sure he'd know about it. He definitely would.

"Kids make up stories," he says. "The ones who end up here are just better at it."

"Right," the Colonel says. "That's what I keep telling her. Only, I remember you had him in one of the rehearsal rooms for a few days…." The Colonel trails off and looks at Donovan expectantly.

"If you want to know something, just ask me flat out," Donovan says. "At least have the balls."

"OK," the Colonel says. "What happens to the kids in those rooms?"

What happens in those rooms. Donovan's surprised he hasn't been asked yet. He's taken just three kids in there so far, only the hard cases, and each time the Colonel hasn't been too concerned. A few days later, when the kid comes out completely changed—respectful, obedient, no more attitude—the Colonel gets to reap the benefits. Even the parents get to reap the benefits. So right now Donovan doesn't feel like explaining himself or being second-guessed.

"You don't need to know," he says. "You're admin, I'm ops, right? Isn't that how you set it up? If I'm a partner, I get to run my part of the camp my way. As long as the kids come out of here with some discipline I figure I'm doing my job. The day you want to start telling me how to do that job, that's the day you make me an employee, and *pay* me. Otherwise, I'll handle it."

The Colonel's about to say something else, but Donovan heads for the door, cutoff cammies in hand. "And I want an air condition-er," he says over his shoulder. "This isn't over."

*

"You lit some grass on fire?" William says. "That's it?"

"It wasn't just lighting grass on fire," Loren says. "It was a symbol."

"A symbol of what?"

"Of how he couldn't fuck with me."

William nods and stares at the cabin ceiling. He seems uncon-vinced.

"I'm telling you," Loren says, "the details were perfect. You could see it from an airplane. You could practically see it from space."

"And the pro wasn't mad?" William says.

"Oh yeah, he was way pissed. But he knew he couldn't do any-thing. He knew I was just getting him back for being such a hand job."

William nods again, scratching at his side. His allergies have been getting worse since the first day. He has big, continental blotch-es on his stomach, and his neck is candy-striped with welts. Loren's never heard him talk any other way except congested.

"So if he couldn't fuck with you," William says, "how'd you end up here?"

A pause. Loren can't think of anything to say, and the silence swells around him. His shoulder aches in waves from hitting the fence post yesterday. He thought he could get some credibility back with the kids by telling them stuff he's done in the past, but now that's backfiring too. The quiet drags on, until William mercifully ends it by coughing up some phlegm.

It's after lights-out and all six boys are locked in the cabin, sweating stains into their bunks. Ty, the kid who rocks, is the only one asleep so far. As soon as Donovan left them, Ty shook out a few pills from one of the orange bottles stashed below his bunk, then rolled onto his side and was out in minutes.

On the other side of William is Jeremy, who keeps sighing dramatically, every once in a while declaring that he's trying to sleep so would everyone please shut up? Jeremy has his socks (three pairs, dark) and T-shirts (three crew necks, white) folded neatly under his bunk, precisely the way Donovan wants them.

"So what about you?" Loren says to William. "What'd you do to get sent here?"

"I stole some stuff," William says.

"Yeah? What kind of stuff?"

"Comic books."

Across the cabin, EK snorts in the dimness. "What, like X-Men? Archies?"

"No, these were really valuable," William says. "Really old. One of them, a Flash #63, near mint, was worth about sixteen hundred dollars. It came out in the 1930s."

Loren's not sure how much he can believe. It sounds true, but he doesn't know anything about comics, and he exaggerated his golf course story by a lot. He said the damages were two million dollars.

"How'd you steal them?" he asks.

William sits up in his bunk.

"I had a job at this store called Ink Bomb," he says. "It's in Baltimore, where I'm from. I know a lot about comics, so I hung around there a lot. The owner, Giorgio, was this fat guy who used to sweat like a horse. He sometimes left little marks when he touched the pages. But I started helping him—sorting things, sweeping up— and pretty soon Giorgio was asking me to watch the place while he ran out to do stuff. If anyone came in I had to tell them he'd be right back. It was easier than setting the alarm."

"So you helped yourself?" Loren says.

"No way, I liked it there. I was thirteen and I had a job."

Jeremy rolls over in his bunk and sighs heavily. The animal under the cabin makes scratching noises. Someone farts—Loren's pretty sure it's Ty.

"So this one day a collector comes in," William says. "Somebody big. Giorgio had his regular armpit stains spreading across his chest, about to meet in the middle, and as soon as the collector comes in, he goes in the back and puts on a clean shirt. They start talking about Marvel and the Golden Age, all that. I'm dusting shelves, and the collector finally notices me and says who's this? Giorgio says—him? He's the maid. The *maid*. They have a big laugh and the collector says they should put me in a costume. Black skirt, apron, all that. Ha ha. They're laughing it up. Even though I know way more about comics than Giorgio—more than both of them, probably."

William stops to deal with some new itch on his leg. He made a flyswatter from a stick and the bottom panel of a Saltines box smuggled from the cafeteria. It doesn't work at all against flies, but it does let him scratch his bug bites while lying down.

"That was the afternoon I took the comics," he says. "Giorgio left me alone while he went to get lunch. I took a few Avengers, one Infinity Quest, and the Flash #63—about twenty-five total, worth like maybe thirty thousand dollars, give or take. All in a milk crate, balanced on my handlebars. Giorgio was at my house an hour later. I just denied it and denied it, even though everyone knew. My *parents* knew. When Giorgio said he'd go to the cops, I said good—then they'll know you had an underage employee. The comics were insured, but he couldn't file a claim without a police report. Child labor, he didn't want that.

"For a week my parents told me to give them back. The whole thing would be over, they said. Then they threatened to send me here, which they knew is like the last place I'd want to spend six weeks, stuck outside with the bugs and the pollen. Even in the parking lot, the day we showed up here, they said all I had to do was tell them where the comics were and we could drive home."

"Why didn't you?" RK says.

"I couldn't."

"Yeah you could," Loren says. "You just didn't want to."

"No, I seriously couldn't," William says. "I don't technically have them anymore."

"Why not?" Loren says. "You sold them?"

"I wish. No, they're just gone. I buried them in this box that was supposed to be waterproof but wasn't. It rained for two days, the books got soaked. They were bagged but that didn't matter. I tried to dry them with a hairdryer, which only made it worse. The pages all stuck together, and when I tried to separate them the paper basically dissolved. It turned to dust. Massive damage—no restorer would touch them."

"Jesus," EK says. "You are such a dumb-ass."

"I know. But I can't tell anyone now. Not my parents, definitely not Giorgio. Even when I get out I can't. I'd be paying him off the rest of my life. Anyway it doesn't matter. I'm glad I did it. He insulted me, the fat asshole."

William sets his flyswatter down and stretches back in his bunk, and the cabin goes quiet again. Loren watches two feathers from William's pillow fall from his bunk and drop in a straight line to the floor. The cabin has nothing in the way of airflow.

"It sort of serves you right," Jeremy says to William. "You shouldn't have taken them. They weren't yours."

RK picks up an empty water bottle by his bunk and throws it at Jeremy's head.

"Quit it," Jeremy says. "They weren't his, all right?"

"What'd you do to get sent here, Germ?" EK says.

"Why do you want to know?" Jeremy says.

"Because I bet you've never broken a rule in your whole life," EK says. "You're a parent's wet dream."

"Sometimes I'm not," Jeremy says.

"So what'd you do?"

Jeremy sits up, cross-legged in his pajamas. His sheets are jammed in a ball at the foot of his bunk.

"I had a party," he says.

"For who?" EK says. "All your imaginary friends?"

"No, people showed up. A lot of people. My parents were away. It got pretty wild."

"Right."

"It did. It was huge."

"So why'd you get sent here?"

"My parents found out. Some stuff got broken. They were mad."

"Bullshit," EK says. "No one gets sent away for six weeks because of a few broken glasses."

"Wait a minute," William says. "You're that kid."

Jeremy says, "What kid?"

"Didn't you say you were from D.C.?"

"Bethesda. Outside D.C."

"You're the kid that had that party," William says, pointing across the cabin with his stick. "It was in the papers. He had a party because he didn't know anyone at school and wanted to be popular. This is you, right? Eighth-grader. Except people came from high school, and like three other high schools. And it got out of control."

"I told you it was huge," Jeremy says.

"No, huge in the bad way," William says. "Like kids trashing stuff, going through all the rooms, putting on your parents' clothes. They were gone for a long weekend, right? Where'd they go? New Mexico?"

Jeremy pauses and then says quietly, "Just regular Mexico."

"That's right. The *Sun* did this big thing about it. Plus, people at my school know people who know people who were there. It's already like a legend."

RK says, "So what happened?"

"Nothing," Jeremy says.

"No, stuff happened," William says. "A lot happened. All these people show up. Jeremy here sees that it's getting bad. It's packed, people in every room, and he's had his, what, like first-ever beers that night. So he decides to take control."

"I told them to get out."

"More," William says. "Tell the whole thing. He went around with a meat fork, holding it up to people's throats. All these people he doesn't even know. Big kids, football players, most of them wasted. Not the best idea."

"They wouldn't leave," Jeremy says.

"Not after the meat fork. Instead they took it out on the house. Someone threw a TV through a window, people were drilling holes in the wall with his dad's tools. A kid flushed a loaf of bread down the toilet, so the plumbing got stopped up. Which was like an invitation to start pissing everywhere. What else? Oh yeah—the mower. There was a riding lawn mower in the garage, so two kids started it up and rode it into the pool."

Jeremy's shaking his head. "The place was destroyed," he says.

"You let them into your house," William says.

"Not all of them. Not to do that. But some of the stuff in the newspapers didn't really happen."

"Did a football player put on your mom's wedding dress and throw up all over it?" William asks.

Pause. "OK, yeah. That one's true."

"Did the patio furniture get cut up with a chain saw?"

Jeremy doesn't say anything.

"Did someone take a dump in the upstairs tub?"

More silence.

RK says, "No way, that's sick."

"It's probably good you were sent here," William says. "You would have gotten lynched at school. His parents tried to press charges against everyone who was there. They wanted the kids to name names."

"They tried to press charges against *me*," Jeremy says. He's slouching back down onto his bunk. "Anyway, it doesn't matter. That's why I'm here, but it's over. End of story."

Loren watches the feathers from William's pillow, motionless on the floor. When he waves his hand over them they shift and settle again, like they're underwater. The cabin grows quiet, the kids tiring at last, but Loren asks one final question.

"Did you give up any names?" he says.

"What?" Jeremy says.

"People who were at the party. To your parents or the police or whoever."

Jeremy hesitates in the darkness before he says no. It's very slight, almost imperceptible, but still enough for Loren to think he's probably lying.

*

In the Colonel's house, two of the phones on the card table are ringing, but Kitty doesn't answer either one. Instead she stands over the table and looks down at her hands, which she holds out in front of her like strange new attachments. She's wearing surgical gloves, each filled with two capfuls of sesame oil, with rubber bands around the cuffs to prevent leaks. Every other night for the past few weeks Kitty has put the gloves on. She got the idea from a women's magazine, which is in her bedroom, folded open to a story on at-home spa tips. The caption next to the photo says, "Wait two hours while your pores drink in the healing moisture."

The phones in front of her are ringing in sync.

"Are you going to answer those?" the Colonel yells from the top of the stairs.

"I can't," she yells back.

"Why not?"

Kitty wriggles her fingers. A few bubbles move around the knuckles. "I just can't," she says.

Descending footsteps on the stairs. By the time the Colonel gets into the room the ringing has stopped. It's just Kitty and her gloves, and ten silent phones lined up on the card table.

"Hon, we've talked about this," he says. "It's one thing. And you *like* talking on the phone."

"I can't do it right now," Kitty says with a shrug. "The stuff would get all over."

"Why don't you try wearing the gloves during the day, when you're at the pool?"

"Weird tan lines," she says. "My hands would look English."

"But even when your hands are free you don't answer the phones. I don't think I've heard you pick one up yet."

"That's not true. I talk to people all the time."

"You call your friends maybe. Or your mother. That doesn't count."

Kitty gingerly taps a pack of cigarettes with two fingers and pulls one out. The Colonel watches her fumble with the matches and walks over to light one for her. When she leans in—his angel, his devotion—she touches his hand and her glove makes a squishing sound.

The phones were the Colonel's idea, a way for potential new clients—he never calls them customers; Laundromats have customers, gas stations have customers, but Camp Ascend! has *clients*—to get the reassured feeling of checking references without calling any real references. He bought ten phone numbers, plausibly spread out around the country (including two in Los Angeles, which he's targeting as his next growth area). All the numbers are forwarded up to the compound, to ten local lines the Colonel had installed at the house. He could host a telethon if he wanted.

Taped to the table next to each phone is an index card with fake info that someone answering that phone might conceivably have about the camp, including a quick anecdote showing how much that person's conceivable son or daughter thrived under the Colonel's guidance. The card for the Chicago phone reads:

Midwest accent (long vowels), single mom Daniella Roiphe, son Christopher, 13, stole from local stereo store. Say "Professional staff" (like STEE-aff), say "Safe, clean operation," (EE-YAPP-eration), say "Colonel puts a lot of heart into it" ("LAT of HURT")

Kitty's supposed to pick up the phones whenever she's in the house, but she has a long list of reasons why this never happens. She's tired, she says. Or she doesn't hear them ringing, or she can't do the accents. When the Colonel wrote up the Chicago card, she told him that she didn't—and he believed her on this—remember which letters were the vowels, which is why he spelled the words out phonetically for her. The Colonel's good with accents—occasionally he'll field two calls at once, putting one on hold and talking to the other, sounding convincingly like he's from both Boston and Texas. He tells Kitty you just have to act like you know what you're doing and other people believe you. If anyone questions it, just pinch your nose and say you have a head cold.

Deep down, he knows, the main reason Kitty doesn't answer the phones has nothing to do with moisturizing or accents. No, the truth is that she doesn't really care if any other kids come to Camp Ascend!. She's never said it directly (though she's said it indirectly, in a thousand small ways), but she'd probably prefer it if they *didn't* come, if the camp ended tomorrow, so she and the Colonel could leave this place and move on to their next gig, one with no bats or bugs or mold. Whenever she asks the Colonel about leaving, he says soon, and when she asks him what that means, he says, "Soon means soon." At which point she goes outside to stomp around the compound, and he wonders if this might be the time she really loses it and burns down one of the empty cabins. She's made threats before.

"What about this?" he says. "How about you get every *other* call that comes in from now on? You don't have to answer every one."

Kitty shrugs and says sure.

"Trying to compromise with you here. But if you say yes, then you really have to answer them. For real."

"Yup."

Kitty reaches for the remote control, which he knows will be glistening soon. Already a bunch of the doorknobs in the house are slippery with sesame oil.

"Because the point is, I can't wait around here to make sure the phones get answered," he says. "I have stuff to do."

"What kind of stuff?"

"I don't know—checking the kids, finishing those medical records. This is a big operation. Lot of day-to-day responsibilities."

Kitty shrugs. "Then it sounds like you should get busy," she says.

"OK, but I can't do it all—"

He's cut off by the back door opening. Donovan appears and marches past, leaving a trail of dripping pool water. His hair is swirled on his head in a way that shows his hairline, which isn't receding at all but looks more like it's *proceeding*—working its way down his forehead.

Donovan says nothing to either of them, just storms upstairs.

"You know," the Colonel says, "between you and your brother, I can't decide who should be employee of the month this time around."

She gives him a withering look and says, "Why don't you vote for yourself?"

His beauty queen, his wildflower.

Instead of letting himself get dragged into the fight he knows she wants, he picks up the phones and starts checking voice mail. It's better than he thought—a lot of fish in the net. One call from Pittsburgh (shoplifting and marijuana; parents ready to liquidate their retirement account), another from Portland (general misbehavior; teacher threatened with Chinese throwing stars on a field trip), and two from L.A. All anxious parents, looking for a solution and ready to sign on to the Camp Ascend! program. The Colonel does the math in the margin—four times seventeen thousand works out to…sixty-eight thousand dollars. Even half of them would help fill out the next class nicely. Oh happy day.

On the couch, Kitty's taking in a QVC show about closet systems. When she stubs her cigarette out on a saucer, a trickle of oil leaks out of one glove. The Colonel watches her reabsorb it by hunching over and rubbing her inner wrists together in a way that reminds him—an unpleasant image, one that he wishes didn't spring to mind—of flies. The way a fly landing on a piece of food immediately does that weird rubbing-its-forelegs thing, like it can't believe its good luck in finding an old jelly smear on the kitchen counter. The Colonel has a lot of opportunity to study fly behavior. There are about four hundred of them in the house at any time.

"Hon," he says, dismissing the image. "Here's an idea. You convert just one family, based on a phone call they make, and I'll send you to any spa in the city. The best one—you can take the Jeep and stay all day. Get yourself scrubbed, buffed, wrapped in grass clippings, whatever you want. But you have to get a new client to sign for me. Just one, out of the net and into the boat. Is that a deal?"

Kitty looks at him. "I guess. Yeah."

"That's my girl," the Colonel says. "Teamwork."

He moves to kiss her. Before he's halfway across the room they hear a crash. It's behind the house but close, loud enough to make Kitty jump from the couch.

*

The air conditioner in the Colonel's bedroom looks heavy but feels much heavier once Donovan picks it up. It's a monster, fifteen thousand Btus, all digital, with a filter alert and a remote control and enough power to chill down a warehouse. When Donovan pulls it in through the window frame, a bunch of condensation water spills onto the Colonel's carpet, smelling like stale plastic. Donovan can come back and clean it up later, or have Kitty do it.

He feels zero guilt about this. There's no real reason the Colonel needs two of these things, one for each window. It's so cold in their bedroom that Donovan shivers, and his shorts, dripping from the pool, feel clammy. He gets the metal box all the way in from the window frame and stands slowly, one knee cracking loud enough to be heard over the hum of the remaining unit. The outside casing is still warm from the outside air, and Donovan has to be careful where he puts his hands—some dried bird shit has crusted onto it in spots.

A handful of moths takes the opportunity to flit in through the open window, plus a couple of buzzing black flies the size of raisins. The air conditioner is ridiculously heavy—the Colonel will never be able to carry it back, even if he wanted to. Donovan thinks this is an advantage he needs to exploit a little more. He's stronger than the Colonel, and not afraid of animals or bugs or the woods at night. Just yesterday, the Colonel called him in from marching the kids around the perimeter to kill a cricket hopping around in the kitchen sink. The Colonel is so lacking in raw strength that Donovan sometimes doesn't get how he's been so successful, while Donovan's had nothing but bad luck as far back as he can remember. It's like the Colonel believes his own bullshit, and because of that he gets other people to believe it too.

By the time Donovan gets back to his room and sets the air conditioner down, it has pressed dark pink lines into his forearms. He starts sweating freely again as soon as he's in the room. The box fan rattles in the window frame, spitting bugs onto the carpet. Donovan points the plug of the air conditioner at an outlet near to the window, then realizes it's wet with condensation. A little congratulations to himself on being smart enough to wipe it on the carpet first. People say Donovan's dumb—he's heard it his whole life, even from family—but just look at that right there. He feels like whenever he does a smart thing it's always small and no one's ever around to see it, but when he does something dumb it's big, it has consequences, and there's always an audience.

The compressor thunks on and cool air immediately blows around the room, beautiful gray streams of vapor chill. Donovan kneels and hangs his head in front of the vents like a dog. So quiet—you barely know it's on. He presses the blue "cool" button and watches the digital display count down, each one-degree change registering with a faint beep, until it bottoms out at "55 F." Perfect. Could he just leave the AC on the floor and run it from there? Donovan thinks about it and decides that that probably wouldn't work, though he can't quite explain why not. When he pulls the box fan in from the window some bugs stream in after it, and he realizes he's going to have to hurry if he doesn't want to be swatting at them all night.

Without bothering to unplug the unit, Donovan picks it up again. Metal corners press into the same pink lines on his forearms, and his knee cracks again as he stands. The motor groans from being tipped, though the vents keep blowing coolness against his chest. He sets the back edge on the window frame and slides it slowly out, an inch or so at a time, the metal casing squealing against the sill. He makes one last adjustment, another half inch on the left, and the unit plunges backward out the window.

It hangs for the briefest instant by the stretched power cord—not suspended, just barely slowed—before the plug wrenches free and whips out after it. The outlet makes a popping noise and some blue sparks light up just as Donovan hears the metallic crunch of the air conditioner hitting the ground outside. His pulse is racing from the panicked stupidity washing over him. When he looks out the window he can't see anything at first, but then someone downstairs turns the outside light on and he can see everything.

The ground is soft from the rain yesterday, though apparently not soft enough. The air conditioner hit at an angle, the upward yank from the power cord enough to spin it slightly as it fell. It's mostly in one piece, in the same way that a car is in one piece after a big wreck. Shattered plastic is spread in a rough circle around it, and some mud has splashed up onto the side of the house in a brown sunburst pattern. A shitburst, it looks like.

"Donovan?" a voice yells.

It's Kitty, coming up the stairs. The back door opens and the Colonel's head appears in the yard. Donovan tries to think of some explanation, something that could make this seem less bad, but everything he comes up with sounds stupid even to him, even as the thoughts are forming. They had two. It wasn't fair. He wanted to sleep and it was hot out and they had two and that wasn't fair.

CHAPTER 7

It's Chore Day and all nine kids are lined up on the ring, waiting for assignments. They've just finished breakfast (curried pancakes from Riap, the Indonesian cook), and already it's tropically hot out. The air vibrates with cicadas, and the shadows of the pine trees are drawing in as the sun climbs in the sky. Loren's trying not to move as a single droplet of sweat tracks slowly down the bone behind his left ear. Donovan is behind them, watching, and if anyone moves it means squat thrusts for the group.

The chores suck as much as anything else in the camp, in that the Colonel doesn't seem to own any tools. They have to pound nails using flat rocks, or dig weeds using jagged pieces of a cut-up milk crate. The linoleum was the worst so far—Loren and the twins were ordered to scrape linoleum up from the floor of the Colonel's screen porch. It was put down decades ago, so it didn't, as Loren had hoped, roll up in nice long sheets but instead came up in about a million petrified flakes, each no bigger than a dime. The three of them scratched away for five hours using nothing but stubby screwdrivers, and Loren's hands got so nicked up it looked like he'd been in a knife fight.

"Stand at attention," Donovan says now, even though they're

already standing at attention.

The Colonel appears from the barn, wearing cargo shorts and running shoes, which Loren thinks saps his authority presence a little. He looks like a suburban dad on errand day. In one hand he has a list, and in the other is his sword, unsheathed and rusty and glinting a little in the sun.

"OK," he says. "Lots of good stuff today, so let's get started. First, I need one person to clean the pool. Skim and vacuum and then shock it—Donovan'll help with the chemicals. Who wants to volunteer?"

Loren thinks about it for a few seconds and then steps out. He swore early on that he'd always resist, but then he realized there was maybe a more sophisticated way to fight back. If he volunteered sometimes it would throw Donovan and the Colonel off, and maybe give him access to higher levels of matériel—and more advanced forms of sabotage. With the pool, he didn't even have to think too hard. He could put his boot through the filter. He could loosen the bolts on the ladder in the deep end. If nothing else, he'd be around water on a hot day.

Donovan appears behind him and yanks him back into line by the scruff of his sweatshirt.

The Colonel pretends not to see. Instead he keeps waiting, a patient expression on his face, until Jeremy steps forward, guided slightly less violently by Donovan.

"Great," the Colonel says. "An eager beaver. I like to see that."

"Wait," Loren says. "What about me?"

"Next," the Colonel says. "Two people to paint the porch."

"Hold on," Loren says. "I volunteered. Why can't I do it?"

"Basic white," the Colonel says, "but I don't want any drips. Who's up for it?"

"Colonel!" Loren says.

The Colonel looks up from his list. "Yes?"

"Can I ask a question?"

"No."

"OK, then can I volunteer for a job?"

"Yes."

"Great. I volunteer to clean the pool."

"That's been decided," the Colonel says. "You're too late. We're on to the next job—porch painting."

"Great," Loren says. "I'll take it."

He'll paint army insignia all over the windows. He'll climb onto the roof and write, "HELP US," in six-foot letters.

Donovan appears behind him and pulls him back into line again using one ape paw.

"No more volunteering," Donovan says, breathing into Loren's ear. "Don't move and don't say anything else. I'm telling you right now."

Instead Ty gets the painting job, along with Meredith, the tall girl with knock-knees and stringy hair, who EK calls Morticia and who Loren is almost certain has some kind of eating issue going on. Meredith is about a foot taller than everyone else, almost as tall as Donovan, and so skinny she looks bug-eyed.

"This is bullshit," Loren announces.

The Colonel looks up again. He walks in front of Loren and says, "We don't use language like that here. Do you understand?"

"I'm just saying—"

Donovan grabs the sword from the Colonel and points it at Loren's chest. "The next words coming out of your mouth better be that you understand," he says. "Right now. Say it."

Loren stays silent, and Donovan pushes the sword forward so that the tip—dull, corroded—rests in a notch between two of Loren's ribs.

Loren looks at the Colonel, who seems as surprised by this as anyone (though he doesn't stop it). Everyone else on the ring stands frozen, watching.

Loren quietly says that he understands.

"Good," Donovan says. "So shut the hell up and do what you're told."

He hands the sword back to the Colonel, who accepts it blankly and collects himself and returns to the list.

The next few jobs get handed out quickly. William and the twins "volunteer" to seal cracks in the driveway, and Liz has to help Riap in the kitchen. In the distance, Loren can see Riap leaning against the cafeteria door, smoking as he waits.

"Everyone who already has an assignment," Donovan says, "take one big step forward. OK, right-face. Now march forward. Go."

The kids shuffle off the ring, not at all in step. Loren tries to make eye contact with Liz as she passes, but if she notices him she doesn't show it. After they're gone, he glances around and sees one other person remaining with him—Becca.

The Colonel wads up his list. He's holding the sword awkward-ly in one hand.

"No fun, right?" he says to Loren. "It's like I told you kids—this place can be summer camp or San Quentin. Your choice. Now, the last item on this list was supposed to be replanting the window boxes for Kitty. She's been asking, and I thought it would be a nice thing for her. But we're going to change things up here and give you both something a little more…unpleasant."

"I didn't do anything," Becca says. "Don't lump me in with him. I'm not a troublemaker."

"Yes you are," the Colonel says. "Kitty says you have a bad attitude."

"She took my lipstick and won't give it back."

"She confiscated it. You're not supposed to have that here."

"Then why's she wearing it? I saw her with it on yesterday."

"No more talking," the Colonel says. "And you." He gestures with the sword at Loren. "In your case it's even clearer."

"What did I do?"

Loren thinks the Colonel maybe knows about the boot polish on the camera, or about the loose plank in the boys' cabin. But he tells himself to play dumb and let the Colonel tell what he knows first.

"You mouth off," the Colonel says, "you question orders. Like just now. We hand out the jobs around here as a form of reward and punishment. So some kids get to clean the pool on a hot day, and others—well, you'll see. Come with me, both of you."

Loren hangs his head and does his best impersonation of a defeated kid. The Colonel knows nothing. He's safe.

They get led off the ring and across the dead grass. No right-face, no forward march—they walk like normal people. Up close Loren can see that the Colonel's hair is starting to go gray along his temples, and that one earlobe is bigger than the other. He walks slightly bowlegged in his sneakers, and his legs are pale white, especially compared to the mahogany tan on Kitty.

When they're close to the Colonel's house, Loren shifts into reconnaissance mode. You're supposed to memorize floor plans, points of egress, whatever intelligence you can gather. The Colonel must be reading his thoughts, though, because he stops on the steps and tells them to look down while they're inside the house.

"No glancing around," he says. "Eyes on the floor. It's a sign of respect."

Becca and Loren drop their heads in tandem, and Loren hears a door creak open. The air-conditioning hits him in a wave. He watches his own boots advance onto a yellow tile floor and sees the bottoms of cabinet doors—they're in the kitchen. Next he steps onto a thin carpet. Chair legs. The curved edge of a wooden table. A TV is on, shouting at them. The air-conditioning is unbelievable—it's like walking into a refrigerator. Loren hears the Colonel fumble with a dead bolt and takes a chance on looking around. On the kitchen table he sees the Jeep keys, house keys, sunglasses, breath mints. More important, he sees a wallet—a man's wallet, black leather. It's so close that Loren can touch it.

His thoughts get interrupted by a smell, powerfully sweet and rotten. Bad food? Mold? Becca lifts her head too, but the Colonel sees them and tells them to get their eyes on the floor again. He opens a door off the kitchen, which leads down to the basement, and the odor magnifies a hundred times. It almost knocks Loren over.

"It smells like something died, right?" the Colonel says. "That's because something *did* die, somewhere down there. We don't know what, so that's your job—to find it."

He starts to say something else, then closes his eyes and pushes the door shut again. "Ooof, that is really rank. It wasn't this bad a few days ago—too bad you couldn't search for it then. Anyway, there's storm doors on the far end, leading to the backyard, but they've got a padlock on the outside. The only way out is back up through here, but you can't come out until you find it. I'm locking you both in." He takes a deep breath and pulls the door open, then lets enough air leak out of his lungs to wheeze, "Call me when you're done. I'll be up here the whole time."

Loren can see the top few steps leading down into darkness. Bare Sheetrock walls—white spackle marking the seams in right angles.

"Where's the light?" he says. Becca swallows a bunch of times in a row. She looks like she might get sick.

"Walk down about three steps and reach up. It's on a chain."

Loren and Becca glance at each other.

"Hurry up," the Colonel says. "Now."

Loren starts breathing through his mouth and heads down the stairs. A few seconds later he hears Becca clomping after him.

*

On the walk to the cafeteria Liz rehearses her speech. *I'm not going to do anything involving meat,* she'll tell Riap. *I'm a militant vegan and I think it's gross to even touch the stuff. I'll chop vegetables until midnight if you want, but there's no way I'm going to do autopsy pro-*

cedures on dead animal parts just so other people can eat them.

But when she gets to Riap at the screen door, ready to argue her case, he stubs his cigarette out in the dirt and goes inside before she can start. In the kitchen, he positions her in front of a big box grater with chunks of coconut in front of it and mimes the up-and-down motion.

"Shredding coconut?" she says. "That's it?"

He nods without expression and she starts in, tentatively at first and then a little faster.

The kitchen is a big industrial setup that could probably feed hundreds. Riap works out of one corner of it, the only part that's clean—a single metal countertop and four of the sixteen original burners, plus one walk-in fridge. In the wall above the sink is a giant fan the size of a car hood. It's not turned on but the blades rotate slowly from the cross breeze, idly slicing up pieces of the sky. Liz is surprised the kitchen isn't warmer.

Next to her Riap chops celery, moving his knife so fast it looks blurry. She has no idea how he's going to combine celery and coconut, but with the food at Camp Ascend! she's stopped asking questions. Last night they had yam-and-shrimp soup. (She ate two rolls and a banana.)

Coconut comes off the grater like snow, and Liz finds the mindlessness of the work sort of relaxing. Just turn your mind off and do one thing, over and over again. There's a big bowl of coconut shells on the counter, with a bunch of approximately flat pieces for her to grate next.

Riap has three pots going on the stove, and he's stirring two of them at different speeds. When he sees Liz looking over at him he asks her, "OK?" and she shrugs and says, "Yeah, OK." Then he says it again, almost as a confirmation to himself: "OK." Riap's English is pretty rough, so he mostly speaks in one-word sentences, either commands or questions. Liz knows almost nothing about him, but when she asks to go to the bathroom, she gets a hint about what his life is like.

He gestures to a hallway, and she wanders tentatively down, some-how taking a wrong turn and ending up in a freezer, where she sees an old sack of tater tots the size of a bag of lawn fertilizer. It's open and covered in fuzzy ice that looks years old. Some of the tots have fallen out and now stick to the floor like animal droppings. She remembers watching a nature show where she first heard the word *scat*.

Outside the freezer she takes another wrong turn, into a pantry, but it's there that she makes her discovery. On the floor is a thin camping mattress with a sheet on top and some folded T-shirts for a pillow. An AM radio and some pictures—little Indonesian kids and a beaming wife. *Holy shit*, Liz thinks. *He sleeps here.* Next to the mattress is a shoe box of letters and a flashlight and a guitar with two missing strings. It's like the Colonel ordered him out of the back of a magazine. Finally she starts to feel like she's invading and backs out into the hallway.

When she returns to the kitchen, Riap is slicing apples. He's using a wooden cutting board that has a giant cluster of scratches on it, and he's going through the apples almost as fast as a food proces-sor. As she watches, he cuts one of them into eight perfect segments, then fans them around a small plate for her. When she reaches for one he holds up his knife to stop her and folds a strip of apple peel into a tiny chrysanthemum, which he sets on top.

She smiles, but Riap just shrugs and keeps chopping. She eats a few segments and reaches for the grater again.

Just then Riap freezes. His knife hangs suspended above the cut-ting board. She's afraid she did something wrong, and then she hears a noise outside. Riap runs to the window, and when he turns back around he's a different person. He starts yelling at Liz, about four-fifths of it in Indonesian with a few barked English commands mixed in.

"Fuck is wrong with you? Faster, OK? Smaller pieces. Go faster."

Liz doesn't know what's happening, why he got so schizo all of a sudden, but the screen door opens and Donovan steps into the kitchen. Riap keeps shouting at Liz, then pretends to notice him.

"What the hell is going on in here?" Donovan says.

Riap shakes his head, exasperated.

"Is she screwing something up?"

"OK," Riap says, holding out a hand and waggling it. "Mostly OK."

"As long as you keep her hopping," Donovan says. Riap gives him a confused look, and Donovan says loudly, "*Keep her hopping, understand?*"

Riap nods. Donovan goes to the fridge for two Cokes and grabs a fistful of coconut from the pile in front of Liz. He pushes the screen door open again, and Riap goes back to shouting. His eyes are fierce, and he yells for a few more seconds while Liz's face gets hot. She has no idea what's going on, what she did. Then Riap glances out the window again, looks back at her, and does something astonishing.

He winks.

"OK?" he says. A half smile, teeth as white as porcelain.

Jesus. He faked the whole thing. Air leaks out of Liz—she didn't even know she was holding her breath—and she feels her fists relax. She wants to throw something at him.

"OK," she says. "OK."

*

Donovan makes his way across the compound, boots crunching in the dead grass. The cans of Coke are already sweating from the heat, and the coconut doesn't taste anywhere near as good as he thought it would. It's not sweet at all—it's more like bitter. He tosses it and dusts his hand against his hip, half suspecting that maybe the girl did something to it. He wouldn't put it past these kids. His attitude is that he needs to be on their backs 100 percent of the time. That's the only way you establish authority. That's the only way you instill some discipline and respect.

Approaching the pool, Donovan hesitates, making sure Jeremy doesn't see him yet. No hitting, he tells himself one last time. The Colonel gave him an order. No screaming, no scare tactics, no throwing anyone against any fences. If Donovan was in charge, he wouldn't use snitches or bribes—none of this bullshit. It would be hard for everyone, period, end of story. Instead the Colonel anoints one kid as being trustworthy and from then on Donovan has to treat him like a prince.

Don't even raise your voice, the Colonel said. *Rein yourself in a little. Bring him a cold soda, find out what he knows.*

Jeremy's skimming the shallow end. His sleeves are rolled up (illegally), and his face and forearms are already sunburned. It's like a joke, Donovan thinks—what's black and red and weaselly all over, ha ha. Kitty has retreated inside. Her two red chaises are empty and in their usual places, near the deep end and angled to catch the sun as it moves past. The hose of the pool vacuum is wrapped around the legs of one of them. This won't take long, Donovan thinks. No hitting.

"Do I see someone's skinny white forearms?" he says, stepping forward.

Jeremy flinches. "I didn't know you were there," he says.

"Someone's always there," Donovan says. "You're always being watched. You know that."

"Right. I forgot."

Jeremy rolls his sleeves back down and Donovan takes a slow walk around the pool, peering down at the water. "Doesn't look too bad," he says.

"I skimmed and vacuumed twice," Jeremy says. "But the hose has a leak, I think. It's got all this tape on it. Otherwise the sides would look better."

Donovan can sense Jeremy staring at the Coke cans. Above them a pair of birds flies past, flapping hard.

"Thirsty?" he says.

Jeremy nods.

Donovan sits down in one of the chaises and says, "Why don't you take a break?"

He's expecting to have to persuade Jeremy, to convince him that it's OK, that big bad Donovan doesn't want to hurt him. But all too readily the kid says sure and drops the skimmer into the pool and flops down in the empty chaise next to him.

"Who said you could sit down?" Donovan says.

Jeremy looks at him like a kicked puppy. "I thought you said...."

"I said take a break. That doesn't mean you get to just drop wherever you want. Go get that and set it down properly."

The skimmer is a few feet from the edge, bubbling faintly as the long handle fills with water. Jeremy starts pushing up his sleeve again but Donovan says no, just hurry up and grab it. By the time Jeremy reaches down the skimmer has sunk beyond his grasp, and he stands back up again, water pouring from one sleeve.

This is exactly the kind of thing Donovan's talking about. He *wants* to like these kids. He wants to find the one he can stand to be around for thirty seconds without his fists starting to clench. Instead he gets this.

"I can jump in for it," Jeremy says.

"Not an option," Donovan tells him. "The pool's for staff only, and the day one of you punks gets in there is the day we change the water."

Jeremy eyes the Coke.

"Can I still have—"

"No," Donovan says. "Not yet. Maybe not at all."

He spins the chaise around so that he's facing away from the sun and Jeremy's facing toward it, then puts one soda out onto the concrete, directly between them. It looks like an ad in a magazine—glistening and wet.

"You can look at it," Donovan says. "You can watch it get warm.

And you can think about this—we've made this place pretty easy on you so far, but it could get worse. Like immediately, today, right now. You could be digging toilet ditches. Or we could send you down to patch the driveway with the twins and what's-his-name."

"William."

"Right, him. So if I were you I'd try to do nothing until I tell you. Absolutely nothing. Don't speak, don't sit, don't scratch your ass."

"OK."

"OK what?"

"OK, sir."

"Fucking-A right."

Donovan opens the second soda and guzzles half of it. No more subtlety. No more soft touch. He wipes his mouth with the back of a hand and burps and thinks to himself—screw it. Just ask the kid straight out.

"So what do you know?" he says.

"Sir?" Jeremy tilts his head to one side.

Donovan sits up in the chaise, one leg on either side. "What do you *know*? I want to know what you know about the other kids in camp. Don't act confused—the Colonel talked to you a few days ago, and he said you had no problem remembering shit then."

Jeremy hesitates. His waterlogged sleeve hangs down farther than the dry one. It covers half his hand, and water drips from his fingers.

"Is anyone else around?" he says, glancing across the compound.

"Nope. Just you and me."

"OK. Who first?"

"Let's start with that one with the red hair."

"William. I just told you, remember?"

"Don't push your luck."

"Yes sir. William's deal is, he's too sick to cause trouble, I think. The allergies are really bothering him. He's loyal to Loren, though. I hear them talking a lot."

"Talking about what?"

"Not sure," Jeremy says.

"OK, who else? The shaky one."

"Ty. Weird but harmless. He doesn't say much, just rocks. I don't think I've heard him talk the whole time we've been here."

"That doesn't count as inside info. I know all that."

"He says stuff in his sleep, though. Did you know that?"

"Like what?"

"Like I don't know. Weird stuff. The other night he said, 'Don't drop the dog.' Sometimes I think he's just acting. No one's that weird, right? Here's another thing—my bunk is right next to his, and sometimes when we all think he's asleep, he's not. He's awake, paying attention. I can tell from the breathing."

In the distance, Donovan can see Ty and Meredith on their hands and knees on the porch, each holding a brush. Donovan watches Ty dip his head down to the paint can and inhale a huge lungful of the fumes, then sit back and close his eyes.

Jeremy's staring at the Coke. "Can I have some of that now?" he says. "I'm pretty thirsty."

"Uh-uh. Talk first."

Donovan pulls the can a few inches toward him, away from the kid. It leaves a dark ring of condensation on the concrete.

"Seriously," Jeremy says, giving a cough that sounds faked. "My throat's dry."

"Wring some water out of your sweatshirt," Donovan says. "What about the girls?"

"Not much to say. The tall one, Meredith?"

"Walks like a stork?"

"Yeah, her. She eats some crazy stuff. I see her sucking down spoonfuls of sugar, straight from the bowl. But she's so skinny. I don't get it."

"That's it?"

"That's all I know on her."

"Who else?"

"Becca, the one who's chubby. She complains a lot. She flirts with the twins. I think she's probably kind of skanky, if you know what I mean."

"And the other one?"

"That's Liz. She hates this place a lot. And she's tough—she handles the workouts better than half the boys here. I think she was some kind of gymnast or something."

Donovan reaches out and moves the Coke can farther away.

"Your information sucks," he says. "I thought you had something better than this. I don't care what they eat or who complains or when they take a crap."

"You want me to make stuff up?" Jeremy says.

"No, but if you don't have anything better you might stay thirsty. And you might start digging toilet ditches."

"OK, how about this? Liz also thinks it's stupid that we have to fix up the Colonel's house when the rest of the place is such a dump. She says we should all try to screw things up. Break stuff, make messes, so we won't have to do it anymore."

Donovan nods slowly. "Better," he says, repositioning the Coke can six inches closer.

Jeremy takes a deep breath. "And here's something else," he says. "The twins have an MP3 player."

"Where?"

"Taped under one of their bunks. I can show you if you want. It's in a big ziplock bag."

"How'd they get it in?"

"No idea."

"And they use it?"

"Doesn't work anymore. Dead batteries. They've already had two fights about who was supposed to bring new ones."

The Coke can gets moved again, even closer. Jeremy watches it and swallows hard.

"Also," he says, "Loren's found a way out of the cabin."

Donovan looks the kid straight in the eye.

"I told you not to make stuff up."

"I'm not. He did."

"How?"

"There's a plank," Jeremy says. "Under one of the bunks next to his. It has some stuff written next to it on the floor. It just pulls up."

"How do you know?"

"When I found out about the MP3 player, I figured I should check under the other bunks too. He already stashed some stuff down there—a Swiss Army knife and some rope."

"You're dead certain?" Donovan says. He's pretending not to be surprised.

"Get a Bible," Jeremy says. "It's true."

That little fuck. There's no way the kid's escaping. Donovan would be on his ass like a pit bull on a piece of bacon.

"We saw it," Donovan says. "On the cameras, remember? We're always watching. I just wanted to confirm it with you and see if you'd really tell us. So here."

He picks up the can of Coke and tosses it to Jeremy, who catches it and fumbles with the flip-top, then starts guzzling. A few seconds later Jeremy winces and pushes his fingertips into his eyelids.

"What's wrong?" Donovan says.

"Fizz headache, from the bubbles. I drank too fast."

Donovan stands up. The pool skimmer now rests on the bottom, looking wavy and bent. Instead of getting it, Donovan thinks he'll head over to the boys' cabin, do a little investigating.

"You know what?" Jeremy says. He's red-eyed and blinking.

"What?"

"If it's OK with you, can I get a Pepsi next time? Or maybe a Mountain Dew? I really love Mountain Dew. It's so much better than Coke—everyone knows that."

Donovan watches his own hand reach out and grab the half-full can from Jeremy. He turns and hurls it toward the woods, and the can pinwheels, trickling out a glittering, sunlit trail of soda droplets like brown gems leaked from a sack. It finally lands in the distant trees with a soft, snapping crash.

"What?" Jeremy says. "What'd I say?"

Donovan's already walking away.

"I would have drank that anyway!" Jeremy says after him.

*

In the basement, Loren stares around in disbelief. It looks like an earthquake just rolled through. Stuff is piled in every corner, along every wall. A bare bulb illuminates about half the space, and in the dimness he can make out shapes—a rack of sagging metal shelves, an unplugged freezer with rust stains trickling down the front, a bunch of green Selmer instrument cases heaped up like clamshells. The dead-animal smell is so strong his ears are ringing.

"Is he fucking kidding me?" Becca says. She's standing in the middle of it all, hugging her elbows and making a face.

"It won't last," Loren tells her, trying to make himself sound certain. "Smells don't last. You get used to them, right?"

"Not yet. Not this."

"At least it's cooler down here," he says. "If it was hot it would be worse."

"Yeah, that's great," Becca says. "You're right—I wish we could stay here forever."

The Colonel wasn't lying about the storm doors being locked. When Loren pushes against them, a padlock on the outside bounces flatly off the hasp. A gap between the doors lets in a sliver of air and light, though, so he jams in a piece of cardboard to keep it wedged open.

Opposite the doors is a crawl space that leads under the house, with a dark opening framed by two-by-fours, like the entrance to a mine shaft. But that's not a way out, no egress there, and even if it were, Loren would have a hard time climbing in. Just the thought of it is enough to trigger low-level claustrophobia alerts in his head. Beneath the opening, centered on the back wall, is an ancient water heater with a turkey pan underneath to catch drips. The heater is twenty years old at least—the gauges on it look like something off a riverboat.

"Any ideas?" he says.

"Maybe we can tunnel through to China," Becca says.

It's impossible, Loren realizes, to live in a place like this and not have any tools. Even just the basics: screwdriver, wrenches, a pair of pliers. The house is old and far from town, and things break. The Colonel can't fix stuff himself, but someone must have known how, back in the music-camp days.

If Loren found some tools down here, he could turn this into an opportunity. The loose plank in the boys' cabin means he can get out at night. He now has access to the entire camp. He could stash the tools someplace and use them to launch strike ops. It's a good idea and he wants to tell Becca, but he's not sure she'd appreciate it.

Instead he says they should probably get going. "You take that half and I'll look over here," he says.

"I'm not looking anywhere," Becca announces, settling onto a low step by the storm doors. "I'm sitting down right here." She has eye makeup on that looks slightly vampirish in the low light. Loren doesn't know how the girls get to keep stuff like that.

He starts going through the piles of junk, trying to be systematic. When he comes across a tool, he wraps it in a rag and stashes it in an old French horn case he's found. Without the foam padding, there's a lot of room inside. After a few minutes he already has a pair of needle-nose pliers and a hacksaw blade and a can of kelly green spray paint. Becca's not paying enough attention to notice.

"What do you think about this place so far?" Loren asks her, partly just to fill the time and partly to gain some human intelligence (HUMINT). He doesn't know if he can trust Becca yet.

"Shit burger," she says. "Shit burger with lettuce."

Loren sees a small propane torch, which could be promising, but when he picks it up it feels too light. Probably empty, and anyway the top seal is rusted over. He crouches down and blows out the pilot light on the water heater without making a big deal about it. Let the Colonel figure it out when he's taking cold showers. Upstairs, almost in response, someone flushes a toilet and water whooshes through the pipes above their heads.

"Some of it's not so bad, I guess," Becca says. "The other kids seem OK. Like the twins—do you know what their deal is?"

"What about them?" Loren says.

"I don't know—aren't they kind of rich?"

"I guess so, yeah. They say they are."

"Like *really* rich?"

"Richer than most people. They go to prep school. Their dad owns a paper company."

"I think I would do them," Becca says. "I think they're doable."

Loren drops the screwdriver he's holding and pretends he meant to. She intimidates him a little, the way she's so blunt about this stuff. Becca always picks sweatshirt tops out of the clean box that are too small for her. She has bigger boobs than most grown-up women, and Loren figures she wants to show them off. She once tried to flirt with Donovan, which didn't work at all. He made her scrub the foundation of the Colonel's house with a toilet brush.

One of the rusted shelves is loaded down with paint cans, and behind them he sees a big canister of potassium nitrate.

"Know what this is?" he asks her.

She doesn't. She's examining her nails and barely bothers to look over.

"Saltpeter," Loren says. "People put it in food sometimes."

"What for?"

"It's like a preservative. But they also do it to, um, make boys calm down."

"Oh."

He's not sure she understands, but he doesn't feel like explaining it.

"How do you know this stuff?" Becca asks.

"I used to make smoke bombs from it," Loren says. "You mix it with sugar and boil it, stick a fuse in as it dries. They're pretty effective —you can make them as big as you want, in any shape you want."

The canister is unopened and old, which makes him think the kids aren't getting it in their meals. Maybe that was someone's rejected idea from way back. The part about it going into food at camps is probably just a myth anyway. He thinks about trying to smuggle the canister out for future smoke bombs, but it's too big.

"Do you know anything about Liz?" Loren says. As soon as the words are out he regrets them.

"Why? You like her?"

"No. I'm just asking."

"You do. You like her, I can tell. She could probably kick your ass, but I think it's cute. I'll say something to her."

"No, don't. It's OK. Definitely don't say anything."

He spots an electric buffer for brass instruments, plus some old, fuzzy circular pads with black wax hardened into the fibers. Next to that is a box of funnel-shaped metal things that turn out to be trumpet mouthpieces. Underneath them he finds (bonus points) a socket set, with only a few of the sockets missing. It gets wrapped into a rag and dropped into the instrument case with the other tools.

The animal smell is suddenly stronger. Loren shifts a box of sheet music and there it is—a possum, totally dead, not faking at all. He guesses it's been here maybe a week, and is so decayed that it's puffed up in spots. He'd have a hard time identifying the head from the tail except for a few angled teeth sticking out of a pointed snout. The smell hits him like a shovel, so he puts the box of music over it again and tries to sort his thoughts.

The tools, good. The loose plank, good. Things are coming together. But before he and Becca leave here, he wants to try one more thing.

"You know this place is bullshit, right?" he says.

"Yeah."

"But we don't have to just sit back and take it all. There's some stuff we can do to fight back."

"Like what?" She's not looking at her fingernails anymore.

He reaches for the socket set. "Like, we could figure out how to get in and out of certain places. The cabins, this house. You could sneak out to go see the twins sometime."

"I don't get it."

Loren unwraps the socket set and brings it over to the storm doors. The lock is on the outside, but the hasp that holds the lock in place is through-bolted, with the nuts on the inside. He tries two sockets before he finds the right size. It snaps satisfyingly into place.

"I'm saying we could get out of here right now," Loren says. "If we wanted."

"Yeah but, dummy, where would we go? Donovan's out there. He'd see us."

"What about this then?" Loren says. "We could undo the bolts and leave them off. That way we can get back into the basement anytime. And the Colonel and Donovan would never know."

"Why do we want to get back down here? It's gross. It smells."

She probably doesn't want to hear about the tools and the sabotage operations. Loren realizes he should have thought for a second before opening his mouth. He can't sell it now.

"Let's just see if these come loose," he says, fitting the wrench handle onto the socket.

"Don't," Becca says. "I don't want you getting me in trouble again."

"No one's going to know," Loren says. "It might not even come off anyway."

He forgets which direction is loose and which is tight. He has to try both. If the nuts stick, there's probably WD-40 down here some-where.

Becca stands up. "Stop it," she says. "I'm telling you. I don't want anymore dead-animal projects because of your stupid stunts."

Lefty loosey, right tighty. When Loren gets the first nut to turn, Becca starts yelling.

"Colonel!" she shouts, cupping her hands at the ceiling. "Colonel! He's trying to escape!"

"Shut up," Loren says. "I'll stop, OK? Look—I'm stopping." He steps away, taking the socket wrench with him. "Just relax for one second."

"You're a jerk," Becca says. "I just want to go home. I fucking hate it here."

"Me too. You think I like this place? I'm trying to fight back."

"Whatever, but just leave me out of it, OK? I don't need to be involved in your POW shit."

Loren leans against the wall by the stairs. The concrete blocks feel cool against his back. He turns the wrench a few times against his fingers, listening to the click of the ratchet. This didn't work, but at least he got something in the category of HUMINT—he wanted to find out if he could trust Becca and now he knows.

"Just sit here and I'll find the animal," he says. "Seriously. You don't have to do anything else—I'll get us out of here."

Becca looks like she doesn't believe him, but she sits back down anyway.

*

William leans on the handle of his busted mop. "You did not," he says.

"We did too," EK says. "Both of us."

"At the same time?"

"No, three days apart. Last Easter weekend—our whole family got together. She asked us not to tell each other, but of course we had to. RK told me like ten minutes after he was done."

RK grins at the ground and shakes his head. The three of them stand in the fractured shade of a dying elm tree. They were issued a bucket of driveway sealant and one soup ladle each, and they got as far as opening the bucket and pasting over two cracks before EK decided they should take a break. That was twenty-five minutes ago.

William doesn't get how the trees and grass around the compound are all dying and yet the weeds in the driveway manage to come up full force, hard enough to crack pavement. He also doesn't know if he should be impressed or disgusted that the twins both had sex with their first cousin.

"How old was she?" he asks.

"Seventeen," EK says. "She'd just come out of rehab." EK is more or less the spokesman for the two brothers, especially when it comes to stories like this.

"How old were you?" William says.

"Thirteen."

"And you weren't grossed out at all? Wouldn't the kid come out with like four heads if she got pregnant?"

"She couldn't get pregnant," EK says. "I pulled out."

"Me too," RK says.

"But there's still the disgustingness factor," William says. "I think it's illegal."

"It was her idea," EK says. "Anyway, what should be illegal was how big her rack was."

RK nods. "Definitely heavy-teated," he says.

William's not sure how much of this he can believe. All the twins' stories seem a little exaggerated—nothing normal ever happens to them. Personally, William has never seen a breast in real life before. Giorgio had some X-rated comic books in the bottom drawer of his file cabinet, which William got into whenever he was left alone, but they didn't do anything for him. They were just drawings.

"It's officially hot as fuck out here," RK says. He picks up a rock

and whacks it into the parking lot with his mop. RK is not only bigger than his twin brother but more athletic too, without really trying too hard. He hits half a dozen more rocks, each one sailing farther and farther away, until they're landing in the woods on the
opposite side of the pavement. It's fifty yards at least.

William notices a massive, volcanic pimple on RK's neck, bigger
than any zit he has ever seen. The rest of RK's skin is clear, but it's
like all the pimples in his body joined forces to come up with one
Vesuvian monster, purple and angry-looking, the size of a nipple.

EK sees what William's staring at and says whoa. "Tell me before
you pop that thing," he says to his brother. "I want to get into a haz-
mat suit."

RK touches it gently with an index finger. "Eric, hit puberty first
and then we'll talk, OK?"

"Bite me," EK says.

William instinctively steps away. The twins make him nervous—stuff has a way of getting broken around them—and he can't
tell when they're teasing and when they're about to start whaling on
each other. The two of them get into fistfights about once a day, and
from the stories William's heard these aren't even that bad. They've
put each other into the emergency room before. RK once broke his
hand punching the back of EK's head, and EK snapped his collarbone when RK pushed him off a garage roof. They were nine.

"We should probably get back to work," William says.

"Five more minutes," EK says.

William shrugs. "Do whatever you want." He takes a ladleful of
sealant out to the driveway and trickles it onto a crack and sneezes
twice. The driveway sealant might be a new problem for him. It's
like thin tar but worse-smelling, in a bucket with a bright green lid
the color of Astroturf. William looks down into the shiny surface,
where a few bugs have gotten stuck. He sniffs faintly, trying to meas-
ure his reaction. A few drips of snot leak from his nose, and he wipes
them away with the back of one wrist.

"Dude, it's probably the *air*," EK says. "Are you allergic to oxygen? Are you allergic to planet Earth?"

William ignores him. EK picks up some rocks and tries hitting them with his mop handle, missing a bunch of times in a row. RK says that's like five strikes right there, but EK swings twice more and finally tags one. The rock goes soaring. He drops the mop and starts leaping around, yelling, "A walk-off home run! Dodgers win the pennant! Dodgers win!"

William doesn't see what happens next but he hears it. There's a thunk, and he looks up to see EK stumbling to the ground and the bucket going over, spilling sealant onto the dead grass like an oil slick.

"Holy shit," EK says. One side of his leg is covered.

"You're an idiot," RK says.

"Fuck you. Help me clean it up."

The twins try to corral it with the mops but it's no use. The stuff has thinned out from sitting in the sun and it spreads fast, pushing black fingers through the dirt in every direction. The bucket sits on its side in the middle like a shipwreck, and the tarry, chemical smell floats up around them. William just stands and stares, mop in hand. He saw this coming. Maybe not *this*, exactly, but something.

Someone's approaching from the top of the driveway. It's Donovan, on his way back to check on them. William pretends to focus on a tiny fault line in the pavement, repairing intently, but Donovan can tell something's up, even from a distance. He walks faster down the hill until he gets to them.

"How'd it spill?" Donovan says.

"It just did," EK says.

"It tipped over by itself?"

"Yeah, just about."

RK tries to take the blame. "I did it," he says. "It was me."

"Shut up," EK says.

Donovan cuts them both off. "On the ground," he says.

"What?"

"Get on your stomach, now."

"What for?" EK says.

"Just shut your mouth and do it." He points over to William. "You too."

"But I didn't do anything," William says.

"He didn't," RK says. "He did nothing wrong."

"*On the ground*. Facedown."

William drops the mop and comes over. Donovan arranges the three kids in the dirt so their feet are pointing away from the spill and their faces are directly over it. They're like three hands around a stopped clock—hour, minute, second. Then Donovan takes three sets of plastic zip cuffs from his pocket and handcuffs the kids behind their backs. William's face is inches from the sealant, close enough to see oily rainbow swirls in the surface. The fumes are worse than he would have imagined. He feels like he's swimming through a vat of it.

"Don't move," Donovan tells them. "You can put your face down into it if you want, but don't move anything else. I'll be back, and if I find out you moved you'll be out here all night."

William's allergies kick into overdrive. His nose runs freely from both nostrils, and his eyes are on fire. Donovan's boot steps fade out of hearing.

RK says to his brother, "Eric, you are such a fucking asshole it's unbelievable."

EK says nothing.

William knows that Donovan's not coming back for a while, but that he'll be checking on them from the trees. There's no way William can hold his head up this way for long. He guesses that RK will be able to hold out, he's tougher, and that EK will give it a go but quit after a few minutes. William decides it's not worth trying. His skin feels like a million ants are crawling on it. Maybe a million ants *are* crawling on it. He picks a shallow spot in the spill, where tiny hillocks of grass poke through, and very gently sets his chin down.

*

"Found him," Loren says.

He's been rehearsing the line in his mind for the past few minutes to make sure he gets the right mix of surprise and relief.

Becca comes over to check it out and stops before she gets too close. "Man," she says, wrinkling her nose. "Nasty."

"Can you get me some bags or something?" Loren says. "Like black garbage bags?"

He has the French horn case waiting, with a bunch of tools and the can of green spray paint, all rag-wrapped so they don't clink against each other. The possum will go on top—he'll get the whole thing out at once. To cut down on the smell, Loren finds some old tile cleaner and spritzes it toward the furry carcass, which accomplishes exactly nothing. The air must be saturated with stink molecules. His sweats and his hair and his skin will probably reek until his next shower tomorrow morning.

Loren's realization here is that Becca's right. The kids think he's making things worse for them, but mainly because he hasn't pulled off something big yet. No one trusts him, which makes sense—he hasn't given them a reason to. But now that he has assets and a rough plan, he can stage something significant. He can get the other kids to believe.

"All the bags have stuff in them," Becca says from across the basement.

"Just dump it out. It doesn't matter. I only need two or three."

Loren uses a hoe to rake the possum toward him like a set of craps dice. The body isn't completely dried out and stiff, the way he guessed it might be. It's actually plump in spots, which he doesn't want to speculate too much on.

Above him he can hear the television—laughter, people clapping, bells ringing. It's a game show.

Becca drops two bags by his feet and runs back to the storm doors, a hand pressed over her mouth and nose.

"Almost done," he tells her. But when he gets the possum into the bags, one inside the other, and the bags into the French horn case, he can't close the lid.

"Hurry up," Becca says.

"Hang on, I'm trying."

He repositions the possum but that doesn't help. Even with the tools rearranged, it doesn't fit. Finally he puts everything back in and kneels on the case. The air gets slowly squeezed out of the plastic bags, and then the outer one pops and the halves of the case come close enough together that Loren can snap the buckles shut.

At the top of the stairs they pound on the door. After a long minute it opens and they see Kitty, not the Colonel. She's in a kimono, smoking a cigarette.

"He's outside," she says. "You're done down there?"

Loren holds up the case as evidence and something shifts inside. There's a soft clink of metal, but not loud enough for Kitty to notice. The smell is more than enough for her to notice though, because she suddenly says Jesus and takes five steps back.

"Get that thing out of here. Now."

Loren lets Becca go first. When she passes through the kitchen and Kitty's turned around, blinking from the stench, he takes another long look around the room. Chilly air-conditioning, dishes heaped in the sink, a smear of something shiny on the counter.

The kitchen table is right next to him, with the checkbook and car keys and sunglasses. As Loren walks out behind Becca he can't resist one last act of sabotage—taking the black leather wallet and stashing it up the sleeve of his sweatshirt.

CHAPTER 8

Saturday night, 11:15, and Donovan quietly pushes the Jeep toward the slope of the driveway. He's got the door open, steering as the car picks up momentum. It's like a big beast he's trying to herd forward. The only sound is his grunting and the click of pebbles as they're picked up and dropped by the advancing tires. The rain stopped half an hour ago, but mist still hangs in the sky. Halfway down the driveway the Jeep is moving fast enough for Donovan to jump in, though he waits to turn the engine on until he's coasted into the middle of the parking lot. It's twenty-one miles to the main road, another thirty-three to the city—he'll have to motor if he wants to make it on time.

Initially Donovan thought about asking the Colonel to borrow the Jeep, or asking Kitty, but he knew he'd have to make up some story about why he needed it, and they always saw through his lies. That afternoon Donovan tried a couple of options on his reflection in the bathroom mirror—he wanted to blow off steam, he was meeting someone, there was something he needed to buy—but he knew none of them would work (even though the truth is basically a combination of all three).

Kitty was so bored up here that even someone else's trip to the city was big news, and she'd grill him for details—or worse, she'd want to come. And if it was anything business-related, the Colonel would ask what and how many and where, plus Donovan wouldn't know a business meeting if one fell on his head. So eventually he said screw it, he'd just *take* the Jeep, just sneak out and not worry about it until he got back. If he was quiet enough they might not notice. When he let himself out, Kitty and the Colonel were watching a movie with the surround sound turned up loud enough to rattle the windowpanes.

Trees along the dirt road are zipping by. He feels like he's moving fast, though it's hard to tell exactly how fast—the dashboard lights of the Jeep don't work anymore, so he can't see the speedometer. Kitty hit an ambulette two years ago (the dent in the front right fender is still there), and since then the Jeep hasn't been the same. No inside lights, no radio, no alarm. She nags the Colonel to fix it up, but he's too cheap. Donovan helps out when he can, but electrical stuff is hard for him. Last spring he put a new water pump in, saving the Colonel a few hundred bucks. He bails the Colonel out like this a lot, but does he ever get any credit for it? Once he drove the Jeep twelve hundred miles, from Pittsburgh to Fort Worth, because the Colonel needed eighty-seven thousand dollars in cash delivered right away. And after all that Donovan didn't even get a plane ticket home. The Colonel made him take an overnight bus.

At the end of the logging road, just over the Camp Ascend! property line, Donovan turns onto the two-lane blacktop headed northwest. The road is smoother now, and closer to straight, so he guns the engine. The Jeep gulps a few times underneath him before it gathers itself and accelerates.

He has a feeling he's forgetting something, that he left something important behind. That would be a good invention, he thinks—a device that reminds you of stuff you forgot. Press a button and it would say, "It's your car keys," or "Go back for the sunglasses." Donovan smiles in the dark just thinking about it.

Someone could make a pile of money on that. But he knows he'll probably see it on a shelf soon—some fucker will steal his idea and make a million bucks. It happens all the time.

Though some of Donovan's ideas—he can admit this—work better in his mind than they do in the real world. After he found out about the loose plank in the boys' cabin, he wanted to do something significant to Loren, something in front of the other kids that would make an example of him. He dreamed up a couple of options and ran them by the Colonel, who vetoed every one. That deaf kid's mom was calling all the time lately, and the Colonel wanted to scale back the threats and the violence. He sat Donovan down for a talk.

"As long as they're not"—the Colonel searched for an example—"I don't know, *stealing* from us, you don't have to always play the hard-ass." He said that from a business perspective it was better for kids to leave this place unchanged than to leave hurt. Because an injury, even a minor one, could put the whole operation in jeopardy. "Besides," the Colonel said, "any idiot can get kids to listen by hitting them. But that's never going to work long-term, for you or the kids or me. So stop."

Donovan had to settle for nailing the plank back into place and checking the rest of the floorboards in both the boys' and girls' cabins to make sure they were secure. Totally unsatisfying, and the worst part is that he doesn't even know if Loren's found out yet—though he'd pay money to be there when Loren does, just to see the look on his face.

Mist floats over the highway like in werewolf movies. Donovan starts seeing more streetlights—he's getting closer to civilization. The Colonel always tells him, "Everything you'd ever need is right here on the compound—food, shelter, recreation. This place is like Club Med. What else could you want?"

At least one thing, which is why Donovan's racing toward the city right now at a speed he can't see in the dark but that must be eighty or so.

*

Loren hears the Jeep leave. He hears the grunting as it rolls down the driveway, the single door slam shut, the engine kick over. Someone who has no idea how to conduct a night operation is trying to sneak off the compound. Sound travels, especially in the woods. Loren doesn't know who it is, but he has a decent guess. Process of elimination: Kitty's not strong enough to push the Jeep by herself. The Colonel maybe could, on his best day, but he owns it—why would he sneak out? That leaves only one (slightly ape-like) option.

For the past hour Loren's been awake, standing at his window and waiting for the blue light to go out. The light means someone from the Colonel's house is up. Loren has watched from this window for the past few nights, until he realized that the blue reflection on the ground outside wasn't really a light but the glow of a TV. About every ten minutes it flickers rapidly and then steadies out again. Loren watched and watched and finally figured out that those were commercials.

His plan tonight is to wait until the blue light goes out and then start the mission, the orders of which are already drawn up in his mind:

Step one: Egress the cabin via hidden plank

Step two: Retrieve tools from French horn case, currently in garbage shed; avoid smelly, dead possum to maximum extent possible

Step three: Snip "power" cord on two to three security cameras around compound; ensure that fake-ass, battery-operated green light keeps blinking on each

Step four: Cache tools under frame of garbage shed

Step five: Return to base

The Jeep is a curveball, though, and Loren thinks he should

maybe abandon the mission and wait for another night. Donovan might not be back for hours. He doesn't want to stand at the window until then, but he also doesn't want to be out on the compound when Donovan comes back. If that happens, though, he'd probably have time to hide, or even to get back into the cabin—he would hear the Jeep coming for miles. It probably makes most sense to stick with the current plan. When the blue light goes out, Loren thinks, it's go time.

Three bunks over, Ty says something in his sleep that Loren can't make out, but that sounds like, "He's sorry." *Sorry for what?* Loren wants to ask.

"He said he was sorry," Ty says again. "He told me he was."

Next to Ty, Jeremy rolls over and sighs. He sleeps in pajamas, even when it's hot out, the only one in the cabin who does. In the bunk closest to Loren, William makes ticking sounds as he breathes through all the snot in his head. The air in the cabin feels deoxygenated and thick, like the air inside a submarine. Loren's bone-tired. His mattress—Nerfy with lumps, smelling of dried sweat—calls to him. But instead of lying down and sleeping, he tries to keep his mind clear by driving a thumbnail into his earlobe.

Where would Donovan be going in the middle of the night? More important, does Donovan know his wallet's missing? Just about everything off the compound requires money or ID or both, and Loren knows Donovan has neither.

After he took the wallet yesterday, Loren went through it in the latrine. Inside he found Donovan's driver's license (who would have guessed his middle name was Albert?) and three credit cards with strange names on them—either fakes or stolen. Loren also found an old PBA card from Tennessee dated 1994, and some receipts for gas, plus three hundred dollars in rumpled twenties. The bills were still cold from the air-conditioning in the Colonel's house. Finally, tucked into one pocket Loren found a tiny scrap of paper with three names written on it:

Edmund Killian, 1ˢᵗ Caymans
Elgin R. Kallinet, Belize F
E. Raymond Koller, B Bermuda

Partners? A trip he was planning? Loren didn't know, but he thought it had to mean something. A person wouldn't write something down like this and stash it in his wallet without a good reason. He memorized all three names, whispering them to himself until he had them down, then stashed the wallet in a cement block under the latrine, cash and cards intact.

The light's out.

Loren is shaken from his thoughts by the realization that the wet grass outside his window is dark. No more blue light—the Colonel's TV is off. Loren checks his navy SEAL watch (extra-luminescent dial, waterproof to two hundred meters). It's 11:48. Go time.

Suddenly wide awake, he kneels by the bunk next to his, finds the knothole, and pulls.

The plank doesn't move. He adjusts his grip and puts his elbow down to gain some leverage. Maybe the board swelled up in the humidity. Another tug, still nothing. When Loren feels around the edges of the plank he realizes what's happened. About thirty-five nails have been hammered down to hold it in place. Loren's fingers slide along the perimeter of the board and come across a nail head every few inches, metallic and slightly cool against the warmer wood, surrounded by a bunch of crescent-shaped dents left by an angry hammer.

Whoever put these nails in was either pissed off or rushing or incompetent, which can only point to one (slightly ape-like) option. Loren's mission is over for the night, and now he has a new one—figure out how this information got leaked.

*

Donovan races down the highway, under streetlamps that give off dandelion-shaped balls of light in the mist. He holds his hand out the window under one of them and checks his watch: 11:52— almost late already and he's barely halfway there.

He starts weaving in and out of traffic to make up time, going around a camper and cutting off a logging truck. He runs right up to the back of a minivan with a sleeping family inside and holds down his horn for half a mile until the van finally moves over. The father raises a middle finger and Donovan yells "fuck you" at him and keeps going. In ordinary circumstances he'd force the guy to the side of the road and maybe bend that finger back for him until it snapped, in front of his wife and kids, but right now he's late. He'll take it out on the next person, when he can be more leisurely.

Donovan's definitely forgetting something—that feeling won't go away—but he's not turning around now. Not when he's already come all this way. Five miles outside the city the streetlights start appearing more frequently, and Donovan sees a sign for the downtown exits. A few straggly buildings rise up in the bug-stained windshield. It's not much of a skyline—low and squat, with big gaps in the middle.

The directions are written down on an envelope, which he peers at in the dark interior of the Jeep while advancing down the highway at almost ninety mph. When he can't read the writing, he tries holding the envelope out the window, but it flaps around like a car-lot pennant, and he's afraid it's going to blow right out of his hand. He picks an exit at random and guesses right—twenty minutes later, after winding his way through a few seedy neighborhoods and one that looks flat-out abandoned, he finds the address and parks.

There's a Laundromat, with a sign in the window that says, "Coin Op," above a row of faded detergent boxes. The sidewalk has broken glass on it in a lot of different colors, and the store next to the Laundromat is sealed over with plywood that looks like it's been there a while. Same with the store next to that. It's the kind of street that makes Donovan wish the car alarm worked. He'd have a tough time explaining to the Colonel what he happened to be doing in this part of town, on the off chance he comes down in an hour and the Jeep's gone. But he's here now, so after locking the doors he points the keys back at the Jeep and makes a conspicuous beeping noise, in case anyone's watching.

The apartment is above the Laundromat, same address but with a separate entrance off the alley. Donovan finds a grimy lobby the size of a phone booth, where he checks his envelope one last time and presses the doorbell. No name next to it, just a bare metal slot. A squeal comes through the speaker—feedback through old wires, barely identifiable as a woman—and Donovan gives the fake name he always uses in situations like this: Tony, like Tony Montana in *Scarface*. It's not that he doesn't like his name—he does, especially the Don version. That's the same name Marlon Brando had in *The Godfather*, Don Corleone. All those top mafia guys are named Don, which Donovan realized a few years ago and thinks is kind of cool. But sometimes it's better to keep your real identity out of stuff.

The buzzer sounds, and Donovan pushes the door open into a dark, narrow stairwell. Three flights, gum-covered tiles on each step, and metal riser plates that are only loosely screwed in, so they clack as Donovan hits them. At one point his foot comes down on something that crunches—a dead bug, or part of a blown-out light bulb—but he ignores it and keeps going, sweating faintly in the airless space. Donovan's wearing a new shirt for the occasion. It has wrinkles down the front from being folded up in the package, and it makes his neck itch.

At the fourth-floor landing stands a woman framed in the light of an open doorway. She's wearing a bathrobe and high heels. From the silhouette Donovan thinks she has really big, weird-shaped tits, but when he gets closer it turns out she's holding a cat.

"Tony?" she says.

"Yup." Donovan's huffing.

"I'm Debbie. Hi."

She hugs him loosely, and Donovan checks her out without bothering to pretend he's not. OK face, dark circles under her eyes, stringy hair. He's paid for worse.

She leads him into the apartment, and Donovan sees an enormous man on a couch, eating fried rice with a plastic spoon. The man looks like he weighs three hundred at least, and not all of the extra is fat. He's bald but not accountant-bald. More like badass-bald, with the kind of neck muscles that bunch up at the base of his skull. The TV's on—some sports show of people playing pool. The whole room smells like a litter box.

"This is Jerome," Debbie says. "Jerome, Tony."

The man glares up at Donovan but doesn't say anything. On the TV the announcers explain how to put English on a shot. There's a diagram of a white cue ball, with yellow arrows pointing to different parts of it.

"Jerome doesn't have any manners sometimes," Debbie says. Jerome looks up and flicks a spoonful of rice at her, and she calls him a stupid prick. The cat shifts in her arms, and in the light Donovan can see that one of its eyes has crusted over. It eats a few pieces of rice off Debbie's bathrobe.

"Come on," she says to Donovan. "Let's go back." He follows her toward the bedroom, and as they leave he sees Jerome reach for the remote. A second later the TV volume cuts off.

"He one of your customers?" Donovan asks, pulling her bedroom door closed.

"Jerome? He's sort of a ex-customer. Now he just looks out for me. I work on my own, so I need someone like that. Sometimes he's my guardian angel, but other times he's just a prick."

Debbie spills the cat onto the floor and starts rooting around in a nightstand. The smell is a lot stronger in the bedroom. There's a litter box in the corner that looks like it hasn't been cleaned in months, with cigarette butts and clumped turds in it. The rest of the room isn't much better. The bed has a single sheet on it, no blankets or pillows, and the floor is so sticky that Donovan's shoes make peeling sounds as he walks. The same painting hangs on two different walls—a beach scene, waves, a lighthouse. Even the frames are identical. "I used to work out of this one motel a lot," Debbie tells him, "and I got to know the people there. When the place shut down they let me take some stuff home, so I got those. Pretty nice, right?"

The light's a little better here, and he can see that the woman has bruises up and down her legs, and a light mustache. Still, he can work with this. He can turn her around, bend her over. There's lots of things he can do. Anyway, he wasn't expecting Las Vegas. He hasn't gotten laid in months, and he's thumbed through the magazines he keeps back at the house so many times the pages are falling out. A woman would basically need scales and webbed feet for him to go back now.

The bedroom door is thin as cardboard, and Donovan can hear Jerome out there, listening in on them. Whenever Jerome shifts, the couch springs complain underneath him. Something's rubbing against Donovan's leg, and when he looks down he sees the top of the cat's head. A few smears of eye gack have come off onto Donovan's pants. He pushes the cat away with his foot, a little more forcefully than he probably needs to. It travels a few feet in the air and lands on its side. When it stands back up, a few clumps of shedded fur remain stuck to the floor.

Debbie finally turns from the nightstand. She has a string of condoms in one hand like a necklace.

"OK baby, in you go," she says, and at first Donovan thinks she means him. But instead she picks the cat up and locks it in the bathroom. Right away it starts scratching at the door. A plastic bottle of something gets knocked to the floor.

"I don't want him staring at us," she says to Donovan. "People get spooked. A month ago Jerome hung him out the window by his tail. So now I do this as part of my customer service." From behind the bathroom door there's another crash. "But he doesn't like it too much, *do you baby?* I know, Virgil. I hear you in there." Donovan picks up the warm, ammonia scent of new cat piss.

"OK," Debbie says. "I'm ready."

She unties her bathrobe and lets it fall open. Saggy boobs and a gut, but it's not until he sees her pubic hair that Donovan's mouth falls open—it's the darkest, thickest bush he's ever seen. The size of a bandana, practically hip to hip, and puffed out like uncut grass. She could probably use it to scrub pots. Donovan imagines reaching in there and pulling out stuff that's been lost for a long time—a condom wrapper or some nickels, or maybe an old pretzel.

She puts her hands on her hips, holding the robe open, and he starts to unbutton his shirt. He can't stop staring at the thatch. Because the shirt is new, the buttons are sticking. He only gets a few of them undone before he thinks, screw it, and just pulls it over his head.

"He-man, huh?" Debbie says.

Behind the bathroom door there's a ceramic thunk, something falling into the tub. "Virgil," she says. "You behave in there."

Donovan's fumbling with his pants. He feels like a teenager, like he could fuck a goat right now if it came to it. His face is getting warm. The couch outside the bedroom creaks again under Jerome's bulk, but Donovan doesn't care. Let the bastard listen if he wants.

When Donovan's pants are puddled around his ankles he steps free of them and toward her, but she holds up a hand.

"Wait," she says. "Almost forgot. Before we get going here, I need 180 in cash or 200 on a card."

Donovan's caught short. He almost forgot about the money. "Oh," he says. "Right. Hang on just a sec." His dick is pointing out idiotically, like a dog tugging on the leash. He picks up his wadded pants and pats them with both hands, feeling for the flat slab of his wallet. When he comes up empty he feels his face get even warmer.

He shakes the legs free and reaches into each pocket. Still no luck. The Jeep keys are in there, and the envelope with his directions, but that's it. His heartbeat speeds up.

Debbie closes her robe and crosses her arms. Show's over—no more free samples.

Donovan pulls each pocket inside out, and pulls the pants inside out too. "Where the fuck?" he says. He tries the pocket of his itchy new shirt, where he knows he wouldn't put his wallet in a million years. He looks in and under both shoes. Then he looks up at Debbie.

"I don't…" he starts.

"Sorry," she says. "Pay to play."

"But I came in here with it. I definitely had it." He's looking at the floor around his feet like the wallet might leap up at him.

"You're a terrible actor," she says.

"What the hell are you talking about?" Donovan freezes. He points at her with both an index finger and his rapidly deflating dick. "Wait a minute," he says. "You stole it."

"What?"

"I had it when I walked in. Now I don't. So do the math—either you have it or that goon out there does."

The woman doesn't bother to argue. Instead she looks down at the floor and says one word: *Jerome*. No urgency, no alarm. She says it like he's right there in the room with them already.

Donovan hears the couch springs release on the other side of the door. He's practically naked, defenseless except for his socks. He looks around for something he can use, but the only thing he comes up with is a cat toy, a stuffed green parrot with a bell inside. The bedroom door flies open and Debbie gets a few words out— "cocksucker says we"—before Jerome advances like a bull, head down, shoulders low. Donovan throws the cat toy at him, which jingles slightly and misses.

When Jerome's almost on top of him Donovan manages to land one punch that half skids off Jerome's bald head and doesn't slow him down at all. Jerome wraps his arms around Donovan and lifts, and it's like Donovan's being hoisted on a winch. Then he's dumped on his ass and Jerome is holding him down with one hand and punching him in the face with the other, windmilling his arm again and again. It would probably look cartoonish, except that it loosens three of Donovan's lower front teeth and spills about a quart of Kool-Aid-red blood all over his face and the floor and his brand-new shirt. The woman stares down at the scene, arms crossed, face completely neutral.

After less than a minute it's over. Jerome lands twenty or thirty punches and is barely winded. He sits up on Donovan's chest and flexes his fingers, checking them for damage.

Donovan is swallowing a lot of blood, warm and coppery and thick. He groans and tips his head to the side and spits a mouthful of it onto the floor. The odor of cat piss from under the bathroom door is working like smelling salts. It keeps him clearheaded, even as Jerome drags him out of the bedroom by his hair and deposits him on the stairway landing outside the apartment. A few seconds later his clothes get thrown out on top of him and the door slams again. Donovan tries to think about what to do next, but he can't line up two thoughts in a row, so instead he slumps against the wall and passes out.

When he comes to again it's like a computer rebooting. Stray images, randomly placed, none of them making much sense. Donovan sees a light fixture on the ceiling with dead bugs in it. Stairs. Gum-covered tiles. His eyelids are sticky and hard to open, and eventually he realizes that it's from dried blood. Only then does he start to remember where he is and what happened.

He has no idea how long he's been out here—it could have been hours. The TV is still on inside the apartment, but it's a different show now, no more pool lessons. Donovan peels himself off the floor and starts getting dressed, pulling on clothes in the order he finds them. Every movement comes with a wince. He's been beaten up before, but not in a while, and almost never so one-sided. In the past, he could almost always get a few shots in. He has a headache that thumps with his pulse, and his tongue won't stop pushing around the newly loosened teeth. Everything on the left side of his face is sore, and his left eye is swelling shut—Jerome's a righty. Donovan wipes his face with his shirt and figures there's no point putting it on. He'd just get the blood all over himself again.

On the street downstairs, the Jeep waits patiently in the broken glass outside the Laundromat. Donovan reels toward it like a drunk, bloody and shirtless and bruised. If a cop were around right now there could be problems, but he guesses no cop has been to this neighborhood in a long, long time. When he's unlocking the driver's door, Donovan sees something. A shape, skulking along the weeds in the alley. It's the cat from upstairs—Virgil. It must have come down the fire escape. The cat stops when it sees him, and Donovan realizes what he has to do. The same thing Tony Montana would do. The same thing Donovan Corleone would do.

He steps away from the Jeep and crouches down on the sidewalk, extending his hand with the wadded-up shirt in it. The cat is tentative at first—it walks a few feet toward him, not directly but at an angle, and stops again. Donovan whispers softly but doesn't move. Finally the cat gets curious enough to come and sniff at the bloodstains.

In one quick motion Donovan wraps the shirt around it, making a small bundle. A set of fanned-out claws immediately pokes through the fabric and sinks into his forearm, but Donovan ignores them and ties the sleeves together around the squirming shape. When he's sure the cat can't get free, he puts it on the sidewalk and unlocks the tailgate.

In the back of the Jeep is a bunch of old crap: catalogs, empty boxes, a flashlight with exploded-battery crust caked onto the handle. All of it gets pushed aside, and under the carpet, in the well where the spare tire is kept, Donovan finds what he's looking for.

The tire iron feels nicely unbalanced, with the weighted end pulling at his hands. He waggles it a little—give him a decent pitch, a fat fastball down the pipe, and he'd put that ball into orbit. The street is completely empty. No people, no cars. On the sidewalk, the cat has somehow managed to somersault itself forward a few feet. Its head has worked free, though all four paws are bound up and flailing. Donovan stands over it and adjusts his grip, and they look at each other—him and the cat, with one good eye each.

He could still stop if he wanted to, just get into the Jeep and drive away, but he doesn't. Instead he folds the shirttail back onto the cat's head and raises the tire iron straight up and swings it as hard as he can, hard enough that the motion gives off a whoosh. The cat stops crying after the second hit but doesn't stop moving for five or six more. Donovan keeps going—a dozen swings, fifteen, twenty —until the bundle is flattened, until the tire iron has gone all the way through in spots and starts to make metallic clanks against the pavement on the other side. When he finally lets up, it's only because his hands hurt.

CHAPTER 9

"This smells like armpit," EK says.

"Suck off," Liz tells him.

EK sniffs at the white bowl again and passes it to his brother. "Two armpits," he says. "It does. I'm just saying."

Liz ignores him and tries not to pay too much attention as the bowl gets passed around. It's lunchtime on Sunday and all nine kids are at a long table in the cafeteria. Riap made pork dumplings and sweet potato fries, and Liz—who would starve before she'd eat pork or anything fried in lard—made a vegan eggplant salad. It's the first thing she's ever cooked (though Riap helped, a lot). She watches the white bowl go from person to person, and thinks maybe she made too much.

Meredith has nothing on her plate but a few fries, which she keeps arranging into triangles and capital As. When the white bowl gets to her she says she guesses she can try some. Liz watches her pick out the three smallest cubes of eggplant she can find and transfer them delicately to her plate, like specimen samples.

Finally the bowl gets to Loren and he helps himself to a massive portion, a plateful, more than any eggplant farmer would ever eat. He takes a bite and chews thoughtfully and says, "Mmmmm." Liz acts like she doesn't notice and Loren acts like he's not aiming the compliment straight at her, but still it makes her happy.

Today is the first time the kids have gotten to eat by themselves since they showed up at Camp Ascend! sixteen days ago. Usually Donovan spreads them out over a couple of tables in the cafeteria, and if anyone talks he makes them all do squat thrusts on the gritty floor. But Donovan is mysteriously absent today—none of the kids has seen him since dinner last night. They got to sleep in this morning, no ring workout, and the Colonel marched them through two very slow laps around the perimeter loop before locking them into the cafeteria. "Sit wherever and eat slow," he said. "I'll be back in an hour. Maybe two."

The kids all have theories for where Donovan might be, but none of them sounds believable to Liz.

"Church?" EK says.

"Right," his brother says through a mouthful of food. "He's a fucking altar boy."

"Maybe he just took a day off," EK says.

Jeremy says, "Or maybe he's here somewhere, watching."

"Why would he do that?" William says.

"To see what happens," Jeremy says. "To make sure we do what we're supposed to even when he's not around."

"I don't think they work like that," William says. "It seems a little too, I don't know, sophisticated. The first time one of us coughed wrong he'd come out of the trees."

Becca announces that the whole conversation is stupid. "He's gone," she says, "We don't know where, so why not just enjoy it?" Then she changes the topic by asking the twins if they have any tattoos.

The white bowl—mostly full—makes it back around to Liz, who sets it down and listens to the echoing clink of silverware. She thinks the cafeteria seems more abandoned than the rest of the compound. It has tables for a hundred people or so, a hundred happy musical

campers, but with just nine Camp Ascend! kids in one corner the
space looks lonelier to her than if it were empty. A few of the tables
are pushed to the walls, or propped up on their ends, or sagging to
the floor on broken legs. Dust has collected into clumps and strands
and small, animal shapes that swirl faintly when the doors open.
There are letters painted on one wall, faded and chipped, that read:

If musi be he fo d of lov , play n.

Loren, she notices, is looking at her every few seconds. She
ignores him and asks William to pass the salt. It's hard to stop herself from blushing sometimes.

"So Ty," RK says, between bites of food. "What did you do to get
sent here?"

Ty looks up from his food.

"Why do you want to know?" he says.

"I just do," RK says. "I bet it's something drug-related."

"No, nothing like that. I pissed in the food bins at Outward
Bound."

"What?" EK says. "Why?"

"I didn't want to do some stuff and they tried to make me. It was
always like—go climb those trees, go slide down a rope, go sit alone
in the woods. I didn't want to."

"So tell the story," RK says.

"There's no story. I pissed in the bins. That's it."

Ty's rocking to himself and looking past them at the far wall.

"Did that food get eaten?" RK says.

Ty shrugs.

"How'd they find out?"

Another shrug. More rocking.

William coughs slightly and reaches for his water glass.

"Good story, Ty," RK says. "Way to weave a tale."

Liz sees that Loren is halfway done with his eggplant salad and slowing down fast. On one side of his plate are a few bits of chewed-up skin, black and wrinkled and looking like olive pits.

"OK, so Meredith," RK says. "You're up."

Two seats over from Liz, Meredith at first doesn't hear. She's arranging the fries on her plate into amputee starfish, and she hasn't touched her eggplant. When she realizes that the focus of the conversation has shifted to her she looks around at everyone and her face goes crimson. Liz watches her drop her head and stare holes into her plate.

After a long silence, EK makes a conspicuous gagging noise, and Liz tells him to shut up. She could willingly kill him sometimes.

"I'll go," Liz says, stepping in to rescue Meredith. "I set some minks free."

"Free from where?" Loren says, suddenly interested.

"From a mink farm. People raise them just to kill them and make coats. I thought they should get to keep their coats. Plus, you know, live."

Loren nods intently. Liz doesn't know what to make of him yet. He's curious about her and doesn't bother hiding it—he's like a puppy that way. And he does some strange things, grown-up things he must have read about somewhere. Like, he holds the door open for the girls, or he takes harder jobs so they can get the easier ones. At meals he stays standing until all three of them sit down—Becca and Meredith and Liz. It's right on the line between cute and weird.

"You know what the real problem with mink is?" EK says from the other end of the table.

No one answers. Jeremy is wolfing his food down. He hardly stops to chew it.

"They don't taste good," EK says. "So once you get the skin off, there's nothing to do except throw the bodies into a pile."

"Maybe someday you could stop being such a dick," Liz says. "Do you think? Ever?"

"It's an issue," EK says. "If they tasted better you could do something with them. Mink fajitas, mink stew, sloppy joes with ground mink. It wouldn't be such a waste. Pulling the skin off is so much work, but right now they're lucky if the rest makes it into dog food."

Liz starts to say something and decides not to. It's not worth it. When RK takes thirds of the pork dumplings and sets the platter down in front of her, one of them slithers onto the table. She uses a serving spoon to push it back onto the platter and drops her napkin over the dark liquid on the table. What some people call "juice" or "gravy" she knows enough to call "processed blood." She can't stand even looking at it.

"So how'd you get in?" Loren says. "To the farm?"

"I scoped it out for a while and made friends with the girl whose dad owned the place," Liz says. "It wasn't even that hard. I knew her for a couple of months. She started inviting me over to do homework and watch TV. They were nice people, so I felt bad, but then one day I saw that she had mink coats for all her stuffed animals. Little tiny ones, like the size of doll clothes. She told me they made them from the scraps. After that I didn't feel bad anymore."

"How many minks did they have?"

"I don't know, a few hundred maybe. All in these pens out back, behind the house. The whole yard smelled like shit sometimes—it stung your eyes. Her dad hired a security guard to walk around at night, really just a rent-a-cop. He saw me the night I broke in, but he thought I was there to do algebra. He actually waved at me. When he went past, I had bolt cutters in my backpack, so I used them to cut through the fence."

"So it was like a covert operation?" Loren says.

"A what?"

"It happened at night? No one knew?"

"I'm not going to tell them I'm doing it, right? I'm not going to go there in the daytime."

Loren seems overly excited, and Liz thinks he's getting close to the line again. Less cute, more like just weird.

Meredith, comfortably ignored again, pours nine packets of sugar into her iced tea, until it piles up in a gray slush on the bottom of the glass. Ty has a twig in his hair from the morning march. He sits across from Liz, holding his plastic spoon caveman-style in one fist.

"OK, whatever," Loren says. "So anyway."

"So anyway, the problem was that some of the minks wouldn't go," Liz says. "They were packed in really tight. I got behind them and shooed them all toward the hole in the fence, but they were scared. When I picked one or two of them up they bit me." She holds up one hand and shows him the thin ridge of scars, a curve of tiny raised white bumps in the webbing of her thumb. Loren stares at her hand just to the point where it becomes awkward, then looks down at his eggplant.

"But you got them out?" he says. "They all made it?"

"Sort of," Liz says. "I wanted them to all go toward the woods. But instead they went in like eight thousand different directions. Some of them circled right back and went into the pens again, and others got hit by cars. The place was close to a county road, and a lot of them went running for it. I couldn't believe how many. It was like they wanted to get hit—they just all took off for the pavement. And some of them would see others going out onto the road and getting hit and they just *would not learn.* They'd head right over too. I think they'd been locked away so long they didn't know how to get along in nature. Anyway, being run over is better than getting stunned and having the skin ripped off your body for some rich bitch."

"I think that's a toss-up," EK says.

"We weren't talking to you, fucko," Liz said. "How many mink coats does your mom own?"

"A lot," EK says. "About three hundred little minks' worth."

Liz sighs and pushes her plate forward on the table. It's fake wood grain with old initials carved into it. In the kitchen, she can hear pots clang against the sink—Riap's doing the dishes again. Technically she's supposed to do that, and because the dishwasher doesn't work anymore she has to do them all by hand. But sometimes Riap washes them for her while the kids are eating, then pretends they were never dirty in the first place.

"I think my mom used to have a mink coat," Loren says. "Some guy she was dating gave it to her. But I'm pretty sure it was fake." He seems like he's confessing something to Liz, something he thinks she should know.

"If it's fake then that's OK." Liz says. "I have a fake one too."

*

After lunch Loren has a lot of time to replay the conversation in his mind. The Colonel put them all in the barn to watch a movie—a little R & R, he said. He wheeled in a tall cart with an old Fisher-Price-looking VCR the size of a suitcase, and a dusty box of tapes, all with musical themes: *Fame*, *Amadeus*, highlights of the 1987 collegiate marching-band regional championships (southeast division). The Colonel cued up *Mr. Holland's Opus* and left them on their own. All the windows and doors were locked.

The TV's old and the color's bad, so Richard Dreyfuss's skin is the orange color of life jackets. No one watches the movie. Ty stretches out and falls asleep, and Becca sits between the twins, whispering with them. But Loren can't stop thinking about Liz and the minks. A covert op! A night mission! She put the whole plan together and executed it. Her story doesn't even seem exaggerated—she aired out all the mistakes and showed her mink bites. He has to admit that it makes some of the stunts he's pulled seem a little pointless. He never helped anyone or rescued anything. Mostly he just blew stuff up.

Her story puts Liz immediately at the top of Loren's list, which has nothing to do with the fact that she's beautiful, that her black hair is so shiny—except for the purple streak—that he can practically see his reflection in it. The list is all the kids he thinks he can trust, sorted by the HUMINT he's been able to gather on them. And in that group of possible team members for the rebellion, Liz—two rows down from him in the darkened room, a silhouette with very good posture—is now officially number one.

Loren has some other names on there, like RK, who Loren is pretty certain about. (And most likely if RK signed on, his brother would too—though EK talks too much to be fully reliable.) William, probably. Counting Loren, that makes five. He's less sure about the other kids, though. Becca can't be trusted, based on what happened in the basement. Meredith's a question mark, and Ty, a bigger one. Ty is a question mark the size of a billboard. In the two weeks they've been at camp, he's talked more to himself than to anyone else.

Which leaves Jeremy. The last of the group, and the one whose HUMINT all points in the wrong direction. Loren thinks Jeremy could be the leak. He doesn't know for sure, but the evidence is there: Jeremy gets the easiest jobs around the compound, almost always working alone, conveniently out of sight from everyone else. And after those chores, some infraction usually gets "discovered" by Donovan or the Colonel. The loose plank in the cabin was the biggest one so far. Someone else might have told Donovan, but Loren doesn't think so.

Still, he needs to find out for sure, before any other ops can go down. Even the most perfect plan, with all the other kids signed on, would fall apart if the staff got tipped off. Loren would be crucified, not just by Donovan but by the kids he inadvertently got into trouble. So that afternoon, with Richard Dreyfuss looking tangerine-colored and swinging a conductor's baton on the TV, Loren comes up with a small plan.

A few hours later in the boys' cabin, as the kids are leaving for dinner, he pulls Jeremy aside and asks if he wants to see something.

"We have to catch up with everyone else," Jeremy says. He seems nervous, but he's always nervous, so it's hard for Loren to tell if this is different.

The other four boys are filing out, lining up outside for the march to the cafeteria. The Colonel's on his way. No sign of Donovan—they haven't seen him all day.

"Just hang back a sec," Loren says. "This is good."

"What is it?" Jeremy says.

"You have to promise not to tell anyone."

"I won't."

"Swear."

"I won't. Get a Bible if you want."

Loren reaches under his mattress. That's the lamest hiding spot ever—for something like this it's *conspicuously* lame—but Donovan's wallet isn't going to be down there for long. After Mr. Holland finished his opus today, Loren retrieved the wallet from the concrete block under the latrine. He carried it around in his sleeve the rest of the day, and stashed it under the mattress twenty minutes ago. A bad hiding spot, definitely, but Loren doesn't think he has to bait the hook too carefully. He has a pretty good idea what's going to happen once this conversation is over. The only question is how long it'll take.

"Hurry up," Jeremy says.

Outside the cabin, the Colonel yells for them to get going.

Loren opens his hand. Inside is a driver's license (vacant gaze, sloping forehead) and an old PBA card from Tennessee, dated 1994.

*

The payoff doesn't take long. It takes hours, not even.

That same night, when Loren and the other kids are getting ready for bed, the cabin door opens and the Colonel steps in. Donovan comes in too, looking like hell. He has bandages on his face, crusted in spots with dried blood. His jaw is swollen, and his left eye almost perfectly blackened, like someone drew the bruise in—oval-shaped, purplish black—with a marker.

"Random search," Donovan says. "Everyone away from your bunks."

"What is this?" EK says.

"It's a random search," Donovan says. "I just told you."

"You never did one before."

"That's why it's *random*," the Colonel says. "We can debate it later. Right now just step away from your bunk."

The Colonel's wearing his dress blues, the ones with the faded left shoulder.

"On the center plank," Donovan says. "Let's go. Now."

The other kids look stunned, but Loren's relieved. Now he knows for sure. He put a piece of swiss out on a metal lever and Jeremy ran right up and started gnawing.

EK kicks something under his bunk. The Colonel sees it and walks over to pick it up. It's a glossy card, with a picture in bright, lurid colors. Loren looks over and sees blond hair and a phone number that starts with 900.

"Have you been calling this place?" the Colonel asks EK.

"No."

"Why do you have it?"

EK thinks for a minute and says, "That woman's my aunt."

"No more wising off," the Colonel says. He rips the card up and puts the pieces in his pocket. "This is going to cost you. Big-time."

The other boys are all on the center plank now. Donovan hovers over Loren's bunk, but the Colonel says no, they'll start at the other end, closest to the door.

"That's fair, right?" he says to Donovan. "We don't want to single anyone out."

Donovan starts to argue, but the Colonel's already moving away.

At RK's bunk they lift the mattress up to look under all four corners. They punch down systematically into his pillow. They sift through his clothes and kick his boots over. At the end of it, they find nothing, though Donovan points out that RK's socks aren't folded properly.

"They're dirty," RK says. "I just took them off, like two minutes ago."

"No more talking."

Next they move on to William's bunk, where they find, in his pillowcase, a stash of pills.

"Zyrtec," William says. "For my allergies."

"Why didn't you declare them when you got here?" the Colonel says.

"I figured you'd take them away. I told you about some and they got confiscated. That's why I saved these ones."

"No contraband," the Colonel says. "Sorry. That's the rule."

"But I need them."

"File a grievance."

"That's not fair!"

"Shut your mouth," Donovan says. "We'll tell you what's fair."

Loren notices that Donovan's words come out a little slurred, from the swelling in his jaw.

At Ty's bunk they find more pills—three orange bottles stashed inside his pillow.

"I didn't know you all were running a pharmacy in here," the Colonel says. He asks Ty what's in the bottles.

"A lot of stuff," Ty says. Even standing at attention he rocks a little, front to back.

"You can say that again," the Colonel says. He shakes some out into his hands. Loren sees different colors—greens, yellows, blues. It looks like fruit salad.

"Prescription?" the Colonel says.

"I have one back home," Ty says. "Not here."

"You'd need about sixteen prescriptions for all this." The Colonel peers at the bottle. "The name on here isn't yours. Who's...Aurora

Bixley?"

Ty hesitates. "She's my aunt."

The Colonel shakes his head. He pours the pills back into the bottle and caps it and says, "Ours now."

Ty merely shrugs.

"Let's get going," Donovan says to the Colonel. "We're wasting time."

"Patience, grasshopper," the Colonel says.

Under EK's bunk they find nothing but some sheet music. It says "Finger Exercises for Flute." Someone penciled in an arrow and the word *skin*. Finger Exercises for Skin Flute. The Colonel leaves it in place and searches the rest of EK's stuff—poking the pillow, kicking floorboards.

When he finally gets to Loren's bunk, Donovan's already there.

Loren can't resist turning around to watch. They peel up the bottom corner of his mattress, and Donovan hesitates. There's nothing there. The Colonel stands and watches as Donovan lifts the mattress corner higher, then hoists the whole thing by one end and shakes it. A rusty metal button pops free and rattles to the floor.

The mattress gets tossed to one side, and Donovan drops to his hands and knees to look under the frame. Nothing. He kicks onto the floorboards, punches the walls, throws Loren's pillow across the cabin. The exertion brings new blood up through his bandages— bright red mixing with the darker scabs.

The Colonel seems to realize what's happened. When Donovan moves to frisk Loren the Colonel says no. "We're done with him," the Colonel says. "This is over. Let's get going."

Donovan stands frozen. The Colonel's halfway to the door when RK speaks up.

"Aren't you going to search Jeremy's bunk?" he says.

RK comes through again. Loren thought the Colonel and Donovan might go through Jeremy's stuff too, just to make it seem fair, but if they didn't Loren figured he'd have to speak up. He didn't want to, though, because that would seem too obvious. And then RK did anyway.

"Yes," the Colonel says. "Yes, we are."

He lifts a corner of Jeremy's mattress and there, like a turd, is Donovan's wallet.

"Huh," the Colonel says. "OK. All right, then."

Donovan's swollen mouth hangs open.

"No way," Jeremy says. "I didn't take it. You know I didn't."

The Colonel hands the wallet to Donovan and asks if anything's missing. Donovan goes through it quickly, checking the cards, flipping through the cash. He doesn't bother to count it.

"I think it's all here," he says. More blood is leaking into his bandages.

The Colonel takes Jeremy by the arm. "Come with us," he says.

"But I didn't—"

"Just shut up and let's go," the Colonel says.

Donovan is so baffled that the Colonel has to grab him by the elbow too. On their way out the door, the Colonel turns off the light and tells the remaining five boys to get into bed and say nothing. "Not one word," he says. "I'll be checking, and if I hear anything you'll be out there on the ring until sunrise. Understand?"

Once the door's closed, the kids listen until the footsteps recede and start whispering at once. They can't believe how messed up Donovan's face was. EK thinks he must have got beaten up in a bar fight, or it was maybe an insubordination thing. "Like, Donovan got too uppity and the Colonel had to put him back into his place," he says.

"You don't know what the fuck you're talking about," RK says. "This morning you thought he went to church."

No one can figure out what happened with the wallet either. EK says he's almost proud of Jeremy, until William points out that there's no way Jeremy took it.

"He's right," RK says. "Jeremy would never. He doesn't have the gonads."

"Then who did?" EK says.

"I don't know," RK says. "It's weird."

Loren keeps his mouth shut. He wants to tell them, but he's afraid to make big announcements to the group before he knows for sure who he can trust. Finally William says that Loren's being too quiet. "So quiet that you had to be involved in this somehow," William says.

"Not really," Loren says. "The only thing I'll say is this. Did you see those bandages? The new blood?"

"Yeah, pretty gross," William says. "He looks like he got run over by a truck."

Loren rolls over in his bunk.

"I did that," he says. "I made him bleed."

CHAPTER 10

Over the next few days, the Colonel tries to reestablish control over the camp. He makes sure the kids do the same thing for a few days in a row—ring workouts at dawn, marching until lunch, camp repairs in the afternoon. He watches Donovan more closely than normal, even going so far as to walk a perimeter loop with him and the kids one day, huffing along behind them to make his presence known. Throughout it all, Loren consistently gets treated worse than the other kids, but that's as far as the Colonel's willing to let things go, punishment-wise.

Donovan tells the Colonel that his own personal approach would be less subtle. He'd force a confession out of Loren.

"By taking him to the rehearsal room," the Colonel says. "Am I right?"

"He'd crack in there," Donovan says. "I know he would."

"Probably, but you can't just grab a kid at random for some selective, special punishment. I thought you wanted to be systematic. Parris Island, discipline, all that."

"Yeah," Donovan says, "but you and I know he took the wallet. And he knows. We're the only three who matter."

"Think of it this way. Everyone in that cabin saw us pull it out from under Jeremy's bunk. So now you take someone else away. A few hours later, a day later, he comes back and says he did it. No one's going to believe him. They're going to think you beat it out of him, and they'd be right. It won't accomplish anything."

"It would show he can't get away with this," Donovan says. "Plus make me feel better."

The Colonel says those aren't good enough reasons. He can't stop thinking about how the wallet came back to Donovan with everything inside. The whole thing was one big prank, nothing more. What Loren probably wanted most from it was attention—same as any kid who acts up. So giving him attention for it would just be rewarding him.

"What about Jeremy?" Donovan asks. "What happens to him?"

"Nothing. He didn't do anything wrong here. I believe him."

This was based on both the number of times Jeremy swore that night that he didn't take the wallet ("Get a Bible. Get *ten* Bibles"), and the urgent, high pitch of his voice when he said it.

"But he was wrong," Donovan says. "He made us look stupid."

"You make us look stupid, all the time. I don't punish you."

In the end, the Colonel gave Donovan five hundred dollars ("a spot bonus," he called it) to make sure they were in agreement: Loren could be given low-level punishments, but only when the rest of the kids were around. He could, and did, lead the conga line on all marches through the woods, tripping on weeds and peeling spiderwebs from his face every hundred feet or so. He could do squat thrusts by the hundreds, and Donovan could scream at him pretty much at will. In the cafeteria two days ago, Loren said something out of line, and Donovan hurled his breakfast (eggs with cayenne, mango coconut muffins—Riap was getting creative) across the room before making Loren eat it off the floor. But all this had to happen in front of witnesses. No secrets, no hauling Loren away for private punishments. The Colonel ordered Donovan to agree to it, and Donovan did.

Four days after the wallet episode, the Colonel's in his office when Mrs. Diehl calls again. He's going through some bank statements, adding up numbers in the margins. The Cayman account is swelling impressively. When the phone rings he picks it up without thinking.

"Colonel, this is Miriam Diehl."

He doesn't know how she got his office number—usually she calls the house. She sounds strange this time. Extra static on the line.

"Ah, Mrs. Diehl," the Colonel says. "I do love to hear your voice. It's the sound track to my life."

"Don't start your stories. This is a courtesy call, to tell you that I won't be calling anymore."

"Really? That's a shame. I'll miss you."

"Because from now on," she says, "I'll go through my lawyer. I should have done this weeks ago—people told me to. But I'm not one of those people who races to the courthouse whenever something goes wrong. I know Matthew's no saint."

The Colonel peers out between the blinds of his office window and sees the kids marching across the compound. Through the glass he can hear Donovan calling out a cadence, yelling at them to get in step. Donovan's face has healed a bit—most of the bandages are off, and his black eye has started to fade.

"Mrs. Diehl," the Colonel says, "we've been through all this, a couple of times. Kids grow up so fast these days. I'm around them all day and even I can't believe some of the things they come up with. If I could give a truth serum to your son I might believe whatever tale he's dreamed up. Until then, I don't think we have much to talk about."

"You can explain all that to my lawyer."

"OK," he says. "I'll look forward to that. Have him call me."

Even if she has a lawyer, the Colonel thinks, he can stall. And if it comes down to it he'll offer a few thousand bucks to make her go away.

"Actually," Mrs. Diehl says, "he's right here on the phone with me."
The Colonel sits up.

"He's snooping on this line right now?" the Colonel says. "He's eavesdropping? I think you better get another lawyer, Mrs. Diehl, because that's illegal."

"I'm sitting in his office," she says. "We're on speakerphone."

The static. Of course.

"Afternoon, Colonel. This is Robert Wollinger."

Deep voice, middle-aged. The Colonel pictures rows of leather-bound books, soft lighting, a wooden desk as big as a bed. He's been in a few lawyers' offices in his day.

"Bob," the Colonel says, "I don't want to tell you how to do your job, but I think step one on your end is you maybe check out that waiver Mrs. Diehl signed. It's seventeen pages long and pretty much gives us blanket—"

"I've read the waiver," Wollinger says. "That doesn't excuse the kind of thing that happened to my client's son. No waiver would. So here's my idea for step one: we come onto that camp and have a look around."

"Impossible," the Colonel says. "Out of the question. We've got a session going on right now, with lots of kids to manage. We can't just shut that down to start giving tours."

"I figured you'd say that," the lawyer says. "So our next phone call is to the sheriff up there about getting a warrant. I've already spoken to the state's Department of Childcare Services, and they say they're waiting on some medical records you were supposed to send two or three weeks back. Now, if what my client says is false, it seems like you'd want us to come onto the property, right? To straighten this whole thing out. But if it's true, we need to get on there anyway, and fast. It's a bit of a dilemma, no?"

A bit of a dilemma, yes. Outside his office window, the Colonel sees Loren running in place while holding his arms up over his head. Donovan's in his face, screaming, while the rest of the kids watch.

The Colonel turns around and cups his hand around the receiver so the yelling can't be heard.

"I'll tell you what, Bob."

"Robert."

"Whatever. My point is, I don't think you're in a position to dictate terms here. You do what you've got to do—run up the hours on poor Mrs. Diehl's dime. If I hear from the sheriff, we can talk. In the meantime, I've got a lot to take care of around here."

"You'll be hearing from us," Wollinger says.

"I bet I will."

The Colonel hangs up and takes a deep breath. It's a complication, but not horrendous, not yet. He has some things he can do—he's not just going to lie around and wait for the place to fall apart. Starting with those medical records. On the floor of his office, by the door, is the ramen-noodle box from a few weeks ago, still half full. He brought the files out here from the dining room a few weeks ago but never got around to them.

For the next hour, the Colonel calms himself down by finishing thirty-seven records, basically everything that will fit into the box, which he'll ship out first thing tomorrow. He also throws in an old "CPR-certified" patch he found in the back of a desk drawer, and a fire department sticker that says, "Pets Inside," plus fake résumés for the nurse (Johns Hopkins) and doctor (Mayo Clinic) that the Colonel says he keeps on staff full-time.

Finally, he types up a letter, on Camp Ascend! letterhead and spell-checked twice, saying that he—along with all the well-trained, thoroughly competent people he keeps on staff—is proud of the operation and everything he's been able to accomplish so far, because nothing's more important than the youth of this country, and that, as always, he remains entirely willing, *eager* even, to discuss the safety and medical procedures of the camp with anyone, anytime, but that in the meantime the enclosed material should establish for any remaining doubters the pride and professionalism with which he runs Camp Ascend!. Signed, sincerely.

When the box is ready to go he looks around his office at the paper trail—the blank records, the ones with misspelled names. The bottom drawer in his desk is full of bank statements from the off-shore accounts, and under all of them he finds one of his old to-do lists ("#17: Open a second location?"). Documents everywhere, lots of evidence, and the Colonel imagines what would happen if a lawyer really did make it onto the property. It all adds up to a decision.

Outside the barn he finds Donovan making the kids do squat thrusts near the cafeteria. They must have been there a while— they've all dug small holes in the ground from moving their feet around so much.

"New plan for the afternoon," the Colonel announces. "We're cleaning this place up."

*

An hour later, William and Jeremy are on the ring, burning papers in a green metal garbage can that says, "Dept of Parks Do Not Remove." Every few minutes the front door of the Colonel's house opens and Kitty appears in a kimono and throws another armful of stuff onto the porch. Boxes, magazines, catalogs—it all gets burned.

William thinks he must look like a homeless person right now. His sweats smell, he has a new hole in his boot, and he's scratching himself almost nonstop. Meanwhile, Jeremy's poking at the fire with a stick, and his face is smudged with ash. If they had a wine bottle in a brown bag, they'd look more like bums than real bums do.

The other kids are scattered around the compound, all with different tasks. Liz and Ty clean the kitchen and haul food trash out from the cafeteria. (Riap keeps it in giant bags in a spare freezer— Liz says they have the room, and this way it doesn't stink in the heat.) Becca and Meredith pull weeds up around the compound.

The twins have to cut down the dead trees that look closest to falling over. Loren has the worst job of all—shuttling trash over to the garbage shed and burnable stuff to William and Jeremy on the ring. He uses a wheelbarrow with split handles and a flat tire. Donovan calls him the Garbage Man.

William makes another trip to the porch and gathers up an arm-load of papers, trying not to think about how much his skin itches. Ever since the Colonel confiscated part of his Zyrtec stash a few days ago, William has tried to hoard his remaining pills (grape-flavored, 10-mg chewables). He breaks them in half, but somehow the math on that doesn't work. Half a dose equals zero benefits. So he goes through the day feeling like he's being chemically, anaphylactically tortured.

Based on his in-depth knowledge of comic books, William can say for sure that no superhero ever has allergies. They have weak-nesses—that's what makes them interesting as characters—but Kryptonite never made Superman's skin break out in hives. The X-Men don't go around with inhalers in their tights, worrying about pet dander. When William was five a nurse gave him a comic book about allergies, Annie Histamine fighting the evil Dr. Spore, which even at that age he recognized as lame.

That's the worst thing about allergies, he thinks: you can't fight them. You can avoid situations that might get you in trouble, but you can't go kick ass on a ragweed plant. Instead you have to be so passive all the time. William monitors his body like a nuclear reac-tor, waiting for the gauges to start twitching. This leaf might bother you, or it might not—just wait and see. Two nights ago a mystery rash flared up between his shoulder blades and itched like nothing he's ever felt before. He used a wire coat hanger and scratched him-self until he bled, and the scabs are now infected and his back looks like someone went at him with a meat tenderizer.

But no matter what happens, William thinks, he can take it. The one thing he does have control over is that he never bitches about this stuff. That's his superhero power—the ability to keep his mouth shut. When he and the twins were zip-cuffed facedown over a pool of driveway sealant and his nasal passages felt like they were being scrubbed with lye and EK was bitching so much he got the stuff in his teeth, and the whole thing was *not even William's fault*, he didn't complain. He didn't then and he won't ever.

Twenty feet from the fire, the barn door opens and the Colonel appears. William's stomach jumps, either from hunger or from nerves. Jeremy stands up straighter and pretends not to see him. The Colonel's carrying four brown grocery bags, each the size of a pillow and sealed with a surprising amount of duct tape. When he drops them on the ring they make a puffy sound, like they're filled with paper.

"Do these next," he says. "I'll wait."

"I thought you said the catalogs," Jeremy says.

"No, these."

Jeremy picks one up. "The whole thing in at once?" he says. "What if the fire goes out?"

The Colonel rubs his eyes. "Then we'll light it again," he says. "Stop worrying and burn the fucking bags, OK?"

Jeremy drops the first bag in and some sparks float up around it. William watches him stab at the bag intently, like it's an animal he's trying to kill, until finally it catches in an orange bloom. The Colonel stands next to them, arms crossed, and peers over the rim to watch. William can look straight into the part of his graying hair, where his scalp is pale white.

When the second bag goes in, the Colonel looks toward the front porch of his house, which is now completely covered by catalogs. He seems to relax a little.

"Did you ever see so many catalogs in your life?" he says. "Jesus, the number of trees that have to die just so one woman can shop."

William blinks and tries to hold off on scratching himself for a few more seconds. The Colonel sounds almost like a relative, an uncle teasing his wife at the family picnic.

When bag number three is almost done, an upstairs window of the house slides open and a TiVo box floats down to the ground. Kitty appears in the window and yells, "Hon? You want to come in here a sec?"

The Colonel gives the two kids a sheepish look. "The old ball and chain," he says.

William blinks again and gives a faint shrug.

The Colonel sets off, watching over his shoulder to make sure Jeremy drops the fourth bag in. The fire's really rolling now. William can feel the heat radiating onto his face. Jeremy's stick makes hollow knocking sounds against the sides of the can. It's possible this fourth bag is not completely sealed, because when it catches fire the outside splits open like a steamed potato and a few pages flutter out in the updraft.

The Colonel's already halfway to the porch, not looking back anymore. William thinks the pages are like escapees—they're making a break for it.

"Go get those," Jeremy says. "Bring them back and throw them in. Hurry up."

William collects a few of the pages. One of them lands perfectly centered on a hexagonal stone a few feet away from him. It's black-edged, with a few orange sparks pulsing along one side. William steps on it to put the sparks out, careful to avoid the hole in his boot. The page is official-looking, with a logo and lots of numbers in a column. Along the top he can make out a name—Edmund Killian—and the words, "First Bank of the Caymans."

*

"Every pea off the ground, Dogface," Donovan says. "I'll wait."

Loren's on his knees, looking around for tiny green balls of ice. A few minutes ago, he let a bag of frozen kitchen trash fall off the

wheelbarrow in front of Donovan. Purely accidental, not even a
resistance tactic. The bag broke open and pieces of thawing nasti-
ness spilled out, including a chunk of ice-covered peas that hit the
ground and shattered, the peas scattering like ball bearings. About a
hundred of them are glistening in the dead grass. Loren collects a
few and lets them rest in his hands while he looks for more. His
palms are blistered and pinched from the split handles of the wheelbarrow, and the ice feels stingingly good.

When he thinks he has them all, Loren stands, and Donovan
says nope, he sees one more. Donovan walks over and picks up a
solitary pea and tosses it toward the twins, fifty feet away. "Go get it."
he says. "Don't come back until you find it."

So Loren sets off.

All day long Donovan has been serving up shit sandwiches and
Loren has eaten every bite. He's pushed the wheelbarrow around the
compound for miles, and he lost track of how many trips he's made
to the garbage shed. He hasn't wised off to Donovan, and he smiled
through his four hundredth squat thrust.

When he gets to where the twins are working, EK asks what he's
looking for.

"A stupid pea," Loren says, peering at the ground. "I dropped
some trash. Donovan sent me over here to look for it."

"Sucks to be you," EK says.

Loren watches EK try to push over a dead sapling. It's stuck at a
forty-five-degree angle. The twins were initially supposed to cut
down the trees—the Colonel gave them each a butter knife, saying
they couldn't have anything sharper, for security. They sawed away
for ten minutes before realizing it would never work. Now EK
grunts and shoves and gets nowhere, until RK comes over and does
a Jackie Chan on the tree—one side kick to the lower trunk and over
it goes. That'll be the next thing Loren has to haul to the ring to be
burned.

"I could've gotten it," EK says.

"Right," his brother says. "In like a week."

They haven't had a fight in a few days, Loren realizes, so they're probably due.

Fifty feet or so away, Meredith and Becca kneel by the pool, untangling weeds from the chain-link fence that surrounds it. Beyond them, William and Jeremy are on the ring. They have their backs turned as a swirling column of smoke rises from the garbage can. William sneezes twice.

"What the hell are you doing?" Donovan yells at Loren.

"Still looking," Loren yells back.

He hasn't found the pea Donovan threw over here, but he brought a few extras with him, cupped in one hand. He takes a few steps, bends down, and makes an exaggerated gesture of discovery.

"Got it," he says. He hoists a pea in Donovan's direction, like it's a piece of evidence.

Donovan tells him to get back and re-bag the stuff that spilled, then hustle it over to the garbage shed. "After you do that, that dead tree goes over to the ring," he says. "Get moving."

Loren trots back and picks up the handles of the wheelbarrow and heads for the shed. He decides he's eaten enough shit sandwiches for one day. For the past few hours he's been weighing a couple of options, and now he's settled on one.

The garbage shed is where the old landscaping stuff used to be stored, from when the music camp was running. There are stray bits of long-dead grass clippings in the corners, aged and yellowed to the color of hay. Once he's inside, Loren finds the French horn case, the one he took from the Colonel's basement almost a week ago. It's been out here ever since, with the dead possum inside, and the tools Loren managed to smuggle out. He's a little nervous about how the carcass might smell, and it turns out to be worse than he could have imagined.

When he gets the buckles of the case freed, the lid pops open like it's spring-loaded. The animal has bloated, cooking and expanding in the heat. It makes the plastic bag crinkle as it stretches out, and the stench knocks Loren backward. He's on the verge of throwing up, so he pulls his sweatshirt collar over his nose and mouth and tries to work quickly.

Under the animal he finds the tools. He needs only a few right now—the socket wrench, five sockets in a sufficient range to make sure one of them will fit, and eight long nails. It all gets wrapped up in a rag and stuffed into his sock. The other tools and the flashlight and paint get stashed under the frame of the garbage shed. He was afraid he wouldn't be able to close the case, given how much the possum swelled up, but without the tools there's enough room.

When he comes out, Donovan's just starting to yell for him.

"Coming," Loren says. "I'm on my way."

The tools in his sock dig into his ankle, but Loren ignores it and tries to walk normally. Now that he's gotten them he has three messages to deliver. The advantage of his current job as Garbage Man is that he can circulate among the kids. It's supposed to be a punishment, but he exploits it.

His first message is to EK, when he stops to pick up the dead tree. "Becca's into you," he says. "But she doesn't officially want you to know about it."

"For real?" EK says.

Becca is at the corner of the pool fence, bent over to yank out a weed. Her butt faces them. It looks padded and cushiony, close to the ground on top of her short legs.

"Every time I go over there she says something about you," Loren says. "She thinks you're funny."

EK's curious, Loren can tell. When the skinny tree trunk is propped across the bowl of the wheelbarrow, he starts hauling it away. "Don't say anything, though," Loren says. "Seriously. She told me to keep it quiet."

Ten minutes later, RK gets a similar message—that Becca has been asking about him.

"Don't fuck around," RK says.

Loren's helping him snap branches so they'll fit in the wheelbarrow. EK is far enough away to be out of earshot.

"I'm telling you," Loren says. "She thinks your brother's a wiseass. She says you're more mature."

Becca, oblivious, is leaning against the pool fence now, rubbing sweat off her forehead. She glances in their direction and sees them looking back. No acknowledgment, nothing registers.

"That's just her playing it cool," Loren says. "But don't say anything, OK? She asked me not to tell you."

The wheelbarrow's full now, and Loren sets off again. He can tell from the silence behind him that RK's thinking about it.

Any qualms that Loren might have kick in right now. He doesn't feel entirely good about tricking RK, who's helped him so far, and who's one of the few people in this place he thinks he can trust (along with Liz and probably William). But Loren knows the twins are going to have a fight again sometime soon. They're overdue. The way Loren sees it, he's just rescheduling something inevitable, like seeding clouds to make it rain. And anyway, in a fight between the brothers, RK's going to come out on top. Loren's seen them go at each other eight or ten times so far, and EK hasn't won yet.

For the next twenty minutes Loren does nothing. He lets the twins think it over as he makes his rounds, collecting and dropping off trash. The tools in his sock press dents into his ankle. But when Donovan ventures over to the ring—far enough away from all involved parties—the conditions seem ripe, and Loren delivers message number three.

"Becca, the twins need help with one of those trees."

"Who said?"

"They did. Go ask them."

She's wearing a sweatshirt that's a size too small, same as usual. Her face is sunburned, the upturned button of her nose redder than the rest. In the wheelbarrow, a bag of frozen trash defrosts in the sun, sweating condensation.

"I don't feel like it," she says. "You do it."

"OK," Loren says. "If that's what you want. But just so you know, they were asking about you."

"They were?"

"Yeah. Both of them. Not at the same time, but yeah."

Loren reaches for the wheelbarrow. His hands still hurt, but he barely notices. When she starts to say something else, he's already walking away.

Now it comes down to timing. He just has to stay away from the three of them and put himself in the right position, near the cabins. It's possible this isn't going to work, but he feels good about his chances. On cue, Becca goes over to the twins and they start talking. Loren concentrates on acting natural. At first nothing happens, but then the twins' voices get louder. One of them calls the other a pussy, and Loren looks up to see EK swing a tree branch at his brother's leg. It's go time.

Donovan sees what's happening, and Loren darts behind a corner of the boys' cabin. His window is covered by a grid of bars, the bars that keep him in each night. Four bolts, one on each corner.

He figures he has less than a minute. Donovan won't break up the fight right away—he'll probably want to watch, but he won't watch forever. The rag comes out of Loren's sock dripping blood (he didn't know the skin was broken) and the contents get dumped onto the ground, shining silver in the dead grass. He tries three sockets before he finds the right one. It slips onto the bolt on the top right corner of the frame and stays there. Loren grabs the wrench and snaps it into place and starts spinning the handle like a NASCAR mechanic. Within a few seconds, the first bolt is undone, and Loren replaces it with a nail. Bolts two, three, and four—same thing.

Unless you looked closely, you wouldn't notice anything different. The frame hangs in place, but he can now get in and out whenever he wants. He kicks the tools and the rag under the cabin—

including the four remaining long nails, which he plans to use on a different window, tonight—and that's it. He's done.

As he comes back around into sight, the fight's just breaking up. EK spits bloody saliva onto the ground through a fat lip and calls his brother a massive ass wipe. When Donovan yells for Loren he's already trotting toward the group again, pushing his wheelbarrow ahead of him.

"Coming," Loren says. "I'll be right there."

CHAPTER 11

"He was a real estate agent," Becca says. "He sold my parents their house."

"Uh-huh," Liz says.

It's after lights-out, and the girls are locked in for the night. This is the time when Becca usually wants to start talking. Meredith is silent, either asleep or pretending to be, with her feet hanging off her bunk. Liz usually tries to ignore Becca too, but tonight she's wide-awake and Becca can tell, so Becca talks to her.

"He's in Avenal now," Becca says. "That's a prison, in California."

"What's he there for?"

"Statuary rape."

"Statuary?" Liz says. "You mean 'statutory'?"

"No, it's statuary. I think I'd know."

Liz doesn't bother arguing. It's late, probably after midnight, and she wants Becca to finish her story and go to sleep. Something's going to happen in about two hours—something Liz can't tell the other two about—and she knows the fastest way through one of Becca's stories is to keep asking questions and jumping ahead. Otherwise Becca will drown in the details.

"So he's old?" Liz says.

"Yeah, but not creepy old," Becca says. "Forty-three. He was forty-two when I met him. I know it sounds weird, but we were in love."

"Uh-huh." Liz sees thinning hair, a paunch, a sports car. She can picture the whole thing.

"The good part was, he had keys to these empty houses all over town," Becca says. "So we had a lot of places to, you know, have sex in. We'd do it on the carpets, sometimes on the stairs. Lots of echoes in those houses, because none of them had any furniture. The keys were in these little boxes, hooked on the front of each door."

"Lockboxes," Liz says. "They're called lockboxes."

"Right, those. He had the combinations, so we could go to any house we wanted, anytime we wanted. Every once in a while a place would go on sale furnished, so we had an actual bed and sheets and stuff."

"And then you got caught," Liz says. Skip ahead. Keep moving.

"Yeah," Becca says. "One of my bitch friends told her parents and they told my parents. It was this big, huge deal. No one understood—we were in love. All of a sudden he had a restraining order and had to stay three hundred feet away. My parents cut my hair off too, to 'cure me of my sexual deviancy.' It used to be down to my butt, but then my mom snipped it all off while I was sleeping. That's why I look like a dyke. Anyway, it didn't work. We couldn't stay away from each other. Our love was too strong. We went to some houses a few more times, and then one day we were on the kitchen counter of this one place, and another agent came in. She had a clipboard and she was showing the place to some couple. We didn't even hear them. I just looked over and there they were."

Meredith rolls over in her bunk. The moon has drifted into the frame of the window, between the bars.

"I thought it was funny then," Becca says, "but that was the last time I saw him. He got two years at Avenal, and I got sent to this dump. He knows I'm here, though. I sent him a letter with the address and told him to get up here and get me out."

"How?" Liz says.

"That's his problem. It's only minimum-security anyway. He says the guards don't do anything all day except play air hockey. Like he can't climb a fence? For me?"

Liz takes the deepest breath she can and lets it out slowly—her way of signaling that she's done listening for the night. Within a few minutes Meredith is asleep, and ten minutes after that, Liz hears Becca start to snore faintly. Liz is tired too, but she forces herself to sit up in bed and stay awake.

*

A little less than two hours later, at precisely 2:00 a.m., Loren is working on the bars outside her window. He spins the socket wrench, careful to keep it moving forward and avoid any suspicious clicking. She whispered to him that he needed to be careful—Meredith was a light sleeper. When the last bolt comes out, he pops the frame of bars free and sets it down by his boot. Liz sticks a leg through the window. Loren takes her hand—tiny, warm—and helps her to the ground.

"What's that all over your face?" she says.

He holds a finger in front of his lips and signals for her to follow. They trot across the compound, under a moon bright enough to cast shadows. The Colonel's house looms silently behind them, windows darkened. Loren knows that Kitty, Donovan, and the Colonel are all asleep—he waited until the blue light went out before starting tonight's mission. A breeze moves softly through the trees, keeping the mosquitoes away and offering some sound cover to muffle their footsteps. Ideal conditions all around.

When they get to the garbage shed, he relaxes a little and crouches down.

"Seriously," she says, pointing at his face. "What is that stuff?"

"Camouflage."

"It looks like dirt."

"That's what it is, pretty much," he says. "Want some? You might need it, if we're spotted."

"I think if we're spotted I'll have bigger stuff to worry about," Liz says.

Her eyes are shiny and clear—she must not have slept at all. Loren can't make out the purple streak in her hair, which is gathered in back and held with a rubber band. The black sweats make her look like a ponytailed assassin.

"So what's our plan?" Liz says.

Loren belly-crawls under the cabin and pulls out the can of spray paint, kelly green. He holds it up for her to inspect.

"I don't get it," she says.

"The plan is that we go to the ring," Loren says, "and paint a green beret on the stones."

He waits to be congratulated on the idea, but Liz has a puzzled look on her face.

"Like a person?" she says. "We draw one of those army psychos?"

"No, just the hat. So they'll find it tomorrow morning."

"Huh," she says. "I don't get what does that does for us."

"It's a sign," he says.

"A sign of what?"

"Of how Donovan can't mess with us. How we're badass, like we're Green Berets too."

"You broke me out of the cabin for that?" she says. "It seems kind of stupid. I mean, I'm sorry but it does."

"I think it's good," Loren says. "I've done stuff like this before."

"But think it through," Liz says. "Donovan sees it—then what happens? He'll know we've been out, or that *someone's* been out. He'll lock up the cabins even tighter. Those bars over the windows will get replaced by, like, steel plates. And we'll all get punished, for nothing."

Loren doesn't say anything. He's thinking about what William said when he heard about the golf course incident, the reason Loren got sent here in the first place. *You set some grass on fire? That's it?*

"If all you want to do is taunt them," Liz says, "you don't need a jailbreak. You can do that during the day, in front of them, even. Besides, a green beret? It's going to come out looking like a pancake."

Loren explains that, no, it's puffier at the sides, with a fold near the middle. "That's how they wear it," he says.

"Then it'll look like a paramecium," Liz says. "We just studied those, in biology."

"So maybe we do a Distinguished Service Cross?" Loren says. "I know what the pattern looks like."

"No painting and no army stuff. It's stupid."

He thinks she maybe doesn't deserve a spot at the top of his list anymore. An hour or so ago, watching for the blue light from the Colonel's house to go out, he thought about how this conversation would go. He ran through it in his mind a dozen times, and in every case her reaction was never less than adoring.

"So what's your big idea?" he says.

"I don't know," she says. "What else is under the cabin?"

"Tools," Loren says. "Wrenches, a screwdriver."

"And you got it all from the Colonel's basement?"

"Yeah."

"Is the basement locked?"

"Not sure. It was when Becca and I were down there, but I don't think it is all the time."

"We should go look," she says. "Maybe we can find something better."

"I don't know," Loren says. "We don't have a flashlight. It'll be dark."

Too late—she's already heading off in that direction. He sets out after her, hunching over and trotting in a zigzag pattern. Liz just walks upright, like she's out for a stroll.

At the basement doors, they find the lock undone, hanging by the hasp. She lifts it—carefully, quietly—and gives him a thumbs-up. The Colonel's house stands impassively above them, air conditioners humming in every window.

"Get going," she whispers, raising the door. "I'll follow and close it behind us. We'll be sealed in."

Loren hesitates. "We don't have a light," he says. The stairwell is a rectangular frame of impossible blackness.

Sealed in.

"So go in and find the switch," she says. "You remember where it is, right?"

He does—he memorized the floor plan, more or less—but the switch is all the way across the basement, on a string at the top of the inside stairway. There's almost no way he can get there in the dark. Stuff is everywhere—boxes and junk, heaps of crap. He'd have to feel his way across.

"It's too risky," he says.

"Why?"

"If we knocked anything over, they might wake up. We'd be trapped."

"Just go slow."

"You're weren't down there. Even with a light it would be hard to get through and make no noise. In the dark, it would take us like a week."

All of this is true, but the main reason Loren doesn't want to go down there (which he doesn't tell Liz) is that he's scared. Stuck in a pitch-black basement, feeling his way across—it's a claustrophobic's nightmare.

"Can't you get matches from the kitchen?" he says.

Liz shakes her head. "Riap sleeps in one of the pantries," she says. "He wouldn't care that we were out, but if Donovan or the Colonel asked him about it he'd have to lie. I don't want to do that to him."

They look at each other.

"So now what?" she says.

"I guess we hold off," he says. "Get matches when you can, or a flashlight. We can come back out another night."

"Whatever," she says. "Sure. I guess."

Loren still thinks they could paint a green beret on the ring and get something out of the night, but he doesn't bring it up again.

Liz closes the basement door and replaces the lock on the hasp, and they start walking back to the cabins. A few clouds drift past the moon, looking nickel-colored at the edges. It's cooler tonight than it's been in weeks, and Loren hasn't gotten a single mosquito bite. Perfect conditions, all for nothing.

The pool is silent, the surface flat as glass. As they pass it Loren gets one more idea.

"You know," he says, "we could go swimming. If you wanted to."

"What would that do for us?" she says.

"Not much. Other than it'd be fun."

Liz says she hasn't been in a pool since last year. "Going through a whole summer without swimming," she says. "That should be illegal."

They walk over and look at the water from outside the fence. Kitty's chaises are in their usual place—near the deep end, positioned to catch the sun as it moves past overhead.

"What would we wear?" she says. "Neither of us has a bathing suit."

"Yeah," Loren says. "Maybe it won't work."

Liz looks down. "Or," she says.

He sees her smiling at the ground.

She walks to the gate and pushes it open and makes him promise not to look. "We'll do it like this," she says. "You go stand at one end, facing out, and I'll take my sweats off and get in. Then I'll turn around and you get in. And we have to stay at opposite ends of the pool the whole time. Fair?"

Loren says fair, trying hard to sound natural. No big thing. He swims naked with girls all the time. His heart is suddenly racing.

"OK, turn around," Liz says. "And no peeking. I'm serious."

Loren stands facing outward and hears the soft rustle of her clothes coming off. One of the posts is bent in from where Loren was thrown into it more than two weeks ago. A few nearby are similarly angled, from the impact with other kids' bodies. Besides that one incident, he's been inside the fence only twice, both times to bring Kitty ice cream. The Colonel said that if he ever caught any kids in the pool, their time at the camp would be extended by a month, automatically.

Across the compound, the tops of the dying pine trees are blue-black against the moonlit sky.

"No cannonballs," Loren says. "We have to be quiet."

"Right," Liz says, through a faceful of sweatshirt.

He can't believe that he could turn around right now and see a real girl on her way to being naked. He won't—he gives himself a direct order not to look—but he *could*. Just the thought of what's happening behind him makes him tremble. He's seen Liz's forearms once and that's it. He has to hold on to the fence and take deep breaths. Don't look, he tells himself. Be respectful. Don't get so excited that you start hyperventilating.

The rustling behind him stops. She says she'll tell him when he can turn around. Loren hears the padding of bare feet on the concrete, steps moving quickly to the edge, and she says, "OK now," in a clipped, breathless way.

When he turns, Liz is in the air, bundled into a ball and spinning. No diving board, she jumped from the side. After one and a half rotations she unfolds her body and slices into the water perfectly straight. Loren gets a fleeting image of her butt, upside down and perfect, before it disappears. Her body makes almost no noise, no more splash than if a knife had been dropped into the water.

Loren feels like he just saw a magic trick. After she surfaces, he says, "How'd you...?"

"I was a gymnast, remember?"

She bobs faintly, treading water in the deep end. Her hair is slicked back on her head, like an otter's.

"Can you see anything?" she says. "Under the surface?"

Loren says no. "Which stinks."

He feels stupid standing on the edge, fully clothed, but he can't compete with an entrance like that.

"Now you come in," Liz says. "I won't look."

She turns away, and Loren peels off his sweats and slips into the shallow end. The water is warmer than the air, and the pool bottom feels gritty against his bare feet. He swims to the other side of the shallow end and then back, then sits on the lowest step, submerged to his neck. It's hard to swim when he's breathing in such quick, nervous gulps. He can't get the image of her butt out of his head.

Liz is twenty-five feet away, treading water and looking at him. Her collarbones have shallow recesses that catch the pool water and then spill it.

"Are you a good swimmer?" she says.

Loren says definitely, which is a lie. Navy SEALs can hold their breath for two minutes, and go down to forty or fifty feet without tanks, but he's not completely comfortable in the water. Not like she seems to be.

Be respectful. Don't stare. He can't see anything under the surface but he wants to keep looking at where he knows certain parts of her are. Instead he pretends to look at the fence above her shoulder.

Liz does a surface dive, feeding herself down into the water— back, butt, legs, feet rising like a tail. She stays down for a long time, long enough for most of the waves in the pool to settle. The night gets quiet. Loren watches, then starts to worry, until finally she pops up a few feet away and spits water at him.

"Now you don't have dirt on your face anymore," she says, backing away.

Loren doesn't know if she's flirting with him, or if this is a signal to do something, like maybe chase after her. It's so hard to know what to do sometimes, and he keeps telling himself to be respectful. Don't be a jerk. Don't be like EK, or the men his mom always ends up dating.

He thinks about this, and overthinks it, and if a moment comes where something's supposed to happen, that moment passes. Loren misses his chance, and from her spot in the deep end, Liz finally says that they should probably get out.

Back in sweats (again with no looking), he picks up one of Kitty's chaises and puts it near the other one—close but not too close, a few inches apart. He and Liz both lie down, barefoot, and look at the clouds moving past the moon. It's chilly enough that Loren shivers.

"If every night could be like this it wouldn't be too bad here," Liz says.

"Yeah," Loren says. He feels clumsy and tongue-tied.

She rolls her sleeves down—he can't even see her forearms anymore—and then pulls a stray thread from her sweatshirt and lets it go. It doesn't drift to the ground but floats up over the fence on some barely felt breeze.

After a few seconds of increasingly awkward silence, Liz asks him how he got his name. "I never knew a Loren before," she says.

He shifts in the chaise and the canvas creaks underneath him.

"It's a stupid story," he says.

"I bet it's not."

"You'd lose—it is stupid—but I'll tell you anyway. When I was born, my mom was dating this guy whose ex-wife was named Lauren. With the girl spelling, 'a-u.' My mom didn't know that. She thought he just liked the name. She found out the real reason when I was a few months old, and by then she didn't feel like changing it. So I was named after the ex-wife of someone I never met."

"Wait, that guy wasn't your dad?"

"No, my dad wasn't around by then. He took off when my mom got pregnant."

"Oh."

An air conditioner at the Colonel's house clicks off, and another one nearby starts up.

"So where's your dad now?" Liz says.

"I don't know. He can't ever tell me. He's in Special Forces, and they go out on missions a lot. They're not supposed to tell people where they're going—it's all secret stuff. Top secret, even."

"That makes sense," Liz says. "I guess."

"My mom says he wasn't really in Special Forces," Loren goes on. "She says he was more like Special Olympics. But she's just mad."

"How do you know for sure that he is?"

"I can just tell. I tried calling the Pentagon once, but there's a million phone numbers there. After two days on the phone, when I finally got to the right person, she said they could only tell me if he was on active duty or not, and only if I had his full name and social. Except I didn't have all that. My mom said I should trust her, that I'd be happier if I never talked to him."

A cloud passes and moonlight shines down. Loren holds his hand out to one side and watches the shadow of his fingers on the concrete.

"Anyway, that was all like fifty boyfriends ago for her," he says.

"Huh."

"I know. It's bad. She tells me she just wants someone to take care of us, but it never works. She's lonely, and most of the hand jobs she dates just make her lonelier. Then she says it's my fault for sending them away."

Liz is looking directly at him.

"It doesn't matter," she says. "Loren's a good name. I like it."

She leans over and holds her face just inches from Loren's. Her eyes look huge to him, this girl who was just naked. She tilts her head almost imperceptibly and leans in more and kisses him—the first time Loren has ever kissed anyone. Her hair smells like chlorine and soap, and her mouth tastes sweet and warm. A drop of pool water falls from her ear onto Loren's neck.

One lingering kiss and that's it. She pulls away and stands up. Loren feels dizzy.

"OK," she says. "Time to go."

He's so stunned that when he follows her out through the gate he remembers to close it behind them but forgets to put Kitty's chaises back. They remain where he left them—a few inches apart, close but not too close, glaringly out of place under the spotlight of the moon.

CHAPTER 12

"After we got kicked out of prep school, we had a few weeks to kill," RK says.

"The new place couldn't let us in until the next quarter," EK says. "It was supposed to be a punishment, but instead it was like one long vacation. Three weeks to sit around and do nothing."

William has wondered when the twins were going to tell the story of how they ended up here, and apparently they've decided it's time. It's mid-morning, and all nine kids are hauling trash bags to the dump. Loren's walking point, and Donovan brings up the back. They've made two trips already and the garbage shed is still half full, so they know they'll be doing this after lunch too. The dump is at the end of a spike trail that branches off from the perimeter loop, about a half mile from the cabins. It's not far, but the bags are heavy, and each trip takes almost an hour. Donovan's in a good mood, so he lets the kids talk as they march.

"We were at our house one day, playing *Brickyard 400*," EK says. "Someone's mom got it on a trip to China, so the instructions were in Chink-ese, but you could basically figure it out. Insanely cool graphics. A few other kids are over, we're drinking Scotch and Red

Bulls, doing hits with the Atomizer."

"What's an Atomizer?" Loren says.

"It's a bong like out of the *Road Warrior*," EK says. "With a propane torch, so you get superhigh heat. It basically nuclear-react-ifies the pot. A couple of hits and you're in orbit. Anyway, the whole thing was RK's fault, because he said he was hungry."

"What the fuck?" RK says.

"You did. And that's why it all happened."

"I was hungry, but that's not why."

William has a knack for picking the heaviest bag each trip, and right now the weight has him bent almost double as they march. Trash juice leaks into his sweatpants, making him smell like a Dumpster.

"Anyway," EK says. "The only car we have is our dad's Beemer. Which is like the BMW of Justice—an M5, shipped in straight from Germany with a supercharger and some other stuff. It goes 200 and he'd just bought it a month before. We weren't even allowed to sit in it. It came with its own TV—this little handheld thing that plugs into the lighter. A giveaway from the dealer. When you spend a hundred grand you get stuff like that."

In front of William, Becca marches slightly pigeon-toed and completely out of step. The trail is sandy, which gives her butt a lit-tle extra back-and-forth. It looks inflated and almost animatronic.

"Your story sucks so far," Liz says. "Get to the point."

"So the point is, RK's hungry, and someone makes a joke about how we should just take the Beemer," EK says. "And then it's like we have to. Two more hits on the Atomizer and then the garage door's coming up. To see over the wheel, RK has to sit on his lacrosse gloves and my lacrosse gloves and one sweatshirt rolled in a ball."

RK says, "The car is so fucking fast you can't believe it. Four hundred horsepower. You just tap the gas and bang—you're down the block, and all those minivans and shit that used to be in front of you are now behind you."

"It's as fast as a NASCAR car, practically," EK says.

"Right turn!" Donovan yells.

They're at the spike trail. Even on their third trip of the day, the turnoff is hard to spot. Loren pushes through, branches snapping, and the kids file behind. The woods have a different feel almost immediately. The trail is shadier and less level. It's not much more than a foot wide, weedy and tangled with roots.

"EK finds the TV right away and starts looking for porn," RK says.

"But I can't find any, because the stupid thing just gets local channels," EK says. "It's not even cable. Spend all that money and you'd think you'd get a satellite link or something. Maybe some Spice Network. Anyway it doesn't matter, because we're almost to the burger place, and it's right then that we see the cops."

"Two cars doing that nose-to-tail thing in the parking lot," RK says. "We pull in and I drive past real slow, trying to be cool, but whatever. They give a little chirp and I guess put their shakes down and pull around behind us."

William says, "It's a new BMW and you can barely see over the wheel? I'd pull you over too."

"Yeah, I guess," EK says. "Other people say that too. Anyway, RK has the brakes on, and they're telling us over the speaker to pull over. I remember the TV was showing cartoons. We're so screwed if our dad knows we were in his car, and we have enough pot in our system to fail like fifty drug tests."

"If you took a urine sample it would come out gray," RK says.

"And on top of it all we're in this fast-as-shit car. So he looks at me and I look at him, and we just know. Neither one says anything. We don't even have to."

RK laughs. "So I hit it," he says.

"So he hits it. Hard."

Ty hawks up some phlegm and spits it onto the trail, where it shines like a yellow oyster. William steps carefully around it. They file past a pine tree that has collapsed against the one next to it—just barely remaining upright, held in place by a few skinny branches.

"Out of the parking lot we put maybe a hundred yards between us and them," EK says. "I think because they were so surprised. And RK, who fifteen minutes ago didn't want to change the seat settings, is now weaving through traffic and jumping medians."

"And what it goes to show is that the graphics on video games have come a long way," RK says.

"Exactly," EK says. "Like when he sideswipes the bread truck, it really does look a lot like what happens when you sideswipe someone in *Brickyard 400*."

"I get onto the 10," RK says, "which is moving faster, and now there's like four cop cars behind us. You're supposed to change roads a lot, to keep them off guard. Otherwise they radio ahead and set up roadblocks in front of you."

"He's driving and I'm holding on," EK says, "laughing my dick off. And five minutes into it I look down and see something you can't believe. On the TV, it's *us*. No more cartoons—it's the BMW of Justice, shot from above, from a helicopter. Just to make sure I ask RK to jiggle the wheel a little bit, and he does, and about five seconds later, I guess because of the time delay, I can watch it on the screen."

The trail becomes sandy and leads down to a stream that gurgles so perfectly it seems fake. William watches Becca stumble on the rocks that lead across it and come out with soaking boots.

"Fucking piece-of-shit motherfucker!" she yells, now trudging like Frankenstein.

"How fast were you going?" Loren asks the twins.

RK says, "Mostly it was like ninety or so. Once, on a straight part, I hit one thirty-five. A lot of the time I didn't even want to look."

"But one thirty-five when you're as baked as we were feels like the speed of sound," EK says. "I thought paint chips were going to start flying off the car. I thought time was going to start running backward."

"For maybe ten minutes we were actually OK," RK says. "We were opening up space between them and us. I tried to just switch roads as much as possible and floor it when I could."

"Seven cop cars following us now, and four helicopters," EK says. "Each filming from a different angle, with a different time delay. So when something happened, when, like, RK swerved onto an exit and started going down the service road, I could watch it live through the windshield, then watch it on TV a few seconds later, then change channels really quickly and watch it *again*, from a different side. The whole thing just blew my mind. I was laughing so hard I was drooling. Factor in the Atomizer for that too."

"On one channel," RK says, "they said we were maybe drug king-pins, because it was such an expensive car."

Jeremy drops his bag, and they have to wait while he adjusts his grip and picks it up again. William's hands are cramping too, but he doesn't say anything. There's no point.

"How far did you guys make it?" Ty asks.

"About forty-one miles," RK says. "By the end they had the high-way patrol on us, county sheriffs—I wouldn't be surprised if there was some DEA in there."

"They must have seen the service road thing coming," EK says, "because they were ready for it. They had it blocked off, and they sort of let us go the way they wanted us to go. They steered us into this big deserted parking lot."

"An old warehouse," RK says. "No cars, no nothing."

"Except the nails," EK says. "They scattered nails over a space the size of a football field and led us into it."

"They set a trap."

"We hit the nails at seventy or eighty. When you get four flats going that fast the tires just disintegrate. Pieces of them fly off, and the car's impossible to control. RK sprained his elbow trying to hold on to the wheel, and we slowed down so quick the air bags popped out."

"The cops all had their guns out," RK says. "We tried to tell them we weren't drug kingpins, but all they said was, 'Out of the car! Get out of the car now!' And they didn't fuck around when they put us on the pavement."

"They were not gentle about it, not gentle at all."

"The nails were poking us. I had all these holes in my chest."

"Now RK can't drive until he's like sixty."

"The car needed twenty-seven thousand dollars in repairs," EK says. "The tires alone were almost a grand each. Plus the bread truck I hit had to be fixed, and some of the cop cars got messed up, so our dad got a bill for those too. Like it's our fault they can't drive."

"Jeez," Jeremy says. "What did your dad say?"

"He told us this place was our last chance," RK says. "If we screw up here, he's giving our trust fund to the Red Cross."

"The Red Cross can lick my left nut," EK says. "He'd never do it."

They're almost at the dump now. William can smell it, even over the trash juice soaked into his sweats. They come to a cut in the foliage, a cleared path about fifteen feet wide, and the kids cross under a set of power lines that runs back to the compound. For a few steps they look up at clear blue sky—no trees, no overgrowth—and then they're back in the woods. It's for maintenance, William realizes, so the power company can get out here and fix any problems in the lines without having to chainsaw their way in.

"You know what the good part is?" EK says. "I think we're going to be on *America's Wildest Police Chases*. The producer called us last week, right before we came up here, and he said it was looking good. So that's one thing anyway."

"If it happens we'll send you guys the DVD," RK says. "We'll sign it and everything."

*

Donovan doesn't figure out that one of the kids has gotten into the pool until that afternoon, when they make their last trip to the dump.

Ever since lunch he's tried to keep his distance from them. He smells a little like perfume and he doesn't want anyone to notice. At lunchtime, Donovan locked the kids into the cafeteria with Riap and went back to the Colonel's house. He was looking for Kitty, and he found her in the TV room, surrounded by half-unwrapped boxes.

It looked like Christmas morning—clothes, jewelry, stacks of shoe boxes—but really it was just the latest batch of stuff Kitty had ordered. She and the Colonel had gone into town yesterday, and while there they cleaned out the PO boxes, everything she'd had shipped to her over the past few weeks.

Kitty was in a yellow dress with tags hanging from it, wearing two different earrings and two different shoes. She stuck one foot out toward Donovan, then the other.

"These?" she said. "Or these?"

"Either one, I guess," he said.

Three phones on the card table were ringing, but they were under a pile of new purses and behind some perfume bottles, and Kitty didn't seem to notice.

"I thought you'd be at the pool," he said.

"I haven't been out there in two days," she told him. "Maybe I'll go later."

She turned sideways in front of a mirror, a hand smoothing her stomach.

"One of the girls says she has cramps," Donovan said.

"The chubby one, right?" Kitty said. "She gets cramps every other day."

"That's what I told her, but I figured for girl stuff I should check with you."

Kitty sniffed the air around her and wrinkled her nose.

"What stinks?" she said. The tags on her dress clicked against each other when she turned to face him.

Donovan took a step back and lifted one sleeve of his cammies to his face. It brought the strong smell of garbage. He hadn't even carried any of the bags this morning. He was just around it for a few hours.

"You need some of this," she said, reaching for a bottle of perfume and spritzing him with it. It came out like mace, all over his hair, in his eyes.

He winced, but Kitty told him he should appreciate it. "That stuff's three hundred dollars an ounce," she said.

He knew he couldn't go back to the kids smelling like that. So before he let them out of the cafeteria he stopped at the pool, knelt on the edge, and dunked his head. Not as good as a shower but better than nothing. There was something off about the pool, something different, but he couldn't figure out what it was, and he didn't have time to investigate.

Now, with the kids approaching the dump for the last time, Donovan feels tired but good. They're almost done for the day, and he can finally see the floor of the garbage shed.

He takes out his air horn, the same one he uses every morning, and blows five quick blasts. Loren's walking point again, and ahead of him a flock of birds lifts off from the rotting trash. There's a rustling sound of animals retreating. Loren leads them underneath the power lines, descends into a short dip of sand and brown pine needles, and finally they're at the dump.

It's basically a huge mound of black trash bags—from a plane, Donovan thinks, it must look like some giant animal took a crap— with other loose stuff mixed in. There's a car chassis that looks prehistoric and always makes him wonder how anyone could have gotten it out there. A flattened trombone that's brown with corrosion, sections of wood fencing, rusted pipes, a bicycle frame looking stripped and geometric in the sun. Donovan counts four mattresses, one wheelbarrow, and three smashed TVs. He wouldn't be surprised to see a hand sticking out from under the pile. There's even a cluttered mound of orange barrels with EPA skulls on them, which

Jeremy notices now for the first time.

"What are those?" he wants to know.

"Nothing," Donovan says. "Just drop your bags and line up again."

The kids all throw their bags on the heap in turns. Loren acts proud that his lands the farthest away. He points this out to Ty, who doesn't seem impressed. William rubs the cramps out of his hands.

Donovan sees a bunch of Kitty's old chaises half buried in the heap. When they got to the compound eighteen months ago she tried three sets before settling on the current ones (teak frame, red canvas). Two of the chairs she tried and rejected were ridiculously expensive, seven hundred fifty dollars each, bought from the same company that supplied deck chairs for the *Queen Mary*. Kitty talked about them for weeks, but when they finally arrived she sat in them once and announced that they weren't good enough.

He's seen the chaises on every trip out here so far, but right now a few things come together in Donovan's mind that haven't occurred to him so far. He's smart—he knows he is, even if no one else thinks so. It's a perfect day, but Kitty's not at the pool.

I haven't been out there in two days, she said.

Someone was, though—someone must have been. That's what was different when he dunked his head an hour ago: the chairs were moved. Those chairs are never moved and now they're in different places. If it wasn't her (or the Colonel—they were both in town yesterday and last night), and it wasn't Donovan, and it wasn't Riap (who would never go in without asking first), then it had to be....

By the time he pieces it together, the kids are in place, lined up for the final march back. He moves toward them and Loren sets off, but he yells at them to freeze.

"Stop," he says. "Stop right fucking now."

*

Two in the afternoon, and the Colonel's too upset to sleep. He's in bed, blinking at the ceiling, and the only part of him asleep is his arm. It's underneath Kitty, who's curled against him and snoring softly. Kitty's mouth hangs open, fillings exposed, Marlboro breath not all that fresh. Her new yellow dress is bunched under one shoulder, with the tags hanging off it. They had a fight just now—tears, screaming, exhaustion—when he didn't claim to love the dress enough.

If it were just that fight, he'd probably be asleep too, but he's got other concerns. Apparently the lawyer Mrs. Diehl hired is not screwing around. The Colonel thought the Diehl kid was lying, thought he could stall forever, but last night that stopped being a realistic strategy. He still doesn't know how they did it, how they knew where he'd be and when. Someone must have been watching from the gate, waiting for the Jeep to drive past.

They'd gone into town to ship out the ramen-noodle box of medical records. While they were there, they also picked up mail from the PO boxes the Colonel keeps in town (under various aliases), plus all the crap Kitty had ordered over the past few weeks. Forty-one packages addressed to one Katerina French-Kellogg, his beloved, his ray of sun. The Colonel got a new bunch of very promising bank statements in the mail, updates on all the offshore accounts. He was feeling expansive, so on the way back they stopped off at the steak place they liked.

It happened after dinner but before dessert. The table had been cleared, leaving a few crumbs and some pink stains from the prime rib they'd ordered (both medium rare). The wine glasses were filmy with fingerprint smudges. Kitty was reading her dessert options from a laminated card. She was the best-looking woman in the restaurant, the Colonel thought. Definitely the tannest.

"Raymond Kellogg?"

A man with narrow eyes who was clearly not their waiter appeared at the table.

Lying in bed in broad daylight while his wife snores her smoky breath onto him, the Colonel can only cringe at the memory. Were there warning signs? There were a lot. The name alone—no one in the whole state knew him by Ray Kellogg. Outside of Kitty and Donovan, he hadn't been called that in months. Plus the man was chewing gum and wearing high-tops, and he had on a fake-leather vest, not suede like the other waiters (who were huddled in a far corner, watching the whole scene play out). The man held a platter high up on one palm, under the kind of silver dome you never see in restaurants anymore.

All of which registered for the Colonel on some dim level, significant enough that he could remember the details later but not so much that they set off warning bells at the time. Instead he sat back, so full of prime rib and red wine that he was practically semiconscious, enjoying the change from Riap's cooking and the absence of any curry aftertaste. "That's me," he said.

"Something for you," the man said. "Courtesy of the chef." His narrow eyes were almost Mongolian. He lifted the dome to reveal a thick envelope, which he slid quickly into the Colonel's lap.

"You've been served," the man said.

As he turned for the exit he dropped the platter to the floor. It let out a reverberating gong, announcing to everyone in the restaurant that Something Big was happening over here, so look now if you haven't already.

The envelope was in the Colonel's lap like a stain, thick and rumpled and dirt-smudged—obviously it had been handled a lot. The return address listed the clerk of courts for the county. He knew right away.

"I don't get it," Kitty said. She was still holding the dessert card. "Served what?"

"It's, ah, a coupon," the Colonel told her. "For a free meal. Next time we come."

He waited until he got home to read it, though he only got as far as page four (of twenty-one). The subpoena laid out the kid's injuries, with a lot of medical terminology the Colonel merely skimmed. *"...otolaryngologist's report...80 percent neurosineal loss ...audiometry results...85 dB attenuation...blunt-force trauma...."* It also demanded that the Colonel present all kinds of records: medical-exam reports for Matthew Diehl, the incident report for the day he was hit, a copy of the Colonel's liability policy for the camp, etc., etc. Which, funny enough, none of that stuff existed. When the Colonel first saw the list he uncapped a pen to circle everything he'd have to forge. But by the middle of page three he stopped circling and put the cap back on again. He'd need a better legal strategy, and the only one he could come up with was: take a nap.

There's calming white noise in the bedroom—just the air conditioners humming quietly—and he guesses that this is what 80 percent hearing loss in one ear might sound like. Permanently muffled everything. Probably good for sleeping in loud places, right? Probably good for ignoring talky people on airplanes—as long as the person was on the right side of your head. Everyone has little things like that that they have to deal with. The Colonel gets colds sometimes, but you don't see him running off to a lawyer.

Blunt-force trauma—Donovan wouldn't do something like that, would he? The Colonel has told him a thousand times to take it easy on the kids. Nothing permanent, no marks. Donovan's problem is that he takes things personally. He lets them push his buttons. He doesn't understand that this is a *business*, that the Colonel doesn't care if the kids all grow up to be serial killers as long as the classes are full and the checks clear, because by that time Camp Ascend! will be a fading memory and the Colonel and Kitty will be on the beach of some third world country, collecting shells and getting pleasantly wasted on rum drinks every morning.

Kitty shifts in her sleep and he takes his arm back from under her. It's so rubbery and numb that it feels almost prosthetic. He tries making fists until the nerves in his fingers start to tingle again. The front of Kitty's yellow dress hangs open, showing him the curve of one breast that's very brown around the edges. The tan lines look like the split on a black-and-white cookie.

Sleep doesn't seem like an option anymore, so the Colonel surrenders and rolls out of bed to go to the bathroom. It's good to be up and around, and he tells himself that maybe things aren't as hopeless as they seem. He can have another talk with Donovan, get him to ease up. Maybe the Colonel can call Mrs. Diehl and make her an offer: five grand if she calls off the lawyer. He'd be willing to negotiate—going by the bank statements, he can afford it. The point is that he'll figure a way out of this. He always does.

But when he turns on the bathroom sink he knows right away that something's wrong. The water barely trickles out. Either the well's acting up again or someone's going through a ton of water somewhere else on the property. He hears shouts and looks out the window down onto the ring. When he sees what's happening he runs for the door, not even bothering to turn off the tap.

*

Liz has never been handcuffed before. Even when the mink farmer pressed charges, her father drove her to the police station himself. Two felony counts, but to Liz it was one big joke—she walked into the courthouse like she was on a field trip. And maybe, she realizes now, the lack of handcuffs had something to do with that. Maybe some physical restraints would have emphasized the gravity of the situation a little more. Because when Donovan puts the cuffs on her, she panics right away and has to force herself to calm down.

"This can stop whenever you want," Donovan says. "One name and it's over."

All nine kids are kneeling on the ring in a long line, heads down. He's zip-cuffing them one by one.

They ran the whole way back from the dump. When the spike trail met up with the perimeter loop they went the wrong way, until

Donovan screamed at them to turn around and keep moving. Ty asked why they were being punished when they didn't even know what they'd done wrong, and Donovan punched him in the chest. Closed fist, full swing. Ty flew off the trail and lay squeaking in the dead leaves until his breath came back. After that, no more questions. They made it back to the compound and came streaming out of the woods like it was burning down behind them.

Donovan lined everyone up on the ring and made them do fifty squat thrusts. Then another fifty. Then fifty more. He seemed to be trying to calm himself down, though his face was purple, and a vein in his forehead was wormy with anger. Liz thought he was losing his mind.

"One name and we're done," Donovan says. "Everyone else can go sleep in the cabins all day. Tomorrow too. I just want a name."

After they finished two hundred squat thrusts the kids were moving slowly. They'd already been hauling trash for hours—they wound down like clocks. And when the entire class was leveled, flat-out exhausted, Donovan made them get onto their knees and took out the cuffs.

"You can't do this to us," Becca says. "We have rights. This is illegal."

"So's trespassing," Donovan says. "I want a name."

"How's it trespassing if we're already on the property?" EK says.

"Put your head back down or I'll punch it down," Donovan says.

"Can I talk to the Colonel?" Jeremy says. He's trying hard to keep his voice level.

"Nope, no Colonel for you today. You're stuck with everyone else."

"But you know I didn't do it," Jeremy says. The whine in his voice rises. "I definitely didn't. I can't even swim."

"Doesn't matter," Donovan says. "Everyone stays until I find out."

Usually Liz can laugh off Donovan's tantrums, but not this time. She has no idea how he figured out that someone had been in the pool, and she can't believe he pieced it together this fast. It hasn't even been twenty-four hours.

The stones hurt her knees, so she shifts her weight from one leg to the other and tries to slow her breathing. In, out, nice and easy. A long time ago she had a gymnastics coach who was into yoga, and he told her that your breath is all you have sometimes. When you're nervous or scared, when you're in front of judges and about to jump up on the bars, your breath will save you. In, out—slowly.

"One of you thinks you're smarter than this place," Donovan says, talking directly to Loren. "One of you is a sneak and a liar. I want to know which one."

A voice from down the line says, "It was me."

"Who said that?" Donovan says.

"Me," Ty says.

Donovan walks down to him. "You were in the pool?"

"Yeah."

"When?"

"Cut everyone loose and I'll tell you."

"Tell me when first."

"A night or two ago."

"Where'd you move the chairs to? Don't look over there—tell me."

"I forget."

"Next to each other or further apart?"

Pause. "Apart."

"Forget it, Freak Show. Nice try. And did you all hear that? Here's someone who *didn't even do it* and he's taking the blame, while the one who did wants to hide and lie. You have one minute to fess up or this gets worse."

He stands in front of them, arms crossed. Liz looks down at his boots and listens to the wind push the treetops around. Her stubby shadow points off toward two o'clock, which she thinks is probably pretty close to the real time. She's become her own sundial.

"Nothing? No one wants to talk? OK."

Donovan reaches into the pocket of his cammies again and walks over to Loren. Liz watches as Donovan pushes him facedown onto the stones and cuffs his ankles. Then he bends Loren's knees and binds his hands and feet together behind him. She's pretty sure this is what the term *hog-tying* means. Loren strains against the plastic in a way that makes Liz think he's got some issues with claustrophobia, but she knows he's not ripping through the cuffs. If you had ten or fifteen minutes and something sharp, you could maybe saw through them, but you'd never get out by sheer exertion. Your shoulders would pop first.

Liz is next in line. She forces herself to close her eyes and breathe while Donovan ties her limbs up behind her. Images flit through her mind of rodeo cruelty, animals in pens, calves lying on their side in the dirt. She wants to apologize to every hog that's ever been hog-tied, because while she knew it must suck she never had any idea how much. Slow breaths—in and out.

A few spots down RK tries to resist the second set of cuffs, but it doesn't matter. Donovan sits on his back and gets him bound up in just slightly more time than it takes to do the others. Meredith sniffles, her hair piled up on the ground, hiding her face. Becca breathes in shallow gasps. The other kids are nowhere near as flexible as Liz, she realizes, which must make this even harder for them. When Donovan's done with all nine she lifts her head and watches his boots walk to the front of the ring again.

"I'm waiting," he says. "Somebody tell me something or this is going to go on all day."

Silence. Another gust ruffles the dying pine trees. Liz's ribs start to ache.

"Whoever went in the pool just say so!" EK says. His voice cracks from the urgency. "Don't put us all through this."

RK tells his brother to shut up.

"Fuck you, I will not," EK says. "If I did it I'd say something. This is more than we're supposed to get here. This is over the line."

"I'm not waiting much longer," Donovan says. "I've been getting screwed my whole life—every day, it feels like. Half the time I don't even know who did it. But that all stops now. This time I'm getting a name. We'll be out here until midnight if you want."

Somewhere to Liz's left, William sneezes twice and then keeps taking big wheezy breaths through his mouth. Ty clicks and grunts—he sounds like he's trying to communicate with dolphins. Liz realizes one of the cracks in the stone under her isn't a crack at all, but part of the initials carved into the ring: "GRSCMI." She doesn't know what they stand for. The upper chamber of the R is right below her face.

"Nothing?" Donovan says. "OK."

Liz watches his boots turn and disappear around the corner of the barn. No one moves. She thinks he's going to leave them here for a while to think about it. Her feet are numb already, and it's spreading to her ankles.

Loren is next to her, so she turns her head and sees that he's already looking over. His eyes are wide and darting.

"Should we say something?" Liz whispers.

Loren shakes his head.

"Never?"

"No."

"But no one else did anything wrong."

"Doesn't matter," he says. "We don't say anything. We don't break."

Donovan clomps back around the corner, dragging a hose. It's turned on full blast, putting out firefighting quantities of water. No nozzle, just a silver mercury stream that spatters on the ground with a noise like sizzling food. Donovan drops the hose and the end rolls over slightly so that it's angled up, the flow arcing out and forming an instant puddle.

"Let's see who feels like they're not getting enough water," he says. To Loren, he says, "You first."

Liz doesn't want to watch but she can't stop herself. Donovan picks Loren up by his bindings and hauls him like a suitcase to the front of the group, where he gets rolled onto his side, facing everyone.

Standing over him, Donovan says, "Was it you?"

Loren shakes his head.

Donovan picks up the hose and points it at the ground a few feet from Loren. Bits of dirt splash up into his face.

"I want to know," Donovan tells him. "Last chance."

Loren shakes his head again, and Donovan points the stream at him, hitting him square in the face. Loren squirms around, trying to get a breath. For a few seconds he's OK, but then Donovan puts his boot down onto Loren's head. Within a few seconds he sucks in some water and starts coughing, and the stream keeps coming, a rope of water. Liz yells at Donovan to stop, but he looks over at her and says that unless she has a name she should shut her fucking mouth.

Loren starts spitting and gasping, eyes squeezed closed. Donovan points the hose away and says, "Was it you?" Loren shakes his head again, as much as he can against the sole of Donovan's boot, and the water comes back.

Liz can't watch anymore. Instead she looks down into the deep groove of the R underneath her. Dirt at the bottom, half of a pine needle so ancient it's turned black. The curve of the lettering is machine-grooved and perfect. She's not looking but the sound is almost worse—Loren chokes as the water keeps streaming down and Donovan asks him again and again, "Was it you? Tell me. I want to know, right now."

Finally he drops the hose and it's over. Loren's face is pale, eyes flat, hair sticking to his head—he looks like he's just been dragged out of some swamp. He lifts his head from the mud and coughs up a bunch of yellowish, foamy water. Donovan picks him up and hauls him back to his spot on the ring, long strings of drool hanging from his mouth. He retches twice more but nothing comes up.

Donovan turns to Liz. "Next," he says.

"I didn't do it," she says. "I swear. You don't have to put me up there."

"Let's make sure."

Breathe slowly—in, out. She's so scared that she thinks she might piss her pants. Donovan picks her up by the bindings and her spine aches from being bent backward. She's light enough that he can carry her with one hand. Three steps and she's on the mud just off the ring, on her side in front of everyone. Donovan's boots make squishing noises, and her sweats soak through immediately. If your breath is all you have, and then you don't have that anymore either, what's left? Donovan stands above her, seventeen feet tall, and holds the hose off to the side. She's at eye level with the grommets of his boots. One of his laces broke and had to be knotted together in the middle.

"You know how this works," Donovan says. "Speak now…."

She looks at the faces in front of her. Ty is still making his dolphin sounds. Bits of sand and dirt stick to his forehead. Meredith is saucer-eyed and silent. Loren seems more scared now than he was before. The pattern on the hose looks a little like snakeskin, or maybe she's just imagining that.

"I didn't—" she starts to say, and Donovan turns the hose on her. The water hits like a slap. It's glacier-cold and smells of minerals. Donovan's saying something but she can't hear him over the splashing. Full-on panic now. She flails around, trying to get some air but can't. This is it—she can't control anything anymore, she's going to drown on dry land. And then she hears someone telling Donovan to stop.

The voice is at ground level and hoarse. It's Loren.

"Don't," he says. "No more. It wasn't her, it was me. I'm the one who went swimming."

Donovan aims the hose off to the side.

"Who else?"

"Just me. No one else."

"Goddamn," Donovan says. "I knew it all along."

Liz can't stop gasping. Some water comes out of her nose as she sees the worn soles of Donovan's boots walk over toward Loren. In the distance, a screen door slams. It's the Colonel, running toward them and waving his arms. Liz wonders where he's been this whole time. Her legs feel suddenly warm—she pissed herself after all.

CHAPTER 13

Loren dreams about his mom again. This time he's younger, six or seven, and they're on a beach. Waves rising and falling, plastic buckets of sand. Towels with smooth round rocks to hold down the corners. He finds a half-smashed Styrofoam cooler that he fills with shells and water and seaweed and pretends is a fish tank. A dead crab goes in too—it seems light enough to float but sinks right away.

Loren's hair is wet and he's shivering. His mom said he could swim, but not too long and not too far out—it was late afternoon by the time they got here, and the lifeguards were already packing up. He didn't really want to go in (it's windy, the water's cold) but he felt like he had to. He's been nagging her to take him to the beach for weeks. So he jumped in and came right out, and his mom said, "Happy now?"

They were supposed to spend the whole day here—Loren and his mom and the man who bought her the necklace (silver loops, all connected). But this morning the man was late to pick them up. Way late, hours late, and then the phone rang. Loren's mom picked it up and disappeared into her room, and when Loren listened all he could hear was her saying, "You won't try? You don't even want to try?" A little while later she stopped talking, though she stayed in the room with the door closed for a long time. When she finally came out again Loren asked if they were still going to the beach, and she said she guessed so. She wasn't wearing the necklace anymore.

The beach is nearly empty now. The sun is low in the sky, all the little bumps in the sand filled with shadows. Loren's mom sits with her arms around her knees and stares at the water. Loren's hungry—he hasn't eaten anything all day, it's like she forgot they're supposed to—but he doesn't complain. Two seagulls stand by the garbage can, perfectly white and so motionless they look stuffed. Happy now? Loren is. It's just the two of them again. They're better off this way. She never believes him when he says it (and he says it all the time), but it's true. He builds a moat for her, a trench that wraps all the way around the towels to keep everyone else away. It's their own private castle.

*

When he wakes it's nearly dark out, and the surrounding gloom is such a contrast from the dream that Loren's disoriented, until he makes out the geometry of ceiling beams above him and remembers. His pillow has damp spots on it from lying down with wet hair a few hours ago. William is asleep in the next bunk, hands folded across his chest in a way that reminds Loren of people laid out at wakes. Through the window a rectangle of bright, deepening blue silhouettes the line of trees—it must be just past sunset.

From the Colonel's house Loren can hear distant shouting. He gets up to look out the window and steps on something wet—his sweats, still soggy. In a far corner of the cabin he wrings them out, holding them close to the floorboards so the dripping doesn't wake anyone. The exertion brings up an ache in his wrists, a leftover soreness from the bindings. When he can't get any more water out he spread-eagles the sweats on a dry patch of floor. With luck they'll only be damp tomorrow.

His eyes are adjusting to the dark now, and he sees something folded on his bunk, dark and square. He pokes at it with a finger, then holds it up to the window and sees that it's another set of sweats—tops and bottoms. They're new and straight from the box, and they smell like cardboard. Maybe someone felt sorry for him and gave him an extra set he's been stashing. But looking around, he sees new sweats left out for the other kids too, on every bunk. EK doesn't seem to have any, until Loren spots a dark shape on the floor and figures out that EK must have rolled around in his sleep and knocked them off.

Pulling the sweats on brings instant warmth—is there anything better than new fleece? Near the door is another mystery—someone left out bottles of water for them, plus a big grease-stained bag of cold McDonald's. Loren picks up the bag and sniffs at the opening, and his mouth waters. He makes sure there's enough for everyone and takes his share back to his bunk, unfolding the wrappers as quietly as he can. The fries are stuck together, the burger squashed flat, but it all tastes better than anything he's had in weeks. When he swallows his windpipe burns, from choking earlier.

Once he's done eating, he puts his head back on the damp pillow to think about the sudden generosity. A peace offering? But who from? Loren wants to mull it all over, come up with some theories, but the sky is quickly turning darker, and he's newly fed and warm, and his conscious thoughts don't stand a chance—he's asleep again within minutes.

*

Over the next few days something happens that none of the kids could have predicted. The Colonel eases up, at first gradually and then completely. They stop exercising in the mornings and instead get to sleep in until the last of them finally wakes (usually EK, around ten). They're allowed to eat as much as they want, and they can talk through meals. No more marching, no more home repairs. In the afternoons they get to sleep some more, or else the Colonel plays movies for them in the band room in the barn. The only rule is that the kids have to stay together, so they're easier to keep track of.

Throughout this stretch Donovan is conspicuously absent, and at first that makes the kids nervous about accepting the Colonel's gifts. When they're let out of the cabin the first morning, they walk outside in their new sweats, blinking and hesitant, and see that Riap has set out breakfast for them. Instant coffee and pear fritters and sausage links and scrambled eggs, all on two picnic tables in the dead grass near the cafeteria. They think it can't be for them—it has to be for the Colonel and Kitty. Or it's a trap, and they'll be intercepted by Donovan halfway to the table and taken to the woods to do eight million squat thrusts. But the Colonel doesn't give any explanation. Instead he simply shrugs and says go ahead, eat up.

When they ask where Donovan is, the Colonel tells them matter-of-factly that he's on vacation. "Taking a break," he says. "Standard part of the routine. He works hard, so halfway through each session we give him some time off. It's in his contract."

Loren asks when he's coming back, and the Colonel hesitates.

"That depends," he says, "on how much fun he's having. But anyway, it doesn't matter—go sit down. Your milk's turning bad in the sun."

The kids have theories about why the rules are suddenly relaxed. Some think that the Colonel's just lazy and that he figures this is the easiest thing to do during the few days Donovan will be gone. Others say he must have felt bad about what happened on the ring and is trying to win the kids back again. A few (actually just Jeremy) say that the Colonel must think that a break would be good for them, and that he would have eased up whether they'd all been hogtied or not. But soon enough the kids stop even wondering about it—they're too busy enjoying themselves.

The Colonel continues to lock them in the cabins for long stretches, but now they get magazines and decks of cards, and Riap brings them milk shakes. The twins teach the other kids how to play spades and euchre, and they stage marathon tournaments—best of nine, best of thirteen, games to a thousand. They even start making requests, most of which get granted.

William wants his Zyrtecs back—he receives a handful—and he asks to fix the holes in the window screens. The Colonel lets him cut down scraps from the unoccupied cabins, which William fashions into patches and weaves into place with wire. It makes the light inside much dimmer, but right away the bug count goes down. He hunts down every last surviving insect in the cabin, and lines up the dead ones on the windowsill. "A warning," he says, "to their friends on the outside." The kids' eyes turn bright from all the extra sleep.

Liz makes a request too: she wants to start helping Riap in the kitchen full-time. In part it's because she simply likes being around him (he occasionally gives her cigarettes, Loren found out) but also because she wants to have some say over what they eat. She puts more vegan things on the menu—a rice loaf and some soy-milk smoothies that are OK, a tempeh-lentil casserole that Loren has to force himself to choke down. And when her dishes require strange ingredients she's allowed to add them to the shopping list that Riap takes into town. The Colonel has Riap do all the shopping now; he seems newly reluctant to go off the property.

Becca wants to sunbathe, so in the afternoons she pulls her sweats up over chunky calves that have gone fish-belly white after three weeks under heavy fleece, and lays a towel down on the cracked stones of the ring. RK wants as many old Dodgers box scores as the Colonel can dig up.

Loren doesn't make any special requests. He thinks the kids might still be mad at him for what he put them through on the ring, and he doesn't want to push his luck. He gets nothing extra during this lull except more surveillance, in the form of Jeremy, who now shadows Loren wherever he goes. Jeremy even has a whistle on a lanyard around his neck, which he's supposed to blow if Loren looks like he's doing something suspicious.

No one mentions what happened with the hose for a day or two, so it's a relief when EK finally brings it up. They're in the cabin one night when EK says, "Wait you guys—look. This is me doing Loren." He takes a drink of water and lies on his bunk with his hands behind his back, then spits it out through his nose and shouts, "Don't hurt my girlfriend!"

"She's not my girlfriend," Loren starts to say, but RK cuts him off.

"Yeah she is," RK says. "Don't lie. And anyway, what about Ty, throwing himself on the grenade for us? What were you going to do if Donovan believed you?"

Ty lies on his bunk and keeps staring at the ceiling. His feet are pointed one hundred eighty degrees apart. He's practically double-jointed.

RK says, "Ty's a ninja. He's the one you don't want to mess with. He'll put you to sleep with his rocking and then fuck you up."

"I can't believe you were out of the cabin and the only thing you could think of to do was go swimming," EK says.

"What would you do?" RK says.

"Something else. Something bigger."

Loren thinks about telling them how Liz was there, or even better, how she swam naked. It would win him points, but he doesn't say anything about it. Jeremy's in the cabin with them, and Loren knows everything he says gets reported back to the Colonel.

"I wouldn't have fessed up," EK says. "No matter what."

"Bullshit," his brother says, "You definitely would have talked. You were already freaking out." He puts on a falsetto voice and says, *"Whoever did it just say so! This is over the line!"*

EK says, "Yeah, but if it was me who did it I wouldn't say anything."

"You would have rolled over like a rag doll bitch."

"No way."

"Yes fucking way."

They start throwing punches, and a minute later EK comes off the floor with a bloody nose. Loren thinks the other kids aren't mad at him anymore—if they ever were—but he also knows that whatever credibility he might have built up is gone. If he wants to lead them, he'll have to start all over.

*

One day when they're bored, the Colonel unlocks an outside storage room off the barn, where they find a bunch of ancient sports equipment left from the music-camp days. Most of it's unusable. The volleyball has deflated into a raisin shape, and mold has colonized one hemisphere of the kick ball. There's a cardboard box of old arrows from an archery set, and some petrified baseball gloves—when Loren forces his hand into one it makes a peeling noise and brown flakes fly off like old varnish. RK unearths a football that has absorbed so much water it wobbles in the air. He lobs easy passes to Ty, who either flinches at the ball or clubs it to the ground with his forearms.

"Good, Ty," RK says. "You want to think about maybe changing your meds."

Finally they find a milk crate of horseshoes that haven't suffered too much from being locked in a dark closet for almost two years. EK pounds the stakes into the ground with an old croquet mallet and gets a splinter in his thumb the size of a horse syringe. They rinse the cobwebs off the horseshoes with a hose (the same hose Donovan used on them three days ago, though no one besides Loren seem to notice). RK says it's an old man's game but he's going to kick his brother's ass at it.

"We'll play doubles," he says to EK. "Me and Ty against you and Riap."

Jeremy wants to play but they tell him he should be referee instead. "That's the kind of thing you're good at," RK says. "You already have the whistle. And besides, my brother cheats."

The four of them take a few practice throws and Loren sits at the picnic table by himself, watching. Riap has this crazy form, where he'll stand quietly and stare at the post for a long moment before unfurling his body and throwing the horseshoe in one quick spasm, like a snake striking. EK tries way too hard, taking practice throws and whispering to himself when it's not his turn. RK's a natural—he gets a few ringers, and when his team is way ahead he starts ignoring the post to throw at his brother's foot.

On the ring, Becca gives Meredith a makeover, rooting through a plastic bag of old cosmetics that Kitty was planning to throw out. The two of them sit on milk crates, Meredith's knees up around her ears, hair back in a ponytail, while Becca brushes tan powder onto her face. Liz is in the kitchen, making something that Loren thinks smells a little like wood chips.

"Germ, I'm going to wrap this fucking horseshoe around your neck in a minute," EK says. "I was not over the line."

"Your foot left a mark, right by that twig," Jeremy says. "That's over the line."

"That's *on* the line."

"On is over."

"On is on. Over is over."

"Tennis, basketball, football. Your foot touches the line and you're out."

"Yo, are we playing tennis here? Do you see a basketball hoop somewhere that I'm missing?"

RK says, "Eric, just do it over and stop bitching. Jesus."

Loren turns his face up to the sun. The sky is a perfect cloudless dome, and the angled afternoon sunlight makes the dead grass look almost decent. Even the weather seems to be letting up on them. Warm afternoons, cool nights. Still, he can't help feeling uneasy about the changes lately. They've been bought off so easily—all it took was a few bags of hamburgers and some movies. Loren's as guilty as the rest. The Colonel throws a few treats at them and they start behaving. It's harder to resist against the good-cop treatment sometimes. You have nothing firm to push back against, and a big part of you is saying, *It's OK. Accept the gifts.*

Of all the men his mom dated, Loren always thought the jerks were the easiest to deal with, because the lines were clear—you knew where you stood. When she was with generous guys (rare, but it happened), they would try to win Loren over by buying him things. He'd ask for outrageously rare, exotic stuff that he didn't even want. One time it was a German telescope that wasn't available in the U.S.—you had to pay for it in euros. When it finally arrived and Loren unwrapped it, the expression on the guy's face was so infuriating, so smug. "You can see the rings of Saturn," he said. Loren used it once, to look in some neighbors' windows, and then deliberately left it out in a snowstorm.

The barn door opens and Kitty makes her way to the picnic table. The kids all fall silent. She's wearing flip-flops that slap at her heels.

"The Colonel wants to see you," she tells Loren.

"Now?"

"Now. He's in his office. Get going."

*

The Colonel rocks back and forth, listening to his office chair creak faintly underneath him. For a long moment it's the only sound in the room. You gain an advantage in certain situations by keeping your mouth shut, he thinks. The other person talks just to fill up the silence.

On the other side of the desk, Loren sits stiffly upright, hands in his lap. He looks well rested for a change, and his new sweats have creases running down the sleeves.

"So," the Colonel says.

Loren says nothing. Instead he looks around at the pictures on the walls. Smiling kids from the music camp, plus squares of dark paneling, a few with hooks still centered in them.

"From previous sessions of Camp Ascend!," the Colonel says, expansively. *Look around all you want. Be impressed. This is my domain.*

"Sure," Loren says. "That's what I figured. But how come they're not wearing black sweats?"

The Colonel falters. "That was…before we instituted the policy," he says.

Loren nods slowly, but the Colonel gets the sense he doesn't believe it. Score one point for the little bastard.

From outside the window, they can hear kids yelling, horseshoes clanging against the post.

He decides to try a different tack. "Getting enough to eat lately?" he says.

Loren shrugs.

"Riap's not bad, right?" the Colonel says. "A little unconventional, a little exotic, but pretty good for camp food."

Another shrug. The Colonel's patience is wearing out.

"You know," he says, "we have rules here, and the rules aren't nego-tiable. You can't just pick and choose the ones you want to follow."

"Are they written down anywhere?" Loren says.

"Is there some confusion about them?"

"I don't know, maybe. You and Donovan talk about these rules all the time, but I've never seen them all in one place. Like in a book or something."

"Did you really wonder about that when you broke out of your cabin? Did you think for one millisecond that that might be allowed? Because even if we had a whole penal code we wouldn't have wasted the ink to put something in that said, by the way, sec-tion 17B right here says that you shouldn't sneak out of the cabins to go swimming, because that's *against the rules*. It wouldn't even occur to me that someone would have the nerve—"

The Colonel can hear his own voice rising. When he stops, the contrasting silence in the office is like an accusation. *You almost lost it right there. The kid's getting to you.*

On the other side of his desk, Loren looks vaguely, casually triumphant. It's in his eyes, the set of his head. The Colonel takes a deep breath to calm down and rocks back in his chair, which lets out a single prolonged creak.

"OK," he says. "Time for a demonstration."

He pulls the top right-hand desk drawer smoothly open on its rollers. From inside, he removes a small tree branch he found on the perimeter loop this morning, two feet long and months-dead and rotted inside. When he sets it on the desk a few crumbs of dirt and dried bark fall off.

"Know what this is?" he says.

Loren hesitates. "A branch?"

"Close. What's another word for branch?"

"Log?"

"No, *stick*. This is a stick."

"Isn't a stick supposed to be skinnier than that?"

"Just try not to be a pain in the balls for one minute, OK?" the Colonel says. "Repeat after me: this is a stick."

"This is a stick."

"Good boy."

A small earwig climbs out from under a piece of bark and investigates the surface of the desk. The Colonel watches briefly and then picks up a stapler and pushes it down onto the bug until it crunches. The noise makes him cringe, but he tries not to let Loren see.

From inside the same drawer he pulls out the other half of his demonstration. Riap usually has carrots around by the bushel—the Colonel has seen him carrying big plastic bags of them in from grocery runs—but this morning he was apparently out, so the Colonel had to go with the next best thing. On the desk, the baby carrot looks childish and penile. It's ludicrously small next to the tree branch, unnaturally orange against the fake-wood veneer.

Loren is nodding already. Everything about the kid is irritating, the Colonel thinks. He's the know-it-all in school, the type the Colonel used to hate.

"I think I get it," Loren says.

"Maybe, but let's make sure. The past few days have been pretty easy around here, right?"

"I guess."

"So that's this," the Colonel says, pointing to the carrot. "Good things. Follow the rules, do what you're told, and that's what it could be like around here all the time."

"But you're just buying us off."

"And? What's your point? People get bought off all the time. Some people *ask* to be bought off. That's how the world works."

From somewhere deep in the barn the central AC clicks on, and cool air drops from a ceiling vent. Two more earwigs come out of the branch now, a search party, looking for their dead brother.

"Anyway, this is option B," the Colonel says, ignoring the insects and pointing at the branch. "Punishment. Every time you step one half inch out of line, you'll be corrected, firmly. It's no secret that Donovan doesn't like you. Even *I* don't like you, but I'm enough of a professional that I can keep my feelings out of this. Him, though, when he gets back here he's going to be itching for a fight. Now, I can talk to him and say—listen, Loren and I had a little sit-down and hashed this whole thing over. I can tell him you're sorry for what you did, that you've already been punished enough and you should get a clean slate. Incidentally, I really believe that. I saw what you went through out there on the ring, spitting up like a two-month-old. Didn't look fun."

"It wasn't that bad," Loren says.

"Sure, you're a tough kid. At least, you think you are. But I'm giving you a free pass here. This is the end of the harsh treatment. The catch is, you have to prove me right when Donovan gets back."

"How?"

"By keeping your butt in line. No more screwing around, no more guerilla resistance. If you do that, then I'll know that you've found the fear of God, and that I was right to ease up. But if you keep doing what you're doing—mouthing off, taking things, trying to lead little insurrections with the other kids—then I'll take Donovan off the leash and that water torture you went through is going to seem like an amusement park ride. Understand?"

More nodding. He's like a bobblehead doll, the Colonel thinks.

"Say, 'I understand,'" he tells Loren.

"I understand."

"I'm not sure you do, but I guess we'll find out."

The two earwigs are at opposite ends of the desk now. When one of them crawls onto the phone the Colonel can't take it anymore. He reaches for the stapler and squishes them both quickly. They stick to it in a way that makes it sit crooked on the desk.

"One thing I don't get," Loren says. "Why do this for me?"

The Colonel doesn't want to give the real reasons—that when the kids do what they're told the place is basically an ATM and, more important, that there's already at least one injured kid out there pressing legal action against Camp Ascend!, one looming subpoena, and it wouldn't take too much imagination to picture Loren getting out of here and giving a deposition to that ambulance-chasing lawyer Mrs. Diehl hired. *Yes sir, a camp employee did in fact bind my hands and feet together behind my back and pick me up by the bindings. Yes sir, the water was cold, and did go in my face until I stopped breathing and then vomited....*

"You want the truth?" the Colonel says. "The no-bullshit?"

"Definitely."

The Colonel sits back in his creaking chair for a dramatic pause before playing his bluff.

"The real reason is that I talked to your mom this morning."

"You're lying."

Now it's the Colonel's turn to shrug. He idly brushes some bark bits from the desk into his hand, and dusts them into the wastebasket.

"What'd she say?" Loren asks.

"She said she's worried about you. She said she loves you a lot, and she wanted to know how you were doing up here."

"And what did you tell her?"

The Colonel says, "I told her about you sneaking out. I had to— I'm legally bound in these situations."

Loren says nothing. The Colonel thinks he might be hooked by the way he slumps back in his chair. It could be time to press a little.

"She said…well, she said she wasn't surprised. She said you used to take stuff from her when you were little, that sneaking around was something you always did. Is that true?"

It's another bluff but a less risky one. A lot of kids take things from their parents—quarters from the change bowl, books with dirty words in them. If you include all kids, the odds are probably better than fifty-fifty, but for the ones who get sent to this place it's almost a lock. Loren's face gives it away—the Colonel's hunting in the right place.

"*Disappointed*," the Colonel says. "That was the word she used. And *mad*. And *frustrated*. She wanted to know what we were doing up here all day. So I explained to her that you'd be getting some special scrutiny, that you'd be under close observation from now on, basically the last three weeks you'll be up here."

"That's Jeremy and the whistle?"

"Partly, yes. He's an extra set of eyes and ears for me until Donovan gets back. Which leads me to the last thing. This might sound rough, but I'm trying to be straight up with you—your mom said that if we didn't think you were responding to the program we had her OK to keep you here."

"What? For how long?"

"That's up to you. Word I got from her was that it's open-ended. You'll be here as long as we think you need to make the necessary changes. Is that clear?"

No more nodding. The kid is finally shocked out of his punk attitude. There's always something, the Colonel thinks. Basic psychology—figure out what this person really wants, then threaten to take it away. With Jeremy, who was in here last night, the biggest threat was that he might lose his favored-son status and become just like all the other kids. No special treatment, no access. The Colonel just had to mention it and Jeremy's eyes went shifty and anxious.

"I said, is that clear?" the Colonel says.

"It's clear," Loren answers.

"Good. You're dismissed."

The Colonel considers asking the kid to take the branch out with him—he doesn't want an earwig army overrunning his office—but he thinks that might undercut the demonstration a little. He'll get rid of it as soon as the kid leaves.

At the door, Loren pauses.

"When does Donovan come back?" he says.

"Soon."

"What does 'soon' mean?"

"Soon means soon. That's all you need to know."

After the office door closes the Colonel sits back, contented for a change. The chair doesn't creak this time. He peers down at the frame underneath it and wiggles, first back and forth and then sideways, until the noise comes back.

*

Back at the picnic table, Loren sees Liz with a tray of blob-ish, tan things that have melted together in the oven. "White bean puffs," she says. Everyone gathers around and plucks them off, juggling them between fingers because they're so hot. They leave smeary outlines on the tray.

"They're a little…greasy," Liz offers. She's wearing oven mitts shaped like lobster claws.

Riap takes a small bite and chews thoughtfully. "Maybe salt," he says.

Ty sniffs at his and discreetly drops it behind his leg.

"Know what these need?" EK says. "Bacon. And gravy."

"Don't be a dick," Liz says. "I spent an hour on them."

"I think they're good," Loren says.

Becca is on the ring, finishing Meredith's makeover. Liz asks if they want any, but Becca says they can't move—she's doing mascara. Meredith has the passiveness of a family pet being put into a dress. Her eyelids are glittery, her lips the color of maraschino cherries.

The boys go back to their game and Loren sits at the picnic table to watch. The horseshoes hit the post with bright, metallic, blacksmith clinks, and Jeremy blows his whistle whenever someone gets close to the line. It turns out that Ty is ambidextrous, but EK says that just means he sucks the same no matter which hand he uses.

After a minute Loren realizes that Liz is still there, sitting at the other end of the picnic table. It's the first time the two of them have been on their own since they went swimming. Loren feels strangely nervous, and for a few seconds neither of them says anything. Finally Liz speaks up.

"In the girls' cabin," she says, "the window I got out of is bolted in again. How come?"

"I did that," Loren says. "Yesterday morning. I thought the Colonel might find it and figure out that you'd been out with me that night."

"Huh. Thanks."

The picnic table is so weather-beaten it's practically silver. The bolts are corroded down to rusty nubs. Loren presses a thumbnail into the soft wood, where it leaves a crescent-shaped indent. Then he crosses it with another indent to make a curved X. Thirty feet away, Riap stands frozen, horseshoe in hand.

"So what do we do now?" she says.

"I don't know. The Colonel just told me I'm going to be here until I'm eighteen, basically."

"But if the Colonel keeps it like this, whether it's three weeks or three months, that might not suck too bad," she says.

"That's not how it'll be, though," he says. "Donovan comes back soon—you think he's going to sit around and watch us do all this? Put movies on, referee our horseshoe games? The weird part is that if we really wanted to do something here—something big, some kind of resistance operation—now's the time. The security's low, minimum surveillance, we can go anywhere we want. But *because* it's gotten so easy, no one's up for stuff like that anymore."

"Plus," Liz says, "no one trusts you."

"Not even you?"

Liz puts the oven mitts on the bench by her boots. They're interlocked—two lobster claws, holding hands. "I half trust you," she says.

The purple streak in her hair has grown out slightly, so there's an inch of black at the roots. The image he can't get out of his mind is of her shoulders when they were swimming, how he watched water collect in the hollow of her collarbone and then spill out. Some of the water that touched her naked body could have touched his. He feels guilty for thinking about her this way but also helpless. He's never had thoughts like this before.

William suddenly appears at the picnic table with some scraps of screening in a pile.

"I think you should look at this," he says to Loren.

"At what?"

William lifts some of the screens to reveal a folded piece of paper.

"The Colonel tried to burn this the other day," he says. "I don't know what it is, but he didn't want anyone else to see it. So maybe it's something."

William turns to leave, screen pieces in hand. When he's gone,

Loren unfolds the paper and says to Liz, "I guess one person here still trusts me."

"He feels sorry for you," Liz says. "That's not the same thing."

The paper is black around the edges. Loren sees a name, Edmund Killian. It's a bank statement. First Bank of the Caymans, current balance: $178,000. Loren has an immediate flashback.

"I know this name," he tells Liz. "I've seen it before, on a piece of paper tucked in Donovan's wallet. Plus two others just like it—I thought they were his partners."

He recites all three names for Liz, and she says those don't sound like partners.

"The names are similar," she says. "Suspiciously similar." Loren gives her a blank look. "Like aliases," she says.

"You think?"

"What are the odds you'd have three people like that, same first and last initial? And the second part—one of those is First Bank of the Caymans, we know that. The others are probably Belize Federal and Bank of Bermuda, or whatever the exact names are. Not the kind of places you send your savings account. People only stash money down there when they don't want it to be found."

At the horseshoes game, EK misses the post on three straight throws, each one landing farther away. He bends over and yells, "*Fuck!*" into the ground. Jeremy is watching Liz and Loren on the table and trying to edge close enough to hear. Loren doesn't hide the statement. It's a piece of paper—from where Jeremy's standing it could be anything, and trying to hide it now would look more suspicious.

"Why would Donovan stash those names away?" Loren says.

"Don't know," Liz says.

"And why wouldn't the Colonel just put money into his own bank account? Why does he need fake ones?"

"Another good question."

"You know who would know?" Loren says. "Someone in town."

"Who?"

"Maybe a reporter."

"Like there's a newspaper in this shit-hole town."

"Or a cop then," he says. "I could get out there and show this to the police, give them the other names and see what turns up. We already know he's not a Colonel. If nothing else, it's more evidence that there's something sketchy about this place."

"You can't just walk out, though," Liz says.

"Why not?"

"Twenty-one miles of woods. No map. No compass. If you stick to the road the Colonel finds you. Plus there's Jeremy and his whistle."

"All that's true," Loren says. "But maybe I can come up with something. Anyway, whatever happens has to go down soon. Donovan gets back in a day or so."

"Just try not to do anything stupid," Liz says. "You're getting a reputation for that."

"I won't," he says. "Trust me."

She smiles. "I'm not supposed to trust you. Remember? No one here does."

CHAPTER 14

William wishes there was one movie on the compound less than ten years old. The night after the horseshoes game, the Colonel puts all nine kids into the band room of the barn for another show, *The Music Man* this time, which as far as William's concerned is basically prehistoric. As the opening credits roll, the Colonel checks the back of the dusty box and says, "I'll be back in...151 minutes. Have fun."

Once the lights go down and the door closes, Loren comes over and sits next to Jeremy, practically on top of him. William is right behind them—he watches the whole thing unfold.

"It's dark in here," Loren says. "You need to know where I am, so we should stick close, right?"

He puts his arm around Jeremy's neck. Jeremy pushes Loren away and says quit it, but before letting go, Loren makes some kind of awkward gesture, a maneuver with one hand. William sees it but can't figure out what Loren's trying to do.

The movie is lame—people singing about trombones—and William's bored right away. It's old, from the early days of color movies, when they didn't have all the bugs worked out yet. Everything looks washed-out and painted back in. William can't help noticing that the movie's about a con man, though—just like the Colonel.

Before long Ty stretches out on the floor and starts snoring softly. RK and Becca disappear into one of the closets at the back of the room, where drums used to get stored. Even with the door closed, the rest of the kids can hear them whispering and laughing and rolling around. Meredith turns the volume up until the singing is loud enough to drown them out. EK sits outside the closet and looks at the door like a dog in the rain, waiting to be let inside.

Half an hour into the movie Loren gets up to go to the bathroom, and Jeremy stands to go with him. "I have to," Jeremy says. "Don't act all surprised. You know that."

William watches two silhouettes make their way past the TV screen. He thinks it's ridiculous that Jeremy has to track Loren so closely—at meals, during walks. Yesterday the kids played dodgeball, and when EK hurled the ball at his brother's face and missed, it rolled all the way down to the parking lot. Loren took off after it, but Jeremy went with him, watching from the top of the railroad-tie steps to make sure he came back right away. And today at snack time in the cafeteria (cumin-cheddar biscuits from Riap, papaya smoothies from Liz), Jeremy dropped his fork. When he reached under the table to pick it up, Loren disappeared. William was at the other end of the table. He saw Jeremy look around, saw him fumble inside his sweatshirt for the whistle, saw him stand up and start blowing it like the place was being robbed. The Colonel came running in from the kitchen, just as Loren stepped out from behind a beam.

"Just looking for napkins," he said, coming back to the table and grinning. "None back there."

Now, though, the two of them are gone a curiously long time. Several songs pass in the movie before Jeremy comes back, alone and breathless.

"Where is he?" he says, standing in front of the TV. William recognizes the nervousness in his eyes.

"Where's who?" Liz says.

"Loren."

"I thought you were supposed to be with him."

"I was, but now he's gone. I can't find him."

Meredith hits pause on the movie. The door to the storage closet slides open. Becca and RK stick their heads out.

"He was in the stall," Jeremy says. "I saw his boots under the door. I had to pee, so I used the stall next to his. The urinal's out— it's just a pipe hanging off the wall. After I was done he was still in there. I could see his boots. After like five minutes I asked if he was OK. No answer. I tried to push open the stall door but it was latched. Finally I crawled underneath, and he wasn't there. It was just his boots and a pair of sweatpants hooked under the toilet seat. He's gone."

"Damn," EK says. "The Colonel's going to have your ass on a plate."

"I can't tell him now even if I wanted to," Jeremy says. "We're locked in. I think Loren put something across the barn door from the outside."

"Why didn't you blow your whistle?" EK says.

"I lost it."

William looks on the floor where Jeremy and Loren were sitting. A tiny glimmer of light from the TV, reflecting off something metallic.

"You guys have to help me," Jeremy says. "What do we do now?"

Pause. There's no vote, no discussion. It's like each of the kids decides independently, but they all decide the same thing. RK and Becca go back in the closet and slowly pull the door closed. Meredith starts the movie again. And William reaches forward with his boot, as casually as he can, and covers up the whistle. It's on the floor, on the lanyard that used to be around Jeremy's neck but was sliced clean through.

*

According to the Code of Conduct, Loren doesn't have a choice. The Code lays it out. He knows because he wrote a paper on the Code back in sixth grade. Other kids wrote about ladybugs or cowboys, but Loren wrote about what the U.S. military tells its soldiers to do if they become prisoners of war. He couldn't read enough about it. The paper had to be two pages, but Loren turned in seven and felt like he left a lot out.

In the Korean War there was no Code, so U.S. POWs didn't know how to resist. They turned each other in and took favors from the guards. They gave up military secrets, sometimes after just a few slaps. When the war was over some of them decided to stay in North Korea instead of coming home. Because of all that, the military wrote up the Code of Conduct, a pledge in six parts, and made everyone in the service memorize it. *Article 1: I am an American, fighting in the forces which defend our country and its way of life. I am prepared to give my life in their defense.* It laid out what you were supposed to do, how you should resist, what stuff you could give up (name, rank, service number, date of birth), and what you couldn't (everything else). Because of the Code the POWs in Vietnam held up a lot better. Only a few became snitches, out of hundreds. Prisoners were ordered by the VC guards to sign papers saying they were war criminals, but most refused. And a lot of them followed Article 3, the one that directly applies to Loren's current situation. Article 3 says that escape attempts are mandatory.

Once he's out of the barn and away from Jeremy, Loren forces himself to slow down and follow through on the first steps of his plan. His instinct is to sprint for the woods, but he has almost two hours before the Colonel figures out he's missing. There's time.

First, clothes. Underneath the garbage shed he finds the extra pair of black sweats he stashed, along with a pair of old running shoes stolen from the front porch of the Colonel's house. The shoes are slightly big—his feet flop around inside them—and, worse, they're white. But he stuffs leaves into the toes and rubs dirt on them, getting them as dark as he can. The bank statement he got from William—the whole reason he's going on this mission—gets stuffed into a sock.

Also at the garbage shed, Loren retrieves his other supplies:

- two water bottles (completely full, so no sloshing noises)
- six leftover cumin-cheddar biscuits (snagged from the cafeteria)
- flashlight (with new batteries that Liz got from the cafeteria)
- three arrowheads (snapped off from the ancient, bone-dry arrows he found in the outdoor closet with the other sports equipment)

When he's ready to go he dumps it all into a pillowcase and moves toward the Jeep. On the far side first, away from the Colonel's house, he squats down and punches the sharpest of the three arrowheads into the front left tire. It makes a sound like a steam leak—he's sure it can be heard for miles—but he tells himself to stay with the plan. When the tire's flat he creeps forward and slashes open the rear tire on the same side, then does the remaining two. The Jeep sighs and settles like it's shifting in its sleep.

Next, Loren walks down the railroad-tie steps to the parking lot, all the way to the opposite corner, where the dirt road leads away from the compound. Semi-conspicuously, not in the road and not in the woods but somewhere in the middle, he drops one arrowhead, the one with the longest bit of bright red shaft remaining. Fifty feet farther along the road he drops half a biscuit. He wanted to leave a stronger symbol, like an ace of spades—the death card—but if he did that it would have ruined the only full deck of cards in the boys' cabin, and made future games of spades or euchre impossible. That afternoon he tried drawing an ace of spades on an index card, but it came out looking like a black, upside-down pumpkin, so he skipped it and figured the arrow and the biscuit would be enough. When he's done, he trots back across the broad expanse of cracked pavement and climbs the steps again.

The woods are darker than he would have guessed, and he almost can't follow the perimeter loop. Everything looks different at night. Loren stumbles a few times and realizes he needs the flashlight. He told himself he'd only use it once he was safely away from the compound—at night even a penlight is like a beacon, visible for miles—but he doesn't have a choice. One sprained ankle and the whole plan would be over. He cups his hand over the end, aiming the beam four feet ahead of him on the trail, and tries to move fast.

In seventeen minutes, according to his SEAL watch, he's at the spike trail, the one that leads out to the garbage pit, and in eight more minutes he's under the power lines, where the trees are cut away, and where he's able to turn off the flashlight again. The cleared strip under the wires is like a wide, moonlit avenue. He has no idea where the wires lead to, but he knows it has to be someplace with people. The Colonel told them no one could ever just walk out of here, because the woods were too deep, too impenetrable, and that's probably true—if you tried going through the woods.

But Loren has a better idea, and now that he's under the wires he knows he'll make it out. No map, no compass, and he'll be OK. He'll follow the poles, travel at night, sleep during the day. Putting the compound behind him feels so good that as he passes the first pole he almost yells. Almost.

*

"Kitty, get out of the car," the Colonel says. "We can talk about this."

"But you promised," Kitty says. "You said to get one family signed up. I did that."

Which is true—an application was faxed in under the name "Bill Jervin," and a deposit check was supposed to be forthcoming. The Colonel doesn't know how she did it—he's never seen her even look over at the reference phones when they ring, let alone answer one—but she must have talked to a couple of families at some point. And now, as part of the deal the Colonel and Kitty struck weeks ago, she has a spa day booked for tomorrow. Donovan returns mid-afternoon, and she timed her appointments so she could pick him up on the way back. The only problem is that Loren's gone, an inconvenient fact that changes everything. When the Colonel said he was taking the Jeep to go look for him, Kitty locked herself inside it instead.

"Open this door, Kit. I'm serious."

"I am too," she says. "I have appointments lined up all day. This place is hard to get into."

"We've got a situation here. Once I find that kid you can take the Jeep for a week if you want. But until then I need it."

"I need it more," she says.

"Right now? It's almost midnight. What are you going to do—drive there and sleep in the parking lot?"

"If I have to, yeah. The body poach starts at seven."

"At least let me get the tires fixed. I'll call a tow truck—someone'll come out in an hour or so. You can't drive there on four flats."

"I can try," Kitty says. "Either way I'm not getting out of this car. Call someone if you want, but they'll have to fix it with me inside."

He's half tempted to just let her go. But she'd probably get stuck somewhere out in the woods, and then he'd have two missing people and the Jeep would still be out of commission. His problems would be escalating.

"Why don't you call Donovan?" Kitty says.

"I did," the Colonel says. "I couldn't get through."

He's lying—the Colonel never called him. He doesn't want a lecture from Donovan about how he should have seen this coming, how this is what happens when you take it easy on the kids. Mostly, the Colonel just doesn't want to ask for help. It's his goal that this whole thing will be resolved by the time Donovan gets back, so he can wave away any questions about it. *Oh, that? That was nothing. I took care of it.*

"What about the sheriff?" Kitty says. "Can't you put out a miss-ing-person thing?"

The Colonel's already considered that idea too, and rejected it. He already has a subpoena, and Mrs. Diehl's lawyer has been calling around for a warrant. The Colonel doesn't want to let anyone in town know that things might be slipping at the compound. It's not an option.

"Kitty, look at me," he says. He steps back from the car door and lowers his voice. "I'm giving you an order right now. I forbid you from leaving."

Kitty rolls her eyes and starts the engine. When she shifts it into gear the Colonel runs around and stands in front of the headlights.

"Don't Kitty. Seriously, don't. Get out of the car."

She eases forward until the bumper touches his knee. The Colonel scrambles up onto the hood and grabs hold of a windshield wiper. His face is only a foot or so away from hers. She cranes her neck to see between his knees. Her expression is oddly calm.

"Are you trying to kill me?" he yells. "Is that what you want? Because—"

Kitty revs the engine and the Jeep lurches forward, bucking and swaying on its flats. The windshield wiper he's holding on to snaps free, and the Colonel rolls to the driveway. He turns to see the tail lights moving away, tracing sideways figure eights, infinity shapes, as the bunched-up rubber of the tires pushes the back of the car around.

Halfway across the parking lot one of the tires peels free. There's a grinding sound, and sparks kick up into the darkness. The Colonel doesn't think she'll get far, not on the dirt road. But she keeps the engine revved and hits the road with some speed and the taillights disappear into the trees. The Colonel waits for the Jeep to shut down, or the door to open—he waits to hear some scream of frus-tration coming from his begonia, his bowl of sugar. Instead the roar-ing of the engine fades slowly until he can't hear it anymore and the silence of the compound settles around him like fog. He still has the windshield wiper in his hand.

*

Loren wakes with the sun in his eyes and black ants crawling across his neck. He's sweating freely, his sweatshirt twisted around and pulled up to expose a triangle of stomach skin that's already burned pink. His watch says it's not even ten, and for a few seconds he wonders if that could be right. He slept less than four hours? The plan was to move at night and rest all day, but it's already so hot out that Loren knows he's not going to sleep anymore, even if he could find some decent shade. Even if the ants weren't all over him.

Last night Loren walked past ninety-four utility poles—that's how he measures the distance—before the sky began to lighten and he stopped to rest. For a campsite he cleared off the most level patch of ground he could find. No moss, and he knows because he looked hard. Moss is the pillow in every story about sleeping in the woods, but instead he had to use a dead log.

Loren never thought he'd consider the cabin at Camp Ascend! comfortable, but compared to where he is now it's a hotel. He's sore all over, and his mouth feels like a dried swamp. Breakfast is one biscuit with the ants brushed off it and two big swallows of water. Before setting out again he rubs some dirt on his face as camouflage and pisses against a tree, darkening the bark in rivulets.

Thirty-five poles in, he can't stop himself from eating the last of the biscuits. It was stupid of him not to realize he'd build up an appetite from all the walking. The survival manuals all say not to hoard your water or your food. Though those manuals also say to learn your berries, which ones are poisonous in a given region and which aren't, and Loren wishes he'd paid more attention to those chapters. There's some sentence he once memorized—All Princes Must Float on Tuesday—but he can't remember what the first letters stood for. (He's pretty sure that the *P* in Princes was for *palmate*.) Maybe as a mental diversion he can force himself to straighten out his memory on all this. In Vietnam the POWs would build entire houses in their mind—every nail, every detail. He should be able to get some berries straight.

He walks up hills and down hills. His feet slide around inside the Colonel's running shoes but he tells himself to ignore the blisters. There are four-wheel ATV marks from the maintenance workers who come out to fix the power lines, plus little piles of trash they leave behind, soda cans and plastic forks. Tired treads—that's what he's putting down, ha ha. He wonders what might be happening back at the compound, and gets distracted by the sight of a hawk swooping.

At pole sixty-six Loren sees his first sign of civilization, when the power lines cross a road. It's a curved section of two-lane blacktop with a double-yellow line in the middle, recently painted. He squats behind the guardrail and sorts his thoughts. The right ride, a sympathetic driver, might take him all the way to town. On the other hand, he left hints that he'd be traveling on the roads—that biscuit and the arrowhead—so if he changes plans now he'll only be outthinking himself. He's never hitchhiked before, but he can't imagine he'll get a lot of rides looking dirty and wearing black sweats. It's no decision, really. He has to stay with the wires.

Still, the smoothness of the pavement as he runs across it is tempting. For twenty paces his footsteps are quiet. No crunching vegetation, no burrs. As he climbs over the guardrail on the other side—curvy galvanized metal, bolts as big as D batteries—he thinks about how connected all roads are. If he had a skateboard he could push himself home from here. This road, no matter how remote, will lead to another, and another, and then maybe some highways, and if he found the right highway and the right exit, he could get all the way to his mom's apartment.

Another seventy poles pass by, moving slower and slower, and the excitement of this whole adventure fully wears off. The boredom is numbing, he's never wanted anything in his life as much as he wants to stop walking right now. But he presses ahead, singing to keep himself company. Finally, at pole one seventy-nine, he spots his first house.

The power lines don't cut through the property but pass along one side on a tangent, so Loren's almost past the clearing before he notices. An old, toothless mutt approaches from behind and barks at him with a rasp that sounds like smoker's cough. When Loren sees it he takes a step back, and the dog walks around in jittery half circles.

In the distance Loren can see a trailer on concrete blocks, with big square patches of bare tar paper in the siding. Nailed to one end is a sheet of blue plastic tarpaulin as a kind of porch roof, strung to poles ten or twelve feet high. In the shade under the tarp are about a dozen motorcycles, all in pieces. A few sit upright, propped with their kickstands set on a plank so their back wheels can clear the mud. Others lie on their side like sleeping animals, and a few are just frames. As far as Loren can tell there's no one around.

The dog barks twice more and sniffs the ground. Loren walks a few tentative feet toward the trailer, and the dog gimps ahead of him, gasping and huffing. They're in the dead leaves, and every step is a crunching explosion. Under the tarp is a red toolbox the size of a dresser. One of the motorcycles is suspended a few inches off the ground by a chain wrapped around a tree branch. Loren thinks the place is all set up for a lynching.

When he's a hundred feet away the side door of the trailer opens and a man steps out. Heavily tattooed and sunburned, wearing jeans and no shirt. He looks at Loren and Loren can't think of anything else to do but wave and shout, "Hi." The man disappears inside, and when he comes out again he has a rifle. He raises it, and Loren hears a popping noise. A branch behind his left shoulder snaps off. He stands frozen while the man draws a bead and the gun pops again—

another branch drops to the ground, this time on the right side. It sounds nothing like in the movies, more like an air gun, like a brown paper bag inflated and popped.

Loren turns and bolts. All his Special Forces knowledge leaves him, and his only thought is—*flee, run.* The dog comes back after him, newly aggressive, taking cues from the owner. Loren's pillow-case hits the ground but he keeps going, sprinting out to the power lines. He can hear the man yelling, "Molly you stupid bitch!" The gun pops again and again. Loren gets six poles out, seven, eight. Any second he expects to hear the roaring buzz of a dirt bike coming to mow him down. When he's half a mile out along the wires he stumbles into the woods, breathless, and collapses against a tree.

*

Donovan sits on a curb at the bus stop and complains to himself. It's not even a real bus stop, just a gas station where the bus drops off whoever's stupid enough to come to this shit-bucket town and picks up whoever's smart enough to leave. He got here more than two hours ago, and since then three buses have come in and pulled out again, and everyone who got off is long gone, while Donovan's stuck on the curb, waiting.

He tried phoning the compound twice already, collect calls both times, because he has no money left and whenever he asks someone for a quarter the crater-faced attendant comes out and tells him that waiting's fine, sitting's fine, but if he's going to beg he has to leave. Both times Donovan got the answering machine at Camp Ascend! and the operator told him she needed "permission from the recipient" before he could leave a message. He had nothing to do but wait, and count up all the stupid, fucked-up things around him.

Whenever a car pulls in and hits the air hose it dings brightly, and the crater-faced attendant trots out and Donovan thinks about how it would feel to maybe step on his throat. The gas pumps are so old they have spooling mechanical numbers inside, little metal dials that cycle around, instead of digital readouts. Sometimes if the cars are positioned the right way Donovan can watch the air above the nozzles move in genie shapes, from the fumes.

The air hose dings and a blue Jeep slows to a stop. Donovan stands, all geared up to start yelling at Kitty for being late, but the Jeep is the wrong shade of blue and too nice—no dents—so he sits back down again.

The vacation was a decent gesture, Donovan can admit that. After coming out to find a half-drowned Loren, with the rest of the kids trussed and lined up for their water torture, the Colonel gave Donovan a round-trip bus ticket and four nights in a motel at a lake town a few hours from the camp. A mandatory vacation, he called it. Kitty said the place was a dump—the Colonel had taken her there once—but better than being at the compound. The Colonel was pretty mad, she said, so if Donovan was smart he'd take the offer. "When you come back it'll be better," she told him. "Just go out there and relax a little. You'll see."

All good intentions, except the motel was scuzzy and the lake was ten feet lower than last year because of a drought, meaning Donovan had to wade out through a quarter mile of slimy rocks that smelled like dead vegetables before he got to water that was deep enough to squat in. There was an unfortunate lack of porn in the motel room (also a lack of cable or a remote control), so he slept a lot and watched staticky reruns he was too lazy to get up and switch. He had pizza delivered and stole sodas from the machine in the breezeway. He bought some pot off the maid, who looked to be Mexican or Hispanic-something, so he figured she'd have connections, except the stuff turned out to be so weak he might as well have smoked grass clippings. After three days he guessed he was relaxed. On the whole it was hard to say.

At the gas station, a car pulls up that Donovan doesn't recognize, a white rental. He doesn't budge. When the car pulls to the curb in front of him, Donovan looks away. He's not taking a ride from some weirdo stranger. The passenger door opens, and the Colonel's behind the wheel, gripping it tightly. He's looking forward, and his jaw is set.

Donovan stands up. "Where's the—?"

"Get in," the Colonel says. "Just shut up and get in."

*

Loren's food situation is starting to suck bad.

Around midday he stumbles across another house, this one empty, and scrapes blackened bits of old food from the grill he finds in the backyard. They taste like salt and charcoal, weightless specks with the gritty consistency of ground-up lava, and he can't tell what they used to be—hot dogs or ribs or whatever. He's now so hungry that he almost doesn't feel hungry anymore, which is less uncomfortable but not a good sign.

Water would be good too. His last drink was this morning, and his tongue is sticking to his teeth. He took the sweatshirt off and draped it over his head, with the sleeves hanging down across his shoulders, to give him some shade. If he thought there was any point in stopping to sleep he'd try, but the provisions are a bigger deal right now. He can rest later.

For another hour he sees no people and no buildings, until finally, at pole two seventeen, he reaches a third house. Loren's feet are so swollen at this point that the shoes almost fit. His legs are covered in burrs, and the sunburn on his face makes the skin feel stretched and tight. Before even checking out the house he makes up his mind that he's eating something here no matter what. If the owners are home he'll ask for food. If not he'll break in and steal it. He wants to go to the cops on his own terms (he has the Colonel's bank statement stuffed into his sock, with the other fake names and offshore banks he memorized written into the margins), but even if he gets arrested, the cops will at least have to feed him and hear his story.

The house is more like a cottage—one story, brown and squat, with crabgrass in the yard. A single power line swoops in and sags deeply, to eight or ten feet above the ground, before arcing back up and connecting near the roof. It makes the house look like it's on a leash.

From around the corner Loren hears voices, a man and a woman. He pulls his sweatshirt back on and tries to rub some of the dirt off his face so he won't look like a savage. A car door opens and closes, an engine starts. This could be lucky, he thinks—if he knows they're leaving he can break into the place quickly. But only one door opens, and the car doesn't seem to be going anywhere. Loren creeps up closer to look, staying behind the cottage. When he peers around it he sees something he almost can't believe.

A small man stands at the end of a long dirt driveway, wearing a banged-up blue football helmet with a skinny face mask and no chinstrap. At the other end of the driveway, forty yards away, a silver van idles with a woman behind the wheel.

"At least twenty-five," the man shouts to her. "Slower's no good. You want to really get on it early, and watch the gauge." He puts something whitish and translucent up to his lips—a mouthpiece. There's no football anywhere around. The man takes some deep breaths and shakes his hands out a few times, the way athletes do when they're warming up. He pulls the mouthpiece out again and yells to the van, "As soon as we hit, get on the brakes. I'll carry a little, but you don't want me going under." The woman in the van gives two quick taps on the horn and nods. Finally, the man turns sideways and gets into a half crouch. One more deep breath, and he waves an arm over his helmeted head. The van surges forward.

Loren thinks he might just be dizzy with hunger. Is he really watching this? He's twenty feet away, not even, close enough to read the lettering on the man's helmet ("Harnish Flooring &

Carpeting—We've Got You Covered"). The man is looking down at the ground, and Loren can see through the face mask that he's squeezing his eyes shut, bracing himself. The woman in the van looks grimly determined—her hands grip the wheel in a way that makes the knuckles turn white. The straight-line acceleration reminds Loren of TV ads that show technicians smashing a car into a wall.

When the van is close enough that it seems too late to stop, when Loren's sure he's about to watch the man get run down, the woman looks up suddenly and stomps on the brakes. All four tires lock, the back of the van floats out to one side, and dust boils up off the ground. By the time the van reaches the man it just barely taps him, with no more force than someone in a crowded room trying to brush past. He gets bumped and takes a slight hop to the right.

"What happened?" he says, looking up into the windshield.

The driver's side door pops open and the woman climbs down. She's tall and solid, bigger in every dimension than the man. She walks to the corner of the house in four giant strides and grabs Loren by the arm.

"Hey!" she says. "What're you snooping around here for?"

Loren tries to pull away but she squeezes his arm harder. His fingers give off nerve tingles.

"Are you with the insurance company?" she says.

"What insurance company?"

"Are you a burglar?" she says. "You're wearing burglar clothes."

"I was hiking," Loren tells her. He's suddenly glad he doesn't have the pillowcase anymore. She would have ripped his arm off.

The man lifts his helmet off and spits the mouthpiece delicately into one hand. He's small, with shoulders so narrow they're right angles. The two of them look like they just stepped out of a white trash nursery rhyme—Jack Sprat and his wife and their silver Ford Econoline.

"Hiking where?" the man says. He sounds more curious than anything.

"George, be quiet," the woman says. Then, to Loren, "Hiking where?"

"From town. Along the power lines."

"We've lived here nine years and never seen a hiker before."

"I got lost. That's why."

"Where's your pack?"

"I dropped it. A few miles back."

"I do stuff like that a lot," the man says.

"George, there you go talking again. What'd I just tell you?"

The woman squeezes more tightly—her fingers press all the way to Loren's arm bone. She towers over him with a face like dough, smooth and shiny. He's suddenly dizzy to the point of falling over. All the blood is draining out of his head.

"He doesn't look so good," the man says.

"Serves him right," his wife says. "Spying on us like that."

"He's no harm," George says. "We should help the boy out. Can't you see he's not right?"

"George, he's not one of your stray animals this time. He was sneaking around here like a thief. And now I suppose you'll punish him by feeding him dinner."

"Seems like he's been punished enough already."

The woman looks at Loren for a long time. "Not if I had my way," she says. But she lets go of his arm.

The inside of the house smells like fish sticks. George leads Loren into a living room, their footsteps echoing on the wooden floors. Loren sees a couch with flattened cushions, and a grandfather clock that doesn't work. A fan in a metal frame blows out of one window and sucks the faded drapes against it. Two sets of crutches lie on the floor, one wooden and one metal, but the woman notices Loren looking and slides them under the couch with her foot.

"Don't be a snoop," she says. "We weren't expecting company."

"Dell, he's no harm," George says.

Dell goes to the kitchen and sets out some stale bread and five slices of American cheese, which Loren inhales, plus a glass of cold water. They refill the glass three times and stare at him as he empties it in huge gulps.

"You'll get sick if you keep going like that," George says.

Loren nods but doesn't slow down. Just getting off his feet and sitting in a kitchen chair feels amazing. His dirty fingers make smudge prints in the cheese as he unpeels each slice.

"Where are you hiking to, did you say?" Dell asks.

She's six inches taller than her husband. They're both wearing the same kind of tan work boots, but her feet are bigger than his, by a lot.

Loren takes a bite to stall for time. The wide wooden floorboards in the kitchen are warped, especially under the windows. He wonders if George and Dell know about Camp Ascend!. They're fifteen miles from it, maybe less. When the silence becomes uncomfortable, he says, with a mouthful of food, "Just to the next town."

"Which is what?" Dell says. "What's that town called?"

"I'm a little lost, so I don't really know. That's why I started following the power lines."

"But you knew where you were going, right? When you set out? You got lost on your way to where?"

"Jamesville," Loren says, as directly as he can. James is his middle name.

Dell raises her eyebrows.

"Never heard of it," she says. "George, where's Jamesville?"

George looks at her and says, "Ummm."

"There's no Jamesville around here," Dell says. "We would know. We've lived in this house for nine years, and I've been in Carlyle County all my life."

"It's small," Loren says. "It's kind of a new town. Pretty new, anyway." *Just shut up*, he tells himself. *You can't lie and you know it.*

"How old are you?" Dell asks.

"Seventeen. Can I have some more cheese?"

"In a minute. You're small for seventeen. I would have guessed more like thirteen or fourteen."

Some of the kitchen floorboards are level, and others are bowed to where a marble would roll off. The silence in the room keeps getting louder. Loren can't think of any way to stall.

Finally he tells them he just turned fourteen. "A few months ago," he says.

Dell nods. "I knew it. You're a runaway, aren't you?"

George says, "Dell, stop grilling him. Sheesh."

"I just want to know," she says. "Someone comes snooping in my yard, dressed like death, sick from hunger, doesn't know where he's going—the whole thing's not right. Did you run away from somewhere?"

Loren knows that anything he can come up with now won't work. He should have thought up a story when he spent all that time walking. Instead he just nods.

"Huh," Dell says. "Course you did. OK, well, listen. We have to take you to the police. We can't just give you some food and send you on your way."

Loren keeps his reaction flat. He can show the police everything he has, the bank statement, the other names. Maybe he'd even get to call his mom. He doesn't want to get too excited because that might make them suspicious.

"I think I learned my lesson," he says, exaggeratedly humble. "I'm ready to go back home."

"At least finish eating first, and get yourself cleaned up," George says. To his wife, he adds, "Looks a little scruffy, doesn't he?" Loren looks at the water glass, where the dirt from his hands has mixed with the condensation and created tiny streaks of mud.

Dell sighs dramatically and says to give her a minute. She disappears into the bathroom, and Loren hears the medicine cabinet open and close. A minute later she comes back out with a bunch of stuff in her cupped hands—gleaming metal things, some half-squeezed white tubes. An orange pill bottle of prescription something clatters to the floor and she stoops to pick it up.

"Did you leave a towel out?" George asks.

"Yes, I left a towel out," she says, mimicking his voice.

To Loren, she says he should get in there and hurry up. "And don't make a mess."

The bathtub has metal claw feet that remind Loren of giant birds. Inside the tub are strange stains in the enamel and dark chips where it's worn away or gotten dinged. He locks the door from the inside and starts the shower, with water so hot that it gives off little wisps of steam. When he peels his sweats off, a black ant crawls from the pile, a stowaway that must have been with him since morning, which he decides to let live. When Dell grabbed him in the yard she squeezed hard enough to leave marks—four bracelet-shaped red rings around his upper arm.

The water's hot on his sunburned face, but he feels like he could stand under the stream for hours, soaking his bones. Serious water pressure, almost enough to hurt. This is what it's like to be in civilization again, he thinks. Back from battle. Loren watches the brown soapy water drain away near his feet. Everything about his existence is better than it was an hour ago, two days ago, a week ago. And it's going to keep getting better. He's not 100 percent free yet, but almost.

Back in the kitchen George has succeeded in making Loren a grilled cheese, which he seems proud of, and which makes the staleness of the bread not matter as much. As Loren starts eating, George apologizes for his wife.

"She's a little shy around strangers," he says.

"I heard that," she yells from the bedroom. Five giant strides and she's back in the kitchen, filling the door frame.

"Anything that comes into the yard he thinks is our friend," she tells Loren, like her husband's not standing right there. "Animals too—he'd invite wolves into the house if he could. He'd set out big jars of honey for the bears."

"We're in their territory," George says. "*We're* the intruders. I'm just being neighborly."

"Was that snake being neighborly when it plunked its fangs into your leg?" she says. To Loren, "The bite swelled up to a bowling ball. He almost died."

"Did I die, though? Am I not standing here right now?"

"If it came back tomorrow you'd probably try to feed it again, wouldn't you?"

"It's not coming back tomorrow, because you chopped it to pieces with the shovel."

"But if its brother came back. If its cousin came back."

"Snakes don't have cousins—sheesh."

Dell's about to say something else, but she sees Loren staring at them and catches herself.

"Maybe we should just get going to the police," Loren says quietly.

"Yup," she says. "Good idea. Finish up quick and we'll go talk to the sheriff. You don't have to hang around here until Christmas."

She stomps back to the bedroom and closes the door. In the silence after she's gone, George gets Loren some potato chips and fills his water glass again.

"Like I said—shy," George says.

Loren nods. "I guess it is a little weird that I just showed up out of nowhere," he says, and immediately regrets it. He wants to change the subject before George starts to wonder too much. Then he remembers the van. "You know before?" he says to George. "When I got here, in the yard? Was she really going to drive into you?"

"No no, nothing like that," George says. He looks at the floor and at Loren and then at the floor again, quickly.

"Because that's what it looked like," Loren says. "It looked like you wanted her to."

"OK, yeah," George says, nodding at the boots. "That was the plan. You weren't supposed to see—no one was. It's a thing we do sometimes to make a little money."

"How?"

"When I was good and banged up, we were going to head out to a supermarket parking lot we know, where they have a lot of fender benders and such. Basically an unsafe setup. So Dell'd go in, buy some milk, eggs, what have you, and come out to find me on the ground. Then we call the supermarket and tell them what happened, like it was a hit-and-run, and let them make us an offer."

"They'd pay you? Just for getting run over?"

"Lots of places do. Medical plus a little extra. Usually the stores want you to be quiet about it, so everyone and their aunt doesn't get the idea they're handing out hundred-dollar bills for sprained ankles. And you want to keep quiet too, so you can go to the place next door and start all over again."

"How many times have you done it?" Loren says. He's starting to wonder if there's an honest person anywhere in the county.

"I don't know—fifteen, maybe twenty."

"Ever get really hurt?"

"Oh yeah, lots of times," George says, and Loren hears a little pride in his voice. "A lot of back stuff. Backs are tricky, because of all the discs and little stray parts. I once broke my kneecap. And listen to this." He holds his elbow close to Loren's ear and moves his forearm back and forth. Loren hears a knuckly rubbing sound, a muffled flex of tendon. "Home Depot, twenty-four hundred dollars," George says. "I climbed up on a shopping cart and had Dell push me off."

"But why don't you just fake the injuries? That'd be easier, right?"

"Anyone can do that," George says. "That's cowardly. You have to play by the rules. If I don't get hurt, we run the whole thing over again until I do. Basically until I hear it."

"Hear what?"

"The thing inside, snapping or twisting or whatever. When you

hear it, then you know. Then you can get yourself looked at by doctors up the yin-yang, even the *company's* doctors, and they'll all say
the same thing—'He's really hurt, so write the check.'"

"So then why the helmet and mouthpiece?"

"Think about it—I don't want to get conked on the head. And
you only get one set of teeth. Those fancy fake ones are no good. I
like eating corn too much."

The bedroom door opens again.

Dell says, "George, what are you telling him all this stuff for?"

"I'm just...." George says. "He asked some questions."

"Great. That's good. He asked and you told him. You want to
give him our social numbers too?"

"Dell, he's just a kid. He's no harm."

"Just a kid that we're taking to the police station. And he's going
to say, 'These nice people brought me in. You won't believe the stuff
they told me.'"

"I wouldn't," Loren says. "I would never say anything like that."

"Sure, we can trust you. A runaway from who knows where."

George is about to say something else but she cuts him off.

"Let's just get going," she says. "I already made the phone calls.
Everything's all set."

Outside the sun is going down—the sky is blue at the top and
orange at the horizon. George's football helmet sits on the ground
in front of the van, and the driveway has four long skid marks in it,
ending at the tires. Dell gets into the driver's seat—George seems to
know to go straight to the other side, no discussion. He walks with
a slight limp that Loren just now notices. Loren sits on an upside-
down wheelbarrow behind the two front seats. Scattered around the
floor are a bunch of lawn tools—rakes and shovels, a weed-whack-
er in pieces. It's a cargo van, no windows in back.

The headlights of the van aren't straight—the one on the right
points in a little, and up—and Loren wonders if it got that way
because of a collision with some part of George's body. The sky is just

dark enough for the streetlamps to start coming on. Dell drives fast, hitting the turns without slowing down much, and Loren has to hold on to a tie ring in the back to keep from falling over. An iron rake slides around by his boots, rusty teeth pointing up, and Loren pushes it away, thinking about how much they would hurt to land on.

They pass a shopping center, and George cheerfully turns to Loren and points out that they did a slip-and-fall at the video store here last winter. "Nineteen hundred," he says. "Very easy money. It all went exactly like we planned."

"Keep talking, George," Dell says. "Why stop now?"

She turns into the parking lot and drives around to the service area in back. Loren looks out the windshield and sees a long, narrow strip of concrete, with a bunch of delivery ramps and some wide gray metal doors—service entrances. A few parked cars but no other people.

"I just want to drop something here," Dell says, turning the engine off.

From beneath her feet she pulls a plastic garbage bag that doesn't seem to have much in it. "George, help me outside for a minute," she says. They very conscientiously take the bag to a Dumpster and put it in.

Loren's alone inside the van. He reaches into his sock to make sure he still has the bank statement. It won't be long now. *I don't know what this is, but he didn't want anyone to see it, so maybe it's something.* He can't believe it's been less than twenty-four hours since he sneaked off the property at Camp Ascend!.

The sky is coal orange, the color of burned peaches, and the shadows are turning heavy. The white wall behind all the stores is apparently a big attraction for graffiti artists—he sees a big spray-painted penis with an arrow pointing to the end and the words *Suck Here.*

From the other end of the parking lot a plain white car approaches. Loren doesn't think too much about it, until he sees

Dell wave at the car. George gives a sad, half-helpless look back inside the van. It takes Loren a few seconds to put everything together, but suddenly he realizes.

He slides the side door open, but Dell is there to block him. She grabs his arm again in the same place as before. The nerve tingles come back immediately.

"Don't make a fuss," she says. "This is hard enough already. I already talked to the commander."

"He's not a commander! He's not even a colonel."

"Either way, you're going back to Bible camp."

"Bible camp?" Loren shouts. "There's no Bibles—he beats kids in there. We have to fix up his house. We get handcuffed."

"Stop lying," Dell says. "The commander went around to some people in town before the place opened and explained how it would work. And he gave out his number and said some kids didn't receive the spirit as well as others, and if any of them found their way out into town we should call him and he'd come to shepherd them back."

"That's what he said?"

"That's what he said. He definitely used the word *shepherd*. I knew where you came from as soon as I saw you."

Loren tries to wrestle free but can't. She has both his arms now, and her hands are like vises. The two of them stagger around ridiculously, a pair of robot dancers. He should have done something with the iron rake. It was right there at his feet.

Both doors of the white car fly open, and Donovan and the Colonel get out. Donovan carries a blanket and a roll of duct tape.

"Whoo! He's a fighter!" Dell yells. "You better come get him quick."

She twists Loren so his back is toward them. Footsteps rush up from behind, and the blanket gets thrown over his head. He hears duct tape peel from the roll. Dell holds his hands down at his sides by the wrists, and the tape is wrapped around him. Three, four, five, six times.

Ringing claustrophobia alerts. Loren can't see, he can't move—it's a primitive straitjacket. Someone grabs a bunch of blanket at the back of his neck and marches him away from the van. A car door opens, Loren's head gets shoved down, and he's torpedoed onto the floor of the backseat. When the door closes he starts kicking furiously—not to escape but more because of the feeling of being so tightly bound up. He can hear bits of plastic on the door breaking off. He kicks his way higher, until his heel shatters one of the back windows.

"What about the reward?" Dell is yelling. The blanket makes her voice sound farther away to Loren than it probably is. "You told us...."

"I'll send you a check," the Colonel says.

Two thunks as the car doors in front close. The muffler hump is hot against Loren's chest. The transmission shifts under him. There's a chirp of tires.

"You don't have our address," Dell says. "You don't even have my last name."

"I'll find it."

"Wait!" she yells. "You get back here."

The car accelerates in a veer, jamming Loren's head against one door, and he hears something hard—the iron rake—come down on the trunk behind him.

INTERMISSION

*In the Colonel's office, late at night, the green "RCV" light on the
fax machine blinks, and squeaking document-feed wheels roll to
life. The Colonel hasn't had time to check it lately, but when he
does he'll find some junk faxes, a few bank statements, and, arriving
now, another transcript from the disbarred lawyer. Same as last time—
the lawyer will first send through a single blank page with a handwrit-
ten note: "This one's definitely bad for your business. Make sure you
read all the way through. And you still owe me $8,700." And then the
transcript follows.*

SHOW: Straight from the Heart (10:00 p.m. ET) — KLS

July 7, 2005 Thursday

TYPE: Profile (Update)

LENGTH: 1,573 words

HEADLINE: Teens on the Edge, Part II: Following up.

ANNOUNCER: Now, from KLS Studios, Pauline Vero and Monty Ong

MONTY ONG: Good evening, I'm Monty Ong, and we're back with another edition of *Straight from the Heart*.

PAULINE VERO: Several months ago, we ran a segment on wilderness camps—remote places where troubled kids get sent for treatment. The thinking is that a change of setting, and some tough love, can turn these kids around. But in the months since, we've received a flood of letters and emails about how not all camps are the same. Viewers told us that some facilities are less than up front about the risks. Others, they said, are flat-out scams.

ONG: In particular, we were touched by one viewer who told us her son had been beaten at a camp and lost his hearing because of it. KLS News decided to investigate. Tonight, correspondent Bill Jervin reports.

(STRING MUSIC)

BILL JERVIN: (VOICE-OVER) For the rest of his life, Matthew Diehl will never hear the sound of laughter in his right ear. Or the latest rock-and-roll song. Or his mother telling him she loves him.

MIRIAM DIEHL: Honey, can you pass the syrup? (Pause) Never mind. I'll get it.

JERVIN: At thirteen, Matthew was like a lot of teenagers. Mixed-up. Emotional. He admits that he got into trouble at school, and experimented with drugs. Then his mom sent him to a place called Camp Ascend!.

MRS. DIEHL: I thought it would be good for him. Instead they made him do chores like cleaning the bathrooms. If I knew that's all it was, I could've saved the money and made him clean up the bathrooms here. And when he didn't do what they wanted, they hit him.

MATTHEW DIEHL: This one guard had a temper. He'd just snap and start whaling on you, WWF-style. One time it was because I didn't want to scrape linoleum off the floor. It would have taken me like a year. The pieces were so small.

JERVIN: Can you describe the place?

DIEHL: Total dump. It was an old music camp, and everything was breaking all the time. The Colonel wanted us to fix up his house for him, except none of us knew how to do that stuff, and he always gave us the wrong tools. We had to put in a deck, but the planks came out crooked and popped up if you stepped on them wrong. When the guard saw it, he handcuffed us to a bike rack in the sun for four hours.

JERVIN: (VO) The Colonel who runs Camp Ascend! is E. Raymond Kellogg, who we found out isn't really a colonel at all. He's never served in the military, and he has a rap sheet with multiple felonies on it, including thirteen for fraud. Chester LoBianco is the sheriff of Carlyle County, where Camp Ascend! is located.

SHERIFF LOBIANCO: What we know as of this point in time is that he's got some kids in there, which their own parents handed over to him. Lawfully. And he has paperwork—contracts, things of that nature—signed by those parents. All of which makes it hard for us to just go in with guns blazing. Much as we might want to.

JERVIN: (VO) However, an attorney retained by Mrs. Diehl has already taken legal action on behalf of the family. Last week the attorney, Robert Wollinger, filed two subpoenas against the camp, asking for documents related to safety and medical procedures.

ROBERT WOLLINGER: Well, that depends on what you mean by "responded." The Colonel has, yes, in fact, turned over some documents that purport to show the camp's on the up-and-up. But we think they're forgeries.

JERVIN: How can you tell?

WOLLINGER: A lot of them were written around the same time, with the same pen. We brought in a handwriting expert who said Mr. Kellogg most likely did some with his left hand and some with his right. Basic gimmickry of that caliber. This is a person who couldn't forge a sick note from school, and now he wants us to believe these are sophisticated medical records? All the kids had poison ivy—every one.

JERVIN: Again, Sheriff LoBianco.

LOBIANCO: He moved in, let's see—a year ago February. So yeah, about eighteen months.

JERVIN: And you've been tracking him the whole time?

LOBIANCO: (Pause) We're aware of his presence in the community and we've been monitoring that presence, yes, sir.

JERVIN: What does that mean, exactly?

LOBIANCO: (Longer pause) (sighs) Early on we thought it was

Bible camp. That's what he told us.

JERVIN: And you believed him.

LOBIANCO: Yes, sir, we did. He can be persuasive; he could sell oil to the Arabs if he wanted, and plus, on top of which, we had no factual basis not to believe him.

JERVIN: But you don't believe him anymore?

LOBIANCO: No, sir, we don't. That's a correct statement at this point in time.

JERVIN: (VO) I wasn't through investigating. We wanted to speak to the Colonel about all this, but he never answered our calls. So I changed strategies. What if I were a potential customer, the father of a troubled child, looking to enroll him in the camp? Not surprisingly, using this approach I got someone on the phone.

(SHOT OF MICROCASSETTE RECORDER. TAPE ADVANCING.)

WOMAN'S VOICE: Hang on a sec. I dropped the page.

JERVIN: What page?

WOMAN: Just this thing my husband wrote up. Things he wants me to emphasize to people who call in.

JERVIN: (VO) This is Katerina French-Kellogg, also known as Kitty. She and Raymond Kellogg have been married since 1986.

FRENCH-KELLOGG: OK, um, here we go: "165 pristine acres of

secluded wilderness. State-of-the-art facilities. Highly trained, caring staff with decades of experience."

JERVIN: What's that squishing noise?

FRENCH-KELLOGG: I have gloves on, for the healing moisture. It works but it's a hassle—the oil gets everywhere.

JERVIN: Huh.

FRENCH-KELLOGG: There's other stuff on here. Like about food, it says: "Five-star, Asian-influenced cuisine. Locally grown ingredients. Dietary restrictions accommodated."

JERVIN: Asian-influenced—what does that mean?

FRENCH-KELLOGG: Does your kid like Chinese? It's basically that, plus coconut.

JERVIN: Well, listen, about my son, does it say anything on that sheet about kids with special needs? Because he's got some emotional issues, and he's hard to handle.

FRENCH-KELLOGG: No problem.

JERVIN: Really? There isn't any type of troubled kid you wouldn't accept?

FRENCH-KELLOGG: My husband decides all that, and I think he mostly goes by the financials. Sometimes a check bounces, or the parents start asking about reduced rates, and then the answer's usually no. He says those aren't the kind of people we want.

JERVIN: But money aside, what if a child had been diagnosed with, say, epilepsy? Or a genetic disorder?

FRENCH-KELLOGG: We don't want every freak under the sun, but sure—bring them on up. We get our share of weirdos. They'd fit right in.

JERVIN: Are you familiar with a boy named Matthew Diehl?

FRENCH-KELLOGG: Who?

JERVIN: He was up at the camp a few months ago and says he lost his hearing because of an incident involving one of the guards.

FRENCH-KELLOGG: Well, I don't know about that, but I do know that kids lie, a lot. You should hear some of the stuff they come up with.

JERVIN: What about training? Do you have any kind of formal education to handle kids like this?

FRENCH-KELLOGG: Everyone here's self-taught. My husband's right, though—you don't need an expert to tell you what's basically common sense. Keep the kids tired, make them work, get them to shut their mouths and show a little respect sometimes. And it works, it really does. We see miracles around here every day.

JERVIN: I'll bet you do. So if a parent really wanted to do this, if I wanted to sign my son up, how would it work? What's the next step?

FRENCH-KELLOGG: For real? I mean, I don't have a good track record with this. I usually don't even answer the phone. But my husband's been up my butt to sign some families.

JERVIN: Up your…

FRENCH-KELLOGG: He said he'd send me to a spa if I got one family to commit.

JERVIN: This is how you bring in new people?

FRENCH-KELLOGG: Not all the time, just lately. We've been slow.

JERVIN: (SHOT OF HIM HOLDING UP AN INVOICE) Monty, we actually did fill out an application and faxed it in, just to see what would happen. About a week later, we got a bill. Seventeen thousand dollars, payable in cash or certified check only. Reporting from Carlyle County, I'm Bill Jervin.

MONTY ONG: Wow, scary stuff. Thanks, Bill.

PAULINE VERO: We'll be right back with more of *Straight from the Heart.*

PART III

CHAPTER 15

"On my command," Donovan says. "Forward march. Ready? *Go.*"

William sets out across the parking lot, with EK on one side and Becca on the other. It's a hundred yards of cracked pavement, Sahara-hot, and they're carrying rusty pipes on their shoulders, which Donovan makes them pretend are rifles. The pipes are six feet long, with hunks of plaster stuck to them and jagged, hacksawed ends. William keeps rotating his, trying to find a position where it won't dig into his collarbone, but so far no luck.

"Get in step," Donovan says. "Left...left...left, right, left."

The morning sun climbs behind them, and the three kids step on their own shadows as they march across the lot. Becca shuffles her feet—her legs are shorter, so she has to take faster strides.

"Switch sides," Donovan says. "Left shoulder...ARMS!"

The kids transfer their pipes over, not quite in sync.

"Now back again. Right shoulder...ARMS!"

EK drops his and it clanks to the pavement. This is the second time he's dropped it—his pipe has an elbow joint screwed to one end, and the excuse he keeps using is that it's out of balance.

"On the ground for a hundred," Donovan says. "All three of you.

You know the deal. If you drop your piece, you have to earn it back."

"But I don't want it back," EK says.

"Yes you do. This is your rifle, your best friend in combat. You're never separated from your rifle, because if that happens and you're in a firefight, what are you going to do, throw spitballs at the enemy?"

"There is no enemy," EK says. "These are pipes."

"There's always an enemy. Now shut your mouth or it's another hundred. Get going."

William's never heard anyone sigh as long or as hard as Becca does now. The three kids look at each other and start their squat thrusts. William's hands are swollen and sore, and when he puts them on the pavement they sting.

"One," Donovan says. "Two...pick up the pace."

William can't help but realize that things just get worse at Camp Ascend!. Sometimes suddenly, sometimes gradually, but they always go downhill. As much as he hates each individual activity and counts the seconds until it's over, the next one is usually worse, or bad in some different way, and he finds himself wishing he could go back to whatever he was doing and hating a little while ago.

After the Colonel found out Loren had escaped, the kids were left in the band room for almost twenty-four hours. He double-checked the locks and yelled through the door for them to stay put. All that night and all the next day, the kids switched back and forth between stress and boredom. They slept a little, woke up, slept some more. The twins put on movies (*The Red Violin*, *Stomp*) but kept the sound turned down. Riap brought the kids food every few hours and took them to the bathroom, one at a time, but he never had any news. William asked and asked, and Riap just shrugged. He didn't know anything, there was nothing he could do.

Around dawn a tow truck showed up in the parking lot, pulling the Jeep behind it on four flat tires. Through the window, they watched the driver change them and then drive off. They yelled but he didn't hear them. Twelve hours later, just past sunset, they heard another engine straining as it raced across the lot. It was the Colonel and Donovan, in a plain white car with a running shoe flailing around in the back window.

The kids were taken out of the band room and led back to their cabins with orders from Donovan to keep their mouths shut—no questions, no talking. That was last night, and in the morning Donovan and the Colonel divided the kids into two groups for close order drill in the parking lot. No more sleeping in, no more horse-shoes. They've seen their last movie.

"...ninety-eight, ninety-nine, OK," Donovan says. "Now on your feet and grab your piece. Next we're going to assault that tree line. Ready? On my command. *Go.*"

The kids give him confused looks and try to catch their breath.

"What does that mean?" Becca gasps. Her face is crimson.

"It means sprint to the far edge of the lot, take up a defensive position, and lay down covering fire," Donovan says. "Let's go—get running. You're under attack. Mortars coming in."

He starts jogging. The kids stay in place and watch him leave. William wipes a significant amount of snot off his face and flicks it onto the pavement. When Donovan sees they're not following, he comes back and yells that if they don't start running, right now, he'll make them dig ditches.

"I'm giving you an order," he says.

The kids grudgingly trot over and lie on the ground and point their pipes at the trees. It's even more pointless than William imag-ined. Donovan tells them to make gun noises, and William coughs through his. The bathrooms up at the compound give off a warm, sewerish smell that floats down and seems to concentrate around them.

"OK, good," Donovan says. "Next, get up and keep marching. Five clicks. Let's go."

"What's a click?" Becca says.

"A kilometer, but for now we'll do laps around the parking lot."

The kids set off, and William is suddenly ferociously thirsty. Being on the hot pavement makes him feel reptilian and baked, and his nose is completely stuffed—Donovan re-confiscated his Zyrtec—so he has to breathe through his mouth, which only makes him thirstier. It's possible he might have hit some point of critical water deprivation, because he feels a dizzy spell coming on. But he doesn't complain. There's no point.

"Stop stop stop," Donovan says. Becca's out of step again. "Jesus fuck. Can't you get this straight? You only have two feet—it's not a lot to keep track of. Start out on your left."

"I'm tired," Becca says. "Can't we have some water?"

"Yeah," William says. "I think I need—"

"Not yet. Soon. You'll get water once you stay in step all the way around the lot. Forward march again. Ready? *Go.*"

Becca starts to say something else, but she's cut off by the sound of EK's pipe hitting the pavement again. This time it's intentional.

"No more," EK says. "I'm done."

"I'll tell you when you're done," Donovan says. "Get back in ranks."

"There's three of us and one of you," EK says. "What if we all just say no?"

"Wheezy here barely counts," Donovan says, gesturing at William, "and Becca's a girl. So really it's just me and you, and I'm telling you to pick up that piece."

"What if I don't? You're gonna punch me? Huh? What?"

"Pick it up."

"No."

Donovan pulls something out of his pocket, scuba-tank yellow, square and stubby, about the size of a pack of cigarettes.

He faces EK and says it again. "Pick it up. I'm ordering you."

"Suck balls," EK says. "I'm done."

Donovan walks over and holds the device up to EK's neck. It lets off a crackling noise, a loud humming buzz, and EK drops to the ground like he's been shot.

Becca screams. Donovan points the yellow stun gun in the direction of the other two.

"Is he dead?" Becca asks.

William crouches down and checks EK, half-afraid to touch him. EK moans and writhes, kicking at the pavement. His neck has two purplish-black marks, from where the terminals touched.

"Make him get up," Donovan says.

"Just give him a minute," William says. His nose is so stuffed up that the words come out funny. *Gib hib a bi-dit.*

EK slowly rolls to his hands and knees, blinking hard. William says he'll carry EK's pipe for a while, until he feels better. The allergies are really rolling now. William's throat is squeezing shut, he feels like he's breathing through a snorkel packed with gravel, and he's thirsty enough to lick the sweat off his arms. Things get worse. You can't stop the decline.

"Line back up," Donovan says. "On the edge for one more lap. If you stay in step the whole way, then maybe you'll get your water. Maybe."

*

Liz stands outside the fence and watches for a moment before going in. If she wants to get any information, she'll need to be strategic. At the other end of the pool, Kitty's on the chaise in a white bikini, with her face covered by a cracked gray mud pack. At first Liz thinks she might be sewing—Kitty's hunched over a pile of clothes. But the pool has cut-up scraps all over the surface, and submerged in the shallow end is something that looks like seaweed, which Liz finally realizes is a pair of shredded green camouflage pants. Kitty's not sewing—she's cutting up the Colonel's uniforms.

A deep breath, and Liz pushes the gate open.

"Donovan told me to bring you this," she says.

"What is it?" Kitty says, talking around her cigarette, not looking up. She has a long pair of scissors and snips intently at a blue jacket.

"BLT."

"I don't want it. Take it back inside."

"I'll just put it down here," Liz says. "You can have some later."

Kitty shrugs and says nothing, weirdly calm and purposeful. She finishes with the blue jacket—it's reduced to shreds, each no bigger than a cocktail napkin, which she sweeps off her lap and into the pool. On the table next to her is a Big Gulp cup, half-full of ice cubes and white wine, with mud marks around the rim. She doesn't seem drunk, Liz thinks, but maybe she is and just doesn't show it. Her hands are covered with tiny pink snips, from where she's gotten careless with the scissors.

Liz decides to play her bluff.

"Oh yeah," she says, like she just remembered it. "Donovan told me to take some food to Loren too, but I'm not sure how to find him. Any idea where he is?"

Kitty looks down into the pile of uniforms, stained and faded but more or less intact. Some ash from her cigarette floats down onto her leg.

"That's a lie right there," she says, almost distractedly. "That's what that is. A big old lie."

Liz feels her neck get hot.

"It didn't make sense at first, but now I get it," Kitty says. "Donovan didn't really tell you to bring that out to me, did he?"

"Yeah he did," Liz says. "He definitely did." It sounds unconvincing, even to her.

"You're just like my husband. Lying his lies, all day long. I don't even like BLTs."

Liz thinks Kitty's going to turn on her, or yell for the Colonel, but instead she reaches for the wine and takes a giant swallow. The mud on her face is dry and cracked on the surface, but underneath it's mixed with sweat, running down her neck in slow trickles. She sets down the cup and takes a khaki shirt from the pile and starts burning cigarette holes through it.

"Do you know how to hot-wire a car?" Kitty says. "One of you kids must. Isn't that what you're all here for—stuff like that?"

"The Jeep, you mean?"

"My husband's hiding the keys from me."

"I can ask around," Liz says. "Someone might know." She pauses. "You know who definitely might? Loren. We should go ask him. I can ask him right now."

"Another lie," Kitty says. She flicks her cigarette into the pool, where it lands with a tiny, clipped hiss, and faces Liz directly for the first time. "Here's some advice. For free. If you're going to lie, get good at it. Treat it like a musical instrument, and practice. Because if you only do it once in a while, like now, it's never going to work. You'll just look pathetic."

"It's just...." Liz starts to say. "OK, look. You hate this place and I hate this place. So maybe we can do something for each other. With Loren, it's weird. I don't know where he's being kept, or what's happening to him, or whether he's getting any food. Just nothing, no one knows anything. And we're all supposed to act normal and not ask. But if you help me out with that—I don't even need to see him, I just want to know how he is—maybe I can do something for you. Like, talk to the twins about hot-wiring the car."

"They know how?"

Liz looks down. "Not sure. But with them, I'd almost be surprised if they *didn't* know."

Kitty seems to think about it for a moment before reaching into the pile for another garment—a pair of dress pants, blue with a red stripe down the side.

"Do you know where he got all these?" she asks.

"Who?"

"My husband."

Liz can't believe Kitty's going to ignore the offer. The warm feeling from her neck spreads up to her ears, her temples. This is when she gets into trouble sometimes, when she's mad and options are sliding away from her.

"On eBay," Kitty says. "Some ex-marine was bankrupt and had to sell all his stuff. Three hundred bucks for the set, including the sword."

"Do you know where Loren is?"

"Yeah," Kitty says, "but I'm not telling you. So if all your whole plan here is to weasel information out of me, you may as well go back to the kitchen."

Liz should walk away, she knows it, but instead she stands her ground.

"You don't know where he is," she says, a sudden edge in her voice. "You don't know anything around here. I probably should have been smart enough not to ask you, but that's how desperate I am."

Kitty looks up from the dress pants. She has the red stripe peeled off one leg already.

"You want me to stop lying?" Liz says. "You want the truth? Here's some truth. Cut up every single one of the Colonel's uniforms if it makes you feel better, but that won't change what happens around here. Which is this: we're leaving soon, and you're staying. We got duped by him, or our parents did, but that doesn't matter. It was a onetime thing and it's almost over, and after that we're leaving."

"No," Kitty starts to say. "We can keep you. We can extend your—"

"No you can't. That's a lie too. You're not much better at lying than I am. No kid has ever spent more than six weeks here, am I right? That's just another threat to hang over us."

Kitty says nothing, and Liz knows she's right.

"Of all the people who got taken in by the Colonel," Liz says, "you're the biggest sucker of all. You know what he's about and still you stick around. He fooled us once, but he's been fooling you your whole life. So between you and me, which one is really pathetic, do you think?"

Kitty's eyes flash under her mud mask. "I'm calling my husband," she says.

"Great. Call him. He'll probably tell you some more lies."

Liz turns to leave, and as she gets to the gate, the plastic cup of wine flies past and hits the ground in front of her feet. She doesn't turn around, doesn't even stop. Her hands are shaking with anger, but she feels better—just a little.

*

Loren realizes pretty quickly that he won't be able to resist in his current state. He's rolled up in a rug that's been duct-taped tightly, like a giant enchilada. His arms are pinned to his sides and he's face-down, unable to turn over or even move his head. The room he's in is quieter and darker than he thought any place could ever be—absolute muffled silence, no echoes. He keeps waiting for his eyes to adjust to the light, squeezing them shut and then blinking them open suddenly, but there's no light in the room to adjust to. He's in solitary confinement, and it's dark as a mine at midnight.

If he had to bet he'd say he's somewhere in the barn. When Donovan brought him in, Loren had a blanket over his head, but he tried to count steps and listen to the opening and closing of doors. He spent his first half hour in the room yelling at Donovan, calling him a motherfucker, saying that he, Loren, would personally make Donovan pay for this. Next he started yelling *for* Donovan, saying OK, he shouldn't have escaped, that was wrong, but cut the duct tape and they could talk about it. Please cut the tape...please? Finally Loren realized that Donovan wasn't even in the room anymore. He'd shouted himself hoarse for nothing.

The claustrophobia alarms in his head started ringing, sirens wailing, and he strained against the tape until he felt something in his shoulder start to pull loose. There was so much dust in the carpet that when he started crying it got into his mouth and eyes and stuck to his wet cheeks. The whole setup felt disturbingly familiar, but he couldn't figure out why. He'd definitely never been here before. It must have been some weird déjà vu. So he focused all his energy on spitting the hairs out of his mouth and trying not to go batshit.

For most of the first night—though it's hard to guess exactly how long, time goes elastic on him, it stretches out like taffy—Loren cries himself to sleep and has awful dreams and wakes up crying again. The cycle happens over and over, with the most intense, vivid images. Sometimes he can't tell whether he's asleep or awake. Probably it's because the room is so black and empty—he has nothing to look at, so his mind plays movies for him. His shoulder hurts and he thinks about a kid in his neighborhood who could pop his shoulder in and out of its socket. When it was out the arm looked rubbery and three inches longer. The kid said it didn't even hurt. In one of Loren's dreams, the kid's arm spools out like toilet paper off a roll, getting longer and longer, piling up in front of him. *It doesn't even hurt*, the kid says. *I swear, it feels like nothing.*

Or Loren dreams of people hanging from trees, like parachutists with their cords snagged in the high branches. He sees Liz's face, and the twins—and then the tree falls over and all the kids float free, balloons cut loose, while Loren's trapped under the trunk. He can feel the cold dirt on his cheek, and smell the hamster-cage scent of newly split wood. The tree becomes a truck, parked on his shoulder blades, with rocks getting piled into the back. The weight comes down onto him, heavier by the ton. Then the truck becomes a tank, and the metal treads mesh with the notches in his backbone.

When he's awake, it takes all of Loren's concentration not to struggle. He tries lamely to fix the small discomforts, spitting and spitting to get the hair out of his mouth, succeeding only in making a damp patch of drool under his face. A creeping numbness spreads through his body—he stretches his muscles as much as he can, but that's not much. The need to piss is growing but not urgent, not yet, and he figures someone has to come back at some point to feed him and cut the tape and make sure he's alive. Right? Doesn't someone have to check on him?

Another dredged-up image floats free in his memory, of mowing his grandfather's lawn. Loren and his mom went to see the grandfather on a summer weekend a few years ago. The lawn was way overgrown, with weeds that came up to Loren's knees. They drank warm lemonade from tall glasses with no ice, and sat on iron chairs that hurt Loren's back. Finally the grandfather said, well, let's get rolling here.

The mower was in the garage, which had a shiny concrete floor and smelled like gasoline and rubber. Loren pushed the roaring machine around the yard for half an hour before it happened—he heard a *THWOK*, and two halves of a turtle shot out in the stream of cut grass. The turtle halves were leathery green and aged-looking, except for the perfect red and white cross section where the blade had gone through. All four legs were still moving, separate but synchronized. Loren threw up his lemonade in the grass because of it.

And then he realizes: he's been here before. Not here exactly, but someplace like this—he knows this feeling. Trapped in a small space, with dust and carpet hair sticking to his wet cheeks. This is why he remembers. He always thought POWs had to try hard to dig things like this up, but it turns out that's only for the good stuff. The bad just creeps back on you....

Loren is crawling under his mom's bed. This isn't a dream—this really happened, same as the turtle. He's four or five, and his mom has asked him not to spy on her. She's told him again and again that it spooks her when he sneaks around, when he goes through her drawers and finds things she doesn't want him to know about. He nods each time and keeps doing it. Right now he's going to hide under her bed, so when she comes home from work he can jump out and surprise her. Usually when she can't get a babysitter she brings him to the restaurant, but tonight she couldn't. Her boss was being mean, she said—one more time and she'd lose her job. She didn't want to leave him alone but there was no other way.

He's never been down here before. It's his biggest spy move ever, but part of him wishes he was back in his own room. The space is dark and dirty—he finds big clumps of dust and old magazines and a broken slat from the box spring. One leg of his mom's bed frame is missing, and that corner is propped up by a stack of books.

Loren's scared but he makes himself keep going. He's not a baby. She's supposed to be back soon—he won't have to stay down there long. But when he's almost all the way underneath he accidentally kicks the books. The frame collapses, with the full weight of the box spring and mattress pressing down onto his tiny back. He's face-down on the carpet, head squeezed, arms pinned. Loren starts crying right away and the dust sticks to his wet cheeks. This is why he remembers. This is why he's always been claustrophobic. The weight, the carpet, the soft trapped feeling.

He tries to scream and whatever breath he has left gets squeezed out. He can't kick, can't move. Now he really has nothing. A million miles away the apartment door opens—his mom's home—but he can't make enough noise for her to hear.

In a few minutes, after she figures out where he is and lifts the bed, she'll cry like Loren's never seen her cry before. On the drive to the hospital she'll come up with a story for him to tell the doctor. It's important, she says, or else bad things will come. They'll be split up, he'll be taken away from her. Loren will do all this, follow her instructions and get his story straight and tell the doctors exactly what she says. For weeks afterward he'll have problems putting an arm into his sleeve, even just breathing will hurt, but right now none of that's happened yet.

Right now he's trying to call for her, but he can't. He can't even cry. She's in the apartment, looking for him, going through the rooms one by one, and his last thought before blacking out is that he's never going to see her again.

CHAPTER 16

"What you do is you wire the money," the Colonel says. "That's fastest. Once it lands in my account —the bank's a little south of here, I'll give you all the info—I can reserve a spot for your son. But definitely wire it, the full amount, because that next class is filling up fast."

"OK, sir," the man says. "Makes sense. But before we talk money I had a couple of questions for you. Real quick."

"Shoot."

"OK, sir—"

"You don't have to call me 'sir,'" the Colonel says.

"I think I do, sir. I was in the corps too, back in the eighties. Third Battalion, first Marines. I didn't make it to colonel or anything like you—I stopped at sergeant. But that's why I call you 'sir,' sir. You earned it. Where'd you serve?"

"Can you hang on a second?" the Colonel says. "I think I'm getting another call."

He makes a clicking noise and puts his hand over the mouthpiece to stall. At one point the Colonel really did know a bunch of Marine Corps bases, at least enough to fake his way through a conversation. Somewhere in the house is a piece of paper with a tree diagram of the whole structure. Seven battalions, six regiments each, or something like that. But he can't remember much of it now. With everything happening at the compound lately he can barely remember his own name.

On the couch a few feet away, Kitty stares at the QVC channel and drools. She's in her white bikini, with the kimono over it and some leftover mud on her face. They've been fighting nonstop for two days—she was mad because she missed her spa day, and though the Colonel initially planned to make it up to her, that changed once he read the second transcript in the fax machine and realized that the family she'd "signed up" wasn't a family at all. It was a TV reporter named Bill Jervin, who made Kitty (and the Colonel) look worse than criminal—he made them look incompetent.

The Colonel waved the faxed pages in her face this morning and said no spa day, ever, at which point she took an armload of his uniforms to the pool and started cutting them to pieces. All morning he watched her through the kitchen window and swore to himself that he wasn't going to react. He wasn't going to let her push his buttons. This time he would be smarter.

So when Kitty came back to the house on a rampage a little while ago, the Colonel was ready.

"I am leaving this fucking place *right now!*" Kitty yelled. "You can't believe what one of those girls just said to me—the mouth on her. If you don't give me the Jeep keys I swear to Christ I'll go up to that safe and set fire to every dollar in it."

The Colonel just smiled and said sure. She could leave. He even set the car keys out on the counter.

"I'll give you these," he said. "You win, OK? I'll help you pack too, if you want. But before you rush out of here, just take it easy for a minute. You're overheating. Drink some of this."

It was an iced tea, with a bit of lemon and some phenobarbital stirred in (which he'd confiscated from Ty a week or so ago). Two pills, 400 mg total, and so far that seems like the right dose, more or less. For the past hour Kitty has been goggle-eyed on the couch, with a bowl of potato chips in her lap and the TV reflecting off her shiny face. She didn't look great, but it was better than her having a melt-down and torching the Colonel's cash. More than anything else, he needed her calm right now so he could figure out his next step. If that required a little amateur pharmacology, he was OK with it.

The Colonel takes his hand off the phone and makes another clicking noise.

"Sorry about that," he says. "Crazy day. Now, where were we? Oh right—the payment. If you wire it, that works best. No writing a check, no messing with a stamp."

"Yes, sir, you mentioned that."

"So anything else? You've got the brochure, right? You've been to the website?"

"We were talking about the corps. Where you served, and when."

"Oh, a long time ago," the Colonel says. "Feels like a former life, practically. It's funny, though—I think about those days a lot. The PT. The guns. All those…uniforms."

He looks out to the pool and sees a few scraps of his khakis floating in the deep end. They'll clog the filter soon. That'll be the next crisis.

Noticeable silence on the other end of the line.

"What was your MOS?" the man says.

"High nineties," the Colonel says. "I always did well on those." He has no idea what an MOS is.

More silence. "That's Military Occupational Specialty," the man says. "It's your job in the marines. Like communications or infantry. It's not a number."

"Right. That's right. Mine was communications, but back when I was in we used numbers. High nineties was for all the communi-cations stuff, like radios. Low nineties was—"

The line's dead. The man already hung up. That's seventeen thousand dollars gone—another fish off the hook. The Colonel thinks he must be losing his touch.

On the TV a blond woman in a pantsuit demonstrates the telescopic handle on a mop. An 800 number appears, and Kitty, chemically stupefied, reaches for a pen and some paper (which is strange—she's never been too curious about cleaning supplies before, or about cleaning in general). The Colonel watches her try to write the phone number down, but the pen has the cap on. She keeps trying, pressing harder and harder, until the page rips.

"Kitty," he says. "I know this is a long shot, but do you remember the initial story I came up with, about the marines? Where I was supposed to be stationed?"

She slowly swings her head around to look at him. It takes her a few seconds to refocus her gaze.

"Wasn't it somewhere in California?" he says. "Or Texas? Was it Texas?"

Blank staring. Frog eyes.

"Kitty, what's seven plus nine?"

It's like talking to a plant. She opens her mouth this time, but nothing comes out. Her lower lip hangs, pink and shining wetly.

The phone rings again, and the Colonel reaches for it. Maybe it's the man he just talked to, calling back. MOS—the Colonel used to know stuff like that. He used to be good.

"Raymond, it's Sheriff LoBianco."

"Oh," the Colonel says. "Not a good time right now. Can you call—"

"I've tried a bunch of times already," the sheriff says, "but you never seem to pick up."

"Well, you know," the Colonel says, pinching the bridge of his nose. "I've got a lot going on right now. Never enough hours in the day."

"Sure, sure. But I've got some stuff going on out here too. Which is why I'm calling."

On the couch, Kitty tries to throw the capped pen at the TV. It drops from her flailing hand down inside her kimono.

"Specifically," the sheriff says, "someone called to complain."

"Oh yeah? Who's that?"

"Couple named George and Dell Mueller. They say they saw one of your, uh, wayward lambs yesterday. He showed up on their doorstep."

"Is that right?" Don't admit anything, the Colonel thinks. *I can neither confirm nor deny....*

"They told me you were there too," the sheriff says. "Said they called you and you gave them the same pitch you told everyone back when the place first opened. That some of your lambs might not receive the spirit as well as others, but it didn't look to the Muellers like there was a whole lot of spirituality going on."

"Well, I don't know if you can believe people like that."

Kitty chooses this moment to point at the TV and say, "Unngggghhhhh."

"I thought we had a deal," the sheriff says. "You keep your business to yourself, and I stay out of it."

"That's right."

"But when kids start running away, that's not good. When you rip people off on the reward you promised them, they come to me and that's not good either, because it makes your Bible-camp story look like the smelly piece of shit that it is. Plus, I've got some lawyer calling now, saying one of the kids up there was hurt a ways back. Lost his hearing."

Kitty turns her glassy eyes toward him and says, louder this time, "*Unnnggggghhhhhhhh!*"

"He's a shyster," the Colonel says, turning away from her. "He's hijacking me for money."

"So the son wasn't hurt?"

"You know kids. He probably had his headphones up too loud. Or he went to a concert and stood close to the speakers. Now they want someone to pay."

"Maybe, but they took that story to a TV network. So what used to be a local problem is going national. You're getting to be a big star, Ray."

"You know, I'm not sure I saw that show," the Colonel says. "We don't like to expose the kids to a lot of pop culture up here. It's not good for them."

"Right. Course it's not. The point here is that you're making me look bad right now, and that's something I can't have."

"OK," the Colonel says. "Get me the Mueller's address. I'll send them five hundred bucks and, I don't know, a cheese basket."

"Not enough. The deaf kid's lawyer says he wants to come onto the compound. He wants to take pictures."

"Nope," the Colonel says. "That can't happen." The words come out more urgently than he means them to.

"That's what I told him," the sheriff says. "I said it's your property. You've got rights. I'm trying to be fair here. So the next step is that he's forcing me to get a warrant. It'll take a few days, a week maybe—the judge won't rush. But at some point we're all going to have to come up there, one big field trip."

"Jesus."

"Right. Which for you means exactly two things. First, don't let any other kids escape, no matter what. And second, clean that place up. When we get there, it better look like Sesame Street. Got it?"

"I've got it."

A cramp spasms through the Colonel's hand. He didn't realize he was gripping the phone so hard.

"Raymond, if you screw me on this, I won't make it pleasant for you."

"I don't think we need to use threats here, sheriff. I don't think that helps—"

"Let's not call it a threat then, Ray. I certainly wouldn't want you to feel threatened. Instead let's call it a guarantee."

After the Colonel hangs up, he stands for a long time and stares into space. Things are coming unglued. The lawyer, the TV show, now the sheriff—multiple enemies on multiple fronts. He thought he could make it through a few more classes, at least a few more weeks to get some kids signed up and pad out the accounts a bit, but that might not be possible anymore. In any business venture, the trick is knowing how long to stay with it, and maybe this whole thing is finally played out.

On the couch, Kitty reaches for a potato chip and misses her mouth, smashing it against her chin instead. She starts moving her lips like fish do, trying to bring in the pieces. If there were a world record for Longest String of Drool between Mouth and Kimono, she'd be a contender.

After all the time she spent bitching over the past sixteen months about when they could leave, it's funny that she's not fully conscious when that becomes a serious option. The tranquilizers would probably help in any kind of exit strategy the Colonel could put together, though. If she were stone-cold sober, Kitty would want to pack all her stuff—clothes, jewelry, pictures. Her shoes alone would fill the backseat of the Jeep. Worse, she'd insist on bringing Donovan, and there's no way the Colonel's letting that brain-dead ape tag along. It's his fault they're even in this situation.

Who knocked the Diehl kid around a few months ago? Who wanted to put the kids into cammies and take them out into the woods for maneuvers? Donovan still whined nonstop about the money and his "stake," but if he'd done what the Colonel said and just taken it easy once in a while, they'd be fine, signing up future classes and collecting checks, instead of plotting their exit strategy. But none of that will matter to Kitty. They're brother and sister, she'll say. They're blood.

Kitty starts coughing, softly at first and then louder. A hunk of chewed potato chip flies out of her mouth and lands on the coffee table, and the hacking gets worse—it sounds like she's scraping off layers of her throat. Possibly the dose was too strong this time. If

they really do leave, the Colonel will need her calm but not coma-
tose, at least able to walk onto a plane without raising any eyebrows.

He sits on the couch and rolls her onto her side—his true north,
his devotion—so she doesn't pull a Janis Joplin on him. He doesn't
know where they'll go yet, but he knows what he wants. Sand like
talcum powder. A cabana with two hammocks, one in the shade and
one in the sun, so Kitty can switch back and forth. He wants something like the place they tried to get to after the credit card scam fell
apart. They were caught at Miami International, both wearing wigs
and holding one-way tickets to Curaçao, with so much money taped
to their thighs that they had to walk bowlegged. He's learned since
then, though. The Colonel whispers to his zombified wife and rocks
her gently, telling her that this time they'll be smarter. This time
they'll definitely get away for good.

*

Loren wakes up when the door opens. There's a clink of keys, dead
bolts sliding open, a faint rush of air. Some light leaks down into the
carpet tube, and he feels pressure on his hip as the duct tape gets cut.
The carpet enchilada unrolls three or four times until it's flat again,
and the sudden light makes him writhe like a bug.

It's a stadium spotlight, halogen high beams, bright as five hundred suns. Even with his eyes squeezed shut and his arm over his
face, the pink glare thrums and overexposes his brain like film, giving him an instant headache. He turns his head to the side and
squints to make out a boot that looks familiar.

"Bathroom," Donovan says. "You can eat once you're done."

The words sound strange, floating above Loren in the muffled
acoustics of the room. He tries to stand a few times but can't. His
numb legs keep giving out under him.

"Go," Donovan says. "Crawl if you have to. I'm not waiting all
day."

Pulling on the doorknob, Loren finally gets himself up. Blood starts flowing to his feet again, enough for him to hobble out to the hallway. In the bathroom he pisses for a minute straight and shits so much it feels like his insides are coming out. Afterward, his head seems to fall naturally down onto his knees, and he listens to the slow drip of the plumbing and thinks about how much he'd like to stay in this position right now. The stall door is open, though, and Donovan waits by the sink. No way would he let Loren out here alone—this is the same bathroom Loren escaped from a few nights ago.

"How long was I in there?" Loren croaks.

"About eighteen hours," Donovan says.

So it must be afternoon. He was brought back just after sunset yesterday. It feels like a month already.

Back in his cell—a plaque outside the door tells him it's the Sarah Uttman Rehearsal Room, one of six lining the hallway— Loren sits on the floor, and Donovan hands him a Cool Whip container full of oatmeal. No fork, so Loren scoops it out with his fingers, like a bear eating honey. His stomach starts to hurt halfway through, but he forces himself to eat it all, for strength. At the bottom is a cut-up apple and some syrup, which he thinks must have come from either Liz or Riap, and which he pretends is dessert. Loren hates oatmeal.

The room is small, maybe ten feet by twelve, lined with acoustic tiles that look like black foamy egg crates. They're everywhere, even on the ceiling, which explains why sound just disappears in the room. The light that was so snow-blindingly bright a minute ago comes from a single bare bulb screwed into a chipped ceramic fixture. In the corner of the room is a piano bench with the lid yawning open, brass hinges locked, and a stack of sheet music inside. Under the bench is a violin bow with split ends, and next to that is a plastic pack of eight rolls of duct tape, six of them unused.

Donovan reaches out with his boot and pushes over a bike bottle. It's warm water, tasting of plastic. Loren takes a few big swigs and lets out a trucker's burp.

"So what do we do now?" he says.

The interrogation must be coming. He's read about these scenes, seen them in movies.

"What do *we* do?" Donovan says. "*We* don't do anything. I leave and you stay here."

"I'm not apologizing for trying to escape."

"Yeah you are. Maybe not now, but you will. Soon."

"You can't make me," Loren says. "I don't care if you keep me here for a week." He's trying hard to keep his voice level.

"You're wrong there," Donovan says. "I can definitely make you. And it won't take anywhere near a week, believe me. The only question is how much I feel like putting you through first. But none of that fun stuff happens yet. We have time."

Donovan stands up and points to an edge of the carpet, a roll of duct tape already in his hand.

"What if I don't want to get back in that thing?"

Donovan shrugs. "Up to you."

Loren tries not to cringe, but when Donovan walks toward him he can't help it. He's a dog, a bad dog, and the master's coming. Donovan only has to push faintly against one shoulder to get him down onto the carpet. It's rolled up same as before, with Loren face-down and immobile, taped in even more tightly. The light goes out, the dead bolts slide shut and he's on his own again. Ten minutes later he's not sure he didn't dream the whole thing.

Except he knows he didn't, because something's different this time—his feet stick out. The carpet roll squeezes everything from the knees up, but Loren can kick his lower legs around. After experimenting a little, he figures out that if he twists them back and forth quickly enough he can roll from his stomach onto his back. Another series of flailing kicks, more experimenting, and he rolls on his stomach again. It's crude locomotion, but it's something.

In complete darkness and muffled silence (except for his grunt-ing), Loren turns himself over three times in one direction, until he runs flush into a wall. Starting back in the other way, he gets better at it, jerking his legs more quickly, generating more torque. After seven turns he's on the other side of the room, with his feet lodged against one wall and his body pointing out perpendicular from it.

Which might be good. Because Loren realizes that by pressing down with his legs, he can push himself forward through the roll a fraction of an inch. He inchworms it back to get his legs reposi-tioned for another push, and shoves himself forward again. After twenty-five or thirty attempts, his head starts to clear the top edge of the carpet. His shoulders, the thickest part of him, get stuck at the top line of duct tape, and for a few minutes he can't move at all. But he jams his feet back and scrunches his shoulders in, and finally he's out. The process takes him more than half an hour, and he emerges covered in sweat.

The light switch is by the door. Loren feels along the walls for it and turns it on, keeping one hand over his face against the bright-ness. After a long minute he can open his eyes and peer around the room. He doesn't know how he's going to get away, but there has to be something. The space is probably air-conditioned—you couldn't have kids practicing the oboe in here in August without it—so maybe there's a vent.

Reaching up, he tugs at the corner of an acoustic tile behind his head. It comes free without much effort, just a dab of dried glue on all four corners, exposing a patch of bare wall behind it. The one next to that comes free too, and before long Loren has most of one wall stripped. He stacks the tiles in the corner, where they pile up weightlessly, each about a foot square and two or three inches thick. To get to the uppermost row, he has to fold the carpet into fourths and prop the piano bench lengthwise on top. If he stands carefully on the end he can even reach the ceiling.

It takes him almost an hour to clear the entire room and find the vent—tiny, about the size of a sheet of paper, way up in a high corner of the room. Loren stands on the edge of the piano bench and stares at it, knowing it'll never work. Even if he could fit through it (a long shot), the vent has a grate over it, held in place by six screws, and Loren doesn't have a screwdriver.

The walls are Sheetrock, too thick to punch through—he tries, until his knuckles bleed—and he doesn't have a knife to cut his way out. He looks at the hinge on the piano bench for a sharp piece of metal he could use, but he'd never be able to pry it free with his hands. It's possible he could kick a hole through the wall, but that would make a ton of noise, and when he knocks a bloody knuckle around he finds studs every eighteen inches—enough room to fit through but too much reinforcement to break the Sheetrock with just his foot. Worse, there's no way to know what he'd find on the other side. Maybe a room just like this one, also locked.

Donovan's coming back at some point, and when that happens Loren will truly be screwed. He can't get the tiles back on the walls, can't roll himself up into the carpet again. Donovan's going to see what he's been up to and come up with some worse punishment, something that will make the last eighteen hours look like a vacation.

On the floor around him Loren sees duct tape, a violin bow with split ends, the piano bench, and stacks and stacks of acoustic tiles. This is a problem, but Loren tries not to panic and reminds himself that he's good at solving problems. He always has been.

*

"Boots off," Donovan says. "Toss them out here."

Five pairs of boots land heavily by the door. Donovan drops them into a milk crate, which he puts on the steps outside the boys' cabin. (Part of the new rules—the kids have to hand over their boots at night, to prevent escapes.) EK's boots come the closest to hitting

Donovan, but he lets it slide. He's bone-tired and doesn't feel like a fight right now. It's just past dinnertime, he's spent most of the day in the parking lot, teaching the kids how to put one foot in front of the other. Once they're locked in for the night he can go feed Loren again and he'll finally be done for the day.

"Can we get some ice?" RK says.

"No," Donovan says. "For what?"

"For Ty's hand," RK says. "Ty, show him."

Ty lifts his right hand, which is shiny and swollen, twice the size of his left. It looks like a clown hand in a tight purple glove.

"Jesus, what happened?" Donovan says. He comes back into the cabin.

"I got bit by some bug," Ty says.

"When?"

"I guess late afternoon. In the parking lot, when we were marching."

"You should've told me then."

"You didn't seem like you wanted to hear it," Ty says. "When we asked for water you made us do squat thrusts. Anyway, it wasn't like this at first. I thought I'd be OK."

Donovan can't stop staring at the hand. It looks dead, with skin stretched so tight the wrinkles are gone, even at the knuckles.

"You're fine," Donovan says, unconvincingly. When he pokes at Ty's thumb, Ty sucks in his breath. "Sorry," Donovan says. "Anyway, this is your fault. You should have said something."

"Are you allergic?" William says. "To bee stings or anything?"

William hasn't said much all day, and he doesn't look so good right now either—he's breathing heavy and his eyes are swollen to slits. This place is like a hospital for runts, Donovan thinks.

"I don't know," Ty says. "This never happened before."

"Here," William says. "Use this." He roots around under his bunk and comes up with something that looks like a giant test tube.

"What is it?" RK says.

"Epinephrine. You use it for really bad allergies, like if you eat a peanut and you're about to die."

"I'm not about to die," Ty says.

"You've been keeping that down there?" Donovan says. "No contraband. Up, get up."

William stands and Donovan lifts the mattress, tosses the pillow, inspects the underside of the bed frame. There's nothing else.

"This is the only one I have," William says. "I swear."

Donovan grabs it—a plastic tube with a covered needle and some fluid, and directions he doesn't bother reading. When he pushes at the covering it sticks, so he pries it free. The exposed needle squirts an ounce or so of clear liquid onto his palm. A few drops spill to the floor. The tube is now empty.

"That's not how—" William starts to say.

"Give me your hand," Donovan says to Ty. "Quick."

Ty holds his hand out and Donovan smears the stuff all over the skin, making him wince.

"There," Donovan says. "Maybe wedge it under your mattress too. For the swelling."

"Are you kidding?" EK says.

"Watch your mouth," Donovan says. "It's better than nothing." He has the stun gun tucked into the back of his cammies, reassuringly solid.

"What if it gets worse?" RK says.

"I'll come back to check on him later. If it's worse we'll deal with it then."

All five kids stare at him. Donovan tries to think of something else to say but can't, so he pulls the cabin door shut and locks it.

Outside the crickets are warming up. The dead grass looks sharper and more angular in the fading daylight. Donovan stops at the cafeteria to pick up another Cool Whip container of oatmeal and makes his way to the barn.

He's exhausted, and the thing with Ty's hand was a fuckup, but still he feels good about the day. When he went on vacation this place fell apart. The Colonel tried to buy the kids off with ice-cream cones and movies, and look what happened. They walked all over him. But Donovan came back, instituted the marching, instilled a little discipline, and the kids lined back up. They were complaining, a lot, but this place isn't supposed to be Disneyland.

Inside the barn it's quiet and dim. Donovan goes past the Colonel's office, down the long hallway to the rehearsal rooms. When he opens the door of the Sarah Uttman room and reaches for the light switch, nothing happens.

The room stays dark. He tries the switch twice more, still nothing. There's some light spilling in from the hallway, so Donovan pushes the door all the way open. He almost thinks he's in the wrong room—everything about it is different. It even *sounds* different. All the tiles are down, the walls and ceiling are bare, and the light bulb hanging from the ceiling has been smashed.

The carpet roll's in place, though Donovan can tell right away that it's not wrapped around a real person—the shape's too bulky and square. He kicks at it and the roll lifts off the ground like a big pillow. It's filled with foam tiles. An amateur-level fake.

So the kid got out. Donovan has no idea how, but the little fucking Houdini is not here. He tosses the Cool Whip container into the hallway and tries to think. All around the room are stacks of acoustic tiles. Which doesn't make sense—if Loren just wanted to leave, why take them down? The walls are all intact, no holes in the ceiling either. He stands in the center of the room, trying hard to figure out what happened and how he's going to explain it to the Colonel.

Something moves behind a stack of tiles in the far corner. Definite, noticeable motion. Donovan realizes that the kid didn't leave, the whole thing's a setup. It's the oldest trick in the book, and Donovan nearly fell for it. He almost walked out without locking the door. Report the escape before it actually happened.

"Nice try," Donovan says. "I see you back there."

He goes to the stack and pushes it over. Behind it he finds no kid, just a leg from the piano bench on the floor. The leg has horsehair around it, two-foot lengths from a violin bow, all tied together and leading away from that corner and over—

A soft footstep behind him. Shadowy motion. The door slams shut and Donovan's suddenly in darkness. He lunges for the door, but with no light it takes him a few seconds to find the knob. When he finally yanks it open, he's immediately hit in the chest with the tub of oatmeal. It splits open, leaking gray sludge everywhere, and Loren bolts down the hallway. Donovan ignores it and sprints after him.

On the ring, a second leg from the piano bench comes flying at Donovan's boots. It sends him sprawling and he lands on his hands and knees and face. He looks up to see a pair of white running shoes heading for the woods. Donovan's fast but Loren's faster, and much more scared right now. He manages to get to the tree line and disappears into the long shadows of the dying pines. Donovan follows forty yards behind, running and running until he realizes he's lost him.

CHAPTER 17

For the next hour, in growing darkness, Loren hides while Donovan stomps around and looks for him, making all the obvious mistakes. He crunches through branches and waves his flashlight like a beacon, he stays on the trail—where no Special Forces soldier would ever travel—and at one point he falls down and yells fuck at the tree root that just tripped him. Absolutely zero noise discipline, basically broadcasting his location to anyone within half a mile. Loren, silent and hidden, could have waited him out the entire night, but eventually Donovan gives up and trudges back to the compound. Fifteen minutes later the Jeep roars to life and heads for the dirt road, and Loren realizes he's safe. They must think he's already gone.

You're supposed to stay operational in situations like this, but when Loren creeps out of the woods, he can't help but look up. After all that time in the dark room, bound so tightly that he couldn't roll over or lift his head, the night sky seems almost dizzyingly limitless and expansive. Trees move quietly in the breeze, and the air tastes as fresh as cold water. Loren's eyes are dark-adjusted, starved for light, and the stars appear to him like a million glittering pinpricks—like every star in the universe came out to greet him.

In the cafeteria, he cleans himself up one limb at a time, using the deep sink of the kitchen. Riap tells him to keep the pantry light on—it's usually on at night anyway, he says. It won't raise any flags. So Loren sits on the edge of the stainless steel sink and turns the water up as hot as he can stand, until it stings his skin. He has to use dish soap, and paper towels to scrub; they turn to soggy pulp and come apart in his hands.

Afterward Riap brings him leftover coconut curry, and powdered milk so cold it makes Loren's fillings ring. When Loren tells him he doesn't have to do all this, Riap says no talking, they shouldn't make any noise. He hands Loren a new toothbrush, still in the wrapper, which at first Loren thinks is supremely thoughtful, then realizes it's probably because his breath could knock somebody over. He hasn't brushed in days, and he spends five minutes scrubbing the moss off his teeth.

Riap has made a bed up for him in a storage locker, hidden under some boxes, but Loren says no.

"They think I'm gone right now," he says. "It's a huge advantage. When Donovan comes back I'll have to stay hidden. I can sleep then."

Riap seems like he wants to argue but doesn't.

"You have to go too," Loren tells him. "Not now, but tomorrow, before sunrise. In the morning, everything's going to be different here. You don't want to be around."

He gives Riap directions to a location in the woods, off the perimeter trail. "On the eastern edge," he says. "By the Colonel's house. Go to where the trail turns sharply, and walk straight out from it, perpendicular to the loop, about a hundred yards or so."

From the expression on Riap's face, Loren can tell he doesn't understand. So Loren spreads flour onto the counter and draws a map in it with his index finger.

"Right here. OK? Where the woods are thick. Go out there at sunrise and wait for me. I'll find you there."

This time Riap gets it.

"Also," Loren says, "bring supplies. Blankets, a tarp, knife, food, lots of water. Don't bring food that'll go bad—cans only. Hide everything, wear dark clothes, and don't make more than one trip. Most important, stay silent when you're out there. Got it?"

Riap nods. The last thing Loren does before setting out again is wipe a palm through the flour.

Outside the boys' cabin, he finds a milk crate full of boots and plucks his out from the bottom. When they're laced up he walks to the window by his bunk and whispers.

"Hey," he says. "Hey, wake up."

"Who's that?" It's William, congested and breathless.

"It's me, Loren. I got out."

"Fuck you," EK yells. "You're out? No wonder—Donovan strapped us to our bunks tonight because of you."

"Keep your voice down," Loren says. "You're really strapped in? Since when?"

"About an hour ago. You want to come in here and check?"

Loren says it doesn't matter, even though he knows it does. "I'm getting you out of here," he says. "All of you."

"Yeah? How?"

Pause. "Not sure. William, you're OK?"

"I'll live. But Ty's hand is messed-up."

"No it's not," Ty whispers. "I'm all right."

"It looks like a Ronald McDonald hand," EK says. "It looks like the Grimace."

"Shut up," Ty says.

Loren says, "All of you, shut up for one second. I need to think."

The straps are a significant problem. He knew the bars on the windows were through-bolted (a modification from Donovan, after Loren and Liz sneaked out to the pool that night), but Loren thought he and the kids could work on them from both sides. By himself, with everyone else strapped to their bunks, he'd never be able to get the bars off. The door has dead bolts, easy enough to address from the outside, but also two key locks, which Loren can't do anything with. He's stuck.

"I'll figure something out," Loren says. "Promise. I'm not leaving this time. Give me a few hours."

"Great," EK says. "You promise. That means exactly dick."

"Just trust me, OK," Loren says.

"Why? You haven't done anything yet."

"Then you know what? Maybe I'll just leave. I can walk to the gate right now if I want. You all can figure it out on your own."

"No, wait. Seriously. It's OK."

"Last I checked I was out here and you were stuck in there crying for help," Loren says. "I escaped three times. So just keep your mouth shut and maybe we can do something. All of us."

A hundred yards away stands the Colonel's house, hugely ominous and silent. In the basement is a ton of junk but also some stuff that Loren thinks might be good to have right now. Tools, paint, the giant can of sodium nitrate (which would be key for making smoke bombs). On the hand-to-hand combat videos Loren sent away for, the instructor said that sometimes you didn't want to maintain any distance. Sometimes you wanted to run right up to the enemy and do things to stun him. It gives you the advantage of surprise and shows you have no fear.

Loren says he'll be back for them, and as he moves away from the cabin, he half expects one of them to do something stupid like yell for him. They don't, though. Maybe they're finally starting to believe in him. Or maybe they *have* to believe in him, because he's their only option right now.

*

The Colonel wakes at dawn, pissed off and nervous. All night he's been in and out of sleep, wondering whether Donovan would really be able to find the kid. When Donovan drove back in the Jeep, around three, the Colonel was wide awake and blinking at the ceiling, but he didn't get up. If there were any good news, he knew, Donovan would come in and tell him. So when the footsteps walked past his door and down the hallway it meant exactly one thing—Loren was still out there somewhere. Donovan had failed, again, and the Colonel would have to make a painful call to the sheriff at some point in the morning, which he doesn't even want to think about right now.

Next to him, Kitty sleeps in fits. He tried to give her another 125 mg of phenobarbital at bedtime, stirred into a chocolate milk, but she said it tasted funny and didn't get past the first sip. "Is this hazelnut or something?" she asked woozily. The Colonel just shrugged. She had slept most of the day yesterday, and though he would have preferred to keep her semi-sedated, he didn't want to force the issue.

When the sky starts to lighten outside his window, the Colonel gets out of bed and heads downstairs. The words on the walls don't immediately jump out at him. There's a chemical smell, but the Colonel dismisses it as something rotten in the trash. He'll have to get Riap to come in and change the bag. From the freezer he pulls out a can of frozen orange juice and slides the pulpy, glistening plug into a pitcher of water, where he chases it around with a wooden spoon. The soft thunking sound is something he always associates with breakfast. Only after he's poured himself a big glass and taken a sip does he glance at the far wall and see his name.

Not his name, exactly, but his alias, or a *couple* of his aliases, spray-painted in kelly green all over the walls of the den.

Edmund Killian, 1st Caymans
Elgin R. Kallinet, Belize Federal
E. Raymond Koller, Bank of Bermuda

They're on the furniture too, and the floors, even the windows—the same three names and the same three banks, over and over. Centered on the far wall is something the Colonel can't make out—an amoeba-shaped logo that looks a little like Florida. He stares at the names and stares some more, until he realizes he's holding his glass at an angle and spilling juice onto the floor.

The kid was in the house. Last night, while they slept, Loren somehow got in. No wonder Donovan couldn't find him—he was looking all over the county, instead of under his own roof. Apparently Loren wasn't leaving, and though he could have done a hundred things to them, instead he simply left a signal—just to mark his territory, as effective as if he'd pissed in the hallways. If these names got out, the Colonel wouldn't get community service, not this time. Instead he'd be looking at a significant jail stint, forfeiture of assets, a lot of bad things that he's managed to avoid so far in his career. Even Kitty, his cherry blossom, his angel on earth, doesn't know about the aliases. He keeps a decent amount of cash in the safe and pretends not to notice when she takes it, but that's only a distraction to keep her from wondering where the rest of the money goes.

From a strip of molding near the doorway, the Colonel flicks away a bit of paint with a fingernail. It's dry, but that doesn't mean much—spray paint doesn't take long. He considers the green flecks on his thumb and thinks, *OK. It's time.* There's no rush, he probably has an hour or two to make all the necessary arrangements (including phone calls to a few offshore financial institutions), but he should definitely proceed with some deliberate purpose toward getting the fuck out of here.

After finishing the orange juice he hasn't yet dumped onto the floor, he pours another one for Kitty—including a 250-mg dose of his new best friend—and goes back upstairs for a suitcase.

*

Donovan's almost always the first person awake in the house, but he opens his eyes this morning—after four hours of bad sleep—to the sound of the screen door downstairs quietly opening and closing. Someone else is already up. He looks out his bedroom window and sees a duffel bag on the driveway near the Jeep. The passenger door is open and Kitty's belted into the seat. One of her legs dangles out, immobile, with a high-heeled sandal hanging from her foot.

Donovan dresses quickly and goes into the hallway to find the Colonel coming back up the stairs.

"There he is," the Colonel says, fakely boisterous. "Man of the hour." He seems surprised but tries to cover it.

"I didn't find him last night," Donovan reports. "I looked all over."

If he's expecting a certain reaction he doesn't get it. Instead the Colonel says that he figured as much. "You did your best though, right?" the Colonel says. "That's all that matters."

The Colonel opens the hall closet and roots around in some old shoe boxes on the floor. Past him, in the master bedroom, Donovan can see a few empty drawers hanging from a dresser.

He hesitates and finally asks the Colonel where he's going.

The Colonel seems to be in a mild rush, but he stops long enough to tap his cigar ash against the white wallpaper of the hallway, where it leaves a mark. Donovan's never seen him smoke in the house before. Kitty never lets him. She says it smells like burning tires.

"Want one?" the Colonel asks, ignoring his question and gesturing with the stub end.

Donovan shakes his head.

"Suit yourself," the Colonel shrugs. "They're Dominican. Hand-rolled, nine bucks a pop."

"I asked you a question."

The Colonel finds what he's looking for—a small black address book—and drops the shoe box to the floor.

"As long as you're up," he says, "you should go check out the walls down in the TV room. Floors too. Funny little message from our friend. Seriously, go see."

Donovan walks downstairs with the Colonel in tow and sees the names spray-painted everywhere. The same names he had written on the scrap of paper in his wallet, except now they're in fuzzy green letters all over the walls and the floor and the furniture. A trickle of green has leaked down from the bottom of one of the *K*s. Donovan instinctively reaches for his wallet and catches himself, but it's too late. The Colonel already saw.

"How do you think he found all these names out?" the Colonel says.

"Don't know."

"I bet you do, though. I bet you've been sneaking around in my business, and now some stuff I thought was secret isn't so secret anymore."

"It's not my fault he took the wallet."

"Is it your fault you kept the names in there in the first place?" the Colonel says. "Is it your fault you let him escape?"

"You let him escape too."

"Once, and then I caught him. He was back here the next day. And as long as we're asking questions, here's another one—how do you think he got into the house last night?"

"No idea," Donovan says. "One of the windows, I guess."

"Good thinking, professor, but they were locked, all of them. Maybe he vaporized himself and came down the chimney. Except whoops—we don't have a chimney either."

"What do you want me to say? I don't fucking know."

"Aren't you supposed to know? Isn't that your job around here?"

Donovan glowers and says nothing. He feels stupid standing in front of the Colonel—a little kid reporting to the principal.

"I'll tell you how he got in," the Colonel says. "The basement. The storm doors were unlocked, so he found his way in downstairs and then the kitchen door up here, well, that was unlocked too. So he just walked in. Middle of the night, while we were *sleeping*. He could have slit our throats, or made one phone call to the cops with these names and I'd be halfway to an indictment, but apparently he doesn't want to do that. Apparently he'd rather stick around a little longer and make us all look like clowns. You have to hand it to the little bastard—high marks for boldness."

"I'll find him."

"No you won't. You might as well have a cigar, because today's a special occasion. After this one I'm leaving for good. Kitty's already in the Jeep. We would've been gone by now, but I came back to get this." He waves the address book from upstairs. "A few names in here I wouldn't want anyone to find."

A small overnight bag sits on the counter. The Colonel unzips a side pocket and jams the address book in.

"Kitty wouldn't go without me," Donovan says. "I know she wouldn't."

The Colonel shrugs. "The plan was to be long gone before you even woke up. For the past five minutes I've been trying to think up some lie to tell you, but it just hit me—I don't need to. I can tell you the truth, which is that we're leaving, you're not coming with us, and if I get my way we'll never see your fat ape face again. That's the story."

Donovan watches the Colonel pause to remove a bit of tobacco from his tongue, which he flicks to the floor before continuing.

"I know," he says. "It's probably hard to believe. I don't have the kind of track record that would make someone trust me. But I swear to you, this is the God's honest. I've got clean documents. Practically virginal, from the Swiss guy in Chicago. Remember him? Passports, driver's licenses, new socials—a whole set for Kitty and one for me."

"What about the kids?"

"Roast them on a spit if you want," the Colonel says. "They're not really a concern of mine right now. Sure you don't want a cigar?"

"Go fuck yourself."

Another shrug. "Up to you," the Colonel says.

"But you still owe me money," Donovan says. "For my back pay and the...equity." He's glad he could remember the word this time.

"Right. I guess there's something to that. If it makes you feel any better you can have the whole place. One hundred percent, it's yours—assuming you can figure out what to do with it, which I know you can't. As for money, no, you get nothing. If anything you should pay *me*. There's how many kids out there with problems? Ten thousand? A hundred thousand? All those worried parents and the stuff they'll do, the checks they'll write, for some help? This place could've run for years, but instead we didn't even make it eighteen months. So no, you don't get money from me, not a fucking hand-shake. If you had any money on you, I'd take it."

"And all this?" Donovan points at the writing on the walls around them.

"I emptied the accounts this morning. You think I'd leave here with those names painted all over? That money's already been moved twice."

"Then I want some of it."

"It's wire transfers, you idiot. They don't just zap a pile of fifties down into my pocket."

"But the safe—you keep cash around. I know you do."

The Colonel's cigar is almost out. "When Kitty told me to hire you I thought, OK, janitor," he says. "I thought, groundskeeper. You could mow the dead grass—how hard could that be? But no, Kitty said you had to be a partner. I would have had better luck partner-ing with a chimp, or a hamster. I could've partnered with a piece of plywood and had an easier time."

Donovan walks toward him.

"You're crazy if you think I'm letting you just walk out of here," Donovan says.

"You're going to hit me?"

"Or worse." Donovan has the stun gun shoved into his back pocket.

The Colonel picks up the overnight bag and slings it over one shoulder. "Now that I think about it, that plywood thing might have worked," he says. "If I'd been partners with a piece of plywood I could have talked my plywood partner into maybe covering a door or two in the barn, so that a fourteen-year-old wouldn't be able to just—"

Donovan punches him in the mouth. The cigar flies against a far wall.

The Colonel drops the overnight bag, and a few drops of bright red blood run down his chin and onto the floor. "Wow," he says. "That hurts, a lot. I don't think I've ever been punched before—all these years."

"Where's the money?" Donovan says. "Go if you want, but I'm getting some of it. You're not leaving me with nothing."

The Colonel dabs at his bloody lip with a finger.

"When you were on my side it was worse," he says. "Your fuck-ups were my problem too. But now that you're trying to stop me, I'm pretty sure I'll be OK. You're like a bad-luck charm. You're instant failure. Even your sister says—"

Donovan hits him in the same spot, harder. The Colonel does-n't fight back or defend himself. His arms stay down at his sides, and when he smiles now his teeth are bloody. "Still time," he says. "You'll fuck something else up."

Donovan cocks his fist, about to swing again, when they hear a car door closing outside. The Jeep engine starts.

The two of them get to the window in time to see it pulling away. The rear bumper bottoms out at the base of the driveway, but the Jeep keeps accelerating across the parking lot and disappears down the dirt road at the far side. A few seconds later they hear a splintering crash. The horn sounds once, briefly.

"Kitty," the Colonel says. "Jesus."

*

When the Jeep starts moving, Loren thinks he might have miscalcu-lated.

For the past half hour he watched the Colonel shuttle bags out from the house and thought about ways to stop him from leaving. Pull the spark plugs? That had potential, but there probably wasn't enough time—the Colonel was bringing stuff out every few minutes. Steal the Jeep outright? The keys were dangling from the tailgate, but if Loren drove off the Colonel would call the cops, and they'd be waiting for him at the highway. Who would they believe, an underage kid in a stolen truck or the local business owner who'd just been carjacked? The whole plan would be over before it started.

But then Loren got a better idea: he could sneak into the Jeep and ride out as a stowaway. All three of them were leaving, he thought—the Colonel, Kitty, and Donovan—for a trip that looked one-way and permanent. If he stayed with them he could at least complicate their escape. So when the Colonel went to the house for another bag Loren climbed behind the backseat and hid under some loose clothes.

For fifteen minutes he lay with his face jammed into a suitcase buckle, trying to take up the least possible space. It was warm under all the layers, and the rising sun meant the car would only get warmer, but Loren tried to fight off the low-level claustrophobia. The Colonel made a few more trips inside, emerging each time with another armload of stuff, and then he came out carrying something heavy. Loren could tell by the sound of his staggering footsteps. It turned out to be Kitty, who got dumped into the front seat with a thunking noise and a wince (her head, Loren realized, hitting the door frame). After she was buckled in, the Colonel went back to the house, and for a few long minutes it was just the two of them— Loren and Kitty, waiting silently.

He thought she was maybe asleep, because at first she didn't move or say anything. But when the shouting began, when Donovan and the Colonel started going at each other inside the house, Kitty let out an exasperated sigh and said, very distinctly, like she'd been awake and faking it the whole time: "OK, that is fucking *enough*."

The Jeep rocked a bit as she got out and pulled the keys from the tailgate, then got in again on the driver's side. The tailgate was open when she started the engine and took off down the driveway. And as the car raced across the parking lot, Loren realized he had just screwed up.

She was leaving, alone. She was abandoning the Colonel and Donovan, and Loren would be carried off the compound with her, like a swimmer caught in a riptide. Suddenly he didn't want to be a stowaway anymore. Kitty was the lowest priority of the three, but while he didn't want to let her get away, he also didn't want to lose track of the Colonel and Donovan or strand the rest of the kids. They were all strapped to their bunks, waiting for him to do something tactical, and instead they would think he abandoned them.

Kitty was already across the lot by the time Loren managed to dig himself out from under all the clothes. She kept accelerating, and he turned to watch through the open tailgate as the dirt road spooled out behind them like a ribbon. A yellow dress with the tags hanging from it got sucked out in the back draft and tumbled to the ground. There was no way he could jump—the truck was going much too fast. If she slowed down, even just a little, he could possibly roll out without being maimed, but after another hundred yards it seemed like she was only going to speed up. Loren had no choice but to rise to his knees behind the backseat and say, "Sorry, but could you—"

Kitty saw him in the rearview mirror and screamed. When she turned around in her seat the Jeep veered into the pine trees lining the road. It had enough momentum to knock the first one over but not the second. Instead it bent the tree and rode up it like a skateboard rail before rolling to one side with a crunch of metal and glass.

After everything stopped moving, Loren found himself upside down in a mound of clothes. His arm was hooked around the strap of a duffel bag. He did a quick inventory of body parts, and when it

seemed like nothing was hurt he scrambled out the back. Kitty followed quickly, gasping hard, on the edge of panic. She stepped on
the horn trying to get free, screaming that the Jeep was going to
catch fire. (It wasn't—he didn't know where she'd gotten that idea,
probably the movies.) In the front seat, the air bags had all popped
and now looked like deflated balloons.

"It's gonna burn," she shrieked. "It's gonna catch fire and go up."

"Just calm down," Loren said. "It's not going to burn."

She was practically delusional, but other than that they were
both OK. No major injuries.

Kitty backed away from him, nearly tripping over a branch.

"Don't hurt me," she said. "Don't mug me. I can get money if
you want."

"I don't want money," Loren said.

"Oh my God—don't be sick. I'd rather you take the money."

"No, it's nothing like that. I just needed to get out of the car.
You're not the one I'm after right now."

"I'm not? Then why didn't you just let me go?"

"I wanted to. I didn't think you were going to steer into a tree."

The Jeep engine was spitting steam—a branch had been
punched into the radiator like a dart. Kitty walked over and peered
down at it and cursed.

"Goddamn, goddamn, *goddamn*," she said. "Can't I ever get out
of this place?"

They heard yelling from the compound. Donovan's voice in the
distance.

"Time for me to go," Loren said.

"Wait. What am I supposed to do?"

"Whatever you want. Go back to your husband, I guess."
Though Loren knew that wasn't an option anymore. Not after she'd
just tried to run out on him.

"He wants to poison me," she said. "He spiked my iced tea and a
chocolate milk and an orange juice a little while ago. I had to pre-

tend to drink it and spit it under the bed."

The yelling was getting closer.

"I don't know what to tell you," Loren said. "Maybe hide. Get behind a bush until they leave."

"What bush? Where?"

"Pick one."

She wore high-heeled sandals and was looking around at the branches like they might grab her. No way could she make it five minutes alone in the woods.

"You can't just leave," she said.

"I think I can. Watch."

He'd have to go off in the wrong direction and then double back, so she couldn't put the Colonel on his trail.

"No," she said. "Please, you can't. I can help you—I know stuff."

Loren thought for a few seconds. He didn't trust her, but maybe she really could give him some useful intel on the compound. If nothing else, the Colonel and Donovan would think he'd taken her hostage. And he knew he was partly responsible for putting her in this situation. If he hadn't climbed into the Jeep, she'd be miles away right now.

"One condition," he said. "You have to do what I tell you. Mostly that means not saying anything. Especially for the next ten minutes, until we're out of here."

Kitty said she could do that.

"I'm not so sure," he said. "But if you yell for them I'll take off running and you'll be stuck. I know my way around in the woods— you don't."

The Colonel and Donovan were closing in. Loren could hear their footsteps in the parking lot.

Kitty swore she would be quiet, and Loren figured he'd take his chances. Before they left, he grabbed the branch poking out of the radiator and yanked it around a few times, widening the hole. When he pulled it out, oily swirls of radiator fluid trickled onto the ground, along with a few final wisps of steam that smelled like cooked rubber. He didn't think anyone would have been able to tip the Jeep upright again, let alone start the engine, but he wanted to make sure. Now, no one was leaving.

CHAPTER 18

"If you can't do anything that helps," Liz says, "at least don't do anything stupid."

"This isn't stupid," EK says.

He leans forward and strains, tugging at the pipe behind him.

"No, it is," Liz says. "It's really stupid."

"She's right," RK says. "You'll never pull that thing out, ever. All you're going to do is make noise and bring them up here."

All eight kids—the entire group, minus Loren—are in the Colonel's house, in a spare second-floor bathroom. Donovan brought them in one by one half an hour ago, so mad the vein in his forehead was pulsing. He forced them to the floor and zip-cuffed their hands behind their backs, then ran a metal chain the thickness of a dog collar through their arms. The chain got locked to a radiator pipe running low along the wall.

"No one moves," he said, once all eight were in place. "No one talks. No one even whispers. If I hear anything, I'll come back and hit whoever's closest with this." He gestures with the stun gun. "You'll all feel it. The charge will go through the chain and everyone'll pay. So don't fuck around."

He's back downstairs now, talking to the Colonel. Their voices resonate up through the pipes, but Liz can't make out specific words.

This bathroom must not get used much, she figures, because the tub is dusty and the air smells like old laundry. Black mold traces a constellation across the ceiling. Some kids were clearly in here in the past, though, doing a repair job. When Donovan carried Liz in, she flailed and kicked and managed to knock some newer-looking tiles off the bottom of the wall. Underneath, carved into gray adhesive, are the words *Fuck everything in this fucking place.* Liz couldn't have put it better herself.

"Why do you think they put us here?" Ty says.

"Consolidate," Liz says. "Round up all their eggs in one basket. Otherwise they'd have to watch two cabins. And look for Kitty. And try to hunt down Loren."

Next to her, William makes Darth Vader sounds when he breathes.

"What's going on William?" Liz says. "You OK?"

"It just gets funner and funner," he says. His head is tipped down on his chest like he's just taken a beating, and his packed sinuses make him square off the corners of his words. *Fudder ad fudder.*

"Where do you think he went?" Ty says. His hand is still purple but the swelling has started to ease, and his shriveled knuckles now look like rotting grapes. He yelped when Donovan cinched the plastic cuffs down.

"Downstairs, dummy," Becca says. "Can't you hear him talking?"

"No, I meant Loren."

"That kid's worthless," EK says. "He's gone, probably."

"He wouldn't just leave," Liz says.

"Maybe he went to get help," Meredith says.

"So what're we supposed to do, sit around and wait for him?" Becca says.

RK says, "For now, yeah. We can't do much else anyway."

"Screw that," EK says. "I can. At least I can try."

He leans forward again and yanks against the pipe, grunting

hard and getting nowhere. Liz watches and thinks about telling him to stop but doesn't bother. It would be a waste of breath.

After a few more seconds he gives up and leans over to yell down through the radiator. "Hey, Colonel! Hey, dickhead! You're going to jail for this, you fucker. You know that, right?"

"Shut up," Jeremy says. "Don't make them any madder."

"No one else is doing anything," EK says. "We're all just going to sit here?"

"What else can we do?" Ty says.

"There's always something," EK tells him.

Liz looks around the room. That's the first intelligent thing EK's said in days.

"Meredith," she says. "Can you maybe reach that cabinet under the sink?"

It's all the way across the room. Meredith looks at Liz like she just proposed gnawing their hands off to get free.

"With your foot," Liz says. "Just try. We'll all squeeze together and give you some slack on the chain."

"No," Jeremy says. "We'll get in trouble."

"Shut up," Becca says. "Don't pull that shit now."

"I'll yell," Jeremy says. "I will."

The kids ignore him and press closer. RK, sitting next to Jeremy, hip-checks him into place, and the chain running through their arms grows loose and clacks against the tile floor.

Meredith slides forward and stretches her stork body full out. She can barely reach the cabinet door with her foot—the kids are all still barefoot—but once it opens a little she's able to put a toe underneath and swing it the rest of the way.

Inside is a bunch of jumbled crap. Cotton balls in a yellowed plastic bag, tub cleaner (unopened), rags, a dirty comb. Meredith kicks the cotton balls out of the way. In the back corner is something with a knotted black electrical cord.

"What's that?" Liz asks.

"Probably a hair dryer," EK says.

"Can you get it?"

The kids all squeeze closer—William's sweaty, feverish arm presses up against Liz—and Meredith takes the added slack and extends her foot another four inches. Carefully, she hooks the cord with her big toe and lifts. It's something none of them has ever seen before, a device the shape of a curling iron, with a small emery board at the end.

Meredith sets it on the floor. A sliver of old soap sticks to the plug.

"No way," Liz says. "It's an electric nail file."

"They make stuff like that?" Becca says.

"Apparently," Liz says. "Shift the chain. Meredith, slide back into place. Give me the slack."

Meredith sits up and the other kids rearrange themselves. Liz now scoots forward from the radiator pipe (which alone is good, as it gets her away from William's sticky arm). Their hands are all bound behind them, but she needs to get hers in front, which means rolling herself into a ball and pushing herself backward through the skinny triangle of her arms.

At first it doesn't seem like it'll work—she's not as flexible as she used to be. When she was little and training all the time, she could do splits and no-arm handsprings and, from a standing position, arch her back until her forehead touched the mat behind her. But that was years ago.

Still, after straining for a few seconds, and shifting her weight, and pulling her wrists out as far as she can, until the cuffs feel like they're slicing into her skin, it happens. She's through—sitting on the floor with her bound wrists behind her knees instead of her back. From there it's easy to maneuver her legs around and put her hands in her lap.

"Damn," EK says. "That was some circus shit."

"Six years of gymnastics," Liz says, winded. "Meredith, pass that thing over here."

"Want me to plug it in?" Becca says, suddenly eager.

"No. The noise."

"If we get caught I'm telling them it was you," Jeremy says. "I didn't want to do this. Everyone heard me."

"And if we get out, we'll leave your whiny ass here," EK says. "Deal?"

The emery board is brittle and old, with dull, worn edges. It takes Liz almost fifteen minutes of solid sawing—she can move her bound hands back and forth only a few inches—until finally the plastic cuff comes loose. Her wrists have livid marks underneath.

Everyone exhales at once.

Liz has to make a decision about who to free next, but it's not hard. The girls, probably not. Neither of them would be much help right now. William's too sick, Ty's hand is a purple mess. Jeremy—no way. That leaves the twins.

Liz steps over EK and starts working on his brother's cuffs.

"What the hell?" EK says. "What about me?"

"Just shut up, OK?" Liz says. "I'll get you next."

RK leans forward and says nothing as she saws away.

The emery board is getting duller and duller. Halfway through, it snaps. The biggest piece is only an inch or so long, not sharp at all. Liz tries for another minute, not making much progress, and then that breaks too.

"Shit," she says. "That's it. I can't do anymore."

"There has to be something else in here," RK says.

Liz looks quietly through the medicine cabinet, under the sink, on the floor behind the toilet. Old toothpaste tubes, an empty bottle of window cleaner, but nothing sharp. No nail clippers, no replacement files.

They try to force it. RK strains against the cuffs—they're sawed nearly halfway through—and Liz steps down into the wedge between his forearms. He grunts, she hops, and finally the cuffs pop free.

"That's why him and not you," Liz says to EK. "He's stronger."

"OK, whatever. Just get me out now." He leans forward, expectant.

"With what?" RK says.

"I don't know," EK says. "Go downstairs and get a knife."

"We're not walking down there," Liz tells him. "Even if we wanted to, we couldn't. The door's locked. We're going out the window."

"OK, whatever, but you have to come back," EK says.

"How?" Liz says.

"Let's just go," RK says. "We're wasting time."

"You're going to find Loren?" William says. *Fide Lored.*

"I have a feeling once we're out, he'll find us," Liz says. "Either way, we'll come back and get you guys."

"Everyone keeps saying that, and I'm still stuck here in handcuffs," EK says. "This is bullshit. I feel like it's overtime and I'm on the bench."

RK slides the window open.

"Just stay here and keep quiet, OK?" Liz whispers. "William, hang in, all right? We'll get you out of here, all of you, even Jeremy. I swear."

*

"What the hell are you doing out there?" Donovan says.

The Colonel ignores him. For the past twenty minutes, he's stood on the porch and looked over his not-so-sprawling empire. Given all the nights he used to sit out here on his rocking chair and contemplate, he's almost never done it during the day. Partly that was because of the heat, but the larger issue, he realizes now, is that in daylight the place looks so much worse—silent and decrepit and crumbling. Another cabin is collapsing in on itself (that makes seven total), and tree branches press against the electrical wires, and the pool is starting to turn green.

"I said, what the hell are you doing?"

Donovan's inside the screen door, and a better question might be what the hell *he's* doing. He has a hunting vest on, and a camouflage expedition hat and shooting gloves. Strapped to his calf is a huge knife with a black plastic handle. He looks like GI Joe with all the accessories.

"I'm scouting the perimeter," the Colonel says. It's a joke, but he knows Donovan won't get it.

"You should be inside," Donovan says. "He's out there."

"You think he's got a sniper rifle trained on us?"

"Just get in. When you stand there like a damn statue, you give away our position."

"I think he knows our position. I think he knows we're in the house."

But the Colonel goes in anyway.

It's dark inside—Donovan has hammered blankets over the windows, with a few slits in each to look out over the compound. He goes to one along the western wall of the house and checks it. There's so much gear jammed into his pockets and vest that he clinks when he walks.

"We're going to get her back from that little bastard," Donovan says. "We've got something he wants"—he gestures at the upstairs bathroom—"and he's got something we want."

"Sure," the Colonel says. "Whatever."

"Don't you care? That's your wife out there."

"I care, you fucking half-wit."

"So how do we do this? Come up with some ideas."

The Colonel gets another ice cube for his fat lip and flops on the couch. He has no ideas. Whenever something occurs to him it leads straight to a dead end. He wants to take Kitty off the property for good, but he doesn't know where she is, and the Jeep's out of commission. He wants to plunge a knife into Donovan's heart, but Donovan's armed to the teeth, and after the punches the Colonel took a little while ago he's shying away from the idea of physical violence. In addition to the swollen lip he has a blinding headache and a loose tooth he'll have to address at some point.

He definitely can't call the sheriff. Money? The Colonel can bribe people—he has about sixty-eight thousand dollars, give or take, stuffed into his socks—but it wouldn't do any good unless he could get out to the highway and flag someone down. Right now, it mostly just makes him itch.

There's a click, mechanical and precise, and the Colonel looks up to see Donovan with a gun. Not a stun gun—an honest to God, no-shit handgun.

"This is my idea," Donovan says.

"Where the hell did you get that?"

"I've had it around. I brought it in with me when I first showed up. Out here in the woods—who knows what could happen?"

"Jesus, put it away. You don't need that. You're going to shoot yourself, or shoot Kitty."

"I don't think you're in a position to give orders anymore."

Donovan lifts the gun and points it at the Colonel, who looks at the oily *O* trained on his face and instinctively jams himself deeper into the couch. The volume on his headache suddenly goes up a few notches.

"Bang," Donovan says.

The Colonel watches him stuff the loaded gun into the waistband of his cammies and says a futile prayer that he blows his own balls off.

*

"All right, he's in," Loren says. "Donovan just pulled him off the porch. Let's go through it again."

He climbs down from his lookout post, in a semi-healthy pine tree forty feet above the ground. For a hiding spot, Riap did better than Loren ever could have. Near the place they agreed on—about a hundred yards east of the perimeter loop, close to the section where it bends sharply—Riap found a shady patch of ground, which he set up almost like a living room. One long log for a couch, a fire pit (unlit) instead of a TV, with water bottles and cans of food lined up neatly nearby. He even sawed off some branches with a tomato knife and wedged them into the trees on the near side, to make them look thicker and hide the site from the compound.

This is their base of operations, where Loren's team is now lined up on the log, waiting to be briefed: Liz, RK, Riap, and Kitty (who's a few feet away from everyone else, on a folded blanket Riap put out for her; she said the bark was too scratchy). One of Kitty's sandal straps broke, and she has mascara tracing muddy lines down her cheeks—either from sweating or crying. Liz, on the other hand, looks fierce and beautiful, like a warrior princess. She looks like she could stay out here for days.

Loren doesn't want his feelings to be a distraction, but when he saw her drop from the bathroom window with RK (he had more or less constant surveillance on the Colonel's house), he could feel his heart roll over inside his chest. From a safe spot along the tree line, he made clucking bird noises until they found him, and then he kissed Liz on the mouth. They were all dirty and tired and still far from safe, but the first few minutes Loren and Liz couldn't stop smiling.

"So, Riap," Loren says. "You first. You'll be in the barn. Aim the speakers out the windows, and turn the volume all the way up. Pick anything loud—the Colonel's got CDs in his office—but make sure the volume's maxed and the stereo is on mute. And fast-forward a little. You want it to be cued up halfway through."

"Got it," Riap says.

"You're the trigger," Loren says. "The whole plan hinges on when you hit that button and start the music. Too early and they'll know it's a trap."

Loren moves down the log and addresses RK. "Next," he says. "RK, you and me are on the barn roof with the smoke bombs. We each get four."

Lined up next to their supplies are eight dirty one-quart milk cartons with lengths of kerosene-soaked string sticking out from each. Loren spent a few hours at dawn this morning in the cafeteria, heating a giant pot of potassium sulfate and sugar (three parts to two parts). After the mixture melted, he poured it through a funnel into the cartons and dangled a piece of string in each. An hour in the walk-in freezer and the stuff had cooled enough to turn solid again.

"The fuses are twisted, " Loren says, "so we can light them all at once, but throw one down at a time, and not until you hear the music."

RK nods. "Ever make these before?" he says.

"Once or twice," Loren says.

"And they worked?"

"Sort of. I think the mixture was wrong then, but it's right this time."

"You're sure?" RK says.

Loren says yes in a way that's supposed to sound convincing but doesn't.

"They'll work," he says. "You have matches or something, right?"

RK holds up Riap's disposable lighter, sky blue with an American flag on it, and clicks the thumbwheel. The flame rises a few reassuring inches.

"Perfect," Loren says. He has another one in his pocket, which he already double-checked. "Try to get them upwind and make sure they're spaced out a bit."

Liz says, "I don't want to step on your whole plan, but I still don't get why we can't just call the police."

"They wouldn't believe us," Loren says. "I've been out there, remember? The Colonel's probably bought half of them off. That's why I got dragged back last time—some people turned me in."

"But those people weren't cops. And plus we have Cruella here on our side now."

Liz points at Kitty, who raises a middle finger back in her direction. Kitty's frosted pink nails are now chipped and broken.

"We don't know who we can trust," Loren says. "It's a small town, and the Colonel has money, and a lot of people out there are convinced we're criminals." He looks at Kitty. "Right?"

She nods and says it's true. "That's what they think," she says. "But to be honest that's what I think too. You really *are* criminals. Or else you wouldn't be here."

"So's your husband," Liz says. "And your brother."

Kitty's eyes narrow. She's about to say something else, but RK cuts her off.

"Couldn't we call our parents, then?" he says. "Instead of the cops?"

"That's basically the same problem," Loren says. "The first thing they'd do is go to the sheriff."

"We could tell them not to," RK says. "We could say just come up here and keep quiet about it."

"They wouldn't make it until tomorrow at the soonest," Loren says. "There's no time—William's sick, and Ty's hand is rotting off his arm."

The kids look back at him and say nothing. A few flies buzz near Riap's shoe.

"Look," Loren says. "We can definitely call our parents and the police and the newspapers, everyone we want, but not until we're done here. That means we achieve our objective first."

"Which is what?" Liz says.

"Capture HVTs."

"What do we need their televisions for?" RK says.

"No, that's high-value targets—Donovan and the Colonel. Before anyone calls anywhere, we get them into custody."

"By luring them onto the ring and then grabbing them?" Liz says.

"Exactly. They'll be disoriented. That's what the music and the smoke is for. RK and I just have to hold them down until the reinforcements show up."

"Who're the reinforcements?" RK says.

"The other kids."

"And they know that?"

"Not now, but they will. Liz, that's you. When this whole thing goes down, you'll be waiting by the Colonel's house, as close as you can get without being spotted. When he and Donovan come out, you run in behind them and cut the other kids free. Take this"—he hands her Riap's tomato knife—"and bring them out to help. You have to be fast."

"How do we get the Colonel and Donovan away from the house?" Liz says.

Loren looks at Kitty and says they have bait.

Kitty's prodding a puffy blister on her foot with an index finger. Eventually she realizes they're all looking at her.

"What, me? No way."

"You have to," Loren says. "You're the one person they'll definitely come out for."

She shakes her head, but Loren says it's her only choice. "You don't need to do anything—just sit there. We'll make it look like you're tied up but you won't be. And they'll never get anywhere near you."

He takes a stick and scratches a diagram in the dirt.

"Like this," he says. "You're here, on the far side of the ring. Riap, this is you. RK, you're up here on the barn, with me. Kitty, after we get you in place and let them know you're there, they'll come in from this side." A long line in the dirt. "Once they're mostly across the ring, Riap hits the mute button, the music starts, and the whole plan kicks in."

"I still can't believe I'm doing this," Kitty says.

"You can quit if you want," Loren says. "Go hike back to the camp. It's right over there."

She turns sullen and says nothing.

"So that's it," Loren says. "Anything else?"

Riap opens a water bottle and holds it out to RK, who takes it but doesn't drink. Liz stares into space. The diagram in the dirt looks like a football play drawn up by kids in a park. *You stay in and block. You go deep.* Loren's never been good at football.

"Sure?" Loren says. "Then let's check everything one last time. We go in five minutes."

onovan's looking in the wrong direction when he hears the megaphone.

For the past half hour he's been patrolling the house—checking locks, scanning windows. Every few minutes he walks outside and sees nothing but the silent, dusty compound. At one point he heard a noise in one of the empty cabins and ran over in full assault mode, but it turned out to be a family of raccoons. Donovan has a feeling Loren's going to come from the woods in back of the house. That's what he would do. Instead the buzzing, electronic voice comes from in front. From the ring.

"Kitty looks sick," the voice says, followed by a squeal of feedback. "You have to come and get her."

The kid's using Donovan's megaphone. Another insult, a tiny fuck-you.

He and the Colonel go to the porch and see Kitty. A few minutes ago she wasn't there and now she is, propped on the folding metal chair on the far side of the ring. She's slumped down, with ropes around her wrists and an unstrapped sandal hanging from one foot.

"Let's go," Donovan says.

"Wait," the Colonel says. "Something's not right."

The Colonel's holding his sword, which he managed to save from Kitty's poolside rampage yesterday.

They hesitate, and the voice continues.

"She just threw up," it says. "All over. Her pulse is really slow. She took some pills or something. You have to get her."

"I'm telling you," the Colonel says. "This doesn't feel right."

"What, you're scared?" Donovan says. "Don't be stupid."

He's already off the porch and moving toward the ring. All he needs is to see the kid—that's it. If Loren's close, Donovan can grab him. Otherwise, there's the gun.

After a few seconds of hesitation, the Colonel follows behind. Donovan hears him coming but doesn't look back.

They cross the yard quickly and get to the ring.

"Kitty?" Donovan says. He pulls the gun from his waistband and holds it with two hands up near his shoulder, pointing at the sky—TV cop-style.

Kitty doesn't move.

Donovan keeps advancing, expecting any moment to see Loren dart out and try to snatch his sister.

When they're fifteen feet from the chair, Kitty lifts her head, and the ropes fall away from her wrists. They're not even tied. "Wait," she says. "Go back. It's a trap—"

Her words are drowned out by a boom, an explosion of music so loud that they all flinch, and Donovan drops his gun to the stones. It's some symphony, screamingly, painfully amplified, with a bunch of buzzes and pops and distortion mixed in—one of the speakers must have blown.

Kitty stands and tries to wave them away, yelling something that Donovan can't hear. He sees the gun, a few feet away on the ground, and then a shadow arcs down and bounces next to it, followed by another. Dirty milk cartons—they hit the stones and start churning out smoke. Within seconds the ring is fogged in and Donovan can't see the gun anymore, or his sister. He can't see anything.

*

There's a flaw in every plan, and usually you don't know what it is until things start falling apart. When Loren sees Donovan with the gun he realizes right away that something big is missing from the current scheme—there's no wave-off option. Once everyone's in place, he has no way to stop it and call them back.

Across the barn roof, RK gives a holy-shit expression, which Loren tries to ignore so he can sort through his options. There aren't many. He could just stand up, yell through the megaphone that they were turning themselves in. That was probably the safest. Or maybe they could wait it out—maybe Liz and Riap would realize that a gun changes everything, and that they should just sit tight. As long as Riap stayed away from the stereo, nothing would happen. Donovan and the Colonel would take Kitty back, recapture the queen, and the kids could reconnoiter in the woods to come up with something else.

Whatever Loren's going to decide has to happen fast, though— Donovan and the Colonel are already on the ring. His thoughts are completely scrambled. What do you do when one side's armed and the other side has nothing but a classical CD and some smoke bombs?

When Donovan's closing in on his sister, near the spot where Loren drew an X in the diagram, the decision's made for him. Kitty stands up and yells that the whole thing's a trap, and inside the barn, Riap pushes "mute." The music roars so suddenly and so loudly that Loren almost loses his footing. He can feel it vibrating through the roof, through the soles of his boots.

Any options he might have had a few seconds ago suddenly don't exist anymore. RK lights his milk cartons and hurls them down onto the stones, and Loren follows. Three of his hit perfectly, but one flies long and lands in the grass. He scrambles after RK toward the ladder and they both race down.

At ground level on the ring, the smoke is choking and thick. The bombs worked almost too well—Loren's basically blind. A boot in front of him disappears into white clouds. Burning smells. Scuffling noises, underneath the soaring, crashing sounds of a symphony that's dizzyingly loud and buzzy. He wanted this to be disorienting for the Colonel and Donovan, but it's way worse than he would have thought. It's disorienting for everyone.

RK yells nearby, and Loren moves toward the sound. He trips over two bodies wrestling in the fog. RK and Donovan, though it's hard to tell who's on top. All three of them roll into the folding metal chair, which topples over onto them. Loren grabs a boot and tries to pull. It's RK—he recognizes the laces—though he doesn't know if he's helping or getting in the way.

A gun goes off, and the ankle in Loren's hand kicks furiously. RK screams over the music—he's hit. The gun skids across the ring and clacks against the wall of the barn.

Through a flickering patch in the smoke, Loren sees the Colonel moving away in the distance, heading for the trees. He should have known the Colonel would never fight, he'd run instead. Riap is moving after him. The Colonel throws his sword back helplessly, and Riap closes in.

The milk cartons are starting to burn out, and as the smoke lifts and things become visible again, Loren realizes how bad his situation is. RK's writhing on the stones a few feet away, pressing red hands against his hip. Liz is somewhere in the Colonel's house— Loren hopes—sawing away at the kids' cuffs to set them free so they can come out and help. Kitty's gone into hiding, and Donovan has disappeared. The whole plan is coming undone.

Loren kneels over RK and presses his hands down onto RK's hands, over the wound in his hip. Twenty warm red fingers, but still the blood keeps seeping up. RK's gasping, with white flecks of spit all over his lips. The gun is close, not even twenty feet away, and

Loren wonders if he should stay with RK or go get it.

Suddenly he's tackled from one side. It's Donovan. He grabs Loren's neck with one hand and wallops him with the other, and Loren feels like his jaw just moved two inches over. No more messing around—he's about to be thrashed, with no one to stop it or help him. It isn't even really a fight. Loren's quickly pinned on his back with Donovan over him like a school-yard bully, knees grinding into Loren's arms, fingers wrapped around his throat.

"You little fucking bastard," Donovan says. "You thought you were going to win? You thought you could beat me?"

His hands are baseball mitts, gorilla paws, big enough that his fingers overlap at the back of Loren's neck. They touch the bony ridges of his spinal cord.

This is how dogs give respect to the alpha male: roll onto your back and show your throat. What that really means is, you can kill me if you want.

RK still screams in pain a few feet away, but Loren barely hears it anymore. He tries to fight back but can't—he's completely outmatched. There's a throbbing sensation in his heel, which he realizes is from kicking against the stone tiles. The skin on his neck gets folded over itself and squeezed like an Indian sunburn.

Once blood stops flowing to the brain a person loses consciousness in about a minute. Loren read that somewhere, a martial arts book. The colors in his vision start to fade—the sky looks white instead of blue. Donovan has a scrape on his forehead that's black, not red. Chocolate sauce—that's what they use for blood in black-and-white movies. Loren doesn't kick as much anymore. Any day now the other kids will come streaming out of the house to help him.

He thinks the grip might be letting up, but Donovan just focuses again and squeezes harder.

You can kill me if you want.

"What are you going to do now?" Donovan says. "Huh? Huh?"

Loren latches onto this word—huh. *Huh. Huhuhuhuhuhuhuh-uhuhhhhhhhhhh.* It must feel so good to be able to breathe out enough to say that word. Strangled people always have finger marks on their throat. A purple necklace, ring around the collar. *Strangled*—that would be a good word to say too.

RK isn't shouting anymore. Or maybe he is and Loren can't hear it.

There's someone nearby, but Loren thinks he's imagining things. His mind is playing sound effects for him, just like when he was wrapped up in the carpet. Yelling, footsteps. The smoke is mostly gone now, and Loren sees Ty holding the metal chair, folded flat, by two legs. Ty rears up over Donovan and swings the chair and hits him square in the temple. His head dents in a little, like a pumpkin hit by a pipe. Donovan's fingers release and he rolls off, motionless. Ty tries to swing again, but Riap and Meredith step in to stop him. A few seconds later, EK shows up, carrying the Colonel's sword and looking for someone to hit.

Loren's throat reinflates and he starts coughing, and the coughs burn so bad they make him cry. It's over.

CHAPTER 20

The place is a German restaurant and they keep bringing out more food. Schnitzel, sausages, potatoes. Who eats sauerkraut when it's not even noon? Becca is the only one to touch the stuff, plus a few of the deputies, but William realizes that people don't know what else to do, so they figure food is a way to help. The mayor's wife drops off a plate of walnut blondies. Women in town keep arriving with casseroles. Every five minutes the cook sets out another platter of something weird—meats or cabbage or fried whatever-it-is under gravy. The tables at the restaurant are all pushed against the walls, and people stand around the big empty room in groups, talking quietly. William thinks that if you'd just walked in you'd guess it was a wake. A wake for a German kid.

He still has a crinkled Band-Aid on his arm, from the IV. In the hospital last night, he got all kinds of skin creams for his rashes, high-dose epinephrine and albuterol to clear up his allergies. Just being in the room felt like a luxury—a semiprivate with three other beds, though he had it to himself. The shower was set up for handicapped people, so he sat on the plastic bench and let the hot water stream down on him for half an hour. When William mentioned that his pillow was a little too thin, an orderly appeared five minutes later with a cart of different pillows for him to choose from, like a dessert display.

"Take them all," the orderly said. "Seriously. I'll get you more if you want."

In the morning the doctors said they were all free to go (except for Loren, who would have to stay for another day of observation, and RK, who needed surgery but would be all right). The kids looked at each other and said—go where? So the mayor talked to some people in town and settled on the German place. That was where they would face down a long row of heaped platters, sauerkraut slowly crusting over in the air-conditioned air, small pyramids of bakery cookies, and where they'd wait for their parents to come and get them.

Every thirty seconds another cell phone rings—a constant chorus of chirps and beeps and snippets of electronic songs. A TV has been set up in one corner of the restaurant, and when the local channel cuts in with news updates every half hour the sheriff appears on-screen, florid and sweaty, talking into a bouquet of microphones. William thinks some of the TV stuff is a little overdone ("I'm Pauline Vero with the latest developments on the torture camp…"), but he keeps watching anyway.

The mayor didn't tell them certain details, so the TV was the only way William would have learned that the kids had all been at the same hospital where Donovan, under police guard, was operated on yesterday to remove some tiny shards of bone from his brain. He was stable, the doctor said. At the 10:30 a.m. update William found out that the Colonel (whose real name was E. Raymond Kellogg; the network had mug shots of him going back ten years) was no longer in jail awaiting charges but was now in the psychiatric wing of that same hospital, after a botched suicide attempt. Apparently he'd tried to hang himself using his socks.

There's not much to do in the restaurant except wait. The sheriff says he's sorry it has to be this way but he can't have them running around on their own, and anyway, there are too many reporters in town. So the kids try to keep themselves occupied. One of the deputies brings in a stack of comic books for William. They're completely lame—Archies and Jugheads, basically fish wrapping as far as William's concerned—but he acts grateful and pretends to read them anyway.

"Can I get you some food?" a voice asks him.

William looks up. It's the social worker, an older woman with flitting eyes and owlish glasses and about forty-five jangly bracelets on each wrist. She's hovering over him with an empty plate.

"No thanks," William says.

"Sure?"

"Yeah, I'm sure."

She's been watching him all morning. The kids had more or less official sessions with her, and when it was William's turn she told him, "You're going to need to talk to someone about this. You don't want to wait."

But actually William did want to wait. He'd already told the sheriff and the district attorney and the chief psychology resident everything he knew (while propped on three very comfortable hospital pillows), and he didn't feel like talking about it anymore. She seemed a little let down by this, insulted even, and since then she's come around to check on him every five minutes. She's been almost predatory about it.

The one thing William would maybe tell the social worker, if she weren't such a vulture, is that he's worried about what his parents are going to do when they show up. An hour ago they called in to the sheriff's cell phone for the third time that morning, and when the sheriff handed the phone to William they were yelling about how he shouldn't go anywhere, they were on their way.

"We'll be there as soon as we can!" his mom shouted. "Just stay where you are!"

William had to hold the phone away from his head, and people across the room looked over at the buzzing. He could picture them, driving grimly for hours and hours, and when they finally arrived they'd overreact. That's what they did—that's why he was here in the first place.

He gets up to go to the bathroom even though he doesn't have to go, just for something to do. The bathroom is fruity-smelling and clean and has a poster on one wall that says, "Bavaria," with a picture of a castle rising out of the fog. William has to stare at it a long time to figure out if it's a painting or a photograph. His hands shake a little when he washes them. Because it probably would be a big scare, he thinks. Getting a call from the sheriff saying please come up, don't believe what you hear on the news, the main thing is that your boy's fine, but you should get here just as soon as you safely can. William would probably freak out too—anyone would. So why's he so nervous about it?

Back in the main room, his parents are waiting.

William's mom drops her purse when she sees him. His dad's eyes go shiny behind his tinted glasses. Everyone in the room is silent, watching, and William hears a jingle of bracelets from the direction of the social worker. He still thinks they're going to yell at him, but instead his mom comes over and squeezes him so tight that William can't breathe for a second. She's wearing her pineapple earrings, and he suddenly remembers what she smells like, without even knowing he forgot. His dad wraps his arms around both of them so that William is double-hugged, all three in the center of the room, and he guesses that, no, they're not mad anymore.

*

The clock in Loren's room says 12:09 in red square numbers. Thirteen more minutes.

He's in bed, watching tree shadows chase each other around the ceiling of his room. The streetlight outside is bright enough that he can see leftover thumbtacks in the wall, and corners of Scotch tape, from where his Special Forces posters used to be. While he was at the camp his mom went through and turned his room into a demilitarized zone. His old ammo boxes, his utility cammies, all his back issues of *Soldier of Fortune*—gone. She put up a Shaquille O'Neal poster on one wall instead (though Loren doesn't really like basketball). Since he got home he's been meaning to put new military stuff up, but it's been three weeks and he hasn't gotten around to it yet, and Shaquille is still smiling down on him in the darkness.

Loren has gotten other projects accomplished, though. The phone line, for instance. He doesn't want to wake up his mom with the late-night phone calls, so he spliced a connection off the line in her bedroom and ran it up over the apartment roof and in through his window. During the days he keeps the phone disconnected, in the back of his closet. The cord is buried in a slit in the carpet that his mom would have to hunt to find. Each night he hooks it up and waits until 12:22 precisely. He has two alarm clocks, both synchronized to atomic time, from the U.S. Naval Observatory in Washington, D.C. It's deeply satisfying to him that the minutes roll over at exactly the same instant. Loren knows because he's watched a lot of minutes pass these past few weeks, just after midnight.

It's 12:14 now. Loren's door opens and his mom stands framed in the hallway light.

"Hey, sweetie," she whispers. "You can't sleep either?"

"I must've just woken up." Loren says. He tries to make his voice sound groggy.

She comes over and sits on the edge of the bed, practically on top of the phone.

"Want some water?" she says.

"No thanks."

"I can get you some. It's no trouble."

Loren figures it's probably easier to just say yes. She kisses him on the forehead and says great—she'll be right back.

It makes her happy to do things like this for him lately. When he first got home, she worried about him nonstop. All they did all day was tell each other everything was OK, like they were trying to convince themselves. Loren didn't play on her guilt, but he knew she felt awful about everything that had happened. The pro had been dumped, for one thing. The whole camp idea came from him, she told Loren. It was her fault for listening, but she wanted her son to know that she was sorry, she'd never put him through something like that again, and starting right then she was going to be a better mom. She was going to be around more, they were going to do things together, just the two of them, like a real family. She took him to the movies a lot, they ate out at diners, she made him waffles for breakfast and chicken parmigiana for dinner—his favorites. Loren even found a new book, *Team of Two: Single Moms and Sons*, on her nightstand. You couldn't say she wasn't trying.

But a few weeks later, she hadn't made it too far into the book (the receipt she used as a bookmark was still on page xiii, not yet into the first chapter), and Loren couldn't help noticing that she'd started getting sadder. She wasn't good at being by herself. When it was just the two of them, she was basically OK, but the rest of the time she seemed lonely. At night he watched her playing solitaire on the computer, resetting the game again and again until she got a hand she could win.

Then someone left flowers outside their front door one day, a cheap bouquet that looked like it came from a gas station. Loren's mom threw them away and didn't open the card. The next day, another bunch, and the same thing the day after that. She threw the first seven away and when the eighth set of flowers came she said it was getting to be a waste and brought them inside. A few days later she was suddenly happy, singing to herself in the morning, and on a hunch Loren checked the trash and saw Chinese takeout containers—enough for two people. In the hamper, he found a lime green polo shirt, so bright that it practically gave off light. He didn't even have to check the logo.

Loren's first thought was, acid. There was a website he knew of where you could buy industrial-strength sulfuric, strong enough to burn through the paint on the pro's car and halfway into the metal too. But when he stopped to think about it, he realized he wasn't all that mad. How could he be? His mom was who she was—Loren could never change her—and at least with the pro she was happier. The pro might be a certified hand job, but Loren figured his mom was better off dating just one hand job than a bunch of new ones every month. He pretended he didn't know about the pro—who still keeps a low profile and doesn't stay over at the apartment—and let his mom think it was her secret. Anyway, the acid was always there as a backup.

Four minutes before the phone call, and Loren's starting to get nervous. Finally his mom reappears with a glass of water, and he takes a big gulp.

"Anything else?" she says. "Another blanket?"

"I'm good."

The handset of the phone is warm from where he's been holding it.

"OK, then," she says. "I'll let you go back to sleep."

She kisses his forehead again and closes the door.

Three minutes to go. Why 12:22, Liz asked him early on. Why such a precisely odd time? Loren said you couldn't do it on the hour or half hour, because that was too obvious. That was what everyone else would do. Liz still needs work, but he's bringing her along. He showed her how to sync her watch up to atomic standard time, so the two of them would be coordinated and he'd know exactly when she was dialing in.

The call-waiting thing was her idea. If Loren was on the line already when she called, Liz said, then the phone wouldn't ring and his mom wouldn't hear it. It was pretty ingenious—Loren had to admit. So he calls catalog companies, banks, 800 numbers for magazine subscriptions. He only needs to be on for a minute or so, until he hears the other line click in.

They talk every night now, for hours on end. He has no idea how she pays for the calls, how she keeps them from showing up on her parents' bill, but she says don't worry about it, she has some tricks too. Loren's been emailing her a lot too, and IM'ing. He doesn't want to leave a trail on the computer his mom uses, so instead he rides his bike to the town library four miles away and uses the resource room until the librarians throw him out. Already Loren is scheming a way to get to Minnesota. He has no idea what he'd tell his mom (class trip? faked permission slips?) or how he'd get out there (Greyhound?), but he's weighing ideas, drawing up low-level plans. School starts up again in a few weeks, ninth grade, so that might open up some options.

When there's a minute to go he picks up the phone and quietly dials an 800 number at random. He doesn't even look at the buttons—just pushes them until something happens. The first time he gets a recording telling him the number is not in service, but the second number goes through. It's a seed company, Loren's supposed to push "1" to check on an existing order, or "2" to place a new order. He does neither, though—he watches the red numbers on the clock, waiting for the last digit to change shape. It's agonizing, he's conscious of holding his breath. Finally the number morphs. The 12:21 becomes 12:22, and within a few seconds he hears the other line click in. His thumb is already on the button; it takes very little force to press it.

"Hello?" he says.

It's her.

ACKNOWLEDGMENTS

This book would not have been possible without the help of some people in my life who deserve special recognition, namely Marc H. Glick of Glick & Weintraub, Dan Lazar of Writers House, and Khristina Wenzinger of MacAdam/Cage. Also, Pierre Epstein, Peter Szabo, and Jess Taylor offered invaluable creative counsel and saved me from my own early drafts. My family has been incredibly supportive through the ups and downs of the publishing process. And finally, enduring love and thanks to Pam Bucklinger, who knows how long I have been writing and has always believed in me, and who makes my life better every day.

1/08